Saratoga

M. R. Pritchard

Tracey, I hope you love this! MRPritchard

SARATOGA is a work of fiction. Names, characters, places, and incidents either are the product of the author's imagination or are used fictitiously. Any resemblance to actual persons, living or dead, events or locales is entirely coincidental.

ISBN-13: 978-0615897226
ISBN-10: 0615897223

First Edition December 2013
Pritchard Publishing
Edited by Kristy Ellsworth
Cover illustration by Jorden Pritchard

DEDICATION

For twinkle-toes

"The earth has music
for those who listen."
-Shakespeare

CHAPTER ONE

When I was eight, I planned to escape the house. I could see myself in my mind; running across the lawn, smiling and laughing just like the other neighborhood kids, the normal ones. They weren't like me. They had no secrets. I could tell this from the way they ran free throughout the neighborhood.

We lived in the suburbs just north of New York City. At night we could see the glow of the city lights and during the day a strong breeze would bring a hint of the fetid smog of ten million people. We were just far enough away that my parents could afford a large house with a great expanse of lawn and Mother could stay home and school me.

Schooling at home was almost unheard of at the time, an archaic practice for the northern country folk and religious nuts. But I wasn't allowed to go to the public school. My parents wouldn't permit it. I couldn't be free to do whatever I wanted for eight hours a day. They knew this would only bring trouble: people might *see* something. I might forget the rules. I might step on the grass or take a flower from a classmate's hand or-heaven forbid-we plant seeds in science class. People might see, and then they would ask questions, questions we can't answer, because even we didn't know how to explain any of it.

You see, there is something wrong with me when it comes to things that are green.

So instead, I watch the neighborhood kids every day running in the green grass, barefoot and smiling as the soft blades tickle the sensitive skin of their soles. How I long to do the same, to feel the soft grass under my feet. After all, it calls to me, beckons me to the windows each day. The grass *wants* me to run outside and play. It always has. The trees too. Even the shrubs in front of our porch. They all speak to me. They all call me to go outside and escape the confines of our suburban home. They call me to be free.

I look away from the window and try to squelch the longing by rubbing my bare feet across the shag carpet of the living room. Nope. It doesn't help. I glance out the window again, trying to crush the feeling in my chest.

I know what will happen. I can still remember the first time I felt it. I was three and Mother had taken me to the park to play. I remember walking away from the playground. A planter box of spring flowers had caught my eye. I remember reaching out to grasp the stem, which should have broken with my tugging hand. But instead it shot right up out of the ground, towering over my head. Mother watched in horror, running to me, leaving her gaggle of other mothers behind. They didn't seem to notice anything. Much like most mothers at the park, they were too busy gossiping to notice what trouble the children were getting into.

I also remember that was one of the last times I was allowed outside.

But now, now I have a plan. I sit on the couch, book in hand, waiting for Mother to carry the laundry to the basement. I try to hide the fact that I was watching the children outside. She knows that I want to run down the street more than anything. I want to rub my feet in the grass. It is still calling me, after all, with a tugging deep in my chest.

"I'm going to the basement to start the wash," Mother tells me on her way through the living room.

"Okay, Mom," I respond, burying my face in a book of history.

"What?" She twists her head sharply towards me.

"Mother!" I lift my head and smile innocently at her. "I meant Mother." I correct myself. I know better. Her schooling is strict; no slang, proper speech and all that. I bet those kids outside called their parents Mom and Dad. I bet they said other things too, like 'nuff, and 'cause. I bet they even dabbled in the occasional curse word.

Mother smiles, satisfied with my correction, and continues on with her task. I close my book and slide off the couch. I tiptoe, headed for the kitchen. Glancing back towards the couch I see my shoes lying on the floor. I don't bother with my shoes-it will be better without them. I make it through the living room without a peep. But the kitchen floor, it's been known to tattle. I slow myself, taking large steps, avoiding the spots that I know have creaking joints. I've been studying them, rubbing my feet all over the floor when I bring my plates to the sink. I've been planning this escape for weeks.

I make it to the back door just as I hear Mother close the lid to the washing machine.

"Demi?" She calls up the basement stairs.

I don't respond. My heart is beating fast, really fast. I know I'm going to be in a load of trouble when they find me. They won't punish me though. They never do. Usually the looks of disappointment are enough. Plus, I think they feel sorry for me since I'm not normal, since I can't live the ordinary childhood they had hoped for me.

The back door is right in front of me. My moment of freedom so close I can almost taste it, like cake or chocolate! I can't hold back any longer. I don't wait, or hesitate, or think. I only know how good it feels to finally give into the urge which has been haunting me for so long. I push down the door handle and leap off the back stoop onto the cement patio. *Freedom*!

The grass and flowers spring up under my bare feet as soon as I leap off the patio. The greenery of the lawn bursting upwards with each step I take. At first it isn't too bad, only similar to walking in deep snow the way it makes your knees bend funny as you try to balance your body. But with each step I take, the green continues to grow and within minutes I'm propelled into the sky on top of a great wave of thick grass and tangled weeds. I lean over the side of the swaying grass mountain, unable to get down, unable to stop it from growing further.

It seems this power has only gotten stronger with age.

I hear Mother's light footsteps as she runs for the door. She must've sensed the trouble I was in.

"Oh no!" she exclaims when she finds me.

"I'm sorry," I tell her from atop my green mountain.

"How am I going to get you down?" She asks up to me, her voice a crescendo of worry.

My eyes only widen with fear.

"I have to call your Father." She runs inside for just a few moments and returns talking hurriedly into the telephone receiver.

There was nothing we could do but wait for him to arrive.

Thankfully the grass mountain did not grow any higher than our two-story house and we seemed to be hidden from the street and the view of others.

Father was there within a few minutes. He began by walking around the tangled mess, scratching his jaw, trying to figure out a way to get me down. He tried ladders, but they just sunk into the tall grass as though it was warm butter. He chopped at it a few times with his garden shears, but it just grew back underneath me. It refused to let me down.

I lean forward, hot tears in my eyes. "Maybe I could just climb down?" I ask them.

"No," Father replies. "Stay where you are. We'll get you down. I don't want you to-"

But it was too late. I had leaned too far over the edge, the edge near the cement patio. The blades of grass bent under my weight, unable to sprout new shoots underneath me due to the thick cement of the patio. I felt the grass give and let loose. And then I was overcome by the distinct sensation that I might be flying. That is, until I struck the patio. I don't remember the pain. I only remember the sound of the bones snapping in my left arm. The groan Father made as he picked me up and carried me to the car. He tucked me in the back seat, yelling for Mother to hurry. I could see the concern on their faces as he closed the door and turned to Mother. She was crying, saying something about the *papers*, they didn't have my *papers*. That was all I could make out, between the muffling of the thick window glass and my own sobs.

~ ~ ~

Even a nine year old can tell when her parents are scared. There are the anxious looks, the hushed whispers, the click of the bolt on the door and the latches on the windows. Then there are the silent dinners where the clang of heavy silverware on the plates is the only noise.

It was easy to see I had done something terribly wrong when I escaped the house.

I waited until bedtime. When I knew Father would be leaving the house again-he had to work two jobs so Mother could stay home and watch me. So she could keep me safe. But I really knew it was so she could make sure I didn't touch anything green.

She hadn't left my side since my escape two days earlier. I watched as the laundry piled up next to the basement stairs. And with my shame getting the best of me, I even offered to go down with her. But Mother scoffed at the idea. Instead she pushed pillows under my cast arm. She brought me sandwiches to eat and books to read when my school work was complete. I think it was the first time I ever felt truly guilty for what I could do. I seemed to be ruining their lives. They couldn't leave me alone. They took turns watching me so the other could complete the simple tasks of life. So Mother could go to the grocery store, or Father could mow the lawn which seemed to grow unnaturally fast around our house. Through it all they always smiled at me, hugged me, and kissed my forehead. They never stopped showing their affection towards me. Just like normal parents would with their normal children. It was painful for me to watch, almost more painful than this secret I keep, that they help me keep, from the rest of the world.

I lie in my bed and watch as she prepares my room for the night. Closing the closet door, placing my slippers by the end of my bed, checking the window to make sure it is locked; a second, third and fourth time. She walks to my dresser to the fish tank where Nixie lives. My blue-eyed puffer fish; she is my only pet, my only friend. I watch as she swims to the front of the tank, her small fins fluttering in anticipation of a late-night snack. But Mother does not feed Nixie. She simply clicks the tank light off.

"Good night, Demi," she tells me, pulling the sheet up to my chin since I cannot do it myself, not with the broken arm. She bends down to kiss me on my forehead just like she does every night.

I decide now is the time. "Mother, have I made you angry?" I ask.

"Why would you think such a thing, Demi?" She sits on the edge of my bed, her brow wrinkled in worry.

"You and Father have been acting…" I run my finger over the textured, pink cast on my arm, searching for the right word, "sad."

"All mothers and fathers worry about their children, Demi," she tells me, tucking the strands of pale hair behind my ears. "You are no exception. Your father and I just worry a little more because you are so special."

"And that makes you sad?"

"No. It does not make us sad. It is because no one else can do what you can and that makes you very unique in a world that isn't so kind to those who are different." Mother tucks my old stuffed bear under my arm. "You need your rest. Goodnight, my sweet." She kisses me again, this time on the tip of my nose.

I watch as she walks out of the room. Her white housecoat billowing about her, it seems like she's floating. The lights go off in the hallway. I wait, knowing that in just a few minutes it will start. Just like it does every night after I've been in bed for a few minutes.

The music.

The songs are familiar to me now: *Moonlight Sonata*, *Für Elise*, and *Swan Lake*. She starts with *Swan Lake*, she always starts with *Swan Lake*, it's her favorite.

I reach under my pillow, grasping the small flashlight that's hidden there. I slide out of bed, and just like in the kitchen, I know just the right steps to get to the door without making the floorboards squeak. I crawl on my knees, the flashlight held in my free hand, the cast arm clutched close to my chest. I lay on my stomach, at the top of the stairs.

I have a perfect view of the empty dining room from here. I catch a glimpse of Mother floating through the house. She stops here and there to pick up a few things. She rearranges the magazines in the living room and my pile of school books next to the couch. She makes her way to the dining room. I hear her turn up the music, just a tiny bit, so she doesn't disturb me, I'm guessing. She takes off the house coat, folding it neatly and placing it on the floor. She bends, slipping a pair of well-worn ballet shoes onto her feet. She stretches her arms, her legs. Then, she *dances*.

Every night it's always the same, the same songs, the same movements, like she's trying not to forget. I watch for a few minutes mesmerized by her long arms and long legs which seem to stretch to unbelievable lengths. She stops to twist her long black hair up and pin it to the top of her head.

I walk back to my room. I no longer have to sneak. She won't be able to hear me now, not with the music, not while she is consumed in her dancing. I shine the flashlight around my room, stopping it on Nixie, who must've been sleeping, her blue eyes bulge open with the sudden illumination of her water. I walk to her tank and sprinkle a few bits of food in for her. It's a bribe to keep her quiet, as if she could talk and tell my parents what I've been up to at night.

I walk to the window, unlatch it, and push it open, letting the cool breeze of the autumn air inside. I can see our neighbor, old Mr. Hawthorne's house, from here. I wait as he turns his lights off. He does the same thing each night; first it's the kitchen, the living room, the stairs, the bathroom, and finally his bedroom. How do I know? Just like in the other suburbs, all the houses here are exactly the same with the exception of the colors on the walls.

I return to the task at hand. The second story is just far enough away from the grass in the yard. It's not like when I'm on the ground, that's when things happen fast. And now I know they happen much faster than before. I reach my arm out the window, knowing I shouldn't. But I just can't ignore the feeling, not after feeling the gloriousness of sinking my feet into the backyard. Even if it did result in a broken arm, it was worth it! I watch as the goose bumps appear on my skin from the cool night air. I take a deep breath in.

It starts as just a small tingle in the tips of my fingers, a little zap, like I touched my tongue to the top of a nine-volt battery. It gets stronger, travelling up my arm, electrifying the muscle, the bone, making the hair stand up on the back of my neck. I stick my head out the window, watching as the plot of grass two stories below me starts to shudder. It starts to wave and bend. It starts to grow as if there were an invisible string stretched between my fingertips and the blades of grass.

I would be in so much trouble if I got caught doing this, especially since I just broke my arm. But I can't help it, the overwhelming urge is too strong to deny. I wiggle my fingers and watch as the grass reaches for me.

I'll stop when it gets as high as the kitchen windows below my room, at least that's what I tell myself.

A few drops of water hit my arm. The streetlight flickers. I look around and see someone on the street. I pull my arm in the window and duck under the windowsill, holding my breath. After a few seconds I peek my head up, looking out into the night. It's dark but my eyes find the dark figure immediately. He's tall, wearing a long, black coat with the hood up, covering his face. He just stands there, looking towards my house, looking right towards *my* window!

The goose bumps return to my skin. I reach up and slide my window closed, hearing a few raindrops hit hard against the window glass. Just as I get it closed and locked, the night sky erupts into a downpour.

I watch from the floor, waiting to see that cloaked man on the street walk away. But he doesn't. Bad guys never just walk away. I know this because I've read it in my books. There's always a bad guy, standing in the rain, wearing a long coat. I see a glint of something from inside his coat, a stick, no...a cane, which he twirls in the air, tapping it down on the cement sidewalk. I can see the glint of the metal bottom tip of the cane and what looks like a stone... no it has to be a gem, glowing from under his hand. The gem glows changing from green to blue and purple. It seems to pulse as though it's a heart in his hand.

I want to turn away, to hide in my room, but for some reason I'm drawn to it, to him, so much that I feel the unexpected coolness of the window glass press up against the tip of my nose. I blink hard, try to end the enchantment. My heart is beating fast, much faster than when I escaped, faster than ever. I reach up and flick the lock on the window, taking my eyes away from the street for just a moment. And when I look back, it's empty, the person is gone.

I crawl back into bed and hide under the covers. I lay there, praying that whoever that was on the street didn't see what I was just doing. Because Mother and Father would be furious, especially if someone saw me and found out my secret.

~ ~ ~

I wake early the next morning. Just as the sun starts to rise, filling my room with a dull light. I feed Nixie and use the bathroom, put on my robe and slippers. I can hear Father's voice, which is strange this early, usually he's at work by now. I leave my room, walking down the hallway and the stairs to find the living room filled with boxes.

Mother and Father are packing all of our belongings. The pictures are gone from the walls, the trinkets gone from the tables, my books gone from the end tables. The pale oak kitchen cupboards are open and empty. My parent's actions are rushed. They barely notice me as I wander through our house. Father pulls the junk drawer out of the kitchen cabinet and empties it into a box. He doesn't even take the time to sort through it.

"Demi?" Mother calls me from the dining room.

I follow her voice and find her packing the small CD player in a box, placing it gently next to a pair of black ballet slippers.

"Take a box to your room," she tells me, worry evident in her voice. "We must pack, quickly."

CHAPTER TWO

We left behind our moderately sized house in the suburbs and moved to the city, New York City. The big apple, the city-that-never-sleeps, whatever you want to call it, that's where we went.

There was no grass in the city by the time we got there; no trees, no flowers. The thick layers of cement, stone, and steel that the city was built with were the perfect barriers for me. Almost every inch of the land was built upon. With the stone walls of our apartment and the fourth floor rise from the ground, there was no more trouble for me to get into. No more sneaking my arm out the window in the night compelling the grass to grow towards me.

The city changed me. I stopped desiring the feel of the cool grass under my feet, I stopped experimenting, and instead of answering the beckoning of the green things, I grew to fear them. After all, I had caused my parents enough grief. I could see it on their faces. And it was already bad enough that that strange man on the street saw me.

My parents got reprieve in the city. They were no longer in charge of shielding me from the few lone trees left on the sides of the street or the occasional flower box on the stoop. This was my problem and I finally took responsibility for it. I stopped planning escapes. I stopped watching other people and their reactions to the trees and the flowers. I learned to shy away from them. I learned to dread the feeling of the green things calling me and tugging at my insides, to fear it, to fear it as much as children fear the night and monsters and the boogeyman. Much to my parents' relief, I learned to hide who I was and what I could do.

While the city kept me in check, there was one downside: I grew slowly in the city, much slower than I did at our home in the suburbs. This was apparent by spring and the fact that I had not quite grown out of last year's clothes. My arms and legs stayed limber and thin; my skin, an unlined paper-white, porcelain. Still, my green eyes were replicate of emerald jewels, as father would say, and my hair stayed like that of bleached corn silk. I really hadn't changed much at all, with the exception of my new fear.

~ ~ ~

This afternoon I sit at the dining room table, engulfed in a story of wizards and witches. This is how I spend most of my days after the few hours of homeschooling are complete. This has become my hobby, my escape from the four brick and steel walls of our home. I may not be able to go out there by myself, into the parks, the forests or even the few grass covered yards on the outskirts of the city, knowing what I could do, but I could read about it. There was no danger in reading and it seemed there were so many stories where people could do magical things; they had powers and abilities beyond the normal people of the world in which I lived. It made me think that maybe I was in the wrong place. It made me wonder, if maybe I wasn't so different, maybe I didn't have so much to fear about myself and what I could do.

Mother sits across from me. She sips on a cup of tea, her free hand smoothing over the newspaper in front of her. When she clears her throat, I look up.

"Would you like to learn how to dance, Demi?" She asks, her eyes hopeful.

Looking over the pages of my book I shrug my shoulders and remember how graceful she was when she danced at night in our old house. She has stopped since we moved. The apartment is much too small to accommodate her long limbs flexed in dance. I'm certain that I can't dance like that. I'm too different, too different from both my parents, too different from anyone I have ever met. I'm not graceful enough to move my body the way she did, swaying and waltzing and twisting. I'm too short, too skinny, and I'm sure I would be nothing more than another disappointment.

"It would be a nice way to get out of the house." She glances out the window and I hear the sound of a city bus pass, vibrating the wall. Her pink crescent shaped mouth frowns slightly. "We spend far too much time in here." She sighs, picking up the newspaper again and continuing on with her reading.

"I don't think I'd be very good at it," I tell her as I turn the page of my book.

"Well, Demi," she says with a smile. "You won't know until you try." She flicks the paper, the seam of it popping out as she lays it on the table and folds it in half. "And I don't think it's very good for you to be indoors so much."

I take a deep breath and turn to look out the window.

"Okay," I tell her, facing her again. I watch Mother's face spread into a smile; not just her lips, but her entire face seems to light up; mouth, eyes, cheeks. Maybe, I can give her a little bit of happiness after all the trouble I've caused.

The next morning Mother puts on her best dress, a black sheath that flares at the knee with a red belt secured across her middle. She wraps her dark hair up in a tight bun. And as I put my coat on I see her slip the black ballet slippers I remember from my childhood into her purse.

"Demi?" She turns as she reaches for the door handle.

I step back, expecting another long lecture about staying away from the flowers and the grass and the trees. I give her a slow blink and a short sigh. I'm not sure she realizes how much I have come to fear those things after what has already happened. When I open my eyes, I feel her soft hand on my cheek.

"Do remember to smile, Dear." Her hand grazes to my forehead, tucking a lock of long blonde hair behind my ear. "You are very pretty when you smile."

"Yes, Mother," I reply as she turns and opens the door.

I try not to slow her down as I gaze at my surroundings: the gray-blue sky, the tall buildings. It has been so long since we last left the apartment. Outings are far and few between, usually we only go to the library every few weeks to stock up on books, or the museums, or art galleries when the opportunities arose for Mother to enrich the syllabus she taught me.

We walk an odd route, indirect to say the least; avoiding the parks, the flower boxes, the one or two trees which still stood by the street.

I expect that they would be gone soon. Just as everything green has left the city, removed, tore up by the roots and covered in cement and rock; there is no room for it here, too many people.

I look up as we walk under the scaffolds stretching across the street.

"They're building new apartments," Mother says. "Soon, they will have to light the streets in the daytime!"

Thankfully, right now, the sun still shines on the streets which are busy with people walking to work, riding bikes, and waiting at bus stops. Remembering that dark man in the street not so long ago who always seems to linger in the back of my brain, I'm hesitant of the smiles from the few who look at us.

That was five years ago, but I can still remember it as though it was yesterday: Mother's music in the living room, the feeling of the constrictive cast on my arm, the hum of Nixie's tank filter on my dresser. The feeling of it starting…

"Demi!" Mother takes my hand, pulling me across the street, nearly missing a speeding bus. She stops and turns to me. "I can't very well have you sleepwalking out here." She squeezes my hand, her eyes wide with concern.

"I'm sorry," I tell her, glancing ahead of us. "It's just… I thought I saw a robin… or something." I try to make an excuse for my lack of focus.

Her lips start to downturn, a few wrinkles appearing on the sides of her mouth. "I'm quite sure the Common Robin is extinct, Demi. They haven't been seen in years. We covered this in your science studies last spring." She raises a hand to my forehead. "Are you feeling sick?"

"No, I just…" Trailing off I think to smile at her, just as she reminded me to before we left.

Mother squints a skeptical eye at me. "I think we should get you out more." She steps back to look me over and I know she's not looking at my clothes, because she picked them out for me before we left. Dark leggings, flats, and a light pink boatneck tunic. It's not the most fashion forward outfit for a fourteen year old, but the best we had to work with since I've barely grown out of the children's sizes, even though I'm heading towards my teenage years.

"I'm fine," I tell her with a renewed focus and taking a few steps ahead of her, I start walking again.

Mother makes a sound of exasperation as she walks up next to me. "Sometimes you are odd, Demi," she whispers out of the corner of her mouth. "Maybe it's all those books you read-" she stops short, looking up to the building next to us. "We're here already!" she says with renewed excitement.

I follow her gaze to the sign above us. *The Off Broadway Dance Academy*, the sign says in bold black font. Underneath the lettering is an image of a ballerina standing on her toes, one leg pulled behind her back, touching the back of her head. It looks like an uncomfortable position.

Mother takes my hand, dragging me behind her as she pushes the door open. A small bell jingles and a dark haired lady, sitting behind a tall desk, greets us, her eyes lighting with cheer when she sees my mother's face.

"Fiona?" the lady asks my mother. "Is that you?"

I have never heard anyone else call Mother Fiona before, except for Father, when he thought I wasn't listening.

The woman stands, hurrying around the desk and embracing my mother. "Gosh, how long has it been? Twenty years I think?"

"Yes, nearly," Mother responds as she steps back. She and the woman grasp hands, their knuckles turned white in their grips. I begin to wonder if-despite my mother's youthful image-maybe my mother is older than I think; to almost have a teenager, yet know this woman from twenty years ago.

Suddenly seeing me there the woman turns towards me. "Is this your child?" the lady asks Mother.

She smiles, placing her hand on my shoulder and removing my jacket. "Yes, this is Demi," she tells the woman. "Demi, I would like you to meet Ms. Angela, we used to dance together."

I keep my expressions reserved, giving a smile to the woman as Mother suggested. She looks into my eyes and down the length of me, not that I'm very tall.

"She is so fair and delicate," Ms. Angela replies, inspecting every inch of me as she shakes my hand slowly. "The makings of the perfect ballerina. Just like her mother!" Ms. Angela beams at Mother.

"Yes, well…" Mother starts. "That is why we are here. I was hoping we could talk about lessons."

"Yes, come, come!" Ms. Angela beckons us down a hallway and walks into a small office.

"Wait out here, Demi," Mother tells me, pointing to a chair by the door.

I sit, barely listening as they chitter and chatter, updating each other on their lives and what they've missed over the years since they've been apart.

I didn't pay much attention to their conversation. I was too busy looking at my surroundings-I had become accustomed to doing this, because sometimes people kept plants, much like how I keep a fish for a pet. And I couldn't risk being surprised. The space seemed simple enough, bright yellow walls lined with chairs. Across from the row of chairs was a large expanse of window which gave a view of a dance studio. The floors were shiny and smooth; there was a wall of mirrors with an attached ballet bar.

Becoming bored I turn, peering into the small office. Ms. Angela was sitting behind the desk, my mother in the chair in front of the desk. I waited, patiently, trying to listen to as much of the conversation as I could. They spoke of dance, of lessons, of money and a job.

"How old is she?" Ms. Angela asks Mother.

"Nearly fifteen," Mother responded with an odd tone.

Ms. Angela's voice dropped to a near whisper. "Fifteen, usually we start them much younger. You know this, Fiona, you yourself started when you were three."

"I know," Mother responds.

"Why did you wait so long?"

Mother pauses. "There were… we had to…" She searches for the right thing to say since she can't very well tell the truth. She can't very well tell Ms. Angela that the grass grows under my feet and flowers spring up in my steps and tree branches grow towards me when I pass by them. Or that this is why we moved, why I'm kept indoors, why my parents take such care to make sure I stay inside and out of trouble.

Their voices stop. Mother and Ms. Angela leave the office, walking across the hallway to a door in front of me.

"Just one more minute," Mother tells me as she passes. "Stay here."

Mother follows Ms. Angela onto the dance floor. She removes her black dress shoes and places the ballet slippers on her feet. The music starts and I find myself straightening in the chair to watch. Mother stretches for a moment, her movements graceful, sublime. I haven't seen her dance in so long, not in all the years since we've moved. I almost forgot how beautiful she is. The lines seemed to melt off her face as she spins and twirls. She is happy dancing, truly happy.

My memories are interrupted by a familiar feeling, a tugging deep in my chest and the smooth feeling of something sliding across my arm, the sound of a soft crackle. I look over to see a small vine running down my arm. The waxy green leaves creeping like a spider across my skin. As it creeps, it grows, in width and length, covering my arm. Delicate purple flowers burst from the vine.

I stand from the chair, startled, tearing at the vine, trying to make it stop. But each time my hands touched it, it only grows longer, sticking to my hands as though they are covered in glue. I can't make it stop, just like the time I escaped the house and ran into the yard. Now I get that familiar feeling, panic and fear, my heart racing, afraid of someone seeing.

Following the vine with my eyes I find a small pot sitting on a shelf high above my seat. Knowing how this would disappoint Mother if her friend sees what a freak her daughter is, I have to act fast. I have to make this stop!

Looking to my side, I see a stack of heavy magazines. Removing the top one, my fingers shaking and using the hard edge of the magazine I scrape the plant off my arm into the garbage can that sits on the floor next to the table. When I am sure I have pulled the entire vine off of myself, I push the magazine into the garbage can, trying to hide what I have done. But the plant continues to grow, creeping around the edges, reaching for me still! I take the entire stack of magazines, throwing them down onto the plant. Only then does it stop. I stand back, moving to the other side of the hallway, waiting for my heart to settle, for the panic to pass, taking deep breaths and trying to quell that darn tugging feeling.

I look down the hallway to make sure no one witnessed what just happened. Thankfully, it is just me.

Mother and Ms. Angela walk out of the studio just as I'm backing further down the hall, away from the garbage can.

"Excellent," Ms. Angela tells my mother, "you can both start tomorrow."

"Oh," Mother grasps Ms. Angela's hands, "this is so wonderful." Mother beams, her whole face smiling and glowing.

Ms. Angela reaches her hand towards me. "It was so nice to meet you, Demi," she says with a smile, shaking my hand.

We said goodbye, Mother beaming as I swallow my dread and that sick feeling that only comes when you're afraid someone has found out your deepest darkest secret. Mother seems to float out of the studio and I can tell from the smile on her face that this is good news. When the bell above the door jingles as it closes, Mother turns quickly to me, grasping my hands.

"They are going to let you take lessons, Demi, for free!" She spins us around in a circle. "They are going to let me teach. Ah! This is such great news."

I smile at Mother. I have never seen her so happy.

~ ~ ~

Three years was all it took for me to become their best dancer. My jeté was always grand, my plié always smooth, my pirouette mesmerizing, and my arabesque, exceptional. "*Watch Demi,*" the dance instructors would say with their thick Russian accents. They would make me stand in front of the class and demonstrate the movements which they had choreographed. The pas de poisson was their favorite. It was the step of the fish. I was light. I could throw myself into the air, arching my back, my legs behind me, straight, toes pointed like needles, looking just like a fish out of water. "*If I didn't know better, I would say you were a fish once,*" Ms. Angela told me.

Mother got to dance again. Father was able to quit his second job. They were happy. I imagine like they used to be before I created such trouble for them. I learned to keep my secret well. There wasn't much here to remind me of what I could do, except for the park, Central Park, which was forbidden.

CHAPTER THREE

"What are you looking at?" Jessica asks me as she stares at the cell phone in her hand.

We were leaving the studio for the day, our dance bags heavy with shoes, leotards, and leg warmers. I still had to walk the twelve blocks home. Jessica was growing impatient; she was going to miss her bus if I took much longer.

"Auditions," I tell her. "We both need to find work. Our last semester is almost finished. Have you applied anywhere?"

She smiles at her phone. "A few places." I wait for her to elaborate. "Don't you need to wait for your mother?" she asks me.

"No," I reply. "She only had a half-day of teaching today. Who are you talking to that has you smiling like that?"

"Oh, just a boy," she tells me.

I can see the blush rising in her cheeks. "Oh." I reply, turning back to the board.

"So when are your parents going to let you date?" she asks me.

"Never, if they have their way."

She gives a slight snort. "I've known you for three years and you've never even mentioned boys."

"I just haven't met anyone that catches my eye."

"*Come on*, Demi," Jess pushes. "There are millions of boys here! We live in New York City. You can't tell me not one has caught your eye."

"These city boys just aren't my thing," I tell her.

I look back at the bulletin board, losing interest in the

conversation. I've thought about it before, read about it in my books, someone always seems to fall in love in books. But that isn't real life, and it's hard enough to keep my secret from the world. I couldn't imagine trying to keep it from someone who wanted to know everything about me, who might want to have some kind of a life with me.

I push a few of the papers aside to see what's underneath them and a flash of blue paper catches my eye. The color isn't bright or bold, just different; subtle and light, like the afternoon sky on a cloudless day. I move the other papers off of the flyer, the bright pinks, the oranges, the dull whites; all advertising jobs, apartments and pets for adoption. *Saratoga* is printed in bold lettering across the top of the paper. I scan the page. It's an ad for dancers needed at the Saratoga Performing Arts Center.

Jessica looks up to see what I'm looking at. "Saratoga, are you kidding me, Demi?" She lets her heavy bag fall off her shoulder onto the floor. Using both thumbs she types something into her phone. "You know how hard it is to get hired there," she reminds me.

"Yeah, I know," I reply, letting the papers fall back into place.

"I'm going to miss my bus. I have to go." She picks up her bag and heads for the door. "You coming?"

I look at the bulletin board one last time. The prospects are grim for us. Barely anyone is hiring, so barely anyone becomes a professional ballerina anymore, the same goes for artists and musicians and writers. The world is too busy with other things: inventions, science, electric cars, and power for the overpopulated buildings and subways.

I have never been to Saratoga. I have never danced there. But, for some reason I feel drawn to that blue piece of paper. *It is mine.* I am almost sure of it, like someone put it there just for me. I reach up, pushing the other papers aside and I pull it off the bulletin board, then stuff it deep inside my dance bag.

The bell on the door jingles as Jessica walks outside. I adjust my bag across my shoulder and follow her out onto the busy sidewalk.

We walk the same route every day, passing the same cement sidewalks, the same stone and metal buildings which seem to reach into the heavens. And just like Mother said there are great expanses of lamp-lit sidewalk, the sun blocked by the expanse of buildings stretching across the walkways and roads.

We have two blocks left until we get to Jessica's bus platform. She has yet to say a word to me, immersed in her phone. She stops typing and grabs my arm.

"Hey, let's run over to the park quick, they're building a new skyscraper. My dad wants me to take a picture of the construction." She starts running, pulling me along with her.

The park is only four blocks away. I know this because I avoid the park at all costs. And right now, I know that I shouldn't be doing this. I should be walking straight home just like I do every evening. I know better than to visit the park. I've done nothing more than glimpse at it a few times from our rooftop or when riding the bus. "*You can't live in New York City and not visit Central Park*," people would say to me. But I learned a long time ago to stay away. This knowledge is what bought me the freedom from our apartment, the freedom to venture out without Mother or Father at my side. I had to earn this freedom.

We turn the corner and stop, both of us out of breath, my lungs burning from the run.

"Holy cow," Jessica says, between deep breaths.

I look up, immediately recognizing her awe. Even though I don't frequent the area I know that Central Park is green, lush, with walkways and acres of trees and flowers and plants. But now there is nothing but a giant dirt hole in the ground. The trees are gone, the grass and sidewalks too. It is all demolished. The only thing left are the bulldozers, the heavy cranes with their giant arms digging into the bare dirt, and dust.

Jessica holds her phone up and starts taking pictures.

I stand next to her, trying to catch my breath, taking it all in. There is no longer the feeling of fear, or shame, or the green things beckoning me. Instead, I start to feel something… something not right. A melancholy, a sadness? And something deep within me begins to mourn the park, the last thing that the city seemed to worship since the temples and churches have all been torn down. The inhabitants of the city may not pray every Sunday but at least the park was filled and they could worship the greenery and the sun and the fresh air. But not now. No one will ever walk through the park on a Sunday again.

"Are you ok?" Jessica asks, looking at my face. "You're much paler than usual," she frowns, "if that's even possible."

"It's gone," I tell her, looking at the demolished park. An ache develops in my chest as I survey the destruction. For some reason I long for the park. Even with all the years of fearing it and everything green, suddenly seems as though I've been wrong to feel that way. "What will they do with all of it?" I ask

"Apartments and housing," Jessica replies. "My parents said we could move back to the city once they are done. The Mayor thinks it will help bring rent prices down, they can fit thousands of apartments in this space." She sighs dramatically. "Sad, isn't it? But, they need more room. Too many people in the city. Can't have us all packed in like cattle."

For a moment I can't believe that she could say such a thing, that she could have such disregard for the loss of the park, for the loss of the trees and the grass! I watch as a large piece of machinery pulls a load of roots from the ground. Dumping the load into another machine, it grinds the roots into sawdust, the squealing of metal machinery substituted for the screams of the trees, screams that I can hear, that I can feel deep in the center of my chest. This is worse than the tugging of the grass and the flowers. It's like nothing I've ever experienced.

"Come on," Jess tugs at my sleeve, pulling me from my trance. "I'm going to miss my bus."

We run in the direction from which we came, headed for Jessica's bus stop. And I can't help but turn and glance behind me at what's left.

~ ~ ~

"What is this, Demi?" Mother asks me as she examines a crumpled blue piece of paper, her brow furrowing.

After arriving home I had dropped my dance bag near the door. She must have been looking for laundry, I assume, from her armful of worn sweatshirts and dusty tights. I stare at the paper remembering how it pulled me, how it beckoned me to rip it off the bulletin board. It's all I can do not to leap up and rip it out of her hand.

"It's for Saratoga," I reply. "They're looking for dancers."

"No," she responds without hesitation, without consideration.

"They need a dancer and I'm going to need to find a job soon." I tell her. "You can't take care of me forever."

"We can't go there." She folds up the blue paper and throws it in the garbage. "You know this, Demi. That's upstate, there are farms and forests and…" She looks at me, her eyes sad as she remembers everything that makes me so different.

"What's wrong?" Father asks me as I slump further into my seat.

"Did you see what happened to the park?" I ask.

I catch Mother standing up straight, abruptly, her arms full of more dirty clothes from my dance bag.

"You're not supposed to go to the park," Father shakes his head in disappointment at me.

"It doesn't matter," I tell them. "It's gone now."

Father's arms lands heavily on the table. "We can't keep you safe if you continue to risk exposure. If you continue to put yourself in danger..." I sink lower in my seat, trying to hide from their looks of displeasure as Father lectures me. "You're old enough to know better, Demi. We've put a lot of trust in you to do the right thing. The last time you did something reckless you broke your arm and we had to…" Father looks towards Mother, both of their faces now downturned.

The tension in the room is suddenly choking me. I know what we had to do; we packed all of our belongings in one day and moved. I can't sit in the small apartment any longer. I need fresh air, the autumn wind on my face. I need more space to breathe.

"I'm going to the rooftop," I tell Father as he stares at his plate of peas and meatloaf. I know he's contemplating moving again, to keep me out of trouble, to keep me safe.

They respond with only silence.

I stand and push my chair in, trying to make as little noise as possible. I slip my boots on and leave the tiny apartment. I climb the five flights of stairs that lead to the rooftop. Pushing open the heavy metal door, a rush of cool air caresses my face. I look to the floor, searching for the half-crumbled brick I use to prop the door open so I don't get trapped out here. My eyes adjust to the dim evening light and, finding the brick behind the door, I prop it into place.

There are lights from the nearby apartments. From the streets and the bright Times Square buildings and signs which aren't far from our West Fifty-first street apartment building. I rub my arms, the sudden chill making me wish I had the sense to grab my coat before leaving.

Even the layers of dance-wear under my clothes aren't protecting me from the autumn chill. I walk to the edge of the roof, looking down to the busses passing. The streets are still crowded with people walking.

I can't help but think that they-the people below me-are the reason the park was demolished. They are the ones who need new apartments for their families, their friends, their relatives that come to join them in the bustling city life. I turn in disgust, facing towards the direction of the park. Even though it's several blocks away I used to be able to see a few of the tree tops from here. Now there's nothing. That longing feeling I had when Jess and I came upon the remains of the park returns and I have a strong urge to see that dusty hole that was once Central Park again.

I walk to the back of the rooftop where our building meets the one behind us. I put my foot on the ledge, which would have been a steep drop off to the street several years ago, but now, it's just connected to another rooftop ledge. Since we've lived here the city has become so crowded that they've started building into the alleyways, across the side-streets, even building bridge-like suspensions of apartments across the double and triple-lane main streets. But this is why we came here, for the layers of brick and steel to hide me and what I can do.

I stare at the sea of rooftops before me, thinking they might go far enough and that I could walk to the park from here on the rooftops. My parents would never know I left. They never come up here to see what I'm doing.

I step up on the roof ledge. The wind grows stronger, ripping through my clothes. Reaching down, I pull my knit legwarmers up and over my knees. I look around me to see if there is anyone else out on the rooftops that might see me. But there is no one up here, I am alone. Taking a few short steps, I step down onto the next rooftop, the gravel of the roof crunching under my boots. I already feel guilty for defying my parents, before I have even completed the act, but the urge to see the damaged park is greater. I can barely contain the curiosity.

I walk across the rooftop, stopping at the ledge to make sure it's not a straight drop to the street before stepping across to the next roof. As I get more comfortable I pick up the pace until I'm running across each rooftop, stopping only for a second to check each ledge.

The park is about six blocks away and then I will have a straight view across Columbus Circle. I count the buildings as I cross their rooftops. In just a few minutes I'm over halfway there and I can already see it: the emptiness.

Skimming the rooftops as I run, light on my feet from the years of dance, the muscles in my legs starting to burn from the running and the cold air. I pace myself, taking shallow breaths in through my mouth, out through my nose. It looks like there are only two more rooftops left in front of me. I cross them quickly, stopping at the last ledge just as I planned. Columbus circle is below me with the busses and cars that still remain on the street circling like dead, rusted fish in a drain, each one waiting for their turn to exit.

I look across the roadway and see the dark park which has been reduced to dirt. There used to be lighted pathways at night, speckled through the trees, but now it's nothing more than a dark gaping hole in the middle of the city. There's not a touch of green. The only things left alive amongst the dirt and rock are the few security guards sitting in trucks, watching the equipment.

I gaze at the bleakness before me, my hand moving over my heart, the feelings which I felt earlier returning, stronger now. But then something catches my eye. Mixed in the dirt, near the streetlight lit sidewalk that still borders the broken-earth hole, I can see the last tiny bit of green left. It's a small blade of grass. For a moment, I'm not sure why, but I would like to teach them a lesson, these people who destroyed the park. I find myself breathing faster, my heart beating harder in my chest, a deep vehemence that I can't control starts growing within me. I wish that I knew how to control my power, the one I promised myself I wouldn't use again. Because I would make the park come back. I would ruin their project. I would re-grow the park. I would raise it from the dead with that single blade of grass. There is a small tug in my center, tiny and faint, but there, telling me that yes, I could do just that.

I look at my hands, trying to remember how it felt those nights at our old house when I would open my bedroom window and beckon the grass. It's been so long. I curl my fingers and leaving my index finger out, I point across the stretch of road at the tiny blade of grass.

Nothing.

I turn my hand, staring at my finger tip, trying to remember. *Grow.* I tell myself, pointing at the blade of grass. Still, there's nothing. I close my eyes, envisioning the tiny blade of grass. The wind bites through my clothes, it stings my cheeks. And then, I feel something, a tiny twinge, a spasm in my gut. The tiny, faint tugging grows stronger. I open my eyes only to see that nothing has changed. I close them again. I squeeze them shut. I focus on that tiny piece of grass. I let the twinge in my gut grow stronger, it moves up my chest, down my arms. My thoughts are broken by the loud groaning of the heavy machinery.

Thinking it odd that they would be working at night, I open my eyes and to my amazement the tiny blade of grass has started to grow! I watch it waver, gaining height, thickening at the stem. I start to notice that it doesn't quite resemble a blade of grass anymore. It must have been a sprouting seed because it grows full up out of the ground into a tree!

Pulling my hand back and closing it into a tight fist, holding it to my chest as though I've touched fire, I watch as the tree continues to grow. It rips through the power lines above it. The long black electrical cords stretch and tangle, pulling at the nearby poles. I watch in awe as one of the poles falls to the ground, shaking the earth under the force of its fall. One of the sprouting branches hits the streetlight, sending a spark of electricity and a shower of lamplight-glass rains down onto the sidewalk.

"Oh crap," I whisper to myself.

Now my heart beats with fear and panic. I squat down, hiding behind the ledge of the rooftop. Just low enough so I can see the security guards run from their trucks. I hear sirens from the fire trucks and police cars. I see the pedestrians stop to watch. I release my hands, letting them grasp the cold stone in front of me, letting them steady my weak legs.

Now another familiar feeling begins to overpower me, the one telling me that I have done something terrible. Mother and Father forbid going near the park, near the plants, and this is why. I scan the street, thankful that no one was hurt. Now there is one thing on my mind: I have to get out of here.

I stand, ready to run back to my rooftop, but something on the street catches my eye. No not something, it's *someone*, a person standing on the far side of the driving circle, away from the commotion of the electrical wire entangled tree. I'm certain I would not have even noticed him if he were not staring directly at me. It's a man in a long black coat, the hood obscuring his face. I wonder for an instant if I know him. And it's when he reaches his arm out, spinning a cane around in the air, a cane with a metal tipped bottom, a cane with a glowing handle… this is when I realize fully that I have seen him before.

CHAPTER FOUR

My mind is telling me to run, to turn around and run home as fast as I can! But my body won't move. I can't take my eyes off the man on the street. Yes, I have seen him before, the night before we moved away, years ago when I was still considered a young child. He was watching me from the street as I played with the grass outside my bedroom window that night.

I hear his voice, not with my ears, and maybe it's not his own voice, but it can't be anyone else's. His voice is in my head. "Is that you?" I hear him ask, smooth and calm. "Yes, it can only be you."

I feel a drop of cold rain hit my face and it's just enough to pull me from his trance.

Run, I tell myself, *run!*

I start off across the rooftops in the direction I came. The rain falling faster, harder and before I've made it two blocks the sky has erupted to a complete downpour. Within minutes my clothes are soaked, my legs cramping from the cold, the wind whipping at my face.

"Child?" I hear his voice, softer, weaker this time. "I will find you again." Hearing his voice in my head is enough to make me run faster, to get as far away from the mess I created in the park and that man as I can.

The rain is coming down in sheets, so hard I can barely see in front of my face. While I was confident in the direction I was running just a few minutes ago, I am suddenly unsure. I stop at the roof top ledges just to make sure I'm still going in the right direction and that there is a connecting roof, that I don't jump to my death.

It feels like my muscles are weakening, the cramps getting stronger, more painful. I grit my teeth with each step. This doesn't make sense. Usually I can go for hours; dancing, performing, and practicing. Running has never been a way to exhaust me. But right now I feel like I can barely make it the few blocks home. My muscles ache, my head hurts, I have to slow to a jog, and then walk. Just as I make it to our building I feel as though I'm dragging myself, that I may have to drop to the ground and claw my way across the soggy roof top.

The rain, it has to be the rain, is all I can think. I have to get out of the rain.

In all of my life I have never been out in a rainstorm. I've always been kept indoors, sheltered from everything. Perhaps if I had I would have known this would happen. I might have checked the weather, or brought a rain jacket. I can feel it leeching my last bits of energy from my body.

I'm sure it's only seconds ticking by but it feels like minutes and hours before I make it to the familiar rooftop door of my building. I reach out, grasping the metal handle, pulling, anticipating the warm hallway, the cover from the drenching rain. But I am only met with the heavy thud of the lock against the frame. I look down to see my brick has been kicked across the rooftop. I'm locked out.

"Crap," I mumble to myself.

I look from side to side at the nearby roofs. A few have doors leading to their stairwells, others have nothing but metal fire escapes leading to the street. I lean my back against the door, trying to prevent the rain from falling on me with the small overhang. It does nothing but prevent the sheets of rain from hitting my face. The rest coats my body, soaking through the layers of clothes: my sweater, the leotard and tights hidden underneath the pair of thin shorts and legwarmers. It drips down my legs, filling my boots with cold water. My arms and legs tremble from the cold and exhaustion, my feet feel numb.

Maybe I could try the fire escape or the nearby doors? I push myself off the door, forcing my weak legs to move. I get halfway across before tripping over my own feet and falling on my knees. The rainwater splashes, hitting my lips. It tastes like rotten fish and bus exhaust. The gravel of the roof grinds into my palms. And during the moment when I think it might just be better if I lay on the rooftop and wait for the storm to end, I hear someone call my name. For an instant I'm afraid it's that man again. That he's found me. But I hear footsteps splashing in the rooftop puddles and the unmistakable voice of my Father.

"Demi?" he asks, pulling me up under his arm. "What happened?"

"The rain," is all I can mumble out of my cold, numb lips.

Father lifts me as though I am nothing more than a sopping wet feather and I am thankful that I am so small and he is so large. The last time I ever remember him carrying me was when I fell off a cliff of grass and broke my arm.

I open my eyes, feel the vibrations of his footsteps, listen to the clang of the metal door. The rain stops falling on me, finally. The weakness doesn't continue but it doesn't improve. I feel the warmth of the hallway, smell the spicy cooking from our neighbors on the seventh floor. I open my eyes just long enough to look at my arm that's draped over my Father's shoulder, it looks pale and gray.

Father pushes his shoulder against the door to our apartment, trying to open it without hitting my head.

I hear Mother's voice. "Did you find her?" she asks, opening the door.

I don't need to look at their faces, just like when I was nine years old, I can hear the worry in their voices.

"Get some warm clothes and towels, Fiona," Father tells her.

"What happened?" she asks.

"Don't know," he says. "She said it was the rain."

"The rain?" I hear Mother's distant voice as she leaves to get towels and dry clothes. "But we didn't know about the rain. The rain has never been a problem before."

"Doesn't matter now," Father tells her.

I open my eyes and see that he is bringing me to my room, laying me on my bed. He pulls my boots off, discarding them on the floor. Mother is at his side, throwing towels over me, helping him pull the clinging wet clothes off of me.

"Why is her skin that color?" I hear her ask.

"Don't know," Father replies. "Need to get her warm."

They dry me. They dress me in layers of warm clothes and pile warm blankets on top. Mother makes a bitter tea, feeding it to me in spoonfuls until I have enough energy to tell her to go away. And when they both leave, they continue their conversation outside my door. My arms and legs finally stop aching. I have regained enough energy to roll onto my side, where I fall fast asleep.

The morning brings soreness and a deep ache. There's pain, more than I ever imagined, more than I have ever felt, the muscle and bone, everything aching so strong that I can't get up. I stay in bed; from the soreness, from the shame of growing that tree, and from the fear of that man. I don't tell them about any of it. I can't. Because I know what they would do, they would pack up our belongings and move away, just like they did last time. And I can't do that to them again. If anyone should have to suffer for my actions, if anyone should have to be miserable, if anyone should have to hide me from the world, it should be me and me alone.

~ ~ ~

After almost a week of Mother pouring broths and teas down my throat, I find enough energy to crawl out of bed and dress myself. I feed Nixie, my poor puffer fish who has been watching me intently from her tank, her blue eyes boring holes into me, wanting to play. Skimming the water with my fingertip, I let her chase it. I pull my finger out and wipe it on my shirt. Staring at the wet spot I wonder why doesn't her tank water affect me like the rain did? I wonder if maybe it's the amount of water, the rainstorm seemed like the ocean was being dumped on the city and sticking my fingertip in Nixie's tank pales in comparison.

Satisfied with my reasoning, I take my brush from the dresser and begin brushing my tangled hair.

"Demi?" I hear Mother ask from the hallway. "Are you up? Do you need help?" She opens the door and gasps.

I turn to find her staring at me, seemingly shocked.

"What?" I ask.

She grabs my wrist, pulling the brush towards her, and suddenly I realize why she was gasping: the brush is filled with clumps of blonde hair, my hair.

~ ~ ~

They brought me to a doctor with an office at Columbia University. There wasn't a sign on the door and most of the people in the small waiting room seemed to speak a different language.

"We don't have her *papers*," I hear my mother whisper to the secretary sitting behind a glass window.

The secretary nods, passing a piece of paper to my mother before typing something into the computer on her desk. I look around the room. Most of the patient's eyes twitch with nervousness; they watch the door and twist their hands in their laps. It is just these few minutes of careful observation which tell me this is a place for those without papers, for those who have something to hide.

I knew I was different. I knew my life was anything but ordinary, that I was not *normal*. But sitting here now, I'm starting to think there's something more; something about me, my parents, our life, my life, there's something more that I'm missing.

The doctor's hands are cold and he has white hair that sticks off of the sides of his head. He's short, plump, with rosy red cheeks and glasses perched on the tip of his nose. I want to reach forward and push them up for him.

Mother told him what happened with the rain. She told him I had the flu, that my skin changed to an unhealthy color and that my hair fell out. I had worn a hat and took it off to show him the bare spots in the back of my head. He sat back on his stool, examining me with his eyes, tapping his finger on his chin. A suspicious look passed over his face as he looked between me and Mother.

"I see she takes after her father, then," the doctor says, holding a strand of my white-blonde hair between his fingers and gesturing to my mother's own black locks.

Her eyes go wide and her skin pales. "Yes, in many ways," she responds.

She lied. For the first time ever she lied right in front of me!

I knew this instantly because I look nothing like my father. And if father wasn't at work the doctor would have seen this, too.

"You're too small for your age, Demi," the doctor tells me. "You don't have much time left for growing."

"What do you suggest?" Mother asks.

"Take her away from here," he says, waving his hand in the air. "Get her fresh air, fresh food, open space. I imagine there won't be much left of any of those in this city now that Central Park is gone.

I'm sure the pollution will get worse. The people that live here will get sicker. Get her out of here while you can. Take her someplace green and let her grow."

If only he truly knew what those words meant to us.

Mother pales further. Her fingers pluck at her purse strings with nervousness. She stands, reaching for me and the door at the same time. "Thank you, Doctor," she tells him in a hurried whisper before rushing me out of the door.

I may have learned a little more about myself at that doctor's office. Because this time I knew what they meant by *papers*. Jessica had told me one day. A person's *papers* are their medical identification cards, and to get a medical identification card you have to have a birth certificate.

Perhaps they lost it. Perhaps I never had one. I've never asked. It never seemed important, but now that I'm older I'm starting to notice a few things that don't make sense. I'm starting to pick up on the little inconsistencies. They are hiding more than just my knack to grow things.

CHAPTER FIVE

I didn't wait until morning to start packing.

I pulled the old duffel bags out of the back of my closet as soon as I heard them talking in their room. As soon as I heard Mother crying and Father trying to console her, I knew it was happening. I'm not sure if she cried the last time we moved. But it doesn't matter now. She's sad and it is because of me, because we have to leave, headed for some other desolate city, some other place to hide me, a fresh place to begin our secrets anew. She would have to give up dancing and teaching. She would have to give up what she loved and what made her happy, for me.

I tried to think of a way that I could leave them, a way to grow some courage and go out on my own, venture out into the world and free them of my burdens. I was certainly old enough, being nearly eighteen now. But I knew nothing else. I had no one else. I couldn't leave them for the single selfish reason that I didn't want to go without them and I didn't want to be alone.

I started with my bookshelf, selecting all of my favorites: stories of wizards, faeries, dragons and gnomes. They are the only other places I know of where someone like me seems to be normal. I pile the first duffel bag full of the well-worn books, smiling to myself when I manage to fit all of them inside, stretching the fabric tight as I pull the zipper closed.

The next day breakfast is quiet, uncomfortable. Father never leaves for work. He and Mother simply clean up after we've finished eating and then started packing.

"Where are we going?" I asked them as I hold the last box for Father to tape.

"Saratoga," he answers in a gruff voice.

I look to Mother, shocked. "But you said we couldn't go there. There are trees and-"

"The doctors say that's what you need," Mother says with her brow wrinkled in worry. "So we'll try it and see what happens. It can't hurt to try, can it?"

I stare at her, my mouth agape, taking in what she's telling me. Finally, remembering that I was asked a question I respond. "No. I don't think so."

I try to hide the joy swelling in my heart, the smile spreading across my lips. I retreat to my room with the excuse of packing the last of Nixie's fish tank supplies and food. Picking up my barely used cell phone, I call Jessica to tell her where we are going. Maybe she could visit. Maybe she could audition and dance there with me.

"I've got a secret, Demi," she tells me, lowering her voice to a hush. "I auditioned in Florida last week, while you were sick. I'm going to work at Disney, on one of their cruise ships!"

"Congratulations," I tell her, mustering as much excitement into my voice as I can. My only friend, besides my pet fish, and now she too is moving away.

~ ~ ~

Somehow, in the short period of time it took us to drive north, Father made a few phone calls and found a small house on the outskirts of the little tourist village for us. Being not far from the performing arts center, it was a strange place, not a tree on the property. The previous owners had laid a large cement pad that extended further than the foundation of the house. They said it was because the wife was afraid of bugs and snakes. They didn't think they could sell it, until we came along.

Staring out the car window as Father drives, I see that Saratoga is green, just as Mother promised, just as she warned me. There are forests, lakes, and rivers. Small houses that each look similar with the exception of the paint on them.

Saratoga is also small; one grocery store, one gas station, one main street, and one… church. I can't remember when the last time it was that I saw a church. Either way, this one is empty, the windows boarded, the grass overgrown.

The ache left my bones and the sickness seemed to seep out of my body with each mile that took us further away from the city. But something else replaced it, something else entirely. That deep wrenching in my gut, the one I felt when I grew that tree in the park, it is back, and stronger than ever.

We unpacked. Father found a job managing the local grocery store. My hair started growing back in. We cleaned out the garage and made it into a studio. Mother trained me, harder than any of my other dance instructors had. A few times it crossed my mind that she might actually be punishing me with the brutal training. But I didn't argue or try to get out of it, because I carried the guilt of ruining their lives and I knew Saratoga was intense and the audition would be hard. I did whatever Mother told me, I didn't have the option to fail. My parents had uprooted their lives for me again and the only option I had was to succeed. It was the least I could do for them since they had already done so much for me.

It only took a few weeks until I was healthy again. But I didn't grow an inch. I didn't gain a pound. Not like the doctor had suggested might happen if we moved away from the city.

My skin remains the same paper white pale as it has always been. Mother and Father still struggle with the fear of things sprouting from the ground towards me, especially now that we are surrounded by the forests and plants. I do too, because I know I can't control it. That had been apparent when I made that tree shoot out of the ground in Central Park.

So, I didn't leave the new house, not even once. Each time I tried I got that feeling; my stomach would ache, my arms would tingle, I couldn't focus on anything but that pulling. My ability, my curse, it was now my captor. I couldn't risk exposing myself in this new place. At first it had seemed like Saratoga was our last chance, but now it's beginning to feel like a prison.

On our second month in Saratoga, Father brought home an assortment of coats and boots, releasing them onto the floor after walking into the living room. In his free hand I noticed a small potted plant-they were forbidden in the house, any house we lived in.

"Demi," Father called me. "Come try these on." A hopeful ring tainted his voice, one that I hadn't heard since he got the offer to run the General Store.

I look through the coats, all oversize and heavy, the boots too. Some of them steel-toed, some heavily lined with some dense material. I press my hand over the jacket currently in my hand; it feels like it might actually be made of some bullet-proof material.

"What are these for?" I ask him.

"An experiment," he replies. "Try on a pair of boots and a coat."

I chose a pair of brown hiking boots and a black parka. Father sets the potted plant on the floor several feet away from me. Far enough so it didn't do anything, but I could feel it, pulling at me, beckoning me, just like green things always do.

"Okay, I want you to walk as close to the plant as you can," Father instructs me.

I turn to Mother, seeking her approval. She nods for me to try, her eyes wide with hope. I walk slowly, taking small steps. I watch the plant, feeling the pull of it as I get closer. I could tell it wasn't working, but they watched, hopeful that it might. When I get about a foot away, it starts. The tingle and twinge in my arms so strong I can't deny it. The potted plant tips over and the small green leaves stretch towards me.

Father picks it up, places it farther away from me. "Try something else," he tells me.

I walk back to the pile of clothes, pull out a new coat, a new pair of boots. They are all too big on me.

"Where did you find this stuff?" I ask.

"The old *Army and Navy* store is going out of business." He replies. "I don't know if this will work but it can't hurt to try."

I put on different combinations of coats and boots. But nothing seems to work. At the bottom of the pile there is a heavy green rain coat. I put it on and buttoned it closed. The stiff material must have been thick rubber, real rubber. Bending slightly I see that it falls to my knees. I am instantly sweating as Mother hands me the last pair of boots. They are a light pink with colored polka dots, tall and made of thick rubber just like the coat. The last thing I would expect anyone to find at an *Army and Navy* store, but, some army men are married, so maybe they were meant for a wife?

I start towards the plant in Father's hand. It is now twice the size it was when he brought it home. I walk closer, pulling my hands up into the long sleeves of the jacket, waiting to feel the pull and the twinge in my gut. But… nothing happens. I walked closer than before, the potted plant resting just a few inches from my boots.

Nothing!

Father looks up at me, his smile widening. "I think we finally did it." He says, jumping up and hugging me. He runs to Mother, hugging her and spinning her off of her feet. They laugh. They wrap their arms around me, lost in delight. We have finally found a way for me to leave the house and lead a semi-normal life.

I raise my arms, feeling the heavy weight of the coat. "I just have to wear this, everywhere?" I ask them.

"It's not so bad," Mother smiles at me, out of breath from her glee. "Just think, Demi, we could go for walks, to the store, you can finally leave the house!"

Looking down the length of me, sweat begins to pool at the base of my spine and in the center of my armpits. I could pull this off in the winter, the fall and the spring, maybe. But walking around in this coat in the summer…that will get people talking. I can only hope that the summers aren't too hot here.

~ ~ ~

I auditioned at the Saratoga Performing Arts Center and, to my amazement, they hired me as soon as I finished. It was odd. They didn't even take a moment to discuss my performance.

Now I am one of the twelve that will practice and perform year round. I try to hide my smile as I walk backstage where the other dancers wait, watching me with hard jealous eyes. I'm sure they want to know how the decision was made so quickly, just like I want to know. I look at the floor as I walk by them on my way to get my bag. They don't say *hello*, or *congrats*, or *hey what's your name*. They just go quiet and stare. And at that moment I make the decision, deep in my soul, that I don't need friends and I don't need to be friends with any of them.

It's probably better this way, I tell myself, *easier to keep my secret, easier to look normal.*

That was a great plan I had, until I met Swayzee at our first rehearsal.

Swayzee was tall, lithe and bony, with raven-red hair and large brown eyes. She was everything I wasn't. Her skin was still tanned from the summer. She was funny, she was outspoken, she was…*normal.* I watched her from afar those first few hours, secretly wishing she would be my friend, even though I had already made a pact with myself: no friends. It was easy to follow through on that pact since most of my new co-workers seemed to give me irritated glances and sour looks, probably because of my strange audition. And since all the dancers had to re-audition each year I'm confident my hiring resulted in another ballerina losing her job. Probably one of their real friends.

That first day at lunch break, Swayzee sits down next to me.

"Hey!" she smiles, flashing a set of bright white teeth at me. "New girl, welcome."

"Thanks," I tell her.

"So, what brings you to Saratoga?" she asks. "I mean, rumor is that you were in New York City, there's no better place to be a ballerina than *The City.*" She exaggerates her words. I heard her talking like this when I first got here, her voice full of delight and…life. Yeah, that's it, *life.* It's not the kind of voice that keeps secrets. It's the kind of voice that would listen to your deepest darkest private thoughts and then blurt them out loud for everyone to hear. "So tell me, what brings you to the sticks?"

I shrug my shoulders at her, thinking of an answer, one that wouldn't reveal my secret. Since I am not so good at this talking-to-new-people-thing, I tell her part of the truth. "Because they cut down Central Park," I respond.

She stares at me, taking a long drink from her water bottle. "Funny girl, huh?" she responds sarcastically when she's done swallowing.

"Sorry," I tell her. "But it's the truth."

"Ok, then." She takes a bite of her apple. "You're pretty good," she tells me as she chews.

"Thanks, my mother trained me."

"Oh yeah, who's your mother?" she asks, sounding genuinely interested.

"Fiona Freye."

Swayzee's hand releases the apple. It bounces off the table and onto the hard linoleum floor, making dull wet smacking sounds. The whole time she doesn't take her eyes off me. "Your mother is *Fiona Freye?*" she asks.

I nod my head at her.

"*The* Fiona?"

"I…I'm not sure what you mean," I tell her.

"Fiona Freye was only the best ballerina who ever danced here. She trained with the Russian ballet, traveled the world. Danced here for years before up and moving to the city, all without notice." She glances around the room with an astonished look. Thankfully no one else is watching. I don't want them to hear all this. "Didn't you look at the pictures on the wall here? She's in every single one of them. Well, except for the past nineteen years. But all the other ones, she's there, right in front."

"Are you sure?" I ask.

Mother had never mentioned any of this to me. I knew she was a dancer, that she was a good-no, great-dancer. I could see it when she danced at night, when she taught at the studio, and during the brutal training sessions she put me through. Now, to find out through a stranger that my mother was someone so special… it hurts even more to know that she gave it all up for me.

"Ask her about it, Demi. I'm sure she'll fill you in." Swayzee reaches behind her shoulders and begins twisting her long red locks into a bun.

I stare at Swayzee for a moment, watching her now that she is so close to me, wishing that I could be as normal as she is, for just a moment in time. I wish that I didn't have to worry about my secret, or my parents, or that man finding me again.

~ ~ ~

The crowd was filled with paying tourists. They visited Saratoga just to see us dance and we were decked out so as not to disappoint. Our hair slicked into buns so tight it pulled at the corners of our eyes. Mine was so tight I could barely blink and the skin of my face felt like it was too small to accommodate the bones underneath. The crystal beads that decorated our heads poked into my scalp. My tutu stuck out so far that I couldn't let my arms fall at my sides. Instead I held them clasped over my stomach as I waited my turn to go back onto the stage.

I blink, my eyelids feeling too heavy for my face. Swayzee had taken to doing my makeup for me since I was a complete failure at it.

For weeks the instructors kept sending me back to pile more on. My lashes were never dark enough, my blush never pink enough, my lips never the right shade of red. After we performed I had to rush home and wash it off or risk a nasty rash.

"I think you have a fan," Swayzee whispers in my ear, poking me in the ribs. "This is the fourth time he's been here. He watches you."

"You counted?" I feel my lip curl in mock.

"Yes, I can count to four." She jabs me again, harder this time.

"Are you sure?" I lean towards the curtain scanning the crowd.

"Yes. He's always in the same seat. Second row, left, end seat."

"I think you're confused," I lean closer and bite my lip.

"I'm serious," she whispers in my ear. "He's really cute or I wouldn't have noticed him."

"Shh!" One of the stagehands scolds us.

I lean to the side, peeking out between the small spaces of the thick, maroon stage curtains. Even from the back stage I can see him watching the edge of the curtains where I wait for my turn to dance. I feel my face flush. To distract myself I stretch my feet, adjust the pale pink tights that stuck to my legs, tuck in the satin tied bow of my Pointe slippers, anything to stop me from staring back at him.

"See," Swayzee leans towards me again, two fingers jab me in the ribs, causing me to jerk and move the curtain. I see him again, still watching. "I told you so."

Out of the corner of my eye I catch the angered look from the stagehand who already scolded us once.

I don't tell Swayzee that I already knew he was there. I could feel him watching me with a steady gaze. But it wasn't the kind of gaze that makes your skin crawl or the hairs stand up on the back of your neck. There was something comforting, something warm about him and the way he looked at me.

As the weeks went by I started getting anxious at each performance, checking to make sure he was there in the audience. I had this strange sense that I might know him, or maybe it was that I *wanted* to know him.

Not long after he showed up, the flowers started showing up. A rose here, an iris there. Always resting on the top of my dance bag. A taunt.

"Have an admirer?" Swayzee laughs at me as I stare at the cluster of purple pansies that have been left today. I'm sure she laughs because it does nothing but makes me angry and brightens the color on my cheeks.

"Why don't they lock this room?" I ask in annoyance.

I'd have to wait until no one is looking so I could kick the flowers across the room. The thin leather of the ballet shoes does nothing to protect me from them. They always managed to grow a few inches as they fly away from me on the wind of a swift kick.

I head for the bathroom, knowing that it will ensure I will be the last to leave. Scrubbing the layers of makeup off of my face, I listen as the other dancers leave for the night. And when the last voices trickle out and the door bangs closed, I make my way out of the bathroom only to find another flower resting on my belongings, a black-eyed Susan.

"What the hell," I mumble to myself.

I take a clothes hanger from the rack of costumes and whip it at the flowers. They fly across the room, hitting the wall, leaving a trail of bright yellow and purple petals on the floor. I collect my things and head for the door. I make my way down the empty hallway, past the auditorium doors and out the employee entrance.

Just as the door closes behind me, I see him walking across the grass towards me. It was like I knew he was there, waiting. The stage lights and dim audience lighting barely hinted at what he truly looks like. He's tall, sinewy, with coppery skin. His eyes the brightest blue like ocean water, and strange silvery hair that's just a bit too long. He brushes it off of his forehead as he walks towards me. He can't be much older than me.

"Hello," he says, looking straight into my eyes, the corner of his mouth turning up into a slight smile.

It was just then that I knew he had been leaving the flowers. There was no question about it.

"Stop leaving those things," I tell him.

"You don't like flowers?" he asks, his voice a smooth baritone.

"No!" I respond, angry at him for testing me, for tempting me, for risking my secret that I had done so well hiding. We finally had a small sense of normalcy. I had a job. My parents had a life again. I didn't want to have to move away.

"So," he responds, smiling still. "It is you."

The sound of Father pressing on the car horn interrupts us. I turn to walk away from the young man, still wondering who he is and how he knows me. He definitely isn't the black coated man with the glowing cane, the one whom I've only seen twice, but who scares me enough to haunt my dreams.

"Who was that?" Father asks as I get in the car.

"Someone from the audience," I respond.

"Oh, like a fan of the ballet?" He asks with excitement in his voice. "Did he want an autograph?"

"Something like that."

I avoid the young man's gaze as Father pulls away, driving us home.

CHAPTER SIX

It took a few weeks before I found the right opportunity to ask Mother about her past in Saratoga, as Swayzee had suggested. I'm not sure if right before dinner was the best time, but it was the time I chose.

"Someone at rehearsal said you used to dance here," I asked her while setting out the dishes, waiting for Father to get home.

Her hands stopped chopping, her back straightened.

"Did you dance here," I pressed on, "before?"

Mother's sighed as she pressed her knife through a loaf of fresh bread. "Yes."

"She said you trained in Russia."

"I did." She sets the knife down.

"Why did you stop?"

"Something happened." She dries her hands on her apron.

"What do you mean?" I press on.

"Well…" She moves away from me, opening the refrigerator and searching the shelves. "We tried for a long time to have a baby, your Father and I. We visited doctors in the city..." She hesitates, closing the refrigerator door yet nothing is in her hand.

"Were you sick?" I ask.

The front windows light up and I hear the sound of Father opening the garage door. I set three plates on the table and Mother moves a hot pan to the table, filling our plates with dinner.

I wait for her to continue.

"Can you get the butter?" she seems to stall.

We sit down just as Father walks in the door, looking tired from a long day's work. And now Mother looks worried from my questions.

"How was everyone's day?" Father asks, kissing both of us on the cheek and sitting down at the table. Oblivious.

"Fine," Mother answers shortly.

Father looks at me, his eyebrows raised in question. I shrug and take my seat.

"You aren't our biological child," Mother says as I butter a slice of bread.

This is followed by the sharp *clang* of Father's silverware dropping onto his plate and the fast beating of my heart.

I look to their faces, examining their dark eyes and dark hair. I knew we were not alike but their love for me has always been strong. I look to Mother, her face twisted with worry; there are slight creases near her mouth that seem to deepen as she presses her lips together. She sighs as though a great weight were just lifted off her shoulders.

Father looks utterly pale, his hands curled tightly into his palms.

I sensed they were hiding something back when Mother lied to the doctor about my taking after Father in the looks department. But I wasn't expecting this. Or maybe, I didn't want to expect this. It was obvious that this was something that they've been agonizing over for some time.

I set the bread on my plate, the knife on my napkin. "Are you telling me I'm…I'm adopted or something?" I ask.

"No, not really…" she struggles with her words for a moment, staring at her plate of uneaten food. "We found you-"

Father clears his throat loudly at Mother's words. Evidently he was not prepared for this conversation happening any time soon.

Mother continues. "We found you under a willow tree in Central Park, your Father and I. We were taking a walk after another appointment with the fertility doctor and there you were: tiny and pink, hidden in the tall grass underneath a large drooping willow. It was a sign. Like you were left there just for us." Mother reaches out and grasps Father's hand. "We couldn't leave you there so we took you home. We raised you as our own. We just didn't expect the thing with the plants, you know, how they grow around you." She makes a gesture with her left hand, mimicking the way the plants reach towards me.

"Why are you telling me this now?" I ask. Sweat starts to collect across the back of my neck and the walls begin to throb at me. I'm suddenly feeling claustrophobic, very claustrophobic. "Why haven't you ever mentioned this to me before?" I push my chair back and it gives a defiant squeal as wood rubs against wood.

Mother looks down at her plate, taking a deep breath in. "You're going to be nineteen soon. You need to know the truth. You wanted to know why I left Saratoga, why I stopped dancing here. This is why. Coming home with a baby out of nowhere…" She shakes her head as though I should be able to piece this all together. "And then when we found out what you could do! We had to protect you, Demi. There could be no questions, no one asking where you had come from. Someone would have called the authorities and we didn't have your *papers*. We didn't have anything that tied you to us. They would have taken you away. Dear *Gods* they would have taken you from us!"

I stand abruptly. "I can't believe you've never told me, never hinted, not once!" I look at their worried faces and lower my voice. "I…I need some time."

Mother stands, following me to the door, reaching for the heavy jacket from the wall hook. "I understand. We understand." She holds the jacket towards me. "Don't forget your jacket." She doesn't let go as I grasp it. "We love you, Demi. All we've ever tried to do is protect you all these years. I may not have given birth to you but you are so special to us. You will never know."

I force a small smile, push my arms into the heavy jacket, and zip it up to my chin. I turn to Father who remains staring at his plate of uneaten food, his dark eyes watery. So this is why I have no *papers*. This is why we move so suddenly.

I slip the rubber boots on and reach for the door.

"Come back," Father yells to me as I walk out the door and out into the twilight.

~ ~ ~

In the city I had the rooftops to escape to; here I only have forests, grass, and long country roads. The things I've been avoiding my entire life. Now I have to find peace in them.

I walk down the empty road, headed nowhere in particular. Just away from this newfound truth. When I am about halfway between home and the dance studio, I catch the sound of water slapping up against something. Turning, I notice a path through the forest. It's dark and narrow, packed dirt. At the end I can see the full moon light illuminating a lake and a pier.

Facing the path I take a deep breath in, collecting the last of my courage just before I run down the path. I run as fast as I can, knowing that if I walk too slow, being this close to the forest, things will grow. The green can reach me from all angles here. The boots and coat help to dull the tugging.

After clearing the forest path I run to the very end of the pier, which stretches almost to the middle of the lake. I take off the boots and jacket, drop them in a pile. I'm never outside without them, since they do such a good job hiding me from the earth. They muffle that feeling I get from the forests. But it seems here on this pier I'm just far enough away that the pull is nothing but a dull roar.

Holding my arms out, the warm evening breeze wisps across my skin before I lie down on the dock and look up at the few stars starting to peek through the darkening sky.

The words of my parents float through my thoughts. *We found you under a willow tree in Central Park*. Strangely, I remember that Mother said *Dear* Gods *they would have taken you from us!* Plural. It's not like she said God, or Messiah, or Jesus, or mentioned any other deity…not that we have ever worshipped one. Still, it nags at me until I force it from my thoughts.

My parents' revelation hurts more than I ever expected. And now it's not like I could go back and find out who I am. It's not like I could go look for clues or ask people who was wandering around the park eighteen years ago and left a baby in a basket. The park is gone, ripped out of the ground by bulldozers and diggers, and with it all hope of finding out who I really am!

I focus on the lapping waves of the water beneath me, slapping on the cracked gray wood of the pier. Soothing, lulling. I start to count the stars, thinking that it might help clear my mind. But counting stars is much like counting sheep and it's not long before I fall asleep.

~ ~ ~

I started to dream that I had wings. That I could fly, fluttering here and there like a hummingbird. Oh, to be a bird. To have freedom and movement! To be able to go anywhere, sit at any feeder, perch on any tree. If I were a bird I'd have nothing to hide about myself. My secret would be nothing more than some bright plumage that all the other birds could admire.

The cool spray of water across my face instantly wakes me. I sit up, gulping at the air, momentarily unaware of where I am. Feeling the wood of the pier underneath my hands I remember. It takes a second for my eyes to adjust, but not for my heart to start fluttering-that occurs immediately.

The full moon helps me see him, his large blue eyes soaking up the pale light, his silvery hair reflecting the moon's glow. Then a slight breeze blows across the pier bringing his scent to me. Clean, fresh, with a hint of something I couldn't quite place. Spearmint, maybe.

He's sitting in front of me, that young man from the audience.

"What do you want?" I ask.

Somehow, even though my heart is beating so fast it feels like it might explode out of my chest, I am not afraid of him. Not as afraid as I should be upon waking to a stranger watching me in the night. But I recognize him from the audience, from the flowers, from that one day that he spoke to me. And really, who is afraid of a handsome young man with his hair dripping wet and his shirt clinging to his skin?

But his shirt isn't just clinging to skin, it's slicked tight against hard muscle, finely worked biceps, toned abdomen, jutting hip bones, hallows and planes...

Stop! I scold myself.

My eyes flick to his and I know my cheeks are red, my eyes wide at the shock of seeing him here looking like he does. But the feeling of having him this close, looking at me the way he is, is something entirely new.

"Were you in the lake?" I ask, noticing the puddle that has formed under his crouched body, thankful for the distraction.

He tilts his head. "The water is where I belong," he replies, leaning in, moving his face closer to mine. I hold my breath. "Do you know where you belong?" He asks. Sensing that his closeness is making me uncomfortable, he sits back on his heels.

I pause for a long time, reflecting on his question. *Do I know*? My parents are not my real parents and I think I've lost all chances at finding out the truth. I have terrible secrets. I have this gift, this curse, which consumes every moment of my life. I'm always taking precautions, avoiding things, hiding it. Still, I feel at home here, so much more than in the city. And I dance. That is all I have in life now, all that I am able to enjoy. But none of this is something I can talk with a stranger about, especially the nice-looking young man sitting in front of me, who for whatever reason won't leave me alone.

"I dance," I tell him, deciding to keep my secrets. "You've seen me. I see you in the audience each weekend."

He smiles at me, the same way he did last time I spoke with him. "You may dance, but it's not where you belong. You come from the earth, like me." He points at his chest. "You don't belong here. You belong in the forest." His speech is odd, perfect English, his cadence choppy, with a hint of some other dialect. And while I am not well traveled I still think he is from some other eastern country. "How do you not know where you belong?" he asks, tipping his head to the side.

"They won't let me near it. I can't go near it." I look back at the dark forest behind him. "Things happen when I go near it. Things I can't control."

"As they should." He nods causing drops of water to trickle down his cheek. "You can learn to control it."

"How do you know?" I ask him. "How do you *think* you know something about me?" The dull roar of the forest tugging is suddenly overshadowed by an anger at him for revealing my secrets to the night and the lake. How dare he! This stranger. I don't care how good-looking Swayzee thinks he is. I don't even care if I agree with her right now. He has no right to risk ruining my life. "You don't know anything about me!" I tell him.

"I've been waiting for you, Demi, expecting you for a long time." He looks up to the sky, mumbling something into the night air.

"How do you even know my name?" I ask, thoroughly annoyed.

He gives me an odd look. "It's in the pamphlet they hand out at all of your performances."

"Oh," I respond, feeling the heat rise in my cheeks.

"I'll see you later." He winks at me and then dives into the water. I don't see him come up for air, not at all.

I stare at his puddles on the pier, watching as they dry, contemplating what just happened. What he said to me. Somehow this stranger knows about me. He knows what I can do. And it seems like he might have some special power too, except he looks to be perfectly comfortable with his.

Pressing my hands to the pier, I tilt my head, watch the ripples of the lake water. I try to quell the tugging, but I can't. My mind is racing with the worry of what that young man just said to me and how quickly my thoughts turn from trying to figure out *who* I am to *what* I am.

CHAPTER SEVEN

"Want to swim at the lake with us?" Swayzee asks me one night after a grueling day of rehearsal.

"No thanks," I smile at her. "I want to go over a few of the routines alone."

"You know the routines like the back of your hand," she says to me, her hand on her hip. She knows I'm just making excuses. She's confronted me about it before.

"I just want to make sure." I tell her.

"If you insist." She picks her bag up off of the floor. "But you need to live a little. There's more to life than just dance."

I look out the window, at the summer wind blowing in the trees dense with foliage. I'd have to wear the coat, the boots, and they would ask questions or laugh at me. No, it is still not a good idea. I never go out with the other dancers, not after practice, not even after a performance, when they all prance off for a night of drinking and fun at the local tavern. They won't miss me tonight. Besides, Swayzee is the only one I speak to.

"Maybe some other time."

"Suit yourself." She throws her heavy red hair over her shoulder and walks out the door.

I walk to the music podium. Scrolling through the playlist on the computer until I come upon a familiar song, *Swan Lake*, Mother's favorite. I press play, wait for the song to start. When the familiar melody fills the room-the one I grew up listening to each night-I dance, mimicking my Mother's flawless movements from so long ago, watching myself in the mirrored wall. Usually this calms my thoughts, my doubts, my fears. But not tonight. I stop mid-arabesque, frustrated with myself and my rambling mind. I walk close to the mirror, inspecting my skin, my hair, my green eyes. At least I look normal. But hiding this, this thing I can do, for so long, sometimes I just feel like it's eating me alive.

My thoughts turn to the man in the coat, the young man at the lake, the disaster I created in Central Park, and the fact that I am nothing but an abandoned child found in a park. I guess it could have turned out worse. I could imagine if someone else had found me, someone not so understanding and forgiving of me and my problems. Maybe that's how I got over the news so quickly after Mother told me, accepting that they really are my true parents, even if they aren't my biological parents. After all they've done for me I couldn't leave them and go in search of strangers who know nothing about me, I never could.

I think of the silver-haired young man. I've tried to ignore him in the crowd but each week he buys a ticket and sits in the same seat. I haven't spoken with him since that night at the pier when he sat in front of me, dripping wet, telling me about all the secrets I've kept hidden for years. I want to stay mad at him. The fact that he continues to show up each weekend is nothing but a threat. He knows my secrets and I can't have it ruining our lives again.

Suddenly, I can't stand to look at myself in the mirror any longer. I turn on my toes then bend to shuck off my ballet slippers. I take the boots. I leave the music on and my bag on the floor. I even leave the heavy rubber rain coat and I head for the door.

The humid summer air embraces my face as I rush through the door of the studio. I don't lock it, although I know I should. But I have the growing desire to run, to run away, away from my life, away from myself, even if it's down the street for a few minutes. I have to have a little freedom right this second.

I take off down the street in the opposite direction from our home. Headed towards the town where I know the streets will be paved, where the sidewalks will be thick, where the green flora of summer will be trimmed back. I run past the houses, most of them dark, the town folk having gone to bed for the night. I run past the gas station and the general store where Father works. They are both closed for the night.

It seems to be just me and the night and since the night keeps secrets well, I am just fine with that.

When I come upon the old football field and see the risers, I think to stop. Sometimes they use this area for baseball practice or flag football on the weekends. I walk across the crumbling sidewalk, making my way towards the risers and just as I step up onto the hollowed metal stairs I realize I am not alone. I see him sitting on the bleachers, a bottle in his hand, his dark hair hanging past his shoulders.

"What's a girl like you doing out here on a Sunday night?" he asks, staring out into the dark field.

"I just needed some fresh air," I tell him, panting as I try to catch my breath, hoping he will leave, and thinking that maybe I should turn around and run back to the studio.

"Yeah, me too," he replies, turning to look at me. The streetlight reflects off the name tag clipped to his shirt. It says *Jedediah.* "Hey, you're that dancer, aren't you? The new one they hired."

"How do you know?" I ask him.

He laughs a little. "Are you kidding me? This town is tiny. That dance center is the only thing keeping it alive. Everyone knows the dancers." He looks me up and down. "Besides, look what you're wearing."

I look down at myself, taking in the clingy T-shirt, the thin tulle skirt, the pink tights. "Oh, I just came from practice."

"Thought they got out earlier than this?" he doubts me. "Had a group of you run through the store earlier buying drinks and snacks. You didn't go with them?" I shake my head at him. "Well, word around town is you're their best right now. Guess that's why, makes others jealous. Practice makes perfect or something like that." He takes a swig from the bottle and leans back on the bleachers. "Out for a midnight run, huh?" I watch as he pulls something from his pocket, a small white box and a thin metal cylinder. "You're lucky the crime in this town is zero or I'd call your father."

"How do you know my father?" I ask.

He simply points at the nametag on his shirt. I didn't notice it said *General Store* when I was reading his name. "He's my boss. I'm Jed. What's with the boots?" he asks. "Those must be fun to run in."

I try to think of a quick reply. "My feet get cold," is all that I can come up with.

I watch as he pulls a thin, white stick out of the box, placing it between his lips, and lighting it. "What?" he asks as I watch him.

He looks young. Not much older than I am. "Aren't you too young to smoke?" I ask him. I stare at the cigarette in his hand as he takes a long drag, releasing a steady stream of smoke from his mouth.

"Definitely not too young," he chuckles. "You want one?"

I stare at the cigarette in his hand. It's something I've never done before, forbidden as always, as everything always was. *Screw it*, I tell myself. I reach out, taking the cigarette from Jed. The smoke curls around my hand, tempting me. It feels strange, my act of defiance, my sudden urge to do something *bad*. But also, my hand actually feels a little odd right now.

I bring the cigarette closer to my face, trying not to wrinkle my nose at the smell of it. I can see a small dark line making its way up my arm, slowly, a vein, turning from blue to black. It feels like my arm is aching. For a moment I want to give it back to him, I want to run back home. But that's what I always do, I hide at home, or I hide at the studio. I'm nothing more than a coward, an invertebrate, a giant chicken. If I keep it up I'm going to wind up like one of those old spinsters with forty cats. This has to change. I have to do something, something different. I stare at the cigarette, determined.

"What's wrong with your arm?" Jed asks, his voice slurring a little, must be from the drink he keeps sipping at.

I look down to see almost my entire hand has turned gray and black veins twist up my arm. It hurts bad, like my arm is on fire. I push the feeling away, trying to be strong, trying to show this boy that I too could be rebellious. *Guys like that*, I think. At least it might make me seem normal. It might make me seem desirable to him, or to any guy for once in my life.

Quickly, I pull the cigarette to my mouth and take a deep breath in just like I watched him do. The smoke burns my nose. It feels like my lips, my mouth, my chest is all burning, all at the same time, just like my arm. I drop the cigarette on the ground, unable to hand it back to him, and begin coughing.

"What's wrong with you?" I look up at Jed, his face is twisted in confusion and repulsion. "Your face, it's turning gray. That's gross." He picks his smoking cigarette off the ground and walks away. He doesn't offer to help me.

The coughing won't stop or the burning. I crouch down to my

knees, trying to catch my breath, the metal risers grinding through my thin tights.

"You shouldn't do those things." I look up, not expecting anyone else since I just watched Jed walk away. But then I see him step out of the shadows of the risers, the guy from the lake and from the audience. "The fumes, the chemicals," he continues, "they damage us." He crouches down beside me, his blue eyes illuminated by the far away street lights.

I cough again and watch the black veins continue to crawl up my arm, the skin turning a shade darker just like it did the night I was trapped out in the rain storm on the roof.

He holds his palm in front of me. "Open your mouth," he tells me. I shake my head, watching as a puff of fog collects in front of his palm. "I'm not going to hurt you."

I want to believe him. But I'm still angry at him. I hold my mouth closed, afraid for an instant, until I fall into another fit of coughing. He pushes his palm at the fog, forcing it in my mouth. A cool, heavy feeling fills my throat. I try to tell him to stop but I can't. The fog has gone down my throat and into my lungs and it feels like I can't breathe. He pulls his palm back and the fog rolls out of my mouth. But instead of it being white, like it was before, it's tinged black and gray.

I take a deep breath, pulling the clean air into my lungs. I look down at my arm, watching as the blackness and the gray skin begin to retreat. I try to wrap my mind around what he just did-he pulled the smoke from my lungs.

"How did you do that?" I ask, pulling myself off of the ground and standing.

He stares into my face, his brilliant eyes penetrating mine. "You still do not know who you are."

"I don't know what you mean."

"You belong in the forest." He points to the far side of the football field where the forest meets the neatly trimmed grass.

"I can't go there," I tell him. "It's not safe."

He cocks his head to the side. "No place is safer than where you belong." His face is so open, and he seems so innocent that it's hard to be angry with him. Especially because he just saved me. I realize this conversation is crazy, between what just happened and what he just did. It's not normal, he's not normal.

But, I tell myself, I'm not normal either.

Still, this can't be real. I must be having some crazed dream. I close my eyes, hoping things might change. But when I open them, he is still there, except he's walking away, out onto the grass of the field. I want to follow him. I want to ask him more questions since it seems he knows something about me, about what I am and what I can do. But I can't step on the grass. I left my coat behind at the studio and the boots are not enough protection on their own.

He stops, bending and pulling something off the ground. I watch as he turns around, walking back to me as I stand on the bleachers. He's carrying something in his hand. I see it better as he gets closer and much to my dismay, it's a small yellow flower-a dandelion. I back away from him, up the bleachers, onto the safety of the metal, trying to get away from the small flower in his hand.

"Sit down, Demi."

"Keep that away from me," I tell him, walking up the steps to the higher seating. He follows me, slowly, holding the dandelion out in front of him, threatening me with it.

"You act as though this is poison," he says so innocently.

"It can be," I tell him. "I can't control it. I've hurt myself, broken things, ruined lives. Keep that away from me!"

He stops, just far enough for me to feel the pull of the small yellow flower. "You just need to learn. I would like to show you something. Sit?" he asks again.

I look behind me, seeing that I am at the top of the bleachers. There is nothing but a drop straight down the ground. I have no way to escape him or that tiny yellow flower.

"Trust me," he tells me, his voice pleading.

I sit as he asks. "I don't want to do this."

"You just need to learn, to practice. I won't let anything happen. I promise."

I give a sigh of defeat. "Fine."

"Close your eyes."

I close them.

"See the dandelion?" he asks.

I nod at him. I do. I can see it as though my eyes were still open. Just like with everything else green it seems to have a voice that calls to me and a magnetism that beckons me.

"Change it into a seed head."

"I don't know how."

"All you have to do is see it in your mind," he responds calmly.

I envision it, the bright yellow flower closing and reopening as a white puff of soft feathery seeds. "Open your eyes," he tells me. When I do I see that he no longer holds the yellow flower, now it's a soft cottony seed head. He holds it out and blows a steady stream of air on it from his mouth, releasing the seeds into the warm summer breeze.

"Send them to the ground," he tells me as he turns back to me, his eyes glistening with excitement in the moonlight.

I close my eyes, envisioning the floating seeds burying themselves into the dirt of the football field. And then I push it a little further. I envision them rising up, sprouting bright yellow buds, then closing again, and re-opening as a fluffy white seed head. I make them burst from their stems, rising up in the air on the currents of the summer breeze. I hear him laugh softly. Opening my eyes I see why-the sky is filled with millions of white seeds, making it look just like a summer snowstorm.

"Do me a favor," he turns to me after all the seeds have settled to coat the ground in white. "Don't smoke ever again."

"Okay," I nod my head at him, thankful for the night to hide the blush in my cheeks. I realize this whole time we've been talking I still don't know who he is. "What's your name?" I ask.

"Dylan Undine," he tells me. "Perhaps I should walk you back now that it is so late."

It's then I remember I ran out of the studio, leaving all of my belongings and the door unlocked. "Yes, I need to get my things from the studio."

I follow him down the risers, watching the way his shoulders flex under his shirt. When he gets to the path leading to the road he steps to the side so we can walk next to each other.

"How did you know about me?" I ask him as we walk down the street.

"I'm not sure." He looks towards the night sky for a moment. "I just knew somehow. I knew I was waiting for someone and then I just had this feeling so I followed it and it brought me to you."

I glance at him from the corner of my eye, taking in his profile; the straight nose, the high cheekbones, the way his hair curls just slightly at his temples. At some other time in history his hair color may have seemed odd but these days people color their hair every hue imaginable. Still, I can't help but ask, "Why is your hair that color?"

He runs his hand through the thick silvery strands on his head. It's just long enough to think he might need a haircut soon. "It's always been this way."

"It didn't change that color as you got older?"

"No." He shakes his head. "It's not much different than yours."

I touch a strand of my own hair, pulling it forward and staring at it in the moonlight as we walk. I can see in this light, it's lost almost all of its white-blonde hue. "Yes, I guess you're right."

"Here we are," he tells me.

I look up, slightly disappointed to see we've reached the dance center already. He waits at the door as I walk inside. I make my way through the reception area and to my pile of things on the dance floor. I collect them, turn the music off, and lock the door as I leave.

"Can you walk me home?" I ask him as I turn from locking the door.

"Yes," he tells me. Neither of us moves. There is just a moment of silence as we stand in front of each other, alone in the moonlight. "Your eyes are green," Dylan breaks the silence.

"Yes. I know."

"I thought they might be more like mine." He turns, resuming our walk out of town. "I guess it makes sense though," he begins.

"What makes sense?"

"You manipulate the green, the plants, so your eyes are green."

"And yours are blue for-" I start to ask.

"Water." He smiles, finishing my sentence.

"What can you do to water?"

"Everything," he tells me excitedly, his eyes shining with pride. It seems he does embrace his power.

I walk in the road, avoiding the forest. Dylan walks on the pebbles and pine needles that coat the side of the road. Normally, I would walk fast, doing my best to pay no attention to the pull of the forest and the way the trees seem to lean towards me. But tonight I want to take my time, I want to ask my new friend questions, questions I've waited my whole life to know.

"Are you going to tell anyone about me?" I ask, worried.

"Why would I do such a thing?" he asks. "You know my secret.

Finally, I have someone to share this with. I've waited a long time."

We walk in silence for a moment as I pray he's telling me the truth. Deep down though, I know I can trust him, I can feel it in my center.

"Ah, the path to the pier." Dylan gestures to the dirt path that cuts through the forest as we walk. "It's nice down there. I like that lake."

"Yes." I reply. "I do too."

"I've seen you there a time or two."

I can't remember seeing him there any other time, except when I awoke with his face in front of mine. But maybe if it was night I wouldn't have seen him.

"We should meet there," he tells me. "Tomorrow, when you are done."

The trees of the forest are starting to thin and I can see my parents' house just past the bend in the road. It won't be long until I've reached the shortly trimmed grass of our lawn. I take a few quick steps, escaping the glower of the pine trees.

"So?" he asks as we reach the mailbox at the end of the driveway. "Will you meet me tomorrow?" He leans on the mailbox, staring at me.

What else do I have to do besides absolutely nothing? "Sure, sounds great. What time?" I ask him.

"Just go there when you're done. I'll be along." He gives me a gentle smile, his teeth straight and white, before he turns around and begins walking back in the direction from which we came.

CHAPTER EIGHT

My days change from spending every moment in rehearsal, to watching the clock ready to run for the door as soon as we are released. For once I am not the last to leave or the sole dancer rehearsing after hours.

"Where are you going so fast?" Swayzee stops me.

"I have something to do," I tell her, shoving my dance shoes in my bag.

"It's a boy, isn't it?" she asks, narrowing her eyes at me. "It's that boy from the audience." She smiles, pointing her finger at me accusingly.

"Don't tell my parents," I tell her, afraid that they might interfere.

"What do they care, aren't you like nineteen?" She makes a face, lifting her eyebrow and lip. "You have a job, Demi. I think you're beyond asking their permission to date."

I smile at her, realizing she's right. Although, I still don't want to tell them. "I'll see you tomorrow," I tell her.

"Have fun," she shouts to me. "He's really cute!"

I walk to the pier where we have been meeting each day. It's secluded, quiet, the perfect spot for two *not-normals* to hang out. It makes me happy, finally having someone to talk to, someone who can share this burden with me. Dylan has taught me how to use some of it and now I don't need the heavy coat. I keep the boots though, just in case.

When I get to the pier it's empty. I drop my bag and kick off the boots. I sit, staring into the forest, waiting for him to walk down the dirt trail. The sun starts to set, dipping behind the trees, bringing night. I search my bag for a sweater, when I hear the soft drops of water splashing behind me. I turn and find Dylan pulling himself out of the lake onto the pier, his clothes soaking wet.

"Did you swim here?" I ask him, pulling an old sweater over my head.

"I've been doing too much talking," he responds. "I needed to stretch my muscles." He holds up a dripping wet arm, flexing his bicep for me to see.

"Nice," I tell him, interrupted by the vibrating of my cell phone. I pick it up, seeing my home number on the screen. I press *ignore.*

"Your parents?" he asks, sitting beside me.

"Yeah, but they're not really my parents," I tell him. "They told me a few weeks ago that they found me. I'm still trying to digest the information."

"You should be grateful. Some never had parents, nor experienced the love that they have for you."

"Where are your parents?" I ask him.

"I have none."

"No one at all?"

"I was found by the ocean in Florida," he runs his hand through his wet hair. "There were no foster homes when I was a child. I was brought to the orphanage, a place no child should ever grow up in..."

"How did you learn about what you could do?"

He shrugs, staring out over the lake. "That's a long story, for another day."

"It started when I was three," I tell him. "And we are the same, so was that when it started for you?" I ask, probing still.

"Similar, not the same," he corrects me. "I have to have the water, just as you need the earth." I watch as he holds his hand out, the moisture from the air collecting in a puddle in his open palm.

"What are we?" It's a question I've been longing to know my whole life.

"I'm not fully certain I know," he flicks his hand, sending the water splashing into the lake, "but I do know that we are not safe."

"What do you mean?"

"There's a man, he's more than a man, really. I've met him a few times. He has this power over me. Manipulates me, like a toy, like I do the water."

His words send a shiver up my back. I know exactly who he's talking about. "I think I've seen him before," I tell Dylan, remembering the man in the black coat and the glowing cane. The one who has shown up each time we've had to move. I wonder if my parents know of this man, if that's why we've moved so suddenly or maybe it's a coincidence, since we've always moved after I'd done something bad.

"I don't want to talk about him." Dylan looks away and I watch as his demeanor changes, from slightly relaxed to tense as he glares over the water as though he's battling some internal turmoil. He closes his eyes and clenches his jaw. I watch as he wicks the moisture off of his body and sends it into the lake with a forceful splash.

"Are you okay?" I ask, worried that I may have upset him.

He takes a deep breath, his chest expanding with the force of it, his features softening. "Sorry," he tells me before turning to look at me. "Sorry."

"Is there something wrong?"

"No." He brushes his silvery hair out of his face and smiles. "It's perfect. Now, it's perfect." He tells me with a tone which seems he's trying to convince himself as much as he's trying to convince me.

~ ~ ~

"Demi?" Mother asks, opening my bedroom door. "Are you feeling sick?"

I roll over feeling groggy and tired, blocking the sunlight from my eyes with my arm. "No, I'm fine." I tell her.

"Well then, you might want to get moving. Rehearsal starts in ten minutes."

"Crap!" I throw the covers back and scoot myself out of bed. I never oversleep, ever. I rush around the room. Nixie watches me from her tank, swimming from side to side expecting her breakfast. I pull on a pair of dirty tights, a black leotard, and I throw a sweatshirt over it all. I have no time to shower or brush my teeth. I pull my hair up into a pony tail and drag my dance bag across the floor.

"Sorry, girl," I tell Nixie as I walk by her tank. "I'll feed you later."

There is no time for our usual family breakfast. Father is already putting his shoes on. Mother is cleaning up the table.

"Running late?" Father asks.

"Yeah." I rub my hand over my face, feeling the imprint left from the sheets. "I must've been tired."

"This doesn't have anything to do with that boy you've been sneaking off with, does it?" Mother asks from the kitchen. I ignore her, slightly surprised that she found out about him.

"You need a ride?" Father asks as I slip on my boots.

"Yeah, do you mind?"

He shakes his head, holding his hand out to take my dance bag. I follow him to the garage. "So," he asks as we buckle into his car, "is it because of the boy?"

"No," I shake my head, hoping he can't see the glowing red of my cheeks.

"You know, Demi," he tells me as he starts the car and begins driving down the road, "you're an adult now. We trust you to make the right decisions and to know the difference between right and wrong."

"Thanks," I tell him, relieved that I may not have to sneak around anymore.

"Just remember, your mother and I aren't getting any younger, it's a lot harder for us to pack up and move now." I look at the grim expression on his face as he drives. He pulls up in front of the dance center and reaches in the back seat. He hands me my bag. "Have a good day," he tells me, as he kisses me on my cheek.

"Thanks."

"Just be careful. I love you, Demi."

"Love you, too," I tell him, closing the door and running for rehearsal.

Swayzee flashes me a thumbs up as I run onto the dance floor, squeezing myself in line for our warm up routine. My lateness hasn't gone unnoticed. I see the choreographer, Mr. Pavlova, glare at me in the mirror. It's the glare of punishment; this rehearsal won't be good.

And it wasn't. The choreographers drilled me. They kept me late for lunch. They kept me dancing after the others had gone home. Mr. Pavlova even took the time to lecture me on punctuality after everyone had left. By the time they released me it was dark outside and I was exhausted from being up late for weeks, from dancing my legs off. The sweat still hadn't dried off my back when I opened the door of the studio to leave.

"Working late?" I hear Swayzee ask as I start walking. I turn my head and see her leaning up against the building. She takes a few steps with her long legs and catches up to me.

"Something like that," I tell her, shaking my head.

"Never seen you be late before." She gives me a devilish grin. "It's that boy, isn't it?"

"Why does everyone suddenly care about who I spend my time with?" I snap at her.

"Jeez," she replies. "I was just joking with you. Besides I wanted to hear about him."

"Why?"

"Because you've been such a goody-two-shoes since you got here. I was wondering when you were going to let loose."

If only I could tell her why I act that way.

"Anyway," she continues. "I'm going golfing on Sunday, you know our *day of rest*, with Jed and I wanted to know if you can come, bring your mystery boy."

Oh no, all that grass, all those trees. "Do you mean Jedediah from the store?" I ask her.

"Yeah."

He's the one who left me to choke after giving me that cigarette. I have to think of an excuse. "Um…"

"You're going to say no, aren't you?"

"It's just that… I'm really allergic to grass," I tell her.

"Fine, suit yourself." She tells me, leaving my side to walk to her car, a red mustang convertible. It looks fun, like her, and the color matches her hair. "Want a ride home?" she asks as she gets in the driver's seat.

"No." I wave her off, looking forward to the quiet walk home. "See you in the morning."

"Don't be late tomorrow, *love bird*." She waves to me out of the sun roof of the mustang, driving off down the road.

I walk in the opposite direction, towards home, since the dance center is only a few miles from my house. It's not long before I wish I had taken that ride Swayzee offered. My legs are starting to feel like jelly from the rigorous dancing. I think they had me jeté a million times and my head is still spinning from the pirouettes. I pass the trail that leads to the lake and the pier where I have been meeting Dylan. I think to walk down it, to rest by the lake and talk with him. He's become the closest friend I've ever had. But, I don't have the time tonight. I can't risk being late again. That will surely get me fired.

I hear the rustle of leaves coming from the nearby forest. A twig snaps, leaves rustle. I look around trying to see who is beyond the front line of trees. I wonder if it's Dylan walking out of the forest to meet me. But there's nothing that I can see in the twilight. The small hairs on my arms start to raise, gooseflesh covering my skin. It's odd, especially in this summer heat. I hear a low sound like a groan or a grumble, more rustling of leaves. That's definitely not Dylan. He would call my name or simply run out and greet me.

A short breeze blows by my ear. "*Demi*," I think I hear, turning around. Nothing's there, just the empty road.

I continue walking, picking up my pace, contemplating running, but I look down, seeing the rubber boots. I can't run very well in these. But if it needs to be done, I have no choice. I pull my cell phone out of my back pocket, searching through the contacts. Mother and Father should be home by now. Just as I press the button to call them there is a great thundering from the forest. It's the sound of something running, something large is running. My heart starts thudding in my chest, my body already afraid of whatever is about to come out.

You have powers, I tell myself. Thinking I might be able to grow something to protect myself, I reach my hand out; envisioning a dense wall of trees so close together that nothing could get through them. I brush my hand across in front of me and the front line of trees starts to fill in. It doesn't stop the thundering sound. Whatever is in there is still trying to find a way out.

Suddenly I see a pair of headlights coming down the road at me in the darkness, the car horn is beeping. I shield my eyes from the glare of the lights as the car pulls up next to me. I recognize it instantly, its Swayzee in her red mustang.

She reaches over, pushing the door open at me, "Get in!" She shouts at me.

I throw myself into her car, pulling the door closed behind me. "Go, now!" I tell her, my heart still beating fast. I turn around, looking out the back window. The wall of trees bulges as though something large is pushing up against them. The tires of the mustang squeal as she pushes the accelerator to the floor, driving down the road, away from whatever was in the woods.

"Did you see it?" she asks.

"See what?" I ask, worried that she might have seen me create the barrier of trees.

"The bear," she tells me. "I was listening to the radio and an announcer broke through issuing a warning that there has been a bear spotted in the area." That explains the sounds in the forest. I let loose a sigh of relief, leaning back into the passenger seat. "They said it already attacked two dogs, killed them, not far from where you were walking."

"Oh my God," I reply, looking at the phone in my hand, realizing that my parents never picked up.

"Did you see it?" Swayzee asks me again, her eyes wide with exhilaration.

"I heard something in the woods, but I couldn't see anything. I think it was running for the road just before you showed up."

"Man, that is some scary shit!" She slaps the steering wheel in relief, giving a nervous laugh.

I stare at the phone in my hand. I bring it to my ear. It's still ringing. I glance at the dashboard clock. It's 7:30 pm. They should be home, they are always home.

"Can you drive to my house?" I ask her.

She must hear the trembling in my voice, the worry. "What's wrong?" she asks, suddenly serious.

"My parents aren't answering their phone." I point ahead of us. "We live just down the street."

Swayzee pushes on the accelerator, speeding down the road. It only takes a minute or two to get there.

"The door's open," Swayzee tells me, pulling in my driveway, shining her headlights on the front of the house. "Dark in there too." She puts the car in park.

I hang up the call on my phone, reaching for the door. She grabs my arm. "You sure you want to go in there? Maybe we should call the Sheriff first."

"You call him," I tell her. "I have to see if they are in there."

I run for the door, stopping on the small front porch. The screen door is ripped. I reach for it, pulling it open. The door wobbles as I pull it, one of the hinges looks broken. I notice a large crack in the heavy wooden front door. My heart starts beating fast, fast with fear and worry. I push at the door, still afraid of what I'm about to see.

"Mother!" I shout. "Father!" But there's no answer. I reach for the light switch, flicking it on. The open living space has been destroyed. The furniture overturned, pictures smashed on the floor.

I hear Swayzee run up behind me, talking on the phone. "How fast can you get here? We're going in now," she pauses, surveying the damage. Her voice lowers, "I think you better get here fast."

I run to the bedrooms, searching for them; the bathroom, the large pantry, even the garage. But they are not here. The car sits in the garage, the keys hanging on the door. Mother's purse is in the closet next to their shoes and both of their coats. It's all here. Everything is here except my parents.

I hear the siren out front. Blue and red lights shine through the front windows, reflecting down the hallway.

"Hello?" I hear a man shout from the front door.

I leave my parent's room to find Swayzee talking with a man who I'm guessing is the Sheriff. He's wearing a tan uniform, a pistol holstered at his side. I wasn't expecting the beard speckled with gray. Or the thick salt and pepper hair. Or the belly paunch. I'm not sure why but I was expecting him to be younger.

"This her?" he asks Swayzee, pointing to me. She nods her head. "Miss, mind stepping outside with me?" He asks me.

I follow him, the numbness sweeping through my body. Never once did I think to be afraid for them, ever. I was always fearful for my own self, because of what I could do. I was selfish, as selfish as they come.

The Sheriff asks me the usual questions. Where was I, what was I doing. When I told him I was at rehearsals he replies with, "I knew that, just have to be thorough." I wonder for a moment, how this man I've never met might know where I was, and then I remember what Jed told me, *everyone knows the dancers.*

He releases me with an apology and a promise of finding out what happened to them. Since there wasn't a drop of blood he doesn't think it was the bear, but there isn't much of an explanation as to where they would go. He suggests I find another place to stay for a few days. *But I have no one to go to*, I think to myself. I haven't seen any of my Aunts or Uncles since I was a child and even the few friends I've had have been distant, not even close enough to keep in touch with when we've moved.

"She can stay with me," Swayzee tells the Sheriff. "Come on," she pulls at my arm. "Let's get your things."

The Sheriff escorts us inside, inspecting the damage, taking notes and pictures.

I take an old dance bag from my closet, filling it with clothes, not paying attention to what I shove in there, trying to hold back the hot tears that are threatening to pour down my face. When I reach for my dresser drawer I realize Nixie is swimming rapidly in the front of her tank. Remembering that I forgot to feed her this morning as I rushed out of the house, I reach for the jar of fish food, sprinkling a few bits into the water for her. She gobbles the food and then, stopping abruptly, her eyes go wide and for the first time ever she puffs up, tiny spikes sticking out of her skin, her fins reduced to tiny wisps of flesh as her belly inflates like a balloon. I watch her, wondering what's wrong. Then I feel it. Something green is in here.

"Do you want to take this?" Swayzee asks. I turn to see her walking towards me with a small potted African violet. I back up, putting distance between us.

"No," I tell her. "That's not mine." She stops, admiring the plant. "Where did you find that?" I ask.

"It was sitting on the kitchen window."

"Just, put it back or throw it out."

"Are you allergic to these too?" she asks me, concerned.

"Yeah," I tell her, thankful I don't need to make something up.

She turns, taking the plant away from me. "Swayzee," I ask her. "You don't have any plants at your place, do you?"

"No, I can't manage to keep anything alive, even the grass in the yard is dead." She notices the tank on the dresser. "You taking that?" she asks, pointing to the tank.

I turn to watch Nixie, her swollen body shrinking back down to its normal size. "Yeah," I tell her. "You think the Sheriff could help me carry the tank?"

"I'll go get him." Swayzee leaves the room, taking the plant with her. I let out a sigh of relief and feeling a hot tear run down my face, I brush it away. I collect my things, stopping to take a framed picture of my parents off their nightstand. I walk through the damaged house, flicking the lights off, locking the doors and windows just as Mother did each night.

I pack my few belongings into Swayzee's mustang, stopping to glance at the house one last time. I get that eerie feeling that someone is watching me from far off in the distance. I take it as a sign to leave.

We drive away, my heart sad, my soul broken, not sure how I can go on in this world without them. Now, it doesn't matter who I am or what I am, because the only people who ever truly loved me are gone.

CHAPTER NINE

I settle in at Swayzee's house as I wait for the authorities to find my parents. It's a single story Cape Cod style house, nice enough, but I'm never quite comfortable. It's not my home and it's hard explaining why I don't want to go relax in the park, or go swimming in the lake, or walking in the rain when we aren't rehearsing or performing. It gets to the point where she stops asking me altogether.

Weeks pass, months. I celebrate my first holiday season alone while Swayzee visits her family in Ohio. I watch TV. I read my books-all my favorites from my childhood. I dance. All my energy, everything I pour into the dancing. I stay late at the studio. I show up early. I dance to *Swan Lake* when no one else is around, remembering the smooth movements of my mother, trying so hard not to forget. I build a bubble around myself, trying to recreate the one that was there before, ignoring the rest of the world around me.

I have this terrible feeling that Sheriff Joe is never going to find my parents. He found the bear, shot it, sent it away to have it dissected. There were no human parts in its stomach, which can only mean the bear did not eat them. But something else happened, I know it. They would never just up and leave. I don't even know where to start looking for them. I have no papers and they aren't even my biological parents. My causing a stir and involving greater authorities, other than our small town Sheriff, would only bring more questions.

They taught me plenty as a child and took me places when they could. Still, I want to blame them for sheltering me, for not preparing me for their loss. They had to know it would happen someday. And now I realize I've been too naïve my entire life, always trusting them. It doesn't help that I can't stop thinking about Father's last words to me that day, when he drove me to rehearsal: "*You're an adult. We trust you to make the right decisions. You know the difference between right and wrong… Just remember, your mother and I aren't getting any younger, it's a lot harder for us to pack up and move now… I love you.*"

It didn't sound like they were going anywhere, like they were planning on going anywhere. If anything it sounded like he expected *me* to go somewhere, or do something. I just don't know what it is.

~ ~ ~

"Whatever happened to your cute boy?" Swayzee asks me during our lunch break. I stare at my uneaten food. I had forgotten about Dylan, or perhaps I just pushed him from my focus. I shrug at her. Not caring that he was the only other person who knew something about me. Who knew what I could do. It just all seems so unimportant now.

"You know, Demi," she tells me, a bit of annoyance in her voice. "I'm sorry that your parents went missing, but this moment does not have to define your entire life. You're wasting away." She pinches my arm, the pale skin refusing to pucker under her fingertips.

I look at her, irritated that she could expect me to forget my family. She doesn't understand, she doesn't know. She sounds like Jessica did when she easily dismissed the loss of the park.

"Sad people live shorter lives," Swayzee continues. "It's a fact." She gets up, throwing her lunch in the garbage and walking over to talk with some of the other dancers.

Her words burn me throughout the rest of rehearsal. But they also get me thinking that perhaps she is right. I stare out the window into the early spring evening while everyone packs up to go home for the day. When I am alone, I turn back to my image in the mirrored wall.

"Get yourself together," I tell myself out loud, staring in the mirror. "It's time to grow up."

Swan Lake still plays in the background, the music soft, relaxing, reminiscent. I pull myself up onto my toes, taking small quick couru steps to the mirror. Perhaps if I changed something about myself, maybe that would help. I pull the clip that holds my hair back. The straight pale strands fall to my shoulders. Maybe I could dye it or cut it really short, that's something I've never done before. I turn my focus on my pale skin, contemplating getting one of those spray tans when I hear the studio door open. Looking in the mirror, I see the reflection of a person standing behind me. I turn, recognizing Dylan as soon as he steps into the soft light that illuminates the dance floor. I'm not sure why or what makes me feel the way I do when I see him, but I'm filled with a sudden excitement, a great happiness so strong that I can't even contain myself.

"Hello, Demi," he tells me, with his familiar grin and blue eyes.

Something about him has changed. It's subtle, but just enough to notice. I take in his dark jeans, his heavy gray sweater. He's overdressed from how I usually see him at the lake-almost naked and dripping with water. I tell myself that's what's changed, just his clothes. I run at him and, unable to control myself, I throw myself on him, embracing him as tight as I can, my feet dangling in the air. He feels warm and strong and good. His arms circle around me, just for an instant, before they fall back at his sides.

"Sorry," I tell him, letting myself slide down his body until my feet hit the floor.

I hear him swallow hard.

"I thought you were not fond of me," he tells me, backing up and putting a little distance between us.

"I'm sorry, something bad happened." I wring at my fingers. "To my parents-"

"I know," he interrupts. "Your friend told me."

"Swayzee?"

"Yes, she's quite a nice girl. She's worried about you, you know?"

"Yes." I circle away from him, pondering how to apologize for ignoring him all fall and winter long.

"You don't need to apologize," he tells me, somehow sensing what I was feeling. I stop and turn towards him. His skin looks darker, his eyes bluer. I am hit with the sudden impact of how much I've missed him. "Would you like me to take you somewhere?" he asks, raising his eyebrows in question.

"Yes," I answer immediately. I know instantly where I want to go, the place I haven't been since my parents disappeared. "Let's go to the pier."

He waits as I collect my things and change my shoes. I've gone back to the boots and the heavy green jacket, both for comfort and fear. I'm afraid because I've forgotten how to control some of the power since I haven't used it in so long.

I follow Dylan out of the building, expecting to walk since the lake is not far from here. But I'm surprised when Dylan leads me to a truck, a black shiny pickup that looks like it's just a few years old.

"You drive?" I ask him.

He laughs a little, "Doesn't everyone?"

"I guess so." *Except for me.* I don't tell him that I never learned how to drive, there was never a need.

"Should we walk?" I ask him.

"Not unless you want to get wet, it's going to rain later." My stomach seems to drop. He must notice my sudden change of expression at his mention of rain. My memories of rain are not good. The last time I was stuck out in the rain on the rooftops in the city, I think I almost died.

"Don't worry, Demi, I won't let the rain touch you." He opens the passenger truck door for me, ushering me inside with the gentle pressure of his hand on my back.

Dylan parks his truck on the side of the road, right near the dirt path that leads to the pier. I leave my dance bag in the cab of his truck, taking just the boots and heavy coat with me. I stare apprehensively down the dirt path, pulling the coat on.

"You're still wearing that?" Dylan asks me.

"Yes." I don't look in his eyes.

"You haven't been practicing?"

"No." I can feel the pull of the trees as he speaks to me. I zip the heavy coat. "I'm going to run," I tell him.

"I'm going to walk," he replies, locking his truck with the key-fob in his hand.

"Meet you at the end," I tell him. Then I run.

I ignore the pull of the forest around me, the way it beckons me. Somehow, it seems stronger than ever. I run as fast as I can until I reach the solid wood of the pier, running out to the end of it, to the middle of the lake. I turn around, expecting to see Dylan break from the forest, but he doesn't. He must be taking his time. I lean over the side of the pier, staring into the still waters of the lake. The surface is smooth, reflective. I shrug off the heavy coat, letting it fall into a pile and sit cross-legged, waiting.

It seems to take him forever to walk the dirt path. By the time I see him exit the woods the sun has started to set. He walks slowly, strolling, never taking his eyes off me. I simply stare back, waiting, realizing how truly nice he is to look at.

"Just taking a Sunday stroll?" I ask him, as he sits next to me.

"I was just taking my time," he tells me, untying his boots. "Enjoying the view. I haven't seen it in a while." He kicks off his boots and rolls up his jeans, dipping his feet in the lake. For a moment I wonder if he was speaking to me or the forest or the lake because I have never had a guy say such things to me before. But it's not like I wasn't thinking something similar.

"What have you been doing?" I ask him, changing the subject, curious about how he's spent his time.

"I had to travel to Florida. The winters here, they're too cold for me." He looks down at his hands. "Everything freezes." His palm starts to fill with water, from the sky or the lake, I'm not sure.

I watch him, aware that I haven't tried to manipulate anything green in a while. Not since the fall when the bear was in the woods and I grew a fencing of trees. He pours the water out of his palm, wipes his hands on his jeans.

"I learned that the hard way my first winter here, froze to the ground until the spring thaw."

"You froze to the ground?" I ask.

"Yes, I don't recommend it."

"When was that?"

"Long time ago, before the earth warmed, before the winters became nothing but a cold dusting of snow. The drifts used to rise above my head. You would've gotten lost in the snow banks." He stares out at the lake. "Want to swim?" Dylan asks, unbuttoning his sweater.

"No." I tell him, looking to the overcast sky. "I thought people weren't supposed to swim during a rain storm?" I ask.

"*We* are not normal people." He grins at me, standing, pulling the sweater over his head and dropping it onto the pier leaving him in just a thin white shirt.

"We look like people," I tell him

"Fine, maybe we are part people." He follows my gaze, raising his hand to the sky, pushing his palm at the dark rain clouds. They seem to back up, leaving us with a few slivers of sunset. "People can't do that."

"You can control the weather?" I ask him.

"Some weather. Clouds are nothing but water vapor." He pulls the shirt off and I see him reach for the button of his jeans. "The winter weather I can't do much about though. It's just too cold for me to do anything."

"So your weakness is the cold?"

"So far."

I hear the unmistakable sound of his zipper. I turn away, sensing that his disrobing may be some seduction trick. Or maybe he just can't wait to get in the water, his desire to swim is that bad, that strong, just like the trees are for me. I feel the pier sway as he leaps off of it, diving into the water. I turn, watching as he barely makes a splash, his image shimmering under the water, diving deep below the surface.

He looks human, I think to myself. Handsomely human and I can't deny that I am a little bit-no, very-attracted to him. I remember how he told me that he felt I was here, and that was how he found me. It seems I have yet to feel that strongly about him. Or maybe, I just can't sort it from the feeling of the forests.

When he doesn't come back up I turn to the forest expecting it to call to me, like it always does. I think maybe I should try and do something, *practice* as Dylan calls it. I look behind me and see he's still under the water. Somewhere deep down there he's swimming as though he's a sea creature.

There's no better time to try than these private few minutes I have. I hold my finger out, pointing at a pine tree on the edge of the forest, waiting for the familiar feeling. When it doesn't come, I open my hand, facing my palm towards it just as Dylan did with the rain clouds. Nothing.

"You're too far away," I hear Dylan's voice behind me.

Startled, I turn back to him. "You moved the *clouds*. Why am I too far away?"

"I've had longer to practice than you." He spins his body as though he's a seal and dives back down into the murkiness.

"Stupid," I mutter to myself, annoyed that I'm too far away.

I get up and walk towards the forest by the entrance to the pier until I can feel the pull throughout my body. I hold my hand out, focusing on a pine tree, unsure of what I should do. I settle with making it grow. I will it up towards the sky, stopping it just as it clears the height of the forest. The branches hit the nearby trees, sending a spray of pine needles and leaves to the forest floor. I bend it towards me, listening to the deep groan of the dense wood. I push it away, and then make it sway from side to side.

"See," I hear Dylan behind me. "Too far away."

"Stop bragging," I tell him, turning only to find his tall sopping wet frame standing right behind me. Thankfully, he's left a thin pair of boxer shorts on, but it doesn't make me any more comfortable, and I have to work hard controlling my eyes so they don't linger over his body. "Perhaps, you should put some clothes on." I feel the flush rising in my cheeks.

"If you insist," he tells me, jumping back into the water, swimming to the edge of the pier where our belongings are.

I walk, noting the darkness of the sky, the lightning in the distance. It's going to rain soon. Dylan is getting himself dressed. Somehow, without a towel he's seemed to dry himself, even his hair. I pick up my heavy coat, pulling it on just as a few large raindrops fall onto my arm.

"I have to go," I tell him, watching as the raindrops start to drop into the lake, creating tiny pock marks all over the surface. I shudder, remembering how it felt when I was stuck on the rooftop in that downpour, the cold raindrops sucking the life from me.

"I won't let the rain get to you," Dylan tells me, taking my hand as we walk.

He's never held my hand before, and I can't deny the sensation it brings; the warmth, his smooth skin. And I feel something, a spark, a vibration, a quiver. It must have been from him, or maybe from the both of us touching. The rain drops stop splashing on my coat, they seem to float around us, never hitting us, falling onto the ground.

I stop at the end of the pier, where the wood meets the soil. "Let's walk," he suggests. I shake my head at him. I can already feel it, the tugging in my chest. "Try?" he suggests.

"Fine," I tell him, apprehensively.

He starts out meandering, keeping a tight hold on my hand as though I were a child about to run away in a parking lot. I close my eyes, trying not to see the trees. Still, I can feel them starting to bend towards us.

"They like you," Dylan tells me.

"Who?"

"Your trees."

"Are you telling me they have feelings or something?" I ask.

"That is why they call to you." He stops us with a gentle squeeze of his hand. "Open your eyes, Demi."

I open them to find the forest has changed, rearranged itself into a thick tunnel of bark hovering above us, the trees bending as though they were hundreds of monks bowing in prayer.

"Push them back," he tells me.

I reach my hand out, pushing my palm to the sky and ever so slowly the trees start to move back, making the tunnel larger.

"Good," he tells me. "Now, let's see if you can keep them like that until we get to the road."

I try to hold them back, but I haven't used the power in so long and after a short time my arms become weak and the trees start crowding us again, just as the last sliver of light leaves the evening sky.

"Let us run now," Dylan whispers.

We take off, sprinting the few hundred yards to his truck.

"What?" I ask him, trying to catch my breath. "Are you afraid of the forest at night?" I mock him.

"I wouldn't say the forest, maybe what lurks in the forest." He opens the door of the truck, his hand remaining on mine, protecting me from the spring rain until I settle in the passenger seat.

His words remind me of that great thundering bear I heard in the forest last fall. "Can we go to my parents' house?" I ask, as he slides in behind the wheel.

He nods, starting the truck and driving down the road where I once lived with my Mother and Father. I haven't seen the house since that night they disappeared. Dylan slows the truck, pulling up into the driveway, illuminating the front of the house with the truck's headlights. Seeing it brings everything back, the memories of that night, of before, of my sheltered life. I knew little of the outside world and it made me mad, mad that they didn't prepare me for this, life without them.

I stare at the yellow police tape across the front door. "Want to go in?" Dylan asks.

"No," I tell him. I got everything I wanted from there. All that's left are things, and they can't help me find out what happened to my parents. "Let's go."

Dylan drives me to Swayzee's place, parking the truck out front.

"Good to see you," I tell him, reaching for the door handle. The rain has stopped, and I don't need him to protect me any longer.

"Tomorrow?" he asks.

"Sure," I tell him.

~ ~ ~

"Date last night?" Swayzee asks as we sit to eat breakfast.

I shake my head at her, raising my teacup to my mouth and blowing on the hot water to cool it.

"Then why are you blushing?" she asks.

"I'm not," I lie to her. "It's the tea. It's hot."

She smiles, flipping her hair over her shoulder. "Well, it's good to see your mood has improved."

"Sorry," I tell her, apologizing all at once for the months of a foul mood.

"Hey, I'm going to dinner with Jed tonight. You want to come, double date? Bring your cute boy."

"I don't think-"

"*Come on*," she pleads. "You never go anywhere, you never do anything!"

"I just don't think it's like that between us, Swayzee." She cocks her head to the side, raising her eyebrow. "I'm serious. We're just friends."

"Fine." She gives up, pushing out her bottom lip in a pout. "We have to go to practice," she tells me, looking at the clock. For the first time in a long time, I won't be early to rehearsals.

The day is hard from the choreographers pushing me. I can't say I blame them. I'm so distracted I forgot a few steps. I catch Swayzee smirking at me a few times. She knows. I can't hide it from her, the fact that I've been seeing Dylan, and that I want to see him again, soon. Maybe we are more than just friends.

I ignore her for the rest of the day until we get home. Since she's going out with Jed, I plan on spending the evening alone, reading a new book. I watch Swayzee get ready. She layers on eyeliner and lip tints. She chooses leggings and a short sweater dress. I watch as she twists and poses in front of the hallway mirror, inspecting every angle of her body. And just as I open my book I hear a knock on the door.

"Can you get that?" Swayzee yells from her bedroom. "I bet it's Jed."

I throw the blankets off my legs, revealing a pair of old sweats, and walk towards the door.

"Hey Jed!" I say as I open the door, except Jed's not there. Dylan is.

I should have known. I bet she told him.

Dylan's dressed nicely in dark jeans and a dark blue sweater. Somehow the outfit makes his hair look lighter and his eyes bluer. I look down at my clothes, slightly embarrassed.

"I sense you've been tricked," Dylan tells me, before I have a chance to greet him properly.

"You sense correctly." I open the door wide and let him in.

Swayzee walks up behind me. "Hi, Dylan, so glad you could make it." She leans in close to my ear. "You can thank me later," she whispers, and then walks off to continue her prepping for the evening.

"Don't worry, you look…comfortable," Dylan tells me, a smile tugging at the corner of his lip. "But, I wouldn't suggest wearing that to Bellini's."

Great, the nicest restaurant in town. Usually it's reserved for visitors and tourists who dine there after taking in the lakes, parks and performances.

"Demi," Swayzee calls me. "I need your help."

"Make yourself at home. I guess," I tell Dylan. I make my way to Swayzee's bedroom, ready to give her a piece of my mind.

"Surprise!" she tells me in a singsong voice, holding up a dress, grinning from ear to ear. The dress is light pink, strapless, and much too small for her, which can only mean it's for me. She thrusts the hanger at me. "Hurry. Put this on, we have reservations in half an hour."

"What is all this about?" I ask her.

"I'm tired of watching you mope around. You only seem happy at work and when you come home after hanging out with Dylan. I'm just trying to help you out." She stands with her hands on her hips, waiting for me to argue. But I don't bother. She's right.

I put on the dress and let Swayzee do my hair and a little makeup. I try to ignore the way Dylan looks at me when I return to the living room. *Just friends*, I tell myself. I need him to stay that way. I need him to teach me what I can do. What we were meant to do. All this acting and hiding what we are, it's exhausting. I just want to be able to be myself, whoever I am, whatever I am.

Jed shows up in a limo, one of the sedan types that's not too long since there are only the four of us. Swayzee plants a kiss on his lips as he gets out to greet us. I walk straight past Dylan, headed for the door of the limo, and climb in. I stare out the window, worried that Jed might remember that night I ran into him and I tried to smoke a cigarette. But he says nothing, he barely looks at me. Thankfully, he can't keep his eyes off of Swayzee.

Bellini's is fancier than I expected. It reminds me of the restaurants in New York City. The ceiling is strung with tiny white lights creating a romantic glow and slow Italian music playing. We get seated at a corner table, a *locals* table. I stop before sitting, the familiar feeling starting in my fingertips: the pull, the tugging. Dylan sees it before I do, a small ivy plant sitting in the middle of the table. He picks it up, handing it to the hostess casually.

"Could you take this away, please?" he asks her. "I'm afraid I'm terribly allergic."

She smiles, taking the plant to the front of the restaurant with her.

Swayzee and Jed sit shoulder to shoulder and order a bottle of wine.

"You want a glass?" Swayzee offers.

I look at Dylan who simply smiles at his menu. "No thanks."

"Dylan?" she asks.

"Yes, please." He holds his glass out to the server. He smiles at my shocked expression and leaning towards me, he whispers in my ear, "You're probably not old enough to drink, are you?" I feel the heat move to my face as his breath meets my bare neck.

I turn my attention across the table as Swayzee giggles. Jed slips something out of his pocket after the waitress pours the wine. He nudges Swayzee, handing her a black velvet box.

"What's this?" she asks.

"Just open it," he tells her.

She lifts the lid to find a necklace, a single golden Pointe slipper encrusted with diamonds. She squeals with excitement, kissing him on the lips, again and again. "How did you pay for this?" she asks.

"I got a promotion last week," he tells her. "Remember?"

"Congratulations," Dylan tells him, raising his glass of wine.

"What was the promotion?"

Jed looks at me before answering. "Manager of the General Store."

I hold my breath. That was my Father's job before he went missing. Suddenly, it's too much, all of this. The surprise date night, the dress, the plant on the table, now this. I can sense Dylan watching me, waiting for my reaction. I realize that I have two choices: I can leave and continue living my life in solitude or I can suck it up and figure out how to move on in this world. I look around the restaurant searching for the fastest way out. But the place is packed, tables are filled with friends, families, all laughing and talking. Doing everything I've ever wanted: being normal.

"You feeling ok?" Swayzee asks me.

I turn around, forcing a smile. "Yes," I tell her as I lean towards Dylan, reaching over his plate and taking his glass of wine. "Just perfect." I take a sip of the red liquid. It's sweet, fragrant and the alcohol seems to hit me right away, probably because I have never had wine before, or any alcoholic beverage.

"Keep that," Dylan tells me, reaching for my empty glass that the waitress never filled.

The night moves on. We talk. We eat. I finish the wine and Swayzee pours me another glass. I lean closer to Dylan, savoring his smell, his warm smile, the way he looks all dressed up. The wine must be hitting me hard because I can't stop thinking about what he looks like with his shirt off on the pier, dripping with water and smiling in the sun.

Dylan takes the check. Jed leaves a tip. I stand to leave, only to grasp the back of the chair to steady myself. The floor seems to sway under my feet.

"Perhaps you've had too much." Dylan takes my elbow, leading me out of the restaurant.

The feeling gets stronger as the limo driver brings us home. I mumble my words. Unable to participate in the conversation, I give up talking altogether and I lean against Dylan for support. I think they laugh about me, but my head is too foggy to care. I close my eyes, trying to block them out until the limo comes to a stop.

"Can you walk?" Swayzee asks, pulling at my hand.

I shake my head no.

"I'll get her," Dylan says from beside me. I feel his arms across my back and under my knees as he lifts me effortlessly.

"I'm sorry," I mumble to him, trying hard not to slur my words as I sink into his warm arms. "The wine…"

I hear Dylan let out a soft laugh. I hear Swayzee and Jed kissing and giggling to each other, lost in some secret lovers' conversation.

"Where's her room?" Dylan asks as he carries me into the apartment.

"Down the hall on the left," Swayzee tells him. "Be careful with her." She warns as though she knows what we are capable of.

For a second I'm frozen with panic, the events of the night finally coming together. So that's what she thought she was planning, a date night, and at my age date nights usually end in one way. But I have never experienced that. I have never even had a boyfriend. Feeling Dylan's hand on my back and the other against my bare leg as he carries me, I struggle a little, trying to get out of his arms.

"Settle down," Dylan tells me, his voice flat. "I don't want to drop you."

"I don't…" I'm not sure what to say, mostly because I don't know what his intentions were for the night.

He releases my legs letting my feet slide to the floor and pushes open the door to the room I rent from Swayzee. He leads me to the single bed and my heart flutters faster. I watch as he bends down, still holding me with one arm stretched across my back and with the other he pulls the sheets back. I can feel the heat start to rise in my cheeks. With two firm hands on my shoulders, he simply sets me on the bed, pulls my feet up, and covers me with the heavy blanket.

"Perhaps some rest will do you good," he tells me. "I didn't think that wine would affect you this much."

I relax, the panic finally gone. I should have known after all the time we've spent together that I can trust him.

"Is this your fish?" he asks, turning to the tank on my dresser.

"That's Nixie," I tell him.

I watch as he opens the lid, poking his finger in the water. Nixie swims to the top, inspecting his fingertip for a moment, and then, like a dog being petted, she rubs the sides of her body against his finger. Dylan smiles and closes the lid.

"See you tomorrow, Demi." He closes the door to my room leaving me to recover.

CHAPTER TEN

I can smell it from my room. It's familiar, acrid; the memory of it makes my stomach feel ill-it's the smell of Jed's cigarette smoke. Since he gave Swayzee the necklace they've been inseparable. He's been staying over and I didn't have a problem with him staying here, but now I can't even leave my room. This is the first time I've noticed him smoking in the house.

I rush to the window, pushing it open and letting the fresh air in, remembering what happened last time, my feeble attempt at being cool: I choked, I coughed, my skin turned gray. I can't risk going out there and have it happening again.

I look at the clock. It's early, six in the morning. Rehearsals don't start for another three hours and soon Swayzee will be knocking on my door, asking me to come out for tea and breakfast. But I can't. I can't risk them seeing what will happen to me. Jed already has, even if he hasn't asked me about it since that night and when we all went out to dinner a few nights ago, he never mentioned it either. It seems he was drunk enough from the bottle in his hand that he doesn't remember.

I shower in the private bathroom off of my room and dress myself. I pack my bag with an extra set of clothes. Nixie swims to the front of her tank as I pass. Usually, I sit with her in the morning and read. "Sorry girl," I tell her, dropping a few bits of food in the tank. "I'll be back later."

I wait at the door until the smell of the smoke seems to lessen; I take a deep breath and reach for the door handle. I pull my hand away immediately, the door handle is hot! So hot that it burned my hand. I reach for a towel from the bathroom and use it to open my bedroom door. The air is milky and warm with smoke. I look down the hallway, towards the kitchen and immediately realize that something is wrong.

It only takes me a few moments to realize that the house is on fire!

"Swayzee!" I yell down the hall. I wait for her to answer. Hearing no response, I take the towel I used to open the door and press it to my mouth. Dropping to the floor, I crawl to Swayzee's bedroom door, the smoke pouring down the hall from the kitchen. When I get to Swayzee's door I reach up and turn her door handle with the cloth I've used to cover my face.

"Swayzee!" I yell, seeing her and Jed in bed.

"Wha-" she turns groggily towards the door. Seeing me crawl into her room, she sits up abruptly. "Demi?" she asks.

"Fire!" I shout at her, kicking the door closed.

"Holy shit." She turns over and starts shaking Jed's shoulder. "Jed! Get up! There's a fire."

I hear his deep voice as he starts to ask, "A what?"

"Get up! The place is on fire!" Swayzee yells at him as she slips on a pair of shorts and a long-sleeved shirt. Jed scrambles to his feet, pulling his pants on along the way.

I watch them from the floor, remembering how my parents told me that if there is ever a fire you simply get out of the house, you don't bother with clothes and shoes, and here we are, getting dressed…

Swayzee runs to her bedroom window and pushes the window open. We can hear the sounds of the sirens as the morning breeze blows in. "We're going to have to jump." She looks back at me. "Are you ready?"

"No," I tell her, remembering Nixie swimming in her tank just a few minutes ago. "I have to go get my fish."

"What?!" Swayzee yells.

"Get out the window," Jed demands as he helps Swayzee.

"I can't leave her," I tell them.

"There is a fire! You are going after a fish. Get out the window, Demi!" Jed yells at me.

I crawl back to the door and reach for the handle. "Demi!" I hear Swayzee's voice from outside.

"I'll go out my window," I tell them as I pull the door open and crawl into the hallway.

The smoke is thicker now, the heat stronger. I crawl to my bedroom, kicking the door closed once I'm safely inside. I stand to find Nixie swimming anxiously in her bowl. "Hey, girl," I tell her, reaching behind the tank and unplugging the filter and light. I wrap the wires up, noticing when I do that my fingers have turned an interesting shade of gray. I move to lift the tank, but when I do I find my arms weak and noncompliant. Crap, I think to myself. I turn, hearing something hitting my bedroom window. I run to the window to find Dylan standing underneath it.

"Demi!" he shouts. "You need to get out of there."

"I know. I can't lift Nixie's tank." I hold my fingers up so he can see the spreading gray.

"Back up."

I move back, watching as his hands grip the window frame and he pulls himself inside.

"Can't you douse the fire with water?" I ask.

"No." He walks towards the fish and lifts the tank effortlessly.

"But, the water?" I start to ask.

"It's too dry in here, the fire has already burned through the moisture in the air." He grasps my wrist and pulls me towards the window with him.

"Get her out first." I point at my pet puffer fish.

"Don't move," Dylan tells me as he stretches through the window.

I raise my hands, watching as the discoloration creeps towards my elbows. Hearing the sirens headed our way, I know that it will create a lot of questions from the medical personnel.

"Demi!" Dylan shouts from out the window.

I stagger and grasp the sill. Dylan reaches forward, grasping me under the arms and pulling me out the window.

"How did you know?" I ask.

"Let's just say I had a bad feeling."

I hold my hand up to him, showing him the discoloration. "They'll ask questions," I tell him as I begin to cough, feeling the same burn I felt the day I tried one of Jed's cigarettes, and remembering my parents' fears of me not having any papers. "Take it out?" I ask Dylan.

I feel him collect me in his arms and walk me away from the house, laying me down on the grass. There is noise from the front of the house, sirens and shouts. The loud spray of water as it hits the roof of the small house. Dylan bends down to me. "There's a lot," he warns.

I nod and watch as he collects the fog of moisture in front of my mouth. I watch as streams of ashen gray form in front of me. Dylan waves his hand, dispersing it, his forehead beaded with sweat. "There's more," he tells me. He holds his hand in front of my face. I close my eyes and open my mouth, feeling the cool heavy air rush into my lungs, and suddenly I feeling like I'm drowning, I can't breathe at all.

"Demi?" I hear Dylan, panicked as he shakes my shoulders.

The last thing I remember is feeling him lift me off of the ground.

~ ~ ~

"Where is my fish?" I ask, waking to find Swayzee and Dylan standing over me in a pastel hospital room.

"Your fish?" Swayzee asks.

"I've got Nixie," Dylan answers.

I breathe a sigh of relief.

"Are you okay?" I ask Swayzee.

"Great, thanks to you."

I force a smile. "How much damage was there?"

"A lot." Swayzee walks around the side of my bed and sits on the edge of it. "We won't be able to go back there for a long time."

"Where will we stay?" I ask, sitting up.

"Well… I'm going to stay with Jed while the owner fixes the damage to the house." She looks to Dylan quick.

"What?" I ask.

"He only has one bedroom," she tells me, her eyes wide with concern. "I don't want you to feel-"

"I get it. There's no room for me." I look down at my fingers where they pluck at the thin hospital blanket. "I guess I could go back to my parent's old house." I turn to look out the window.

"Don't be ridiculous, Demi," Dylan finally speaks. "You can stay with me."

I whip my head towards them to see Dylan with a shy smile and

Swayzee winks.

"Perfect!" Swayzee walks to the door with a renowned exuberance. She stops, just before leaving, and turns. "We'll get together and go shopping for new clothes. Okay, Demi?"

"Sure," I tell her.

"Great." She flashes a bright smile, her face glowing despite the smears of ash left by the fire. "Toodles, love birds."

I look down at my fingers again, feeling my face turn a bright shade of red.

Dylan sits in the chair next to my bed. "So," he starts. "When are they going to let you out of here?"

"I'm not sure. I figured it would be when they found out that I have no medical papers, but the office lady just came in and said the Dance Center would pay for our medical care."

Dylan leans back in his chair. "No medical papers, huh?" he asks.

"Yeah," I say with a sigh.

He crosses his ankle over his knee and a knowing smile spreads across his face. "Me neither."

~ ~ ~

Dylan's home is a mixture of weathered logs and stone, jutting out over a narrow stream and lake so far it seems as though the entire house may fall in. There's a porch that wraps around the house and it hangs over the lake like a suspended bridge without a railing. Possibly so he could jump into the lake any time he desires.

I thought nothing of the cabin as I stepped up onto the weather-beaten porch or the fact that it was made of logs. And I didn't think much of the few crackles and pops I heard. I assumed it was the shifting of the cabin, or the sound of the stream which ran so close to it. There were large windows, a small open kitchen, and an open staircase that led to a loft. It was small, the pine walls were sparsely decorated with a few paintings, a few pictures of the ocean.

I lay down on his overstuffed plaid couch. In front of me there's a giant cobblestone fireplace. He passes me a blanket and adds a few logs to the already smoldering fire. He tells me he has errands to run and to get some rest. I lay there, inspecting my fingertips, listening to the cracks and pops of the flowing stream, realizing that he was correct. I am suddenly exhausted. I roll over and fall into a deep slumber.

Sleeping was easy that night. I had dreams of green things. Vines growing, faces smiling in the tree trunks, thick moss and wavy grasses. It was soothing, serene. It didn't riddle my body with the anxiety I usually felt when walking near the forest, having the strain of them pulling on me.

It was the morning that brought trouble.

I was aware that the preserved wood of most houses I had no effect on. But this place was not preserved. It was built of large logs, whole tree trunks which had not been soaked in an array of chemicals. I wish I had known. Because I woke to find that the log walls had sprouted green. Vines and green branches stretched across the cabin and cracked through the pine paneling. I rushed to the wall, pulling at the vines, tearing at them, trying to cover up what I had done-I had ruined his home.

I was startled when I noticed Dylan had snuck up behind me.

"I'm so sorry," I tell him. "I didn't know this would happen." I look down at my handfuls of leaves, feeling the red glow of my cheeks.

"It's ok," he tells me, holding my arm down and stopping my attempt to rip down more of the vines. "I like it better this way."

And even though I had told Swayzee we were nothing but friends, he bends down, brushing his lips across mine, kissing me softly. My heart skips a few beats and I can't stop my arms from reaching around his neck. I don't even notice when the vines I had torn at quickly grow back into place.

"We could make this work," he whispers in my ear, clutching my body close to his. His heat warming me and sending tingles straight to my stomach.

"What?"

"You and me. Stay here with me?" He asks.

"Do you think that's a good idea?"

"I think it's the best idea I've ever had."

I hold myself back from saying yes right away. I don't want to sound desperate. *I should think about this*, I tell myself. But this place feels like home and so do his arms wrapped around me. I haven't felt this comfortable since I lived with my parents, and since they're gone what do I have to lose? I found someone, or he found me. And it is hard to deny the attraction we have for each other. It just feels so right.

"I just want to make sure we aren't moving too fast," I tell him.

"Then we won't." He brushes his lips across mine. "There is a spare room in the back of the house with a private bathroom and lock on the door. We could be roommates," he suggests with a smile, pressing me closer to him. It is hard not feeling every angle of him in this position and that makes me sense something deep inside myself that I've never felt before.

Still, this feels rushed, moving in together in a heartbeat. I know we can wait to see if it goes any further since he is like me, whatever we are. And truly, I have no one left besides Swayzee, who already seems to be moving on with Jed. Right now, I can't find any error in taking him up on his offer.

~ ~ ~

Two duffel bags, one box, and Nixie in her tank. That was all I had to call my own and all that I needed to pack to move out of Swayzee's apartment. I got the feeling as I left that she and Jed were more than happy to have the place to themselves.

Although I felt a deep pang of remorse walking away from a friend, of whom I have found few and far between, I know deep down that this is the right thing to do. Finally, I am in a place where I can be myself, where I don't have to hide what I can do because Dylan understands. He has been harboring the same secrets, hiding, just like I've had to do my entire life. Now we have each other. I just wish my parents were here to meet him.

~ ~ ~

We sit on the pier, just as we have done each night after I get done with rehearsals. I watch the rain pour down all around us. Not a drop falls on my skin, thanks to Dylan's hand holding mine.

"How can you do so much?" I ask Dylan. "You control it so well."

"It wasn't always like this. It takes years, years and years of practice and focus. You have to focus, that's always the hardest part."

Someday, I would like to be as strong as him.

"You want to see something great?" he asks, pulling his feet out of the water.

"Sure," I smile at him.

He holds his free palm up and pushes at the rain clouds. They part, headed away from us, leaving just the starred night sky.

"That was *amazing*," I tell him, trying my best to keep my voice flat. I've seen him do that trick at least ten times already.

"Not that." He releases my hand and the night air cools the skin which his hand was keeping warm. I cross my arms and wait.

Dylan closes his eyes, and reaching out with his index finger he touches just the top of the lake. I watch as the water swells, rolls, and then, it stills. He takes three deep breaths and opens his eyes, staring at the lake. The night breeze plays with his hair. It looks almost white with the light from the moon and I wonder if he might let me cut it, just a tiny piece, a few strands, so I can keep them with me when he leaves for Florida in the winter. That way I might have a bit of him here with me, and maybe I won't feel so lonely like last year when my parents disappeared.

"I think it's done," he says.

"What?" I ask, taking my focus off his hair.

"Just watch."

He stands, his toes on the edge of the pier, looking as though he might dive in. I've seen him do this a hundred times. I yawn mockingly at him, patting my lips with my open hand. He doesn't give me a response, just the flick of his brow and a little grin as he steps off the pier into the water. What makes me jump to my feet, feeling like an idiot for mocking him, is that he doesn't sink under the water, he doesn't swim away. No, he is standing on the water!

I meet him at the edge of the pier. The water is still, flat, a smooth mirrored surface illuminated by the moon. I can see the tiny fish and a few frogs swimming underneath, but none break the surface. It's motionless, and even, and miraculous.

"Do you want to come out here?" he asks. I can see the lines starting to show on his forehead, the concentration it's taking him. I hesitate. "Come on," he tells me. "Just… you just can't touch me, not now, not until I've mastered it."

I nod at him, stepping out, my toes touching the water. It feels just like it looks, cool and smooth, like walking on a mirror. I slide my feet across the surface, marveling at what he's created.

"It's amazing," I tell him. He smiles. I look out over the lake noticing the sliver of the crescent moon reflected on the surface. "I want to touch the moon."

He nods. I take it as his indication that I can do it. I run, I slide, I spin myself to the center of the smooth, hard lake, stopping only when my toes touch the soft reflection of the moon. I look up in the night sky and back down again. It's a perfect likeness, no wobbly outlines, no interference from the creatures of the lake. It's wonderful. I touch it with my bare toe, hoping that it might feel warm. But it doesn't. I take a few steps back and with a few skips I jeté, leaping over the moon's reflection.

"Did you see?" I shout back to Dylan. "I jumped over the moon!"

I think I see him nod his head. I jeté again. I pirouette around the reflection, smiling and laughing to myself. Never have I been able to enjoy the lake so much.

Then, suddenly, the image of the moon wavers under my feet. I look up to see Dylan waving to me. The image wavers again, a shudder obscuring the glowing outline. I look at my feet, which seem as though they have sunk into the lake a small bit. It's as though I'm standing in cool mud, but it's not mud, it's some strange phase of the lake water. Not quite liquid, not quite solid. Dylan continues to wave, more frantically now, beckoning me back from the center of the lake.

Oh no! I realize he's losing focus.

At least a hundred yards away from him I run at full speed and with each step I sink deeper into the softening water. It feels as though I'm walking in snow or on sand, my feet dipping deeper with each step as I get closer to the pier. When I get close enough, I see Dylan's eyes are closed, his brow covered in beads of sweat. I only have a few steps left, but I'm sure he can't hold on much longer. I leap for the pier, my toes landing just on the edge. I balance myself, fluttering my arms, steadying my body from falling backwards.

I hear a splash.

Turning, I see that Dylan is no longer standing on the water. I can make out the tips of his silvery hair as he sinks below the surface, which is no longer smooth and flat. It has returned to normal, with small waves lapping against the side of the weathered wooden pier.

I wait, watching the water, watching for him to swim up and break the surface. Nothing. Seconds pass, minutes. He should've come back up by now. I don't usually worry about him when he's been under water for a long period of time, but this is different. He's just pushed himself too hard, too far. I know the feeling, when my arms become shaky and tired after making things grow, after trying things I haven't done before and all that's left is exhaustion. It's a muscle that needs to be exercised, used repeatedly to make stronger. But this is something new he's tried, he hasn't perfected it. That's why I can't trust that he is fine under the water right now.

I look to the edge of the forest, trying to think of how I can help him. There's branches and vines near the shore, I could draw them under the water and pull him out. I could, if I were closer. I don't have time to run down the pier and across the shore. No, there's no time left, he needs help now. I squat on the edge of the pier, taking a few deep breaths. I only have one choice. I have to jump in after him. I close my eyes, readying my body, knowing what I am about to experience and dreading it but at the same time hoping I have the strength to pull him to the surface.

I dive, a poor dive at that, hitting most of my torso, forcing the air out of my lungs-the air I was counting on using to reach him. The water soaks me, through my clothes and to my skin. I adjust my body, facing down, kicking, and doing my best to swim down. The water is dark; the sliver of moonlight does nothing to help me see. I kick, I try to swim a few strokes, my legs feeling like lead, my chest already burning. I push myself, knowing that Dylan can't stay under like this, not even if it's his element. In his weakened state, I'm not sure if he could die, but the panic that is filling me makes me think that he could.

I kick two more times. I pull with my arms, trying to get deeper, the muscles in my arms and legs burning. Finally, I see his silvery hair floating below me. It gives me just enough hope, just enough adrenaline to push, one last time. I can see that his arms are floating above his head. I was right, he's out of it. I reach for his hand, my fingertips barely reaching his. Everything is burning, everything is weakening. I give one last kick, grasping his hand. I let my feet sink below me, until I'm looking up at the surface of the water. I'm not sure how I'm going to make it back to the top. The weight of Dylan's body is too heavy for me. I yank his hand, trying to get enough inertia for his body to follow mine. I kick. I pull with my free hand. Somehow it works. Maybe it is me, maybe it is some invisible force of the water, but somehow I drag his body up and just as I feel as though my lungs might explode, we break the surface. I gulp at the air, grasping for the pier at the same time. Relief hits me when my hand lands on the hard dead wood. I rest on my elbow, trying to catch my breath. When I think I've regained enough energy, I pull myself up onto the pier, never letting go of Dylan's hand. I settle on my knees, pulling him up after me, grasping him under his shoulders. He's far too heavy for me, his thickly muscled body nothing but deadweight. I have to stop and rest, his weight dips the corner of the floating pier under the water. The water rises, covering my feet. I reach forward, grasping his swim shorts at the waist, and I heave, dragging the rest of his body onto the sunken corner of the pier. I push on his shoulder and his hip, rolling him onto his back. He's pale but I can see the small rise of his chest and the slow beat of the artery in his neck. I look to the edge of the pier, towards the forest trail. There is no way I can drag him out of here. There is no way for me to get him home so he can rest. So I can rest. This leaves me with no other option than to sleep on the pier tonight; at least until we both recover.

I sit, staring at him in the moonlight, watching the rise and fall of his chest, the twitching of his eyes as he dreams. I notice my arms are trembling. I lay down at his side, reaching my hand out, stopping just before I touch him, my arm feeling like it's made of lead. I let it fall to the pier and I close my eyes, falling asleep instantly.

CHAPTER ELEVEN

"One should not do such things." I wake to hear.

"What things?" I ask, sitting up, groggy. I realize that we are back at the cabin, instead of sleeping on the cold pier like I remember.

"Distracting things." Dylan sips at his mug. "Like dancing with the moon."

"I didn't mean to." I rub my hand over my face, making sure I'm really awake and not stuck in some dream. "I just… I just couldn't help myself."

He laughs a little, lifting up my feet to sit down next to me on the couch. "I guess we'll have to find another way to spend our time together."

I lay back on the arm of the couch, watching him.

"That was pretty amazing," I tell him.

"Which part? Where I failed miserably at my new trick, or where you saved me?"

"I was talking about the water. It was like walking on glass."

"Yeah." He frowns at whatever is in his cup. "Not that I can remember much of it. But you were pretty amazing too." He pats my leg. "I've never had anyone come to my rescue before."

"I only did what you've done for me, twice now."

"I must say." He turns to face me. "I am a little jealous."

"Of what?" I feel my face twist in question.

"Of your dance partner, the moon."

~ ~ ~

We found another way to spend time together, a way to steer clear from the temptations of the water. He took me to forests, to the valleys and fields out in the countryside where there was no one to watch except the horses and cows. The steel of his truck bed was enough to stand on and protect me while I practiced.

These things we can do, it's a muscle that needed to be exercised and then rested. Each time I tried I got stronger. I was able to do more, more than grow some vines and shape some trees. I asked the plants to do odd things, things they would never do otherwise. I had a giant oak grow up tall, I formed its trunk and branches to look like that of an old man, bent with a cane. I made Dylan close his eyes while I did it, and then glowed in his laughter when he saw the figure completed. I made the field grass grow long as a horse's mane, and then wove it together in a thick mat covering the ground. When we were done I had to work backwards. I had to undo everything, because we couldn't raise suspicions. We knew there was a man looking for us, a man in a black coat, with a metal tipped cane, and a glowing stone grip. Still, that didn't stop us from honing our skills.

~ ~ ~

"It is safe?" I ask, remembering what happened last time.

"I've been practicing, while you sleep, and while you work. I'm quite confident now." He stands up straighter, pushing his chest forward.

"Okay," I tell him.

This time Dylan doesn't close his eyes. He doesn't even take a deep breath. He simply touches his finger to the surface of the lake and it's done. Smooth, cool, reflective glass, just like before. I step out, sliding my feet across its surface. This time the moon is full, a perfect glowing circle in the center of the lake.

I turn to Dylan. "Can I jump over the moon again?"

"Yes, whatever you like."

Just like before, I run, I slide, I jeté and then I turn to find Dylan walking towards the center of the lake.

Suddenly I am embarrassed by my inability to be as strong as he is. I tell myself, *I need to work harder, try harder.*

"This dance I am stealing from the moon." He tips his head.

The crickets sing and the frogs croak the song of a summer night. "Do you know the waltz?" I ask Dylan as he stops in front of me.

"I think I can make do."

I hold my hand out for him to take, but instead he places his hands on my hips, the fabric of my summer dress preventing our skin from touching. I remember what he said last time, that he couldn't touch me, that he couldn't break his focus. He leads with the familiar steps of the waltz: forward, to the side, and then back together. His movements are smooth, sweeping. He even leads me to spin a few times before pulling me back close to him, his arm bent tightly across my back. It feels so right, the both of us like this.

I told him that I wanted to take it slow, that I didn't want to rush into anything, and all this time he has done nothing but comply-giving me my own space in his guest room and the freedom to do what I pleased. Still, I find myself spending every minute with him. If I'm not at work, or sleeping, it's just the two of us, and it feels so good.

I look into his pale blue eyes, wondering if he might feel the same, if he might be thinking the same things as me. I feel his other hand move away from my hip and across my back and just as though he's reading my mind, thinking the same things as me, he leans forward, stopping, just before his lips meet mine. He hovers, hesitates. I don't want him to get the chance to pull away, just as I have so many times with my excuses. So I lean forward pressing my lips to his. Dylan's reaction is immediate, his hands move, trailing up my skin, across my arms, my shoulders, my cheeks. He buries his fingers in my hair, tilting my head just so. I feel his lips part on mine, their soft pressure, and then his tongue flicks across my bottom lip. Electricity, burning electricity-that's what this feels like-running through my body, straight for my heart, making my head foggy.

A strange sound interrupts us. A creeping-crackle, like breaking ice. All at once the solid lake below us lets loose, changing back to fluid water. We fall, plunging down deep under the murky surface as two bricks. I can feel the energy drain from my body as we sink deeper. I open my eyes, but he remains the same, stuck with his lips on mine, his eyes closed, savoring the kiss, not wanting it to end. I don't either, but I can already feel the lake water sucking the life from me.

I pull back, shoving at his chest, he barely moves and my muscles hardly work under the heavy water to break the trance. I see his eyes flick open wide, taking in what was happening before him. *I'm drowning.* By the time he realizes, it's almost too late. My lungs burn, starved of oxygen, my muscles wobbly as noodles.

His action is immediate, much faster than when I dove in the water after him to pull his limp body to the surface. I searched, I waited, I contemplated another way, but not Dylan. He moves swiftly.

I've only seen him swim from the surface but now, under the water with him, I can see he changes and his movements are odd. His body seems to stretch, fanning out, almost fin-like. His skin takes on an odd sheen, it glimmers. I look up, unable to see the night sky, or the full moon. We are deep at the bottom of the lake, the center. He grasps me under my arm, pulling me hard. He swims like nothing I've seen before; maybe like a dolphin, or a mermaid. He's fast, and just as the moon comes into view, my body decides it can't hold on any longer. I close my eyes.

I come to just as I feel the lake water being pulled from my lungs. Dylan's face is hovering over mine, his brow creased, his lips drawn into a tight line. I've never seen him so focused. I notice a small drop of water hit the corner of his eye and run down his cheek. When I look up, I see his hair is dry, his clothes are dry. I move my arms, feeling my clothes-I'm also dry.

"One should not do such things," he tells me, sitting back on his heels, staring at me, rubbing his hands over his face in relief.

The kiss, that must be what he means. I sit up, looking around. We are back on the pier, dry and safe.

"You look different under the water," I tell him, sitting myself up.

"I wouldn't know," he replies, his voice as grim as the look on his face.

"Are you mad?" I ask.

With a dreadful realization I deduce that he's changed, again, like when he came back from Florida. Then, I thought it was his clothes. But now it strikes me backhanded across the face. It's apprehension; about me, about us, about everything.

It was wrong, I guess, so wrong of me to think that I could just kiss him like that. Without warning. After telling him that I wanted to wait. But it was my first kiss, my first real kiss. It wasn't a peck on the cheek, or a quick peck on the lips. It was a real kiss, from a real boy who understood everything about me. I never realized the implications of a kiss, that they could be so dire.

"I'm fine," he replies as he drives back to the cabin. Silent. There's something wrong with the energy between us now. It used to be light, and fun, and enjoyable. But now, now it's different. It's heavy, and sad, and foreboding. I don't like this feeling. I almost wish I had never kissed him.

It's when he closes the front door that I turn to him and demand answers. "What's wrong with you?" I ask.

"I shouldn't have done that…" He runs his hand through his hair. "I've tried too hard, and it's just, just..."

"What?" I plead.

"I just wonder, if… if you were meant for someone else, not me. I don't think you are for me, I think what he said…"

The blood rushes in my ears, drowning out all the other sound around us. "Why would you say such a thing?" I nearly shout. "What who said?"

"Look at all that has happened. What I am. What I can do. It's dangerous for you. You've risked your life twice now." He turns away from me, running his hands through his hair, gripping it at the ends and giving it a slight tug, the tense muscles visible through his thin shirt. "I just don't know if it's safe for us to be together like we are. I think I was wrong."

I simply stare at him, trying to process his words. How could he, after all this time? My silence is interrupted by the blowing of leaves across the window. The walls that grew green since I've been here have pulled back, thinning in the colder weather.

"Winter is coming," Dylan says. "I have to leave for Florida, soon."

"How soon?"

"Tomorrow. I think…yes, tomorrow would be best. I need some time."

I try not to watch him pack. I sit, staring at a book, biting the insides of my cheeks until they bleed. I pretend I'm reading, trying to hide the fact that I'm scared he will never come back to me, just like my parents. I'm scared that I did something wrong. *It was just a kiss*, I want to yell at him. I want to pack a bag and go with him. But I can't risk losing my job. It's all I have, other than him.

The next day, he leaves for winter, for Florida. He doesn't leave a number, or an address. He doesn't hug me, or kiss me on the cheek. He doesn't even say goodbye. His warmth is replaced by the cold blowing northern winds, the snow, and this new sadness in my heart. I am left only with the memory of a first kiss that should have never happened. And I guess it hurts so much because I always thought kisses were innocent. All those books, those fairy tales I've dragged around and read over and over, they seem to be nothing more than lies now.

CHAPTER TWELVE

Maybe I should have moved out of the cabin. Gone back to my parents' place or just gotten another place for myself. Instead, I stayed, wandering the halls, running my fingers over the clothes in his closet. I slept on his pillow, burying my face in it, trying to remember how he smelled. I slept in his shirts, wrapped myself in his blankets. I pulled his sweaters on during those cold days during the winter where you just can't seem to get warm.

I start to wonder if maybe he was right, doubting our relationship. I don't understand how I can be drawn to him so intensely, when the single thing that makes him extraordinary, seems to be so dangerous to me: the water.

The winters are short these days. Or so Dylan had told me. And just as the snow came, it left. The earth warmed, the lakes un-froze and I gave up hope of ever seeing him again. Eight weeks without a word. I was just beginning to accept a life of solitude, alone, without a partner to share my secrets with. That acceptance hurt, it was painful, worse than when I broke my arm as a child. It stung and burned, it scorched my soul. And for all those books I read, fairy tales and stories with people who could do amazing things just like me, like us, they always had happy endings, there was always true love. I've come to find that those books were nothing but lies. It seems there are no happy endings for me.

So I took all of those books, the favorites from my childhood, and threw them in the river behind Dylan's cabin.

~ ~ ~

I stand on the shore of the lake playing with the plants. I weave strands of ivy up and down the tall pine trunks, sometimes stretching in between another, creating a spider web of sorts. A flock of crows squabble amongst the tree tops, stopping every few moments to caw at me, to yell at me for toying with their roost. I would like to tell the crows that they are all I have left to share this secret with. I can't tell Swayzee or Nixie. A fish and a friend, they wouldn't understand this burden I carry with me. I pull the vines down, letting them fall onto the soft pine needled mat of the forest floor in defeat. Suddenly, I'm overwhelmed with the feeling that I miss my parents and I miss having someone else to share this burden with.

To my left I see a shadow out of the corner of my eye. I turn, stopping what I'm doing, recognizing the shape as soon as both of my eyes focus; it's Dylan. We watch each other. Neither of us moves. I only know I stare just to make sure he is actually real and not some figment of my imagination. Not some dream I've seen every night for over eight weeks. I wait to see if his image disappears in a wisp of smoke, or fog, or tears.

He waves, the corner of his mouth up turning into a half-smile. At that moment I forget it all. I run to him, throwing myself at him, kissing him hard on the lips. I let it all slip from my mind, everything that happened, him leaving and never saying goodbye.

"You're back," I whisper to him, sliding down the length of him until my feet hit the ground.

"Yes." He pulls back and I notice his face is tense, his body too. He gives me a short smile. "Let's walk." He shoves his hands in his pockets and begins walking towards the pier.

It takes me only a few moments to notice as we walked down to the end of the pier, he doesn't take my hand. Actually, he takes careful effort not to touch me at all; the entire time, keeping his distance from me. It stings, it stings deep and hard, and it hurts me deep inside.

"What's wrong, Dylan?"

"I met someone," he tells me, looking to the ground, grinding his sneakered foot into the pier. His voice is so soft I can barely hear him. But I get it. I hear enough to know what he's saying. And my reaction is immediate. My heart stops. It doesn't thud, it doesn't skip a few beats. It just stops and I can almost hear the flow of blood in my veins slow from a deafening rush to a standstill. I'm sure if I look at him much longer I might be able to hear the muscle fibers of my heart tear.

I can only blame myself for this, for throwing all of my trust into one single person, the only person like me. He taught me everything. Over one year we lived together, danced together. I forgot everyone. I gave up my life for him and now, with those three little words...

Perhaps, Florida was just an excuse the entire time. Perhaps there was always *someone else*. Perhaps he planned this, after the hurried way he left me, just before the snow blew in. Now, I know I am truly alone in this world.

I don't give him the chance to explain. I don't even ask him why. I simply turn and run, leaving him standing on the pier, our pier, alone.

"Demi, wait!" I hear him shout from behind me. But I can't look at him. I run down the path leading back to the road, growing a dense trail of pine trees in my footsteps, trying to put as much between us as I can. I can't bear to hear one more word come out of his mouth.

I don't take the path to the cabin or the road back to town. I run back to the only real home I know here, my parents' abandoned house. I run up the steps, stopping just as I feel a cold drop of rain hit my arm. Looking up, I see the sky is now filled with dark rain clouds. Maybe it's just a spring storm, maybe it's his response to my ruining the path to the pier. Either way, I know I have to find cover.

I reach for the metal doorknob, noticing that my heart is back to beating again. I'm hoping it's unlocked because I haven't been inside the house since the night my parents disappeared. I turn the handle and I'm flooded with a sense of relief as I push the door open. Just as I step into the open living room, the sky lets loose with a deep rumble of thunder, a flash of lightning and a heavy downpour of cold rain.

I stand in the doorway, watching as the sky lets loose. A car drives by, slowing for the storm. I glare at the vehicle, still angry, still hurting from Dylan's announcement. I can't help but feel as though I want nothing to do with this tiny town, with Dylan, with any of the people. I look to the edge of the cement pad that extends around the small house, wishing I could grow through it, but there's only the spiky crabgrass growing along its edge. The grass will have to do. I move to the center of the room, stretching my arms out, palms up. I focus on the grass at the edge of the cement, waiting until I can feel it with my fingertips. I pull it up over the roof of the house much like a child pulls the blankets over their head when they are scared at night.

That does it. I no longer hear the patter of the spring storm on the roof. I can't even hear the thunder or see the sparks of lightning. Before, I took such care not to reveal what I could do. I hid everything or tore it down. But a house cocooned in grass, that will not go unnoticed.

No longer having the distractions of the outside world-just the echo of Dylan's words in the darkness-I throw myself on the floor, taking deep, ragged breaths and using every ounce of energy I have left to hold back the impending tears of disappointment, the tears of a broken future, of a broken heart. But then...something strange happens and it's not that I hear or see anything. It's the hair rising on the back of my neck, the gooseflesh covering my arms. Someone or something is in the house with me. I should have checked before doing what I did. Because now I have only caged myself in with whatever is here.

I sit up straight, letting my eyes adjust. It's pitch black and I can barely make out anything in the room. A wisp of hair blows by my cheek, from the left, then only a few moments later from the right. I get the sense it's circling me. There are no footsteps, or the padding of paws, or the beating of wings. I should be scared, but for some reason I'm not. Having lost the only few people in my life that I cared for has left me unshakable. I take a few small breaths, noticing the change in the air; it's no longer the familiar stale smell of my home. It smells like earth, mud and rain, pine needles all mixed with some unknown spice I've never smelled before.

Just in front of me is a small glowing light, not much larger than the flame from Jed's lighter. It grows larger, brighter, changes to shades of purples, pinks, and greens. As it brightens I can see the light is attached to a stick, a tall stick with a glinting metal tipped bottom. But it is not just a stick, hovering in the middle of the room, it's the cane to that man I've seen twice before, the one who seems to bring rainstorms, who seems to know who I am, the one my parents have been running from.

I just trapped myself in this house with him.

I move my legs under my body, positioning into a crouch. Now the entire room is illuminated. I can make out the old furniture, the broken knickknacks, every angle of the room, except for the corner to my right. There's still a shadow there. I can see movement, the shine of a well polished shoe. I stand, drying my hands on my shirt, trying to ignore the tiredness in my arms from growing the grass. I don't have the energy to do much, not after pushing myself like I just did. And I know if I escape outside I will only be met with my greatest enemy: a cold, energy leeching rainstorm.

"Impressive, Demi," I hear a deep voice from behind me.

I turn to find nothing, just the emptiness of the kitchen.

"I knew you were ready," the same voice continues.

I turn around to find the shadowed corner has been lit up and there he stands. The man from my childhood, his face covered with the hood of his trench coat, his glowing cane hovering in front of me. He moves towards the cane, reaching up and pushing the hood of the coat off his head. All I can see is the side of his head and his dark, shoulder length hair. As he walks he unbuttons the coat, shrugging it from his shoulders, letting it fall to the floor. He reaches for the cane, grasping it, and finally turns towards me.

He is tall, his features dark, eyes black as a raven's feather. He's wearing dress pants, a white shirt, a double vest of black and gray, finished with a tie that's decorated with varying stripes of silver and black. A shining silver chain holds the buttons of the open outer vest, diamond studded clips hold his collar in place. He's much too overdressed, especially for this town. He reminds me of a fine-looking businessman from the city. One of those men that women swoon at from across the street, that women rush to their windows to watch walk out of his building each afternoon. City men didn't do much for me. Still, I can't find it in myself to look away.

"Do you know who I am, Demi?" he asks.

I nod at him. I've seen him before. I've felt his presence, but I do not know his name. I know that Dylan has met him. That he can control us somehow.

"Yes, well, I figured you would have some sense of me. After all, I am who made you."

I open my mouth, to ask what he means, but nothing comes out. I watch as he flicks his finger up and my mouth closes, my teeth clack together with the force of it.

"Yes, you may have questions," he continues. "I am Baal. I

created you, crafted you from the soil, from the delicate petals of a flower, mixed with the magic of a fairytale creature, and settled all that you are in human form." He plucks the cane from in front of me, tapping it on the floor as he circles me, inspecting me.

I can tell from the way he carries himself, from the way he speaks, that he is quite fond of himself. Perhaps he thinks he is something grand, something great. But he is nothing to me. I have no knowledge of him, or who he is. I've only begun to learn about myself and how different I am from the rest of the world.

I look down at myself, noting that I am severely underdressed for this occasion of meeting my maker. One might hope for more than old leggings and a stained sweatshirt. I might have opted for a dress, or even a shower and clean clothes. I feel him tug at a piece of my hair, twisting it in his fingers. I can feel his breath on my neck, sending a wave of shivers down my back.

"It seems as though you've grown together quite nicely. I had my doubts after seeing you as a child, and then on that rooftop not so long ago in the city. But our friend has taught you many things, helped you grow. I think, not long from now you shall be able to accomplish the task I crafted you for."

I want to ask him, "*What task?*" But I can't open my mouth.

He stops, moving towards the front window, smiling. "I believe we have a visitor," this man named Baal tells me.

I listen and it takes a moment until I can hear the faint sound of metal on wood and a muffled voice. It continues, growing louder, and soon, out the window I can see the ripple in the dense grass covering I made. A small stream of water starts dripping through, the grass wavers. I see it heave as an axe slices through the last few blades, followed by a steady rush of rainwater, and hands pushing the dense blades of grass aside.

"Dylan," I whisper as he steps into the grass covered dome I created. Baal flicks his finger again and my mouth closes, teeth clacking, once again. I try to move my arms, to run and push him away, but I can't move. My limbs are frozen. I want so badly to warn Dylan, even though I was just so mad at him. I watch through the window as he runs up the front steps and pushes open the front door. It is only a split second from when our eyes meet that he drops to the ground on both knees, his head bowed, his arms limp at his sides, his silvery hair dripping with rainwater.

"Master," he whispers to Baal without even looking at him.

"Ah yes, my little stool pigeon has returned!" He raises Dylan to his feet. I notice his eyes flick to me for an instant, then back to Baal. "Dylan, Dylan, Dylan. My little water boy, Dylan. You had told me she wasn't ready. She looks ready to me. And yet, she does not know who I am. Why is this?"

"I hadn't even told her that I met with you," Dylan replies. "I just found her since I've returned."

I think back to a few moments ago and what was he trying to tell me on the pier? Did he say he met someone or he met *with* someone? Did his time away from me only prepare me to hear those words, to skew his voice? My cheeks flush with embarrassment. I wasn't listening to him. I was too busy trying to figure out what was wrong, without even asking him. I should have just asked. Now look at the predicament I've put myself in, that I've put both of us in. Looking around I can't believe this is real, any of it, it just seems like a story from one of my books. But it has to be real.

"Well," Baal continues, "I may have not given you enough time to warn her, but here we are. All of us together just as it is meant to be. And she looks ready to me, does she not to you?" Baal asks Dylan.

He doesn't respond to the question.

"And now my children, it is time to go home." He turns to Dylan. "Take our little friend here and pack her things, as well as yours. Saratoga has done its job having given you both a secluded place to hone your skills. We will not be returning." Baal walks out of the house, his cane clicking on the floor the entire way.

I turn to Dylan, feeling the panic in my stomach, remembering what my parents did every time there was a sense that this man named Baal was near. "We have to run!" I tell Dylan.

He simply shakes his head and a grim look covers his face. "It's no use."

"Why!"

"He'll find us. He'll find me. Which means he'll find you."

"No, we can't go. He just left, we can leave here." I pull at Dylan's arm but he barely moves. "I'm sorry I didn't give you a chance to explain, that I ran off. I'm sorry. I'm so sorry but we have to go now!"

Dylan's arm reaches up and he grasps a piece of my hair. "I'm guessing you didn't feel it when he cut this?" I look down to see a lock of my hair has been cut short, leaving the length uneven. "He has a piece of you now. He can find you anywhere."

Looking into his eyes, my heart sinks, the beating slows. "He will kill us, both of us." Dylan tells me. "Let's go." He places his hand behind my back, leading me out the door, out the hole he chopped in my grass dome and into his truck at the end of the drive way. The sky is clear, the rainstorm gone.

Next to the truck is a Towncar, all glossy and black with the engine running. The back window rolls down and Baal is there. "I expect you at the castle in twenty-four hours, my sprites." The window rolls up and the car pulls away.

"Why did he call us that?" I ask Dylan.

"It's a joke to him." Dylan presses his lips together.

"He told me I was part fairy tale creature."

"That is also a joke to him."

"So what are we? What is he?"

"Get in the truck. I'll talk and drive."

He rushes me to the passenger side, opens the door and ushers me in. He's in the driver's seat, starting the engine before I even have time to buckle my seat belt. I fold my hands in my lap, mostly so I don't have to feel them trembling, and wait for him to explain.

"I can only tell you as much as I know, as much as he's told me." Dylan starts. "It could be a lie, it could be true, but I've only known what he has told me, nothing else. He has every resource imaginable at his fingertips and with this he has given himself great wealth. He has power over the elements of the earth, which is how he formed us."

"But why would he make us?"

"I think that I was his first, a practice model."

"And me?"

He looks at me, his eyes turning dark, fiery with anger. "You were meant to be his bride."

And it happens again, my heart stops. "No," I whisper.

We pass the dance center and I turn to look out the window, noticing Swayzee's red mustang parked in the parking lot. I will never see them again, never get to say goodbye. Dylan returns his steely gaze back to the road, saying nothing for the rest of the short drive to his cabin.

We pack our clothes, the last picture I have of my parents, Nixie and her supplies. I stretch plastic over her small tank so the water won't slosh out. She swims feverishly, anxious, and antsy at another move.

"It's all right, Nixie," I whisper to her.

After the truck is packed Dylan walks through the house, turning off the water, the breakers, locking windows, closing curtains. I stand in the center of the room, waiting for him, staring out over the small lake the house is perched on. He walks in front of me, closing the curtain, obstructing my view. Then, it is just the two of us in the darkness.

"Demi," he stands right in front of me, his voice low, saddened. "It's time to go." I hear his footsteps as he walks towards the door.

"I don't want to be his bride," I tell Dylan in the dark. "Did you hear me?" I ask when he doesn't respond.

"Yes," he whispers.

"I don't want to go there, Dylan."

I can see his shadow in the dark as he turns towards me. I don't give him a chance to say anything. Instead, I throw myself at him, wrapping my arms around his neck, my legs around his waist, pressing my lips to his. Wishing I hadn't left him on that pier, that I had stayed and listened and not run off like a jealous teenager. He is all I have and I ruined it. I can't lose him. I've already lost my parents.

At first he just stands there, frozen, like he's unsure of what to do, until slowly I feel his muscles relax, his arms wrap around my back. He presses me against the wall, his lips kissing me back, hurried and hungry, like he'll never be able to do it again. And then all too soon he's pushing on my shoulders, trying to pry me off of him.

"It's time to go," he says.

The magic is gone. The dread returns. I release my hold on him, letting myself slide down his body, until my toes hit the floor. He reaches for the door, holding it open for me to walk through.

Standing by the truck, I watch as he locks the door to the cabin, then removes the key from his keychain. He steps off the porch, to the edge of the stone walkway. Placing one foot on the grass, he bends, the pointed end of the key turned down, and he pushes the key into the soil.

"Why did you do that?" I ask him.

"Because," he sighs, his shoulders slump, "I don't know if we'll make it back." He looks at me and I can see his eyes clouding. "Ever."

I don't wait for him to open the door of the truck. I get in myself and buckle up.

CHAPTER THIRTEEN

Dylan drives north-west along the main highway that cuts across the state. He also drives fast, so fast that the forests bordering the roadway are nothing but a tugging blur.

We stop once at a highway rest area, just before dark. I stare off into the forest and watch the other travelers walk by me. I want to run to the payphone and call the Sheriff. I want to tell them what we are doing, where we are going. I want to ask them for help. But I know it's no use. They'll think I'm crazy, they could never understand this strange new world I've entered into.

I watch Dylan as he walks towards the truck from the rest room. He's tense. I can see it on his face, his jaw, his shoulders. This leads me to believe he's just as apprehensive about this as I am. Or maybe he just knows more.

"Why are we rushing?" I ask Dylan when we get back into his truck.

"What do you mean?"

"He said we have twenty-four hours. So why are you rushing to get there?"

He shrugs. "I guess I'm just afraid. I don't want him to get angry. I don't want him to hurt you." He looks at me, for the first time in hours, his expression serious. "He's not good, couldn't you feel it?"

Yes, I could definitely tell that Baal was not good. He seemed dark, and malicious, and it was easy to see that his intentions for us were definitely no good at all.

But that didn't mean I wanted to run after him. If these were my last twenty-four hours of freedom, my last day being able to do what I want, then I wanted to do something for me.

Dylan continues driving well into the night and it's not long before we are the only vehicle on the road. When Dylan finally slows his speed, it's after the third deer he's almost hit as it tries to cross the road.

I see the signs for Perch Lake fifteen miles before he reaches the exit. I can't deny the fact that I just want to go somewhere, anywhere besides the place where Baal is expecting us in the middle of the night.

"Let's stop at the lake," I tell Dylan.

"Now?"

"Yes, now."

"I don't think that's a good idea." He looks at the sign on the road, grips the steering wheel tighter.

"This is the last thing I will ever be able to ask of you, so just do it, Dylan!" I want to do something, anything. I just can't let Baal have me without doing something with my life.

He pulls off the exit ramp, muttering something unintelligible, and follows the signs to the lake. Just as I had hoped, it's empty, not a car in the parking lot. Dylan parks at the edge of the lot, hiding amongst the shadows of the trees.

Feeling antsy, my muscles twitching, I open my door, jumping out of the truck before Dylan has time to unbuckle. I run for the beach, full sprint. It's not long before I hear Dylan's footsteps behind me. I figured he would follow and that he might try to stop me. After all, he's taller, stronger, and faster than I am.

"What do you think you're doing?" I hear him as I slow myself just a few feet from the water's edge.

"I want to go swimming."

His eyes stretch wide. "You can't go in the water! Last time you almost died!"

"I don't care," I tell him defiantly. "I'm going."

"You're going to kill yourself," he argues.

"What does it matter? Huh? I'm better off dead than in Baal's clutches!" I reach for the bottom of my sweatshirt, pulling it over my head just like he has done so many times at the pier in front of me. "Besides, I'm not going to drown," I tell him over my shoulder.

"You're coming with me."

Headed for the shoreline, I leave a trail of clothing behind me, wanting nothing more than five more minutes with just Dylan, just the two of us. It's not long before I'm just in my underwear with the cool spring breeze blowing across my skin.

I run into the lake, the sand squishing between my toes, not stopping until the cool water reaches my elbows. With the glowing light from the full moon overhead it almost seems like daylight in the emptiness of the lake. I turn, looking for Dylan. Just as I notice that he's not on the shoreline, I feel something brush up against my legs. His head emerges just a few feet from me, the moonlight glowing off his silvery hair, and his pale eyes reflecting the light.

It was definitely a little devilish of me to demand stopping at this lake, because I know he can't deny the temptation of the water. It is life to him, he craves it. Dylan holds his hand out to me. Placing my hand in his, I kick my feet, letting him pull me towards him until I am close enough I wrap my arms around his shoulders and bury my face in his neck.

This time, he doesn't hesitate wrapping his arms around me and holding me close. Our bodies pressed together, so close I can feel the taut muscles of his abdomen on mine. I can feel his heart beating in his chest. I shiver, feeling another cool breeze. And raising my head, looking into Dylan's eyes, so close our noses almost touch, I tell him for the third time in just a few hours, "I don't want to be his bride. I want you. Just you."

And then, probably from the fear of knowing I will lose him, combined with the effect the lake is already having on my body, tears start flowing down my cheeks. Unable to bear letting him see how weak I am, I press my lips onto his, knowing that this may be the last time I ever have the freedom to do so.

His thumbs brush across my cheeks, wiping the tears away, his lips never leaving mine. I feel his hands on my neck, one reaches into my hair, the other pulls my shoulders against him. But I've already been in the water too long and without his arms gripping me to him I start to slide further into the water. He must notice. I feel him lean back, pulling me onto his chest as he floats on his back. I want to open my eyes, to look at him, but they are too heavy and weak. I feel his arms wrap around me again and he spins us in the water.

It takes a few spins and twirls before I think with my foggy mind that he might be dancing with me and it makes me happy. I never thought we'd be able to dance together again, not after the last time, which scared him enough to leave me. I part my lips, just a tiny bit, and run my tongue across his bottom lip just as he did to me last summer. This time I feel it, it's just like a lightning strike to the chest. I feel the water hit my face. He must've felt it too and dropped me, or maybe he forgot how to swim for that instant.

How could it not mean something, when kissing him feels like this? How could we not be destined for each other? How could I be made for someone else?

"You have to stop doing that," I hear him grumble softly.

Dylan pulls away, his arms releasing me for a second before he reaches under me and pulls me out of the water. He walks onto the sandy shore, carrying me in his arms.

"You didn't learn the last time?" Dylan asks me as he sets me on the sand.

"I learned something. I think you're wrong about us."

The corner of his lip starts to turn up in a sad smile.

He collects a few blankets from the truck and some logs from the forest. He builds a small fire on the beach, wrapping us in the blankets and waits for me to regain my strength.

"I thought you were going to try and run away," he admits to me, bending to press his lips to my bare shoulder. "I thought I was going to have to run after you and drag you back."

"You still might have to," I reply, wrapping my arms around him. "There's nothing I want less than to continue on to where we are going."

What I don't tell him is that this is nothing more than a nightmare, to have found him and now face the reality that he is going to be taken away from me.

~ ~ ~

From the signs on the road I deduce that we are heading towards the Thousand Islands. I know at one time the Thousand Islands area was open for tourists; they would flock there in the summers for boat rides on the river and to explore the giant castles that line the seaway. Now, it has become one of the largest gated communities in the north east. There are no more flyers promoting boat tours, there are no coupons for discounts to tour the castles. There are truly no gates either, but everyone stays away. This place is reserved for the wealthy so that they may get some peace from the twenty billion people that now inhabit this earth. This overcrowded, Central Park-less earth.

We pull up to a guard shack on the highway. A man in uniform steps out, waving for us to stop. Dylan hands the guard a piece of paper.

"Is Mr. Baal expecting you?" The guard asks.

"Yes," Dylan tells the man.

"Are you taking the bridge or heading for Blind Bay?"

"The bay, Mr. Baal has a ferry waiting for us."

The guard hands Dylan back the piece of paper. "Carry on then, Mr. Baal is not one to be kept waiting."

From the highway it's easy to see why some pay so much to call this home. The morning sun glimmers off the St. Lawrence Seaway, making it look as though billions of diamonds are floating on the peaks of the river waves. We pass mansions and seemingly true castles built of stone and rock, with large expanses of yards with flowering shrubs, exquisitely trimmed bushes and winding walkways of stone. We see no one on the streets or out in the yards. Even in all this beauty, it seems barren and empty. And then, there's the continued dread of being here which gnaws at me, it makes my stomach queasy, my temples pound.

"People do live here," Dylan interrupts my thoughts. "It comes alive in the afternoon and evening, the weekends."

"So you've been here before?" I ask.

He looks away. "Yes," he replies flatly.

"You told me you didn't know who he was. It sounded like you had only met him a long time ago. Why didn't you tell me?"

"I was trying to protect you."

"By lying to me?" I ask, trying not to yell.

"If it's the worst thing I've ever done, I don't regret it." He stares straight ahead, his hands gripping the steering wheel so hard his knuckles are white. "I'm not going to apologize. Imagine the dread you would have felt since I've known you, every day, knowing this was coming."

"We could've done something." I tell him. "We could have run."

"No, we can't escape him. It wouldn't matter where we went, he can find me. The only option would have been to drop you off somewhere and hide you."

"So why didn't you?"

"Because," he turns, looking into my eyes, "I have been alone for a long time. I've kept what I can do a secret. I've had to hide and lie and never let anyone in. And you know what that's like. All I've ever known is Baal. He found me when I was a child, he is all I've ever known. And then I found you, just like he wanted me to. Things changed so much. I finally had someone to share this with, someone else who is like me, and…"

"And what?"

"And I can't live without you."

"Then why did you leave me?" I ask him. "You went to Florida, you just left. No note, no number. You didn't even tell me goodbye. That hurt, Dylan. It hurt me in my heart." My hands move to my chest and I feel the organ beating there, faster than it should.

"I had to see if I could do it, if I could be without you. I had to sort things out in my head."

"And?"

"I told you." He grips the steering wheel harder, his knuckles turning white. "I can't live without you."

I don't tell him that I sulked around his house. That I slept on his pillow, wore his clothes. That I, too, was miserable without him.

He pulls into a marina parking lot. Docks extend into the water where there are boats of various sizes tethered. Dylan parks his truck in a corner spot on the far side of the lot. We get out and collect our few bags and boxes. It's not much for two people whose lives are about to change drastically.

I follow Dylan as he walks out onto one of the docks. He stops at an old white motor boat. It sits low in the water, with five rows of seats. Under the white paint on the hull, *Uncle Tom's Boat Tours* is still visible. There's a man inside waiting on one of the benches, reading the newspaper, he looks up at us.

"Help you?" he asks.

"We're going to Dark Island," Dylan tells the man. "Mr. Baal is expecting us."

"Better get on then." The man folds up his paper and starts the engine of the watercraft.

Dylan steps onto the boat and sets his bags on one of the benches; turning towards me he takes my bags and Nixie's tank and I follow him to a bench seat. We sit next to each other, our shoulders touching, as the driver pulls away from the marina.

The boat cuts through the still water, jolting every so often when it hits a wave. I shiver as a fine sheen of spray from the seaway falls on us. At least, that's what I tell myself the shiver is from.

We pass more mansions on the seaway and the islands that are dotted throughout the water. Some are tiny, just rock, or rock with a single tree or bush. Others are large with castles and giant houses from past eras.

I look ahead to see that the driver is directing the boat towards one of the larger islands. There is a large dock and an old wrought iron sign secured to the stone seawall. *Singer Castle* is what it says. I survey the island as we get closer. The base of the island is mostly stone, the land dotted with scrub grass and a few aspen trees. There is a long stone walkway leading from the dock to the castle, where there are patios, archways, and towers, all crafted in a light colored stone.

To the unsuspecting eye the castle looks light and inviting, but the windows seem dark. I worry as to what is inside.

In one smooth movement the captain pulls the boat up to the dock and jumps off with a heavy rope, tethering the watercraft. We stand, swaying as the current rises. Dylan collects our things and hands the boat captain our bags and boxes to take to the castle.

I sit, not wanting to move. Not wanting to take those last steps which will lead me to a new life. It doesn't matter if Baal has all the answers of what I am and where I came from. Right now, it seems insignificant paired with the fact that I will lose Dylan.

"Come on, Demi," Dylan urges me.

When I don't move he holds his hand out. I take it. Savoring its warmth, letting it provide me with some false sense of security. He lets go as soon as we reach the stone walkway. I notice our things have been left by the front door.

The boat captain walks towards us and nods as he passes by. "Welcome to Dark Island," he tells us as he heads towards the boat.

I hear the motor from the boat start, the sound growing distant as we make our way to the castle. We wait at the towering red front entrance, both of us hesitating. I run my hand down my shirt, feeling the dampness from the boat ride and sweat from my nerves. I glance towards the dock, at the rippling water of the seaway, squelching the urge to run and leap in and try to swim away. I can feel a war brewing in my chest, between wanting to leave and wanting so badly to know who I am. Another hard shiver runs through me.

Finally, Dylan reaches forward, grasping the doorknocker, the lower jaw of a demonic looking face that's secured to the door; he uses it to knock twice, eliciting a hollow, empty sound.

The door opens immediately.

"Ah yes," a man greets us wearing a green velvet suit. And although he appears old, I don't see a true wrinkle on his face. "Master Baal is expecting you. I am Herman, follow me."

"But our things," I interrupt as he starts to walk away.

"The Vassal will bring it to your rooms." He waves at the bags, dismissing them. "Come now."

"What are the Vassal?" I ask.

Herman turns, he steps forward, so close to me that our toes almost touch, and being a good foot taller than I am he leers down at me. "You might want to take these next few moments to listen and stop interrupting. It may do you some good now that you've left your godless world behind-"

"That's enough," Dylan steps to my side, pulling me back from the old man.

Herman sneers at him. "Look who has returned to his *Master*, just like a good little pet."

Dylan scowls. "You've forgotten your place here old man. You are the butler. Now, take us to Baal before I have to tell him we were delayed because of you!"

Herman turns on his heel and walks into the castle. We follow him into the towering entranceway.

Inside, I find the castle is even more magnificent. There is an immense marble fireplace and a winding staircase leading to an open area above us. Herman leads us down a stone arched hallway, our footsteps alternating between the hollow and full sounds of walking on the heavy carpets and dense stone floors. We pass paintings, large gothic windows, and a multitude of closed doors. I hear Herman snap his fingers twice. The patter of footsteps follows and a line of small people rush by us.

I watch them as they pass. They look strange, much smaller than I am, being already small for my age. It seems as though they might be similar to the dwarves I've read about, yet finer built, with elfish features.

"The Vassal," Dylan says from beside me.

The last one slows, long enough to stare into our faces. I take in its golden eyes and pale skin. It's black tuft of hair sticking out from under its cap. It smiles a little, revealing a row of small pointed teeth. I take a step back from the creature.

"Don't be afraid," Dylan tells me, "they're harmless."

I smile back at it and turn to watch as it hobbles along to catch up with the rest of its kind.

Herman brings us to a large open ballroom. The walls are glazed oak, the floors a smooth, shiny maple. At the end of the massive room there is another towering marble fireplace. Above us float three sparkling chandeliers, hanging from tin-inlaid ceilings. But my eyes are drawn to the large windows which surround us. They are floor to ceiling, in what seems to be an almost three story room.

"Master Baal will be with you," Herman tells us, "wait here." He gives me one last crude glance before walking out of the room.

"What's wrong with him?" I ask Dylan.

"I don't know. He's always been like that." Dylan starts to wander the room, I follow him.

"He acts like he's someone more important than a butler," I reply.

"I know. He's always been that way. Just pay no attention to him."

I stare out the window at the large expanse of lawn. It seems the one good thing about this castle, with all of its rock and stone, that draw from the green is gone, the one that pulls me to the forest and makes the trees bow over my head.

This is a new feeling. Right now I can tell it's just me, finally free from the green. A small shudder runs through my body and it seems for the first time I can almost feel what's going on inside me, the raw emotions finally separated from those of the forest.

I turn towards Dylan and wonder if maybe here I might feel differently about him. I take a step towards him as he watches me.

"You've been here before?" I ask Dylan.

"A few times." He reaches for my hand and as soon as he touches me I can feel it, that warmth and tingle that I've always felt from him. "You can't let him know about us. It will only make him angry," he warns, his face serious.

"Who?"

He takes both my hands, his blue eyes wide and clear. "Baal."

Dylan's voice dips.

"Ok," I reply, sensing how grave our situation has become.

Dylan gives my hands a light squeeze before releasing them and turning towards the windows, staring at the water which surrounds us.

We wait for a good hour until we hear the sound of a boat's motor and footsteps echo in the stone hallway.

Baal enters the room. "Go, water boy," he flicks his wrist at Dylan. "Find something to busy yourself with while I speak with our new friend."

"I'll find you later," Dylan whispers as he leaves the room.

Now, I am left alone with Baal. This man whom others call their master, whose bride I am to become.

"He tells me you dance quite beautifully," Baal begins. He looks just as he did in my parent's living room, the nice clothes, the double vest, all in varying shades of black and gray and white. I catch the gleam of a diamond studded tie clip as he circles me, inspecting.

"Yes, I can dance," I answer, trying to hide the quiver of my voice.

"Well then, let's see."

Music starts playing in the empty ballroom and I recognize the notes instantly, *Swan Lake*, Mother's song. How could he know? I stare at the shiny floor, trying to hold myself together. He has to know something about them; why else would he choose this song?

"Dance!" Baal yells at me impatiently.

He doesn't give me the chance to stretch my arms, to take off my boots. I feel my arms and legs moving oddly, the movements jumbled, tense, and jagged. I glare at him. I guess the guard was right, you don't keep Baal waiting, even for seconds.

"Let go of me," I tell him. "I can do a much better job on my own if you give me time to compose myself." He doesn't stop. My arms and legs continue to move in his forceful dance. "I am not your marionette!" I yell at him.

"Fine then." He flicks his wrist, the movements stop, and a chair appears behind him. He sits, crossing his arms over his chest, his ankle over his knee, waiting.

The music continues to play. I take a deep breath in and try to get myself together. I remove my boots and socks. I rub my toes across the floor, judging its tackiness since I am not used to dancing on glossed hardwoods, especially in bare feet.

Baal begins tapping his foot in the air, looking thoroughly annoyed.

I wait for a moment, listening to the music, getting ready to pick up at the crescendo when the mood of the music darkens. As I hear the familiar notes, I take a shallow breath, and dance.

As I swiped my bare feet across the polished floor in a pirouette and a jeté, I wish I hadn't seen Baal's reaction, the way his foot dropped to the floor, or the way he leaned forward with his elbow on his knees. I wish I hadn't seen his eyes watching me so intently.

As the music decrescendos to an end, so does my dancing. Finishing with a knee on the ground and my arms flexed above me, I don't look to Baal. Instead I rise and walk to where I left my boots. I pull my socks on and replace the boots on my feet. When I straighten, Baal remains seated in his chair, continuing to scrutinize me.

"It seems to me he was correct," Baal says. He stands and walks to me, his shiny shoes tapping lightly on the wood floor. "You are a beautiful dancer."

"Thank you," I tell him, crossing my arms over my chest.

I take a few steps back, putting more space between us. As with most people, Baal is much taller than I am, possibly one of the tallest men I've seen. His height makes me uncomfortable. I look up, only to find his black eyes are still on me. I take in his high cheekbones, the dimple in his chin, the straight nose and full lips. With his dress, his features, I find it hard that he would want me for his bride. I'm sure there is a line of women, somewhere, waiting for him to pick from.

"I have much to ponder," Baal tells me. "In the mean time, I'm sure you desire rest after your travels. Herman will show you to your room." Almost as soon as the words leave his lips, the butler enters the room. "Good day, Demi," Baal tells me as I walk towards Herman, feeling his eyes on me still.

As I follow Herman into the arched stone hallway he says nothing. He simply leads me down the hall towards the front door and up the marble staircase. I stop for a moment, hearing the sound of soft footsteps behind me and when I turn to look I see the small Vassal creature I encountered in the hall earlier following us.

Herman leads me down hallways with numerous doors and up

stairways, although none as grand as the marbled one at the entrance of the castle, until finally we reach a heavy wooden door at the northeast corner of the castle. Herman pushes it open. I follow him, notice my bags and boxes piled in the center of the room, but one thing is missing, Nixie.

"Where's my fish?" I ask.

"Ah yes, you might want to keep that out of the reach of the Vassal." Herman points to a high shelf near one of the large windows, where Nixie swims in her small tank.

"Why?"

"The Vassal eat fish," he replies with a pinched look.

I look down to the creature which followed us. He nods his head, licking his lips and kneading his hands, hoping that I might drop my beloved pet into his mouth.

"Stay away from my fish," I tell the little creature.

His smile withers. He drops his hands to his sides and bows his head. Clearly upset at my orders.

"Well then," Herman continues, "life in the castle is simple, you may make yourself at home. We are at your service. The one rule is at two o'clock in the morning, you are to be safe in your room and not roaming the halls."

"Why?" I ask. It seems odd being given a curfew.

His voice drops a few octaves, his eyes narrow. I can only assume he's annoyed that I'm asking more questions. "Because other things roam these stone walls in the night. Things you do not want to encounter!" Herman heads for the door to the room. "I will ring you for dinner." He points at the Vassal which followed us. "You, get back to work!"

The Vassal looks at me, then back at Herman, trying to decide which one he wants to stay with. Eventually he gives up and slumps towards the door, turning to look at me one last time, right before Herman kicks the creature in the back side, forcing it out of the room.

"Hey!" I yell at the butler, about to scold him for treating the Vassal so poorly. But he slams the door to my room closed. It's then that I notice the four heavy locks, two with thick chains and two more bolts. They are hefty and look as though they were made to keep something out, something large and powerful.

I wander the room, taking in the luxurious accommodations.

There's a large four-poster bed with heavy bedding, dressers, cushioned window seats and a spacious private bathroom. I walk to the windows, gazing out over the grounds, and stare at the rocks on the shoreline. It's as I stand there, missing my home, that I realize Baal has brought me to the perfect prison, disguised as a beautiful castle, surrounded by river of which I cannot cross without a boat. At first I was enjoying the freedom from my powers, the quiet, the lack of the pull. But now I see the truth: I am trapped here.

It seems a terrible joke that my whole life I always thought I was trapped inside, imprisoned by what I could do, keeping it a secret. Only now do I realize I did have freedom. And now, it's been stripped from me.

I notice movement near the shore and leaning closer to the window I recognize the silvery spikes of Dylan's hair. He turns, looking at the castle. I wave from the window, trying to get his attention. But he turns back to the seaway and dives in the water. I wait, hoping to see him resurface or climb back onto the shoreline rocks, but he doesn't. I sit in the window seat, and pulling my knees up to my chest, I continue to wait.

The sky darkens and still Dylan doesn't return from the water. My thoughts of worry are interrupted by my sudden need for sleep. I get a blanket from the bed and wrap myself in it. Then taking a pillow I return to the window and curl up against the glass, waiting to catch a glimpse of Dylan returning.

CHAPTER FOURTEEN

I wake in the morning to a soft tapping at my door. Sitting up I realize that, somehow, I'm in the bed and not the window seat where I remember closing my eyes. I push the covers back and walk to the bedroom door. The tapping continues. Whatever was roaming the halls last night must be gone by now. I turn the heavy deadbolts, unclasp the chains, and open the door to find the Vassal standing in the hallway.

I count eight of them as they push past me, dragging heavy shopping bags behind them. After depositing the bags in the center of my bedroom they turn and walk out of the room and back down the hallway. The last Vassal stops and looks at me. I recognize him as the one who followed me yesterday when Herman showed me to my room. He smiles, showing his row of tiny, pointed teeth.

"Good morning," I tell the small creature.

He waves, nods his head at me, but says nothing. I'm not sure if they actually speak. The Vassal stares at me expectantly.

"What?" I ask it.

He juts his tiny finger towards the shelf where Nixie swims in her tank, raises his thin, dark eyebrows and licks his lips.

"No!" I tell the Vassal firmly. "You cannot eat my fish. She's my pet. I love her. Now stop begging!"

The Vassal performs another display of disappointment, much like it did the day before, slumping its shoulders and moping out of the room. I follow after it, closing the door and replacing the deadbolts. And as my fingers slip the last chain into place, I realize that I never locked this door last night and Herman never summoned me for dinner. Yet, somehow, I awoke in the bed with the door securely locked. Strange.

I turn to the bags on the floor. They look like nothing more than paper shopping bags, the sides bulging in fullness. I open the first one and empty it on the floor. Out falls a pile of designer jeans. I recognize the tags from the expensive boutiques in New York City. I reach for the next bag and find it filled with cashmere sweaters and trendy shirts. I continue looking through the bags. There are dresses, nightclothes, expensive shoes and boots. There's even a bag of lingerie. I feel my cheeks blush as soon as I pull out the thin laced underwear. I throw them back in the bag and crumple the top of the bag closed. The clothes are one thing. Something I never asked for. But for a man I do not know to buy me something so personal! I can't even bear to look at what else remains in the bag. I stand and walk over to the bed. Lifting the bed skirt, I shove the bag of lingerie underneath.

I shower in the adjoining bathroom and dress in the clothes I brought, an old pair of jeans and sweater, instead of the expensive bribes littering my floor. As the sun starts to peak over the mainland forests I walk to the window to watch morning begin.

The seaway is calm with only a few boats cutting through the deep water. The serene image is interrupted by someone walking across the yard, headed for the shoreline. Judging from the hair, it can only be Dylan.

I knock on the window and yell his name a few times, but he doesn't turn around. I run my fingers along the window frame, trying to figure out how to open it. But it seems there is no way. When he reaches the rocky shore he turns, merely glancing at the castle just before he dives into the water.

He said he would find me yesterday, but never came. Instead, I watched him dive in the water, just as I have now. He must've returned at some time though, perhaps I missed him while I was sleeping?

I leave the room to explore the castle. The hallways seem to wind and blend together much like a maze. I try a few doorknobs but all of them are locked. Finally, I come upon the marble staircase. I walk down it, staring at the large door leading to the outside. I would like to explore the island, but having been confident in my abilities I only wore the simple leather boots I bought to replace the thick rubber ones.

As I follow the hallway Herman brought us down when we arrived, I find a narrow hallway leading away from the grand ballroom where Baal made me dance for him. There's a small kitchen and a dining room. I continue further past more locked doors until I come upon the end of the hall and one final door. I twist the cool crystal door handle and to my surprise it clicks open. I push open the door and enter the room.

To my amazement, I've found what seems to be the castle library. The room is just as grand as the ballroom, decorated with deep red velvets and royal blues and all four walls are lined with books, hundreds of thousands of books. The shelves tower to the ceiling and tall ladders are attached with wheels so one may move across the wall and search for the perfect book. The small sections of wall that are visible are lined with carved walnut panels. There are large windows, another granite fireplace. There are thick carpets, luxurious sofas, and comfortable looking high-backed chairs with footstools. The coffee tables and end tables hold an array of magazines and stained glass lamps.

I walk to the end table nearest me and pick up one of the magazines. It's coated in a thick layer of dust. Brushing it off with my sleeve I check the date. It's over twenty years old. I shuffle through the rest of the magazines only to find similar and older dates on them. I drop the magazine and continue gazing around the room. I think of the box of books I threw in the river when Dylan left for Florida, compared to this collection, mine was pathetic. I'm sure there are more books here than I could ever read.

I wander the room reading the titles on the spines of the books. There are novels, encyclopedias, dictionaries. I count ten bibles, each spine looking a bit more frayed than the previous. I recognize the titles of Patterson, Poe, Darwin, Pyle, and Grimm. But there are others I don't recognize, a whole wall of them, their spines aged so much that I'm afraid to run my finger across them. I lean in trying to read the words and dust floats up in the air, disrupted by my shallow breaths. I can make out Bion, Strabo, Herodotus, but the others are too frayed and aged to identify.

I inspect the fireplace, noticing that inside it remains clean as though a fire has never burned here. A thick pile of dust covers the mantle. Strings of cobwebs cling to the ceiling and the towering bookshelves. It seems as though this may be the least used room in the castle.

As I look around the room, a glass case tucked into the shadowy corner catches my eye. I walk towards it, place my hands on its wooden frame when I get close enough and look inside. There is a town and tiny wooden figurines, men, women, children, even horses, dogs and goats. I press my nose to the glass peering into the box at the tiny wooden people which seem so delicately carved and expertly painted. I notice a small area in the rear of the glass box where I see a man and a woman. The woman wears a white dress, she looks as though she is spinning up on her toes, one hand raised to the sky the other reaches towards the male figurine, which stands smiling, also with his hand outstretched towards the dancer. They remind me of my parents, with their dark hair and smiling faces. I run my hands over the wooden frame, searching for a switch to see if the figurines might move or if the tiny windows of the carved houses might light up, but I find nothing.

I turn away and continue searching the shelves. I come upon an older section of books. I pull one off the shelf and sit with it. The front reads *A Midſommer nights dreame.* The paper is crinkled, aged brown. I scan the first page, most of the font I can't read but the inky black shaded images are enough to entice me.

I set the book on a coffee table and sit to read it. The pages crackle with each turn and I fear that I might risk ripping them. All too soon, just as I spent most of my childhood, I'm lost in the decades old fairy tale. Before I know it I'm almost through with reading what I can make out and the sun has started to set low in the sky. I close the book and replace it on the shelf. I leave the library, stopping at the small kitchen I passed earlier and grab a croissant off the table to eat as I find my way back to the front of the castle and the marble staircase.

Just as I reach the fireplace I hear the front door creak open. I turn to see Dylan walk in. Actually, he seems to stumble in. His clothes are wet and he hangs on the door as though he may collapse. I run to him, placing my shoulder under his arm.

"Dylan, what happened?" I ask, pressing my fingers to his soaking chest, searching for injuries.

"Nothing." He points up the staircase, his face pale, his arms trembling. "I have to rest."

I help him up the stairs and he directs me down a different hallway, to the opposite side of the castle from my room until finally we reach a corner room that's much like my own.

"I need to lie down," Dylan tells me.

"But you're all wet."

"I don't care." His head hangs heavy and his shoulders slump.

I help him to the bed and leave him leaning against the frame as I get towels from his bathroom. I dry his face and hair. Reaching for the hem of his soaked shirt, I pause for just a second before pulling it over his head. I've never stripped a man of his clothes before. Good thing he's too out of it to notice the burn of my cheeks.

"Do you have a change of clothes?" I ask.

He nods and points to a dresser just like mine. I open the drawers and find a shirt and shorts for him. When I turn around he has found enough energy to remove the rest of his clothing and wrap a towel around his waist.

I pull the dry shirt over his head and I can't ignore the cool feeling of his skin as I take his hands and press them through the arm holes of the shirt.

"What's wrong with you?" I ask, lifting his feet to place them in the legs of the dry shorts.

He shakes his head, refusing to answer. Reaching down, he pulls the shorts to his waist, dropping the towel on the floor when he's dressed.

"Dylan?" I ask, terribly aware of his heavy lidded eyes. "What happened to you?"

Still, he refuses to answer. Instead he turns to the bed and falls on his side. I reach for him, brushing away the damp hair from his face, noticing the dark smudges of exhaustion under his eyes. Even the skin of his cheek feels cold and clammy. I pull the heavy duvet over him and try to control the urge to bend down and kiss him as he sleeps, remembering his warning yesterday.

I leave him to sleep and make my way through the maze of hallways towards my own room. When I get to the door I sense someone is there. Standing near the doorframe and giving the door a soft push open, I find Baal standing over the bags of clothing that remain on the floor.

He turns to me as I enter the room. "Did you not like the

clothes?" he asks, his voice deep with concern.

"Uh..." I stutter. He's more handsome than the day before, dressed in a pair of faded jeans, a dark T-shirt stretched tight over his shoulders. "They're nice."

"But not nice enough to wear?" His expression seems concerned.

"I have my own clothes."

He looks me up and down. "I can see this."

For the first time I am a little embarrassed, being in this beautiful castle, wearing my old worn clothes.

Baal reaches down, picks up the bags, and walks towards the armoire. He opens the wooden doors and begins stacking the new clothes inside. I stand awkwardly near the door as he empties out the bags. Soon he has the jeans neatly folded, the shirts and sweaters neatly stacked and the dresses hung. He turns, searching the floor, noticing that the bags are empty yet there are certain garments he hasn't put away, the lingerie. I make no attempt to get the bag from under the bed.

"Yes, well then." Baal turns back to the armoire fingering through the dresses. He pulls out a pale blue one and lays it on the bed. "I would like for you to dance before dinner. Wear this. I'll meet you in the ballroom in ten minutes."

He walks by me and I am only able to meet his eyes once before looking away. They're dark, black, intimidating. His elbow brushes my shoulder as he leaves. I still until the sound of his footsteps echo in the hall.

I let out a breath before closing and latching the heavy bolts of my door. The smell of his expensive cologne still lingers in the air. The thought of spending the evening with him, instead of by Dylan's side, angers me. I don't care if I was meant to be his bride; he makes me uncomfortable, shouting at me one day then thoughtfully hanging up my clothes the next.

I grab the dress from the bed and take it to the bathroom to change. I hang the dress on the back of the door and pull off my boots and socks, undressing quickly and pulling the dress over my head. Then I stand in front of the mirror and look at the pale blue material. It's wispy and thin, meant for a summer evening outdoors or on the beach, not the cold walls of this castle.

Reaching for the door I hear a faint scraping noise coming from the shower. I stop, tiptoe towards the shower. In the dim light it looks like there is something behind the curtain, a shadow sitting low in the tub. I reach for the curtain, pulling it back quickly. Sitting in the tub is the small Vassal which has been following me around.

"What are you doing here?" I ask it.

The creature smiles and shrugs innocently. Then it looks down, rubbing its stomach.

Of course, this thing is intent on eating my lifelong pet.

"No, I have no food for you," I tell it. "Get out!" I point towards the door and watch as the Vassal climbs out of the tub and sulks out of the room.

I leave the bathroom, walking towards the bags I brought with me. I pull out a pair of thick tights, legwarmers and my well-worn Pointe shoes. As I stand and turn, I catch the Vassal staring up at Nixie's fish tank.

"Stop it!" The Vassal looks at me again. I motion towards the door.

As the little creature walks, I pull on the tights and leg warmers. I'm sure they don't match the fancy dress but I don't care much. If Baal thinks I am to be his wife he will have to accept me as I am and with the clothes I feel comfortable in. I select a pair of simple black flats from the shoe bag which was brought to me this morning and meet the Vassal at the door. I unlock the bolts and we step out into the hallway.

I find it strange that this creature seems to be following me, albeit, he does seem particularly interested in devouring my pet fish, but other times it seems as though he may actually like me. I slow my pace so we can walk side-by-side in the hallway.

"Do you have a name?" I ask.

The Vassal turns to me, holding out a small tag on the breast pocket of its shirt. I lean down, trying to read what it says, but it seems to be written in a language I don't know.

"I can't read that," I tell the Vassal. He shrugs at me. I would prefer to have a name to call him by, especially if he is going to become a permanent fixture, lurking around, trying to eat my pet. "Well," I say out loud, "if I can't read your name, maybe I will make one up for you."

The Vassal nods and raises his eyebrows a bit as though he agrees.

"How about… Bill?" The Vassal coils back, spreading his lips in a grimace and shaking his head. "No? Well, how about John?" He makes a similar face, this time adding a small grunt of displeasure. "How about, George?" Same face. I continue on with Alex, Jim, Jack, Frank and what seems like a hundred other suggestions. All of them the Vassal adamantly dismisses with an odd noise in his throat. It's when we reach the marble staircase that I change my name searching to include more pet-like names. There's Buddy, Shadow, Buster and Buzz. The Vassal seems to lighten up to these names, giving a slight shrug and a wave of his head as though he's considering one of the names. "How about Kibbey?" I ask, ready to give up.

The Vassal jumps a little, waving his arms and pointing at his chest. "You like the name Kibbey?" He nods his head up and down. "Ok then, Kibbey it is." By now we've reached the hallway just before the ball room. "Okay, Kibbey, I think now is where you go wherever you go. I don't think Baal wants you at the dinner table." He turns around and disappears down some unknown passage which I haven't explored, yet.

The ballroom is empty, except for a small table with two chairs. Baal sits at one of them, his clothes changed to a suit. I try to shake the image of him dressed so casually, performing the intimate task of putting my clothes away.

I take my place in the center of the room.

"Are you ready?" he asks this time, giving me a chance to stretch.

I nod at him.

With the snap of his fingers the music starts. Another familiar song, this time *Cannon in D*, it seems Baal has an appreciation for classical music. Thankfully, I've performed to this in the past. I find the choreography from deep within my memory and begin. When I am done I remove the Pointe shoes and walk to the table barefoot.

"Please, sit." He motions to the seat across from him.

As I sit, Herman enters the room carrying a tray. He sets a plate of food and beverages in front of both of us. Then he is gone, just as quickly as he showed up.

"You are quite gifted in your dance," Baal says, reaching for his glass. "And other things." His left eyebrow lifts.

"What other things?" I ask.

He smiles, knowingly. "Growing trees and other greens of the earth."

"Yes." I take my silverware and move the food around on my plate. It seems to be some type of chicken and potatoes lathered in a white sauce. I look at the goblet in front of me, so wishing it was water, instead of a deep red liquid.

Baal must notice my hesitation to drink. He raises his glass and sips from it. I force a smile and mimic the action. As soon as the liquid hits my tongue I regret it. I was hoping the goblet was filled with some type of juice, instead, its wine. I set the glass down, eating a few of the potatoes, hoping to soak up the wine in my stomach. I catch Baal smiling from across the table.

He stands, snapping his fingers, the music starts again. He holds his hand out to me. "I hope you don't mind me interrupting your meal but I just can't help myself. Do you care to dance?"

I want to tell him no. I want to sit here and pretend to enjoy this meal with a total stranger. But I am in his house and there is not much of an escape for me here. Hesitantly, I place my hand in his and stand.

He leads me to the center of the large ballroom and turns to me, placing his hand on my hip. I nod at him, trying to ignore the fact that I feel awkward dancing with Baal. One reason being his height. My head barely reaches his chest. The other being the fact that I barely know him and the last time I danced with someone was with Dylan, and it was…magical. This is something entirely different. There's something strange in feeling him touching me, it's just his hand, but it feels so possessive, his fingertips gripping my hip through the thin dress.

"Have you found a way to entertain yourself during the long day?" he asks me as he sways us from side to side.

"Yes," I tell him. "I've found some books in the library."

"Ah! Good, the library has not been used in many years. I'm glad you've found a way to entertain yourself. Mostly I spend my days in the city working. The castle is a weekend home for me. But now that you're here I will make more attempts to visit in the evenings. I want you to be prepared for the weekend, though. I like to entertain. Many of my associates and acquaintances from the city visit here for dinners and boat rides. I would like for you to dance for them, since you do it so beautifully." His dark eyes never leave my face as he speaks.

"Every weekend?" I stare at the knot in his tie, avoiding contact with his dark eyes.

"Yes. It will be an event. Dinner, dancing, entertaining, it's what we do here in the Thousand Islands. This is our sanctuary, our place of respite from the mundane."

I feel as though I have no choice but to nod my head in agreement.

He slows his pace in the dance. "Look at me, Demi." His voice is firm, demanding.

I look up, taking in his dark eyes. I can't seem to help it, but even with all of my feelings of discomfort I am curious about him and how his powers work.

"What are you?" I whisper. I catch his eyes change, for just a split second, the pupils turn a dark red before returning to black.

I had the feeling he is something dark, dark and powerful. Now I know it for certain.

He picks up his pace leading our dance. The grip of his large hand on my hip is firmer, his pace faster. For a moment I'm filled with hope and dread, for maybe finding out what he is and what we are. Maybe we are the same?

"Are you like Dylan and I?"

He laughs from deep within his chest. "You two are far too pure to even hint at what I am."

"Then what are you?" I ask as he pushes me away from his body, spinning me in his dance.

"A Lord of a dark place, darker than you've ever experienced."

"Like a demon?" I ask, falling against his arm, his hand returning to my hip as he pulls me close. "So I'm a demon then?"

"You are far too naïve, as well." He spins me again, this time pulling me back to his chest tightly.

"What are we?" I press on, hoping for an answer.

"You are not ready to know."

"Angels?"

"No."

"Fairies?"

He gives another hearty laugh. "No."

"What then?" I step back, placing myself at a good arm's length from him as we dance.

"Something else."

"Why won't you tell me?"

"It's not my place."

"But you made us come here. You're threatening me with

marriage."

Faster than I have ever seen anyone move he spins me, and stopping, he dips me back, his face hovering at my neck, his eyelids droop as though he's thinking about more than just dancing. My arms stiffen at his closeness, his offering to dance suddenly becoming much too provocative. He twirls me back to my feet.

"Is that what you think of me as, a threat?" he asks.

"I...I don't know."

I've never had a real relationship, just what Dylan and I barely started. But Baal is a man, a dark otherworldly man. And with the exception of myself I'm sure women must drop at his feet. I can only imagine what he wants me for. I notice I am no longer at arm's length, during our conversation he has drawn me closer to him. Much too close.

"You are special for this place. You were meant to be here, with me." He stares at me intently. Then slowly, ever so slowly, he starts to lean in as though he is going to kiss me.

My stomach churns with panic and unease. I can't do this. "I have to go." I tell him, ducking under his arms and running from the ballroom.

Out of sheer luck, it seems, he lets me go. Baal doesn't draw me back with his ability to control my body. He lets me run down the long stone hall, to the marble staircase, and back to my room. I click the heavy bolts into place and lean against the door, sliding down to the floor, out of breath. It's not long before I hear the sound of a boat's motor starting at the dock. I crawl to the window and look out, just in time to see Baal get on the boat and pull away from the island.

"Seems as though he's given up for tonight," I whisper to myself.

I walk to the armoire and replace the dress, trading it for a pair of my old pajamas. I crawl into the bed, shivering from the loneliness and the fear of him almost kissing me.

The ache is back, the one telling me that all I want is to go back in time, when it was just me and Dylan and Saratoga.

~ ~ ~

I spend the rest of the week waking only to watch Dylan dive into the seaway. I pass time wandering the castle, exploring the library, choosing a few books to read. I practice dancing in the ballroom, preparing a few performances for the weekend. Baal doesn't return. It seems my blatant decline of his affections have worked at keeping him away.

I linger by the front door each evening, waiting for Dylan to walk through. He always does. Pale and dripping with water, too exhausted to talk, to tell me where he's been and what he's been doing. Each evening I help him to his room. I dry and dress him.

I hold back the urge to kiss him, to crawl into bed with him and lie next to him, afraid that Baal may find out. After all, if I'm meant to be with Baal, he wouldn't take kindly to my relationship with Dylan, just as Dylan has already warned me. And I could never live with myself if my actions caused Dylan harm.

CHAPTER FIFTEEN

As my eyes open, I am filled with dread. It's not the impending performance making me feel this way, it's the fact that today is Friday and I will have to see Baal again. I will have to face him after running away like a scared child.

I get out of bed and walk to the window just in time to see Dylan dive into the seaway. I was hoping that today might be different. That he might be around for the day. I head to the armoire to find something to wear since all the clothes I brought have been worn, and Herman seems to have a problem with delivering my laundry back to me. I select a pair of the designer jeans and a sweater, gifted to me by Baal. I shower, comb out my hair, and twist it into a bun.

As I leave my room I can see the changes already taking place for the weekend. All the hallway doors that were once locked are now open and the Vassal scurry about, carrying blankets and towels to each of the rooms, preparing them for the coming guests. I stop by the small kitchen and make myself tea and toast, then I carry the plates to the library and settle into one of the high back chairs. I stare at the open book in front of me, the bookmark holding my place. Today, I have no desire to read about the wizard boy in that book. Instead, I gaze out the window as I eat.

When I'm finished I wander the room. I climb the tall ladders to search the dusty books on the upper shelves of the high walls. I open the cupboards along the baseboards. Disappointed that I find nothing to entertain myself for the day, I stop as I come upon the glass case holding the figurines. Staring at them, it seems as though the people are in a different location than they were before. The dancing lady, I could have sworn, was in the back corner of the glass box, not the middle.

I run my hands along the wooden frame. I look under the box, searching for a switch or something that might have moved the figurines. After a few minutes I stand, having found nothing in my search. I stare at the figurines, waiting to see them move. Maybe they are on a timer or shift during certain hours, like when the clock strikes twelve. I stare at their delicately carved faces and skillfully painted clothing. They look so lifelike. Whoever made these must have been of extreme talent. I have never seen figurines such as these before.

Hearing the commotion of boats arriving to the island, I make my way towards my room. I sit in the window seat, dreading the fact that I will be seeing Baal and desperately missing Dylan at the same time. I watch as boats pull up to the dock, men and women get out, most carrying bags with them for the weekend stay. They are all dressed in expensive clothes, the women in dresses and heels, the men wearing suit coats and shined shoes.

Commotion fills the hall as the guests are shown to their rooms.

There is a small knock on my door, and a strange grumbling noise-which I have become accustomed to hearing from the Vassal. I open my door and find Kibbey standing there with two bags in his hands. He brushes past me, bringing the bags in the room. He's wearing a little black suit with a blue sash around his waist.

"What did you bring me, Kibbey?"

He shrugs, making a small yawning noise over his seemingly tedious task. I open the bags and pull out a fine beaded dress in white. There are matching stockings, shoes, and a sparkling gemstone necklace that looks to be made of emeralds and diamonds.

Kibbey snaps his little fingers at me and taps on his wrist, presumably to hurry me along. I get that sickening feeling in the pit of my stomach. Looking out the window, I see the sky is darkening. The party will start soon and I will have to face Baal.

Kibbey crosses his arms and taps his foot.

"What?" I ask. He holds his palm out and uses his other hand to mimic the walking of legs with his two fingers. "Oh, are you waiting for me to get ready so you can walk me down there?" He touches the tip of his nose and nods at me. "Just give me a second."

I take the dress to the bathroom and change, stopping to glance at myself in the mirror when I'm done. I look like a ghost with my pale skin and pale hair, and now the white dress and stockings. The only color left comes from my green eyes and the green emeralds around my neck. I leave the bathroom to find my dance bag. I take out the Pointe shoes and put them on. Lacing the pink ribbons up my legs, at least these will provide a bit of color. I turn to Kibbey who is waiting by the door, holding the dress shoes in his hands.

"Ready or not?" I ask Kibbey.

He nods at me.

Glancing out the window one last time, I'm struck with a feeling of emptiness. I wish Dylan were here. As we walk, I think it strange that Baal would allow these creatures to be out with his visitors, but then, with just a glance, they can be easily mistaken for a human with unusually short stature.

By the time we make it to the ballroom it's obvious that the party has started. There is a roaring fire in the fireplace; tables have been set up with shimmering tablecloths and an assortment of buffet foods and drinks. My eye catches Herman weaving through the guests, offering to refill their empty glasses with a bottle of wine.

I look down the row of tables to see a giant ice sculpture of a swan flapping its wings. A distorted shadow is visible from behind the ice. I walk closer and Dylan steps out from behind the sculpture. He's awake, and walking, and smiling at me as I hurry to him.

"What are you doing here?" I ask. "I was so afraid you'd still be gone."

"Not tonight." I notice his brow is tense. He must be using his power.

I look at the ice sculpture. "Did you make it?" I ask him.

"Yes."

"Why are you concentrating so hard?"

"The fire, it's drying out the air. I can't keep the ice from melting." I look down to see his hands balled into tight fists. "Looks like you have company." He nods behind me.

I turn to find Baal walking towards me.

"Here is my little dancer," Baal greets me, tipping a flute of champagne to his lips. "Are you ready for your performance? Of course you are." He smirks at me.

"Actually, uh, there's one problem."

"What could that be?"

"It's too hot in here." I fan my face. "I need the fire turned down."

"Anything you desire." He snaps his fingers and the roaring flames are gone. The guests turn in awe, whispering to each other about the sudden lack of glowing ambiance. "Now, time for you to dance."

Baal leads me away from the comfort of Dylan, guiding me with his hand on my back. I try to walk ahead of him so he isn't touching me but his stride is too long and each time I get a few steps ahead of him, he catches up, placing his large hand across the small of my back.

He brings me to the center of the room. The guests part to the sides, giving me space. I compose myself, closing my eyes and waiting for the music to start. Again, it's *Swan Lake*, but this version is different. It's a solo piece, a recording of a cellist playing a version that's equally as beautiful as the original but feels a bit darker.

I dance for them, just as they expect, just as I did in Saratoga each weekend. And when I'm done they clap, they nod to themselves, they smile. There are a few whispers as they raise their wine glasses and toast the evening. Perhaps I've won their hearts with my movements, or perhaps they are thinking of letting me into their circle of friends, which is just the place where I don't belong. I am just a performer here. I don't fit in. Just like it has been my entire life, that feeling is as strong right now as it's ever been.

The guests turn back to themselves, giving me the chance to slip off behind the tables and meet with Dylan. Kibbey stands next to him, holding out my dress shoes. I take off my Pointe slippers and exchange them with the shoes in Kibbey's hands.

"That was nice," Dylan tells me.

"I'm sure it was." I try not to roll my eyes at him. "Is it better with the fire out?"

"Yes, much." I search his face, the wrinkle is gone from his brow, but his face still holds some concern.

"Now what do we do?" I ask him.

"I've been instructed to stay with the ice. But I'm sure you can do whatever you want."

I look into his crisp blue eyes, fearing that the rules put in place by Baal are already chipping away at us. Baal has categorized Dylan as nothing more than another one of his servants. And while he may order me to dance for his guests, I am meant to be more to him than

Dylan. No matter how much I don't want it.

"I miss you." I tell him. "You're gone all the time and I'm left here alone. I wish you didn't leave each morning."

"Don't-" He presses his lips together and turns away, refusing to look at me. I watch in confusion as he takes a few deep breaths before turning back to face me, nods behind me. "Your visitor is back. You had better keep your distance from me. You don't want to make Baal jealous."

I hold my breath as I feel Baal's arm wrap around my shoulders. "If I didn't know better I'd think our little water boy is trying to steal you away from me." He guides me away from Dylan and the ice, towards the open floor where couples are mingling and dancing.

Baal introduces me to a slew of people. All whose names I recognize from the socialite papers of the city from when I used to live there, but have never met. I smile and shake their hands. I try to seem interested in their talks of money, and Wall Street, and the economy, and their recent luxury purchases. They speak of islands and boats and cars, things that I have no interest in.

Every now and then I catch a stray eye watching me, probably wondering what the heck Baal is doing with me at his side.

The last group he brings me to is a group of women. They all smile and grin and do their best to flirt with Baal. Placing their manicured and jeweled hands on the lapel of his coat as they spurt their admirations for his castle and the luxuries provided to them for the weekend. They don't pay much attention to me, I think because they tower so far above me with their stiletto heels, and the dress is working well at making me seem ghost-like.

The women flirt desperately with Baal as he smiles and admires them with his dark eyes. He touches their bare arms, their strands of hair, and he kisses the backs of their hands as they each tell him their names. Stepping away from me, he joins their circle and it's not long before one of them boldly asks him to dance, right in front of me. At first I am angered, then grateful for the distraction. I take it as an opportunity to get out of here.

Sneaking along the back wall of the ballroom, I make my way towards the door, then run down the hallway to the library. I find a hiding spot on the floor behind one of the luxurious couches. From here I am out of view should someone walk in the door and look around. I wait, hoping for the time to pass, for the party to end, for the guests to return to their rooms. Not much time passes before I hear the door creak open. I crawl to the end of the couch, peering around the side of it to see who is invading my room. I am surprised to see Kibbey, carrying a plate that's loaded with cocktail shrimp!

"Kibbey," I whisper loudly to the Vassal. He seems shocked to see me but hobbles towards me. "What are you doing?" I ask him.

He points at the plate of shrimp and then his mouth.

"You little thief," I mock him.

He shrugs. Sitting down next to me, he offers me a piece of shrimp from the plate. I pass and watch as he devours the pile of shrimp, tails and all. When he is finished he lets out a small burp and pats his distended belly.

We wait behind the couch until the hall clock strikes midnight. And as we hear the partygoers drift off to their rooms, we make way to my room. I lock the bolts just as the clock strikes two.

I sit by the door, waiting to hear whatever it is that roams the castle walls at night, and it's not long before I feel the floor vibrate underneath me, eventually stopping as it gets closer to my room. Pressing my ear to the door, I think I can hear the sound like air blowing through a large cavern. I think it's breathing outside my door. The hairs on my arms rise as I move away from the door and lock myself in my bathroom.

~ ~ ~

This continues for weeks; the loneliness, the waiting to see Dylan, the dancing for Baal's parties. Baal sends pretty dresses and jewelry. He introduces me to his friends; the rich women seem to scoff and brush me off, they pay no attention to the small girl hanging on Baal's arm. But that's fine with me because I've already created a game out of it. I find the prettiest woman in the room and edge Baal her way, or, sometimes, I go to her alone, so Baal must come and find me. Sometimes I do more than stand awkwardly next to her, I chat with her, ask a few questions, make sure she is enjoying her time on the island. Meeting new people is something I've never been very good at, but it seems to work here. I think it's because the guests are all so inebriated with the rich wine and other drinks. Not long after Baal comes around looking for me, and to escape the threat of him asking me to dance or hang on his arm, I introduce him to my new friend. The pretty women flirt with him, just as they always do, and Baal soaks it up. Soon they are dancing and drinking and I sneak off, sometimes waiting to leave the room until I see him search the room for me one last time before he wanders off with the pretty young things.

Once, I made the mistake of following Baal with one of the distractions I set him up with. Walking past the guest room I saw them enter, I could hear his deep voice inside and that of the woman's. The sounds of them kissing, and other things, it was enough to send me running down the hall.

The next day it's always the same. I have to find a new lady, because whoever he was enamored with the previous night, he loses interest in fast. He ignores them and moves on. Much like I'm sure he would do to me if I ever gave him the chance. Amongst all of this, I find it hard to believe he could ever think I would accept a life like this, being betrothed to some man who has no qualms skipping from warm body to warm body each night.

Each week I watch Dylan swim away in the morning, only to return each evening too exhausted for words. I wander the castle. I stand in his room, wishing he were here with me. He has yet to explain what he has been doing, what is so important that he has to drive himself to exhaustion every single day.

I watch the days turn from spring, to summer, and to a chilly fall. When Dylan returns one day it strikes me, just as the crusty leaves of autumn blow in the door with him; I haven't been outside in a long time. I haven't even practiced growing anything. I've spent all my time in this castle, dancing, reading and avoiding Baal.

Dylan starts to change. I think it's from the exhaustion, but I'm not really sure. Whereas before, I would help him to his room, I would dry him and change his clothes, now he tells me that he can take care of himself, that he doesn't need any of my help. His blue eyes grow dull, his silvery hair grows long and ragged to his shoulders. He grows thin, the bone and muscle visible through his sopping wet clothes. Sometimes I think I am watching him turn into an old man before my eyes. Sometimes I just watch him trudge his way to his room, glancing through the castle windows at the island I have yet to explore. We have only been here a few months, long enough for the summer to pass, but for Dylan, it seems like he's been here longer, like the time here has taken such a toll on him, affected him differently.

I just wish I had known what was about to happen, that I had had some type of premonition. If I did I might have tried to find a way for us to escape. I might have confronted Dylan, snapped him out of his stupor and made a plan. Looking back, I could have done something to prevent this, I just know it.

CHAPTER SIXTEEN

With the increasing coldness, Dylan has to work harder at keeping his ice sculptures from melting now that Baal has returned to filling the fireplace with roaring flames. Tonight I can already see the toll it's taking on Dylan, the silvery hair at the back of his neck curled with perspiration, and the grim look he wears, distorting his handsome face.

I dance, just as I always do. Most of Baal's guests now know me. They've watched me perform for months; they've clapped at my performances, and acknowledged my existence when Baal prances around with me on his arm. Some of them even call me by the correct name. Never the women though, the women simply ignore me, unless I speak to them.

Something about this night feels off, though. Dylan is in a heightened sour mood, and there seems to be an electricity of excitement charging the room. After another performance I change my shoes. Baal escorts me around the room. Except this time he holds me tightly with a hand on my hip, pressing me possessively against his side.

His guests pat him on the back, they wish him luck, and I assume it's some inside joke to which I am not privy. I scan the crowd, looking for a pretty woman to send him off with and just as I spot her, Baal changes my plans. He pulls me onto the dance floor, away from the pretty women and the rich men.

"Where are we going?" I ask, trying to pull away from him, to direct him another way but it doesn't seem to work. "There's someone I want to talk to."

"If I didn't know better, my dear, it seems as though you've been trying to avoid me." He stops in the middle of the dance floor, places his warm hand on my hip and pulls me close. So close I can feel the rise and fall of his chest. I can feel the hard muscle beneath his fancy clothes. I can smell the expensive cologne mixed with the scent that can only be him. It reminds me of burning embers, the cedar wood of the forest, and it's no wonder the women fall so easily for him. It's intoxicating. If it weren't for the burn of Dylan's gaze on my back, I might fall for Baal's tricks.

I wish I could turn around and run to him. I want Dylan to know that Baal may look good to my eyes, but not my heart, he has never held my heart the way Dylan has-the way he still does.

Baal leans down, whispering in my ear, his breath caressing my neck. "I've seen what you've been doing, little dancer. The games you've been playing. Well, it's my turn now." He rests his cheek against my forehead, as though we've danced in this position a thousand times. I try to pull away from him but, like so long ago, I have lost control of my limbs, my arms and legs move for me. Baal is taking control.

"Please, stop," I whisper to him between my teeth. It's all I can make out since he has my jaw locked in a permanent smile.

"This was meant to be. I cannot wait any longer." I feel him let go of my waist. He reaches into his pocket. My heart races. "You cannot deny me forever, this ends now."

Suddenly, Baal is kneeling in front of me, a velveteen black box in his hands. I am frozen in place, not just by Baal's magic but by my own panic because it's obvious what he is doing. The guests whisper to each other, then hush silent. All of their eyes on the two people in the center of the room. I can see Dylan at the ice sculpture, his face stony with anger. He must have known this was coming, he must have sensed it and maybe this is why he's been acting so strangely towards me.

"Demi," Baal starts, he takes my right hand in his, and flips the lid open on the ring box with his free hand. "Will you do me the honor of becoming my wife?"

The crowd hushes. The beautiful women in the audience, who've had their relations with him all summer long, roll their eyes. I can feel the tears welling up in my eyes, not out of happiness or joy, but out of fear and anger because Baal is holding my mouth closed and nodding my head yes.

It must look real and the guests must believe it is true. They clap, they whistle. I watch, bewildered, as Baal places a diamond ring on my finger. It's different from normal engagement rings. Instead of being made of clear diamonds, they are a tarnished brown color. I think I've heard those called chocolate diamonds. But they don't represent sweet chocolate to me, only a dark promise and a murky future without the only boy I'm sure I've ever loved.

So suddenly, my life changes again. I am engaged, against my will, to a man I barely know. I'm sure there will be a wedding, of which my parents will never attend, of which the few friends I have, or had, will not attend.

Baal raises himself up onto his two feet, beaming with pride as the tears stream down my face. To make the situation worse, he takes my face between his hands and pulls me to him, pressing his lips onto my wet cheek.

The joy of the room is interrupted by a loud crashing sound. I look up to see the ice sculpture has shattered. A thousand bits of ice slide across the well polished floor. Herman and the Vassal rush to clean up the mess. I feel Baal's control over me dissipate, the distraction just enough for his hold on me to waver and I pull from his grasp. While others look to the broken ice, I run from the room. I run away from Baal as fast as I can.

I find myself in the library, throwing myself behind the fancy couch. Hiding just like I always do, just like I've done for months. Kibbey is already there, devouring a plate of shrimp, just as he does each weekend. It's our secret: I hide, Kibbey eats.

Sometimes I read to him until the party is over, then we sneak back to my room, avoiding all responsibilities assigned to us in the castle. Except this time I don't greet him with a smile. I don't tease him about the shrimp. I let myself fall to the floor, burying my face in my knees crying. I try to do it quietly, but I'm sure it's not quiet enough.

I hear the gentle *clink* of Kibbey setting his plate on the floor. He makes small gurgling noise as though he may be trying to talk to me. But I can't bear to look at him. I simply hold my hand out so he can see the diamond ring on my finger. In his silence, I look up to see a look of puzzlement on his face. I tell him what happened and I watch as his tiny face contorts from confusion to what can only be irritation.

He holds up his tiny finger, motioning for me to stay where I sit. I peek over the side of the couch and watch as he pushes a chair in front of the library door, hooking it underneath the door handle. He shuffles over to the bookcases near the fireplace, slides the tall ladder into place, then climbs, much further than I ever have, he climbs all the way to the top, to the ceiling. There he pushes a panel of the ceiling up, revealing a hidden area, and pulls down a book. He tucks it under his arm and makes his way down the ladder and back to me where he sits, placing the book in front of me.

I rub my hand across the front of it, wiping away the dust. The book is old, older than anything I have ever set my hands on, some relic from the distant past. The font is cryptic, the images resembling hieroglyphics. I have no way of knowing what this book is about.

Opening the cover I find images of the solar system, the nine planets crudely drawn and scrawled notes all over the pages. Kibbey reaches past me, brushing my hand aside and turning the page. He stops at a rough drawing of the earth; on each side of it seem to be drawings of twelve robed figures. Kibbey points at them. He turns the page again; there is a picture of two more figures, their waists surrounded by a thin looped line. Kibbey points at the picture then at me.

I stare at the images, seeing what seems to be a female, with flowers at her feet. The other image seems to be of a male, three droplets are drawn above his head and he holds what looks to be a violin in his free hand.

There is writing all over the page, but the only word that I can remotely make out is *mūsa.* Which I only know as the Latin word for muse, learned from an experience at the city museum where Mother took me as a child. I flip the page back, trying to see if the one before it may have some clues as to the meaning of the image, but all I find is a tear in the binding, a few of the pages seem to have been ripped out.

"I don't understand," I tell Kibbey. I look up to see him grasp his shoulders in a hugging motion and purse his lips. "Is this suppose to be me?" he nods his head. "And this is Baal?" I ask but Kibbey doesn't have time to answer. The hallway clock dings with a thirty-minute warning. It's almost two AM. We have to get back to my room.

Kibbey closes the book and runs back up the ladder, hiding the book in the ceiling. We rush out of the library and down the hall. In the dim light I can see we are coming up on a figure, they turn just as we make it to the main hallway and my heart throbs in my chest, it's Dylan.

"Dylan!" I grab his hand but he wretches it back. "What's wrong?"

He turns to me, his face stony, his voice deep. "You're engaged now. You shouldn't be speaking to me."

"Why?"

"I told you before." He looks away from me. "I told you that we were wrong, that you were meant for someone else. But you…you…"

"What's wrong with you?"

"I have seen what he does to women, how he entices them, how they keep coming back for him. Until he is finished, and like a child with a broken toy he just flings them aside. Yet they continue to pine for him until the day they die. And now you are one of them, you are nothing but another one of his harem."

I step back in surprise, never hearing him speak to me like this before. "I've done nothing wrong. This is all against my will. You've only seen what you want."

"And why would I *want* to see this? I had hopes, dreams for us at one time, now it is only so apparent they were just dreams." Dylan walks away from me, quickly making his way to the staircase and I suppose his room.

I feel Kibbey tugging at my hand, trying to draw me to my room before the clock strikes two. I follow the small Vassal, numb from Dylan's spiteful words.

When I make it to my room and the door is locked, I sit in the window seat, staring at the floor. Kibbey pats my hand. I catch him glancing to Nixie's fish tank a few times but I don't threaten him to leave her alone. He knows better right now. He climbs up next to me and reaches in his suit pocket, pulling out something tiny and green. He places it in my open palm, making some strange sound as he does.

I stare at the object in my hand, realizing that it is a small seed. The feeling begins, slow and soft in my arms. Pins and needles. The feeling of something waking that has been left dormant for too long. A muscle that hasn't been used. And I wonder if I were to lay down for a year and not move if this is what my entire body would feel like.

I watch as it grows, almost having forgotten what it feels like to have the trees tugging at me, the vines growing towards me, the grass growing under my feet. The seed grows in my palm, curling and unfurling. Soon it is doubled in size, tripled, and a tiny bud starts to appear. It grows larger, the bud gaining size until it takes up half of my palm. The bud starts to crack, the petals inside pushing, trying to get out. I let it bloom, revealing a small violet flower. I stop it, amazed with myself that I still possess the ability to make it stop, after all this time without practice. I pull the plant off my hand and place it in Kibbey's lap. He smiles, his little pointed teeth revealing themselves.

The clock dings a five minute warning just as he touches the delicate purple flower. He jumps down and hobbles to the door. I follow him, opening the door to let him out. He waves, pulling the door closed behind him. I bolt the heavy locks and secure the chains.

~ ~ ~

I can't say that I slept that night. I also can't say that I was fully awake, but I didn't hear the heavy snorts and spittle-breathing of the hall roaming beast. I did feel the emptiness in my chest, the longing and the strange sense that something is terribly wrong.

Today is going to be different, I kept telling myself, staring out the window for the entire day, until it was almost time for me to get ready. And now I have it set in my mind, I am not going to perform tonight. I can't, not after the forced engagement and Dylan's harsh words.

There's a knocking at my door, followed by the snap of dry fingers rubbing against each other. I watch the door to see the heavy bolts unlock themselves. The door opens and Baal steps into the room.

"Dear Fiancée, why aren't you ready for the party?" Baal asks me, taking the time to adjust his tie in the mirror which hangs on my wall.

"I can't dance today."

"Why not?"

"My Pointe shoes are too old."

He snaps his fingers and a new pair of shoes appear on my feet. They feel stiff and cold.

I flex my feet, the rough inner material rubbing harshly against my skin. "I can't wear these," I tell him.

"What is wrong with them?" he asks sweetly. "You asked for new shoes, I provided them. I will do whatever needs to be done to keep my little dancer happy."

"They aren't broken in," I tell him. Every dancer knows you never perform in brand new shoes. They have to be stretched, and worn, and bent. They have to be broken in and broken down.

"You will dance." His voice turns stony. "I have provided you with the shoes. Wear the white dress, the green jewels. Get to the ballroom, now."

"I don't want any of this." I stop him as he heads for the door. "I never did. I just want to go home. I want things to be back the way they were. I want to be normal."

Baal smirks at me. "My sweet little thing, why would you want *normal*? To be nothing but human, when all they want is to be like us. You may not realize it but those godless humans; they aspire to be just like you."

"They have no idea who I am," I tell him. "I've kept it hidden all these years."

"Deep down they know who you are and they know who I am-"

He stops short, looks down at my hand. "Where is your ring?"

I step back. "I-" I start to tell him I took it off but with the snap of his fingers he seems to find it. The ring comes floating towards us, dropping into his open palm.

He reaches for my hand, pulling it harshly towards him. "Leave this on. You are *mine*, meant to be *my* wife."

"No!" I shout at him. "I don't believe you or any of this!" I yank my hand out of his.

He walks towards me, so swiftly I don't have a chance to back up or shield myself from him. "I forget how naïve you are, being so young and all. You are *mine*. And let me tell you this about those humans, my sweet little dancer, in the most hopeful parts of their hearts, they want nothing more than to be like we are." He leaves me then, gliding out of the room with a few long strides, with nothing but an echo of his presence left, and his words ringing through my head.

There was something more revealing in what he just said, even if he didn't mean it, this is the second time I've heard the term godless humans since I've come to this castle, and I can't help but feel like it means something.

I ready myself, an anger growing inside me the entire time. Baal knows what we are, what I am, yet he refuses to give me a definitive answer and he refuses to free us. It's all I want, to know, to have the knowledge of what I am. And it seems my fate has already been determined, sketched in some ages old book. If only I could read it. Maybe I could tell Dylan, maybe he could help, if I could get him to talk to me again. Or maybe… maybe I could convince Dylan that we should just run, run away from this place even if Baal might kill us. I think I would rather have one moment of happiness with him, one more moment where I don't have to see the darkness ripping through Dylan and keeping him away from me. I think that I would give anything to sit on the pier by the lake and watch him dive into the water one last time with his face smiling in the evening sunlight.

Kibbey shows up to walk me to the ballroom, but this time he is not his joyful self. Something is wrong, something is off.

As I enter the ballroom the first thing I notice is there is no ice sculpture. Remembering the shattered ice sculpture littering the floor, my heart drops. I never feared he would be in trouble, but it seems with his lack of attendance, he may just be.

I walk to the center of the room, the new Pointe shoes constricting my feet, the rough material rubbing harshly against my skin. I stand in front of Baal's private crowd, glancing at their faces, noticing a few of Baal's mistresses. I keep my chin up, thoughts of escape fresh in my mind. I try to pretend I might be daring, that I might be able to change this, that what he just told me upstairs means nothing. I wait as the music starts.

When it begins, I notice it doesn't start from the speakers like it usually does. Instead, it starts from somewhere behind me, with the soft plucking of guitar strings, a deep resonating sound that's melodic and sweet. I turn to find where it's coming from and in the corner of the room I see Dylan sitting on a stool, a guitar of dark glossy wood in his hands. He strums, he plucks and after a few chords I begin to recognize the tune, *Hallelujah* is what he's playing. Mother played it often at the dance center, when I was a child. It's a song as old as the heavens, as old as when humans began believing in a God. A song most should recognize, but don't these days, since most churches are gone. I watch him in awe. I never knew Dylan could play, or that he could play so beautifully. But the sound of the music doesn't reflect his demeanor. He sits hunched on the stool, focused on the floor, his silvery hair covering his eyes. I see he is barefoot, a pair of tattered jeans and dark T-shirt dripping with water and clinging to his skin. As I stare I notice he begins to look up, his eyes now haunted and dark as he peers at me through his hair.

This must be his punishment is all that I think, that and the fact that Baal has fully broken him. He is no longer the laughing boy I met at the lake. And as I search my memories I have a hard time recalling the scent of his skin, or the feel of him pressed against me as we danced on the lake frozen by his magic. Finding my fingertips pressed to my mouth, I can barely recall that sensation we experienced kissing for that first time… Oh no, something strange is taking place here and tearing us apart.

Someone snaps their fingers. Pulled from my daze I turn to see Baal watching, waiting for his ballerina to dance. I point my toe, the material stretching against my skin. I swipe my leg, sway my arms, arch my back, extend my legs, pull myself up on my toes. The movements are so easy, matching the melody of the guitar.

A smooth jeté, a lingering pirouette, I don't even have to think. But then… then he starts to sing, the words, his voice, deep, melodic, haunting. I dance, each movement hanging on his lyrics. This version of the song he performs, it's not buoyant like the versions I've heard Mother play, it's not rejoiceful or exuberant. Instead it's a slow, painful burn, burning me deep inside where my soul rests in the center of my body, and it feels like he's ripping my heart in two as he sings.

He has never told me he had this talent. In all the time that I knew him, for all I knew of Dylan and his gifts, he has never performed for me. I never knew about this one until right now. And I'm struck by the beauty of it, that he had this hiding in him the entire time I've known him. It's beautiful. I'm sure more beautiful than my dancing.

Dylan finishes with a few dwindling notes. The strings resonate under his fingertips. I stop and turn to him, but he won't look at me. His head hangs in fatigue. The muscles covered by his shirt slackened and soften. I get the feeling that he's given up.

Slowly, it comes to me, the events of last night, mixed with the events of the past few minutes. The book Kibbey showed me, old and hidden in the ceiling of the library. The other image was not Baal, the male figure with the water droplets and the violin. The male figure, whom I am locked for infinity with, I know without a doubt, in the center of my heart, it is Dylan. It's always been Dylan. We started to feel this before Baal uprooted our lives. But now, Baal has broken him so badly with the engagement, with the labor of exhausting him beyond recovery. I am certain Dylan doesn't know, and in his current state he can't see it for himself.

The guests have yet to applaud our performance. They do not whisper or murmur about my dancing or Dylan's playing. I turn to see them staring, their eyes wide in shock. They don't stare at my face, or my body, or the boy behind me. Instead, their eyes are gazing towards the floor. I look down to see what they are so stunned by and when I see, it shocks me too.

I knew it was wrong to dance in brand new shoes, I told Baal so. Now, fresh blood seeps through the flawless satin of the new Pointe shoes. I had felt nothing while I danced, fully immersed in Dylan's music. But now I am aware of the pain seeping through my feet, the sore ache of blisters being rubbed raw inside the new shoes. I find Baal in the audience, with nothing but a grim look set on his face-not a pleasant gaze for his new Fiancée. But then, it's not love he's looking for in this union. I'm more sure of it now than I ever was. I must have something he wants, that can be the only reason for him keeping apart two people who are destined to be together.

I start for the door, headed for the seclusion of the hallway, limping on my sore feet. Baal makes no attempt to stop me or to help me. I'm sure stopping me would only make him look bad in the eyes of his guests and with all his powers he can't erase what they've seen from their memories. Reprimanding me in front of his crowd of the rich and famous would do nothing but ruin his reputation.

Someone does come to my aid, though. The person whom I least expect, the one who greeted me so crudely when we first arrived, the one who treats the Vassal so poorly, Herman.

He takes me under the elbow, leading me gently out of the room. A row of Vassal rush past us, cloths and buckets in hand. When I turn I see that they are cleaning up the small bloodied footprints that I've left on the glazed Ballroom floor.

I need to go somewhere to rest, to collect my thoughts and figure out what step I will take next. "Take me to the library," I tell Herman.

He does, without much of a word. The Vassal follow, I assume to clean the trail of blood off the floor. He leads me to one of the sofas and leaves the room. I reach for the Pointe shoes, untying the satin bows, winding the ribbon off of my legs. I pull my foot out of the slipper, the lamb's wool padding meant to protect my toes has worked to soak up the blood seeping out of the blisters on my feet. I throw the shoes aside, now staring at the sores, red and raw, covering my feet.

Herman enters the library again, this time carrying a basin and a collection of things under his arm. I watch as he pushes the oak coffee table aside. He kneels at my feet, setting the bucket, steaming with warm water, on the floor. He doesn't ask me to but I slip my feet into the water, welcoming the heat.

"This castle, it has ways of bending time," Herman begins. "There is a magic here of sorts, and it makes some forget their purpose." He looks up at me, his face wrinkled in thought. "I was not meant to be a Butler, but something else. It's slowly coming back to me, but I still can't quite remember. Watching you and that young man, it awakened something deep inside me." He pulls my feet from the basin, and begins patting them dry on a white towel, leaving splotches of blood on the colorless terry cloth. He takes from his collection a roll of bandages and wraps my feet. I say nothing. When he is done, he stretches a pair of socks over the bandages and begins to collect his things. "Master Baal will be expecting me for the rest of the evening to take care of his guests."

"Can you send Kibbey?" I ask him

Herman tips his head in question. "Who is Kibbey?"

"That Vassal who follows me around."

He nods his head and leaves the room.

Kibbey returns, a tray of food for both of us, sandwiches and crackers, not simply a pile of shrimp for him to devour. He sets the tray on the table and turns, pushing a chair under the door handle. We sit on the couch in somber silence. Kibbey doesn't touch his shrimp. He pulls his hand out of his pocket. The delicate purple flower from last night rests in his hand. The vines start inching towards me.

Feeling the tingle in my arms I lean away from the flower. "I've forgotten," I whisper to him, barely remembering the things Dylan taught me about myself. "I've forgotten how to control it."

Kibbey places the flower back into his pocket and stands, making his way across the library. He climbs the tall ladder and brings down the old book he showed me yesterday. He sits next to me turning the pages, again to the solar system, to the page of the two figures tied together for infinity.

"Yes," I tell him. "I see now, it's me and Dylan, not Baal."

Kibbey nods his head, still staring. I notice his eyes moving. He's reading! Whatever language the book is written in, he can read.

"You can read that?" I ask him.

He nods, pointing to his mouth. Gesturing that maybe he speaks it, or could speak it at one time. I've never heard him utter anything except for grunts and groans.

My feet begin to throb. I lean back and close my eyes, trying to think of a way to get out of this mess. Remembering what Dylan told me: Baal has ways of finding us, even if we did escape this island.

Too soon, I hear the hallway clock give the warning chime. I look to Kibbey who stands, climbs the ladder and replaces the old book. He slides another chair in front of the door and a small table. He makes his way to where I am sitting and takes my hand, pulling at it. Feeling exhausted I stand and let him lead me to the glass case where the carved figurines stand frozen in time. He points to the hollow space under the case and back at me.

"What?" I ask.

He taps his wrist, holds his ear as the clock chimes again. He watches the door, concern spreading over his strange face, and points under the case again.

"You want me to hide under there?"

He nods, opening his eyes wide, tugging at my hand to hurry me. I crawl under the case, pushing my back against the wooden wall. Dust blows around my face, cobwebs catch in my hair. I see Kibbey's feet walk away and then return. He shakes out a blanket and throws it over the glass case, engulfing me in darkness. Kibbey does not hide under the case with me, instead, I hear the patter of his small feet as he runs away and the clock chimes again.

It's two AM.

At first, all I can hear is the sound of my own heartbeat, the sound of my shallow breaths, and silence. I can't hear the heavy, wet breaths of the beast that roams the halls like I have before. But, I do hear something, a soft pitter, a tiny murmur from above me. As though mice were dancing and talking in the glass case I am hiding under. I wait to hear the growl of the beast, to feel its thunderous footsteps on the castle floors. Nothing. I crawl to where the blanket drapes over the glass case above me and I pull the blanket back, peering out into the library. The dim reading lights are still on, the chairs and table still in front of the door. I crawl out from under the case and pull the blanket off.

The figurines are there, just as they have always been, frozen in time. I peer closer. It seems they have moved, again. There is something strange with this box of figurines. And then, as though the events of the day don't already have my mind spinning, I think I see the eyes on one of the figurines move, it turns its head to look right at me. I pull the blanket the rest of the way off the case and toss it onto the floor. Reaching for the nearby table lamp and stretching it to the case so I can get a better look, I search for the woman and the man who seem to always be coupled together. They are in the front now. I tip the lamp and shine the light on them. And it happens again! Both of their eyes turn and look at me. They seem to waver, to float a little, their heads turn, their arms move, all of the figurines, they come to life.

I knew it! I knew something was strange with this case. The man and the woman take each other's hands; they skip and run to the front of the case, where my face is watching them. I hear the same tiny sound of mouse chirps. I kneel down to see they are moving their mouths. Unable to hear them I press my ear to the glass.

"Demi!" The man and woman shout with their tiny voices. "It's us! Your parents!"

I remove my ear, looking back at them in disbelief. They press their hands to the glass, looking between me and each other. They smile, they laugh, they say more things, but I can't make it out. Suddenly, their faces turn grim. Mother, covers her mouth, Father, he yells, pointing at me. Their joy at seeing me seems to be gone. They must be filled with the realization that I am huge and they are stuck in a glass case as enchanted figurines.

"How do I get you out?" I ask them.

But now, Mother points at me. They both yell something that I can't make it out. I look behind my tiny parents and see the other figurines are pointing and yelling also. I tip my head and press my ear to the case.

At first it's just jumbled mouse chatter, a collective silence, a small but understandable yelp. "Behind you!" they shout in unison.

Turning, I find a great looming shadow has descended upon the room. I look to the door and see it's still closed, with the chairs and the table in front of it. The shadow materializes, forms itself into a figure, a figure of a giant bearlike creature. I can hear its rasping breath. I can feel its thunderous steps as it lumbers towards me. Snorting, sniffing, growling from deep within its great, furred chest. It lurches towards me, giant arms raised, ready to pound me. I move to the side, the beast just misses, crashing into the glass case.

"No!" I scream at the monster, watching as the figurines drop to the ground and scatter across the floor with bits of broken wood and glass. Some of them run under the furniture and wall cupboards, others seem to turn back into wood, their enchantment gone out of them.

The beast turns to me, growling, roaring, making my ears ring from the noise. I turn and run, weaving around the furniture, but the beast crashes through everything, headed straight for me. I find myself out of space, backed up against the wall and the fireplace, watching as the monster drops to the floor and runs at me on all four legs.

I press my back to the wall, trying to create a distance, bracing myself for the impact of the claws and the bite of its sharp teeth. I know this will hurt, much more than my aching feet, much more than losing my parents, than Baal's engagement, than Dylan's harsh words.

Perhaps, I think for a moment, it is for the best that I should be devoured by this beast, just to be gone would make things so much easier. I wouldn't feel these things of fear, and sadness, and loss. I could just go wherever it is people go when they die, if people like me even go anywhere at all.

I face the beast, staring into its blackened eyes. It shakes its head, and its head appears to morph into three heads with three sets of black eyes blinking in unison as it runs to me, the floor vibrating under my damaged feet. I press my back against the wall, harder. I brace myself for the impact. And then, suddenly, I am falling backwards into darkness. Someone's hand grabs mine, pulling me, dragging me. I hear the beast slam into something in front of me, the wall where I was once standing. The beast roars with anger. Now, this place I am in, it cannot be heaven or hell as I had feared. I've fallen into some strange place that smells of stale dust, of aged wood and decayed rodents.

"Demi," I hear a voice, the voice of Herman. "You aren't supposed to be out of your room this late."

"Where am I?" I ask.

"The walls of the castle contain passages, the Vassal and I use them on a daily basis." He flicks on a small light. "Let's get you back to your room."

Herman pulls me by my hand, leading me through the dusty narrow hallway. Up old and creaking aged stairwells until at last, he stops, tapping the wall, then pushing on it. He pulls my hand and we are in a closet. I recognize the housecoat and the towels, we are in the linen closet in my bathroom. Herman walks swiftly through the room, the bedroom, he reaches for the door and slams it closed, pushing the four locks into place.

"It seems, Ms. Demi, I have the sudden urge to protect you," he tells me.

"Yes, thank you." I rub my hands over my arms, trying to calm myself.

"I must return to where I belong at night. Do not leave your room. In the morning, I hope some plan comes to me."

Herman disappears back within the walls. I open the closet door, unable to see the hidden passage. And for a moment, I wonder if it was even real, or a figment of my imagination, because the things that have occurred tonight seem very much unreal.

I notice Nixie swimming rapidly in her tank. I reach up, shaking some food in for her. "Something strange is happening, Nixie." I place my fingertip in the water and let her rub on me.

I change out of the dress and into a pair of jeans and a sweater. I sit in the window, watching the night. Trying to formulate a plan, an idea of what to do. But my thoughts are interrupted by the deep growl coming from outside my bedroom door. I recognize the spittle-breathing of the beast and I lay my head against the thick glass window, searching my memories for something, but all that comes to mind is the image of Dylan dancing with me on the water and the happiness I felt then.

Whatever he is doing to us, it is wearing upon our souls; we've become tired, soft, and argue against each other. Something in this castle is dark, and we need to escape it.

Somehow, sleep consumes me.

CHAPTER SEVENTEEN

Even in sleep I could sense that someone was close to me. I could feel their breath on my face, the sensation of my hair being twisted around their finger, fingertips brushing across my cheek.

As I slept I dreamt it was Dylan, and we were standing on the pier. The sun made his eyes sparkle and I could tell he was fighting the urge to turn and dive into the lake. He was always fighting the pull of the water, but unlike me, he welcomed his ability.

The heaving of the bed causes me to wake. My eyes flutter open to find a large, dark figure looming over me. I gasp, my eyes wide, focusing on the figure. It's Baal. I scurry off the other side of the bed, my feet dropping to the floor with a heavy thud as I make it to the other side of the room, where the open door is. I remember locking it last night, actually, Herman locked it. But then, I remember Baal unlocked it with his magic on the previous day.

It seems those locks only keep *some* monsters out.

"It seems we have a misunderstanding, Fiancée," Baal begins, smiling. It must be a fake smile, after all that occurred yesterday, I can't think of anyone who might smile afterwards. "Here I have given you so much," he stands and begins a menacing waltz towards me. "Yet, you give me nothing."

I stare at him, noticing for the first time that he's wearing a chain around his neck, and hanging off the chain are two tiny braids. I recognize them, one is silvery, the other pale blonde-they are wisps of mine and Dylan's hair. I must not have seen it before, because he's usually buttoned up to the nines. But on this day, he wears one of those offensive shirts that have been cut so low I can see the tense clench of muscle running down his chest to his abdomen.

The bedroom door slams closed.

"I don't want your things," I reply, backing away from him until my back hits the far wall.

"It seems you need them." He looks me up and down. Of course, I am wearing the expensive clothes he bought me. "I suppose I didn't see it before but now I do." He walks closer to me, slowly. "You are still pining over my boy, Dylan. My sweet little dancer, when will you realize that he can't take care of you like I can? He can't protect you, or keep you safe from the things you don't understand."

"What is it that I don't understand?"

He laughs quietly at me.

"I don't want this. Or these games you are playing." I tell him. "I don't want you!" I shout.

"Oh, but you are so young and naive, you have time to change your mind." He tilts his head to the side as though he's allowing me a few more minutes to decide.

"No," I tell him defiantly.

"You do realize I could put him in the ground with the snap of my fingers." He raises his eyebrows.

"Then, I think you had better dig two graves. I'd rather die than continue on in this life without him. I would rather die than continue on like this… with you."

"You think that is a smart decision, because I could make it happen. I can snap my fingers and it will be just as you wish, my dear Fiancée."

"I've told you before. I want nothing to do with you."

"We are betrothed. You were meant for me. I made you. I crafted you and placed you on this earth for me and only me. He is nothing but my pawn, my errand boy. I sent him to find you, to teach you, to bring you to me. And he delivered you, just like a good little water boy. Does it not bother you that he lied? He did just as I asked, just as I ordered, and he always will."

I stare at Baal, the realization of his words slicing me deep through the chest. I already knew that Dylan lied to me, that he was trying to protect me. *If it's the worst thing I've ever done, I don't regret it. I'm not going to apologize. Imagine the dread you would have felt since I've known you, every day, knowing this was coming.* I begin to wonder if maybe his logic was flawed. He just took Baal's words as fact, believed him, believed that this is our future, our destiny. But it can't be, it feels so wrong.

"I don't care," I tell Baal, moving along the wall, trying to get further from him, until, suddenly I become unable to move. He's frozen me.

"Are you sure?" he asks, walking towards me.

I can see it in his eyes, his pupils changing just for an instant, and I can feel the energy radiating off of him. He's ravenous, an animal, and right now I can do nothing to stop him. I can't even attempt to run away. So I stand, entranced, trapped and waiting as he moves so close to me I can feel his breath on my skin. I don't even have the control of my muscles to cringe as he touches my face, the rough skin of his fingers scraping over my skin. It seems to crawl, to ache, and then… it craves him. *I crave him.* And at that moment I am certain that Baal has put some spell upon me, more than controlling my body. He's playing with my mind. Reaching into depths he hasn't explored, that I don't think I've ever explored. He's making me think, for this one second, that maybe… maybe I'm the one who's wrong.

Baal continues, caressing my cheek, pulling my hair back from my face with his one hand while the other travels down my cheekbone leaving a trail of what feels like static electricity jumping from his fingers. It feels good, but, at the same time, it doesn't feel right. It can't be right. But, all I can think of is how Dylan told me I was just another one of Baal's harem. So why shouldn't I let him have his way? He strokes my cheek, rubs his thumbs down my arms. There's something so enchanting that I can't stop myself from leaning towards him, yearning for more.

"There are things you don't know, sweet sweet Demi. Only I can keep you safe. Only I can keep you happy. You may not love me now, but you will learn to, just as the others learned…"

"Others?" I ask, the buzzing in my mind slowing.

One dark eyebrow rises as he looks at me. He smiles, a knowing smile, and then he presses his lips onto mine, only strengthening his enchantment-I'm sure of it.

I'm sure of it because I know don't want to lean into him. I don't want to press my fingers to the smooth skin of his chest. I don't want the small moan to escape from the back of my throat, but it does. It all happens, and his kiss deepens, his tongue probes into my mouth, investigating, claiming. His arms wrap around my back, pulling me into his chest. I close my eyes, my head spinning, trying to focus for just one minute… until, until he slides his tongue across my bottom lip, just where Dylan did when he kissed me so long ago on the water.

Baal pushes me away. He shoves me so hard that I stagger backwards, my shoulder blades digging into the wall behind me as he turns and spits on the floor. His eyes turn a shade darker than black, his face twisting in anger.

"How could *you*?" he bellows at me.

I simply stare at him, afraid, unknowing of what just happened, still unable to move. And confused, so confused as to how I could even have a moment of desire for this person, this person who I despise so much.

"He has tainted you," Baal continues. "Put his lips on yours. You more than pine for him, you are in *love* with him!" He spits the words at me with venom and in his anger his spell is broken. The fog clears from my head, my thoughts are truly mine again. "I have waited a thousand years for you and now he must pay."

There is movement from the window and my eyes flit to it, seeing the tips of Dylan's silvery hair as he walks to the seaway, just as he does each morning.

Baal follows my gaze.

"Run!" I scream at the glass, praying that he might hear me.

But Dylan doesn't hear me. A great sudden wind begins to blow across the island, brushing the leaves from the trees, and with the wind comes the spattering of ice and snow and cold. I watch as Dylan turns, slowly, too slowly to do much. I feel the temperature drop in the room, which can only mean it has dropped outside. I watch, unable to breathe, hearing only the rush of blood in my ears, as Dylan freezes still.

"No, how could you?" I scream at Baal.

"I will do what I want and I will take what I want and if you cannot find it in your young heart to accept me, then you had better get used to losing the things you love." I watch in horror as he moves to the shelf that holds Nixie's tank and reaching in, he pulls her out of the water. One fist smashes the window pane, letting the freezing air blow into the room. "Your mere existence breaks laws that you know nothing about. This could have been so much easier if you had both listened. No girl should ever love a fish as you do."

I watch as Nixie's eyes swell, they bulge; she whips her tail and wriggles her tiny body. A cruel smile spreads across Baal's lips as he draws his hand back, getting ready to throw my beloved pet out the window.

"No!" I plead.

Then, something so strange happens. Since Nixie is a puffer fish, and it is in her inherent nature, she suddenly swells up like a great balloon, her tiny spines stick out, stabbing Baal through the hand. And since she is my pet, I know her spines are poisonous. Perhaps Baal is just finding this out. He looks at his hand, his eyes wide and dark with shock. Maybe it's the poison working on him, or the stiff spines jutting through his hand, either way it's enough to break his hold on me. I can move my arms and legs again.

I run to Baal, ripping the necklace from around his neck. I pull the braids of hair from their clasp and throw the strands out the window. They catch in the wind, floating over the island, out to the seaway and across to the mainland. Now, our wisps of hair cannot bind us to Baal, they are nothing but nesting material for the songbirds. His hold on us ends, immediately. I see a shudder run through Dylan's body as he looks up at my window.

"Run! Dylan! Run!" I scream out of the broken glass pane.

Perhaps he hears the fear in my voice, or the warning that we are not done here. He doesn't look up, or look back, he just runs for the seaway, just as I remember him doing on the pier, and he dives into the water.

Baal's hold on him is now gone, Dylan is finally free.

~ ~ ~

I had hoped that Baal's hold on me was gone also. Forever removed with the tossing of my pale strands of hair out the window, but it is not. Instead, it's replaced with the harsh grasp of his free hand as he knots it into the fine hair on the back of my neck. He flicks his injured hand and Nixie's lifeless, swollen body flies out the window.

To think that a fish could do so much for one person. Goodbye friend.

Now Baal has no other means to control me than by force. His hand curls into a fist, bunching my hair. He pulls me along with him as I kick and scream. He is tall, lean and strong, and it doesn't seem to take him much effort as he hauls me down the hallway, down the marble staircase, and towards the ballroom.

At first I think he might be bringing me to the ballroom, but he turns sharply, heading down a stone hallway I have never explored. Down a staircase I have never explored because I have never ventured under the ground floor. I never had the curiosity. So now, I see that much like other castles this one is complete with its own dungeon.

Baal throws me into an old withered chair.

"You were meant for more!" He screams at me, his voice deep with anger. "More than this!" He spreads his arms wide. "You were meant to change the world, the earth. We were going to do it together."

"What do you mean?" I ask him, adjusting myself in the chair. "I can't change the earth. You are crazy!"

"You control the plants." He looks down at his injured hand. "The food." He pulls the three spines out. "Therefore you control the people, out of all of *us*, you can control the *godless humans.* They may not listen to the warnings of their gods, but they listen to their earth." I watch as thin drips of a dark, inky substance trickle out of the wounds and the holes in his hand close on their own. He flashes his hand front to back. There's no indication that he was just stabbed with poisonous puffer-fish barbs.

"I'm not going to harm them." I try to stand, but he pokes his finger into my chest, pushing me back into the chair.

"We could make more of them." He tells me, his face directly in front of mine. I can feel his breath on my face. "It's easy to make humans. A little bone, a little flesh, a little sin and magic-"

"I am one of them. I was one of them. I have friends, family-"

"You can't fool me. I know what you are like, how hard it is for you to fit in. Dylan was the same way, awkward and quiet. You both had too many secrets to hide from them. If they knew what you could do-"

"I have parents!" I scream back at him.

"And your parents are dead!" he retorts.

I lean away, as far as the back of the chair will let me, tears stinging my eyes.

"If the humans knew of us, of what we can do, if they remembered, we would be their Gods again! And if we don't act soon, then they will kill us, they will kill the very beings responsible for keeping them alive." Baal's eyes are wide with excitement.

"Why don't you do it?" I ask. "You obviously have powers of some kind, which seem not to be limited like mine and Dylan's."

"I can't," he tells me. "I need you. But this will never work if you continue to pine for that boy."

"I won't." I shake my head at him.

"You will once I find out where your little toy Dylan is hiding. When he is gone, you'll have no choice but to side with me."

"Leave him alone!" I threaten Baal, realizing that my words will do nothing to make him fear me.

"You still have no idea *what* you are."

I watch as he pulls a box from his pocket, much like Jedediah used to, he lights a cigarette, holding the smoking stick in front of me. Just like before the gray line of smoke starts curling in the air, making its way towards me. The dark wisps curl towards me. I pull back, allowing just a few more inches, but it's not enough. I breathe in the offending smolder.

"Has he told you that you are immortal?" Baal asks.

I glare at him.

"You see, he has many secrets also. And there are some things he has yet to learn. I almost wish I could tell you everything right now. But you're still not ready. I can see it in your eyes. You still don't know what you're capable of. You have no idea."

And so I learn a truth about myself. I am immortal. I will never die. I will always be here suffering, without the ones I love the most, while Dylan remains free, while my parents remain wooden figures, while the Vassal clean and Herman tries to remember what he was meant to do. I will remain the same, unchanged, alone, alive, to suffer, presumably in this murky dungeon. Forever.

"We can't be immortal. You just threatened to kill him."

Baal smirks and with a sigh he says, "You may be immortal in many ways but I know you still feel pain. Perhaps you know where he went?"

"I don't know where he is." I tell Baal, choking through the smoke. "He left me, remember? He dove into the seaway and swam away. He didn't even look back. What makes you think he cares about me anymore? You have done your best to break him down all this time we've been here."

"Oh, he cares for you. That was apparent the moment I tasted the memory of his kiss upon your lips. That is something that won't just go away. It's going to burn in his soul until he finds you, until he comes back for you, and I'll be waiting for him."

I turn my face away, watching as the black veins snake up my arms.

"I guess you need some time to think about it."

Baal reaches for me again, but I stand, pulling the chair out from under me and flinging it at him with my last bits of strength. It bounces off his arm. He doesn't flinch. Instead he grips me by the hair and drags me further into the dark dungeon where the rocked walls melt into the soiled depths of the earth. He opens a thick wooden door, complete with an iron-barred window and chain handle. In the dim light I can see it is nothing more than a bare room. But I know this is the worst kind of dungeon for something like me. There's nothing but soil.

"No!" I scream at him one last time as throws me into the dark cell.

The door slams, the chains rattle. Baal's footsteps echo in the hall as he walks away.

~ ~ ~

One thing I have come to learn is where there is soil there are roots. Within moments the roots start poking through the hard-packed floor. I hold my hands out, trying to stop them, but it doesn't work. I'm too weak from the poison smoke, too weak to use my power. I can no longer control them. The months in this castle have made me forget. The roots creep and crawl towards me. I put my back to the door, banging on it, yelling and screaming for someone to help, to make them stop. No one comes. I scream again, louder this time. I scream for Dylan. I scream for Herman. I scream for Baal to come back, begging for him to make it stop.

No one answers my screams.

Within minutes they start to consume me, like a python enjoying a goat. They wrap around my feet, my legs, twisting and yanking. Kicking is no use. They are dragging me to the center of the room, weaving their roots around my body, pulling me to the ground so they can get at me from all sides. I curl up, my face in my arms, trying to preserve a small pocket of air as I feel them twisting and pulling and wrapping.

The roots start poking into me, running across my cheeks, my ears, caressing my scalp. I feel one near my mouth and I clamp it shut, afraid that the roots might crawl down my throat and choke me. I can feel the layers, wrapping and squeezing like a giant wriggling python.

Within minutes I feel tiny pinpricks all over my arms and legs, the back of my neck. It feels like they're growing into my pores, stabbing me. I try to calm myself. I try to remember what Dylan taught me, what he told me. I try to make the roots move away, but it's no use. I'm too weak, much too weak from what Baal did to me.

Now, he doesn't need a lock of my hair. Because I am trapped, unable to move, hardly breathing, consumed by darkness, by the roots, hibernating as a bear in a winter cave. There is no light, no fresh air; only silence, interrupted by the twisting rope-like sound of the roots tightening around me every few minutes.

At times I can only hear my shallow breaths, my screams that cannot escape this living cocoon. Other times, I think I can hear Herman calling my name and the small footsteps of the Vassal, the tiny goblin groans produced by Kibbey. But, if they take the time to look into my cell, I'm sure all they see is a gnarled ball of roots, not a small girl who once danced and made things grow.

The dark does not tell time well, nor the roots, as their tiny fibers ripple over my body. I fear I may be left down here for some time.

CHAPTER EIGHTEEN

The earth may be old, as is the soil and its elements. But the earth carries no knowledge of time and time down here doesn't pass the same as it does above ground. I wonder if this is what it would be like in the heavens, or the underworld; a soul waiting, not sure if the time is even passing.

I know I have not eaten or drank, nor have I stood or stretched for a long while. It's not long before the echo of footsteps pacing the dungeon disappears and I can no longer hear the calls of Herman.

No one comes to rescue me. There is no knight in shining armor, no handsome prince, not even a magical dragon. I have no one but myself.

I try to think of what Dylan taught me when we lived in Saratoga. "*You have to feel them, you have to envision them.*" He told me. But that was a different Dylan. That Dylan was good, that Dylan was truthful, that Dylan may have even loved me, if only for a short time. I wonder how he could be so deceiving, how he could be the way he was, the way we were together and kept so much from me.

The roots continue to poke into my skin and each time I move a muscle, they squeeze me tighter to fill in the space. I try to visualize the roots moving away from me, unfolding and spitting me out. But it doesn't work. So I focus on the tiny root hairs that probe my pores, the ones that still have space to move, and something strange begins to happen…I feel myself leave my body.

It happens just for an instant the first time. I can no longer feel the roots squeezing my body and I can sense the space of the dungeon. While I am sure it is dark as a moonless night down here, I can see the root ball. I see a mouse running across the wall. I can see it not with pure eyesight, but some other type of sensitive awareness. I think of it like the sensitive sonar used by submarines and ocean creatures. That is the only way I can explain what I see and what this feels like.

And then, when I am afraid I might lose my body, or forget how to get back to it, I zip along the root as though I am a tiny electrical impulse and reclaim my body. I breathe, feeling the stretch of my lungs. I blink my eyes, and somehow, after what I just experienced, I am still very much alive, my body safe within the cocoon of the roots.

I do it again, this time venturing further underground with the root. I can sense the moist earth, the bugs and worms which crawl beneath the soil, until the root I am travelling on stops. It comes to an abrupt end, leaving me to turn around and rush back to my body. I feel the rapid beating of my heart, the flush of apprehension. I know I have to find a way out and since I can't get the roots to unwrap, I have no choice but to leave my body behind and search for help, travelling within the tangled roots under the ground.

When I have built up enough courage, I follow the large root again, taking different branches this time. To my disappointment they each come to an end, except for the last one. The last one extends further, growing deep within the earth, until finally I sense that I am travelling upwards. I break the soil, feeling the warm sun. I sense that I have travelled up the trunk of one of the large pine trees which grows on the island. From here I can see the castle, the docks, all the way to the mainland. I travel the tree, the branches, trying to figure out this ability I have. I feel the dense trunk and the pine needles as they shudder in the breeze.

It's not long before I start to fear I may become trapped like this and I travel back underground, surging into my still body within the root ball. I touch my face, lick my lips. I'm still alive. As any immortal being may be, alive without the necessities, alive forever it seems. I stay with my body for a short time, remembering the way it feels, afraid that I may never be connected with it again. And when I can take the solitude no longer, I leave; travelling, exploring every living green thing on the island, the shrubs, the grass, the small trees.

~ ~ ~

What most don't know, what took me months, I assume, to figure out for myself, is that the roots of the earth are old and deep. They extend under the rock, deep down, further than most can dig. They travel under water, under the seabed, under the Hudson River. Roots as old as time, as old as the ice age, before the glaciers tore through this area and dug these waterways out of the crust of the earth. The roots are still here, they may look old and dried up and fossilized, but they are still very much alive.

I travel along these roots, just as an electrical impulse would jump across nerve synapses. Time passes, soon I sense this as the leaves begin falling, the branches begin feeling cold, and the sky fills with what seems to be a white static. Snow, it must be.

I think of who could help me. I had a friend in Swayzee, but she's a normal person. These things I have to relay to her, the help I need to get free, she can't help me. I need Dylan, even if he lied to me. If what Baal told me is correct, if he really loves me, then Dylan will be looking for me. I just can't wait any longer for him to find me on his own. I rest my soul in a spruce, the static sense of a blustery winter storm fizzles around me. If it is winter then Dylan would be in the south-where he won't freeze.

Finally, after I have talked myself into it-the need to find Dylan-I head south to Florida, using only my surroundings to help. I can see geese flying and I know that geese in winter fly south. I travel down the trunk of the spruce, nothing but a spark of energy, a soul without a body. I head in the direction of the geese.

Time passes underground, as I am surrounded by dirt. I envision myself as a corpse-less ghost and the fear of never feeling my own body again rushes me, whatever I am right now. I immediately brush the thought from my mind.

Soon the roots of the ground become dense, healthy, the soil muddy with moisture. I travel up, sensing along the way that it is now warm, my surroundings thick with vegetation. There is just one problem: A giant city looms before me. I can sense that there is not much to travel through close to the topsoil, the plants are gone, their roots stripped from the earth and covered in stone. I will have to venture deep underground, similar to how I got off of Dark Island.

I travel down, far in the depths, where there are no more worms or beetles. I can still sense the rumble of the towering city above me, it's heavy, thick, crushing the earth beneath it. This extends for a long time, before I am able to break above the dirt and when I finally do, I am only met with more disappointment: another city, this one bigger. I savor being above ground, settling my soul in a daisy for just for a short time, a few hours maybe, soaking up the warmth from the sun before I delve below. I stay there, hearing the cities rumble above me. It feels like forever until they fade away and the soil turns sandy and loose. I travel above, finding myself to be positioned in a towering palm tree.

This must be Florida.

I hope this is where I will find Dylan. Trying to find a needle in a haystack is what the task seems like, but what do I have to lose? If I don't try something I will remain trapped in that dungeon forever.

I travel along the coast, searching the beaches from the nearby vegetation, watching the men, the women, the children as they run and play on the beach. I miss the feeling of having my legs underneath me, having a body, of dancing and running. Now, I just have the trees, the plants, the things I had feared for so long, they are finally helping me.

I wait to feel a sense of Dylan on the shoreline. It takes days, weeks, months maybe. When I am certain I've travelled along the entire coast I turn around, travelling up the beach trees, and back under the sandy earth, for another round of searching.

Just as I am about to give up hope, when I consider returning to Dark Island to make sure my body is still safe, cocooned in the root ball, I sense a man on the beach. He stares out over the ocean, alone.

He stands there all night, and all day as I feel the sun warming the leaves of the palm tree I have settled in. The day moves around him as though he is the sun. The people, those *godless humans* according to Baal, they seem to pay no attention to him. They focus on their electronics in their hands, their children, their lovers at their sides.

Night comes again. To stay awake that long, standing like that, it has to be Dylan. Maybe he is practicing some new trick? I sense his mouth is moving, words escaping. I let the wind bring them to the leaves of the palm tree.

"Where are you, Demi?" he whispers in the ocean breeze.

I want to scream, to yell and let him know I am right behind him. That I am here! But, I am nothing but a palm tree right now, my mind separate from my body, a body which remains thousands of miles away, hidden in a dungeon. All I am is this, this nothingness. I can barely call myself a spirit, because at least a spirit could float amongst the living.

He turns to leave the beach. I panic, rushing from tree to tree, following him. I need to stop him. He turns down a path, headed for a parking lot. I can't lose him. I can't risk him walking across that stone lot and me unable to follow. So I do the only thing I can, I bend the tree trunk down, blocking his path. He stops, staring at the bent tree, looking around him.

"Demi?" he asks into the night.

I can't answer. I have no words in this form. No way to speak or communicate. He stands stiffly, peering into the dense southern foliage. I'm sure he is searching, waiting for me to step out and greet him. Maybe he's hoping I will run at him and throw myself onto him just like I did so long ago. But I can't.

The vines, I think. I could use the vines to spell. I use the trunk, to push him back towards the beach. He turns around and walks across the sand. Stopping when he is a few feet away, he faces the trees and waits.

I send the vines, growing, twisting, extending towards his feet. I have so much to say, so much to ask, but this is not the proper way to communicate. I think of the most important, the best way to get him. I start with one word.

Strong. I spell out with the vines.

Dylan tips his head. "Are you asking if I'm strong?"

I shift the vines. ***Yes***.

"Then yes."

Rest.

"Yes. I have rested."

Time?

"Do I have time, or…?"

I shift the vines again. ***Passed***.

"It's been almost a year since you freed me."

Oh no. I've been buried in the ground for an entire year!

I shift the vines again. ***Island***. I don't wait for him to speak. ***Dungeon. Help. Save. Me***.

"You are still there?" he asks.

Save me. I spell out, and then repeat the words over again, shifting the vines.

"How are you doing this?"

Trapped. Roots. Save me. Find Herman. Help.

I twist the vines, repeating the words, over and over again, as fast as I can manage. I no longer care if someone comes across this spectacle, I need him to understand! He ponders the words, a wrinkle stretching over his brow, his hand resting on his chin. I begin to think he doesn't understand, or that he doesn't want to help.

"I'm coming," he says out loud.

Dylan turns, running down the sandy beach, diving into the ocean.

CHAPTER NINETEEN

Dylan must intend to swim all the way north. I leave the tree, delving under the sandy soil. I stay deep, travelling as fast as I can, hoping to reach the castle before Dylan does, afraid that he may find my body without my soul attached. Because if he does, I'm not sure what he would do besides assume that I am dead, and without the connection with the roots I have no idea how to get my soul back into my body.

Travelling faster than I ever have the landmarks become familiar to me, I can sense the rumbling cities above me. I rush away from them, headed north, pushing faster. Until finally, I reach the aged roots that travel under the seaway. I push myself, moving faster than I ever have before. The roots of the island even more familiar, having explored them for some time. I rush back to the dungeon, its familiar darkness and I throw myself back into my body.

Maybe it was the shock from how fast my soul was travelling, or the length of time I was separated from my encapsulated body. It takes moments, seconds, minutes, of just darkness, until I hear the rush of blood in my ears and I feel the beating of my own heart.

Yes, I am back, almost human again.

I wait for Dylan, afraid to leave. It seems to take forever. So long that I'm worried he's not coming. I start to wonder if maybe I should leave my body again and find him. But I know, I tell myself he has to sneak in, he has to find a way, he has to find Herman, and then he has to find the dungeon and the tangled root ball that hides me.

Finally, I hear a noise, a small noise, the creaking of rusty metal. I think it could be the dungeon door opening. My heart thumps in anticipation. It closes and I hear nothing for minutes maybe, or hours. I hear the door open again and I can make out the soft whispers of voices. The root vibrates, it shrinks back. There are groans in the room, the sound of dense wood being torn apart, the roots tearing. A soft light breaks into the darkness of the root ball. I blink, my eyes not used to the light, even in its dimness. Hands reach down, pulling the roots up and away from me. They tear my cocoon open like a great soft clamshell.

I recognize Dylan's face; I reach my arm towards him. My skin stretches, my muscles ache. He pulls me up out of my root bed. I can feel the tiny pricks as the small root hairs are pulled from my pores. Dylan sets my feet on the floor, holding my upper body close to him with one strong arm.

"You came," I whisper, my mouth feeling odd from disuse, my throat dry.

"Of course." He smiles. "I've been searching all over for you."

"I thought you wouldn't, you were so angry before."

"I was wrong, so wrong to not see what Baal was doing." Dylan pulls me closer and leans down, kissing me, his fingers stretching into my hair, weakening my already feeble legs.

We are interrupted by the sound of Herman clearing his throat. "We must go," he tells us.

"Did you remember?" I ask Herman.

"Not much since you both disappeared, but now that you're back, a few things have returned to my memory." He waves at us. "Let's go."

Dylan loosens his hold on me, just enough to look down at my body. "Your clothes, there's not much left."

I look down at myself, seeing he is right. The jeans and sweater that I was wearing have been reduced to a few shards of torn material. Soil stains my skin. The bandages and socks have deteriorated off my feet. I reach down, pulling a piece of the root from the ground.

"What are you doing?" Dylan tries to stop my hand.

"It's ok," I tell him, feeling a confidence like never before.

What did Dylan say the last time the smoke turned me gray? Rest and time are all that would heal me. Well I've had plenty, locked away in here, waiting, resting, and learning how to truly harness my powers. Baal thought he was punishing me, and he did, but it only made me stronger.

I shake the root until it grows out like a long, thick rope. I wrap it around my body, growing it, coiling it, until it resembles a short dress.

"I guess that will do," Dylan says with a surprised smile.

He takes my hand and we follow Herman.

"How did you do that, in Florida?" he asks.

I look to him, a little embarrassed. "I left my body."

He stops, turning to me. "You left your body?"

"Yes, it was so strange, but I did it. I had to do something."

He smiles. "That's pretty cool."

We continue following Herman through the dungeon and up a set of stairs.

"Have you been practicing?" I ask Dylan as we walk.

"Every minute."

"But I saw you just standing by the beach for days."

"You just couldn't see what I was doing."

"What were you doing?"

"Creating a tsunami in the middle of the Atlantic."

"Did you hurt anyone?" I ask.

"No, that's why I did it in the middle of the ocean."

"Baal was planning on using us to take over the world. He has some crazed plan that we could help him destroy and rebuild the humans, be their Gods."

"Sounds like something he would do."

"Dylan." I stop, squeezing his hand tight. "He said we are immortal."

"Yes, I know."

"How old are you?"

"I stopped counting at one hundred."

"You never told me. Why?"

"What good would it have done to tell you? So I could go on the rest of my life knowing that you were always meant for someone else, that we could never be together, so you could know that also. Where would that have gotten me?"

"I just…"

"See," Dylan continues. "What would it have done for you?"

There is a long pause between us as I imagine forever without him. "There's more. He said there are things we don't know," I pull at his hand. "We need to go to the library."

Herman guides us along the back hallways, the stairwells, places within the castle I had never seen. When we finally come upon the library an old friend is waiting inside the familiar room.

"Hi, Kibbey!" I tell the Vassal as he rushes towards me and grabs onto my right leg, hugging it tightly. "Can you get the book," I ask him when he is done, "from the ceiling?"

Kibbey hobbles away. He pushes the bookshelf ladder into place then climbs. We watch as his stumpy body climbs the three stories to the ceiling and pushes up, revealing the hidden space. He pulls out the aged book, locking it under his arm, and climbs down.

We sit on the floor around one of the coffee tables, the old book spread before us. Herman flips silently through the pages.

"Have you seen this before?" I ask him.

"I get the sense that I may have."

He turns to the page with the drawings of the two figures, the muses. I stop his hand from turning the page.

"Dylan, why didn't you ever tell me you were musical?"

He shrugs. "I haven't played in a long time. When I did, before, it got me nothing but trouble, people wanted me to play for them at parties and make records."

"Why didn't you?" I ask.

"What would I have done once they started noticing I wasn't aging?" He pauses to look at his hands, and then taking a deep breath he looks at me. "I stopped so I could hide."

I don't press him further. I know exactly what he's talking about, exactly how he's feeling, because I've felt the same way.

I point to the images in the book. "I think this is us. And you see this-" My finger runs over the thin line that ties us together. "I was never meant for Baal. He has been lying to us, to you. I think this means we were meant to be together."

Dylan stares at the image, I assume the years of lies and deception are unfolding in his mind.

"He's not going to give up easy," Dylan finally says. "Baal has never been one to give up. We have to draw him back here. We have to plan. We have to defeat him."

"He will be back," Herman tells us, "in two days, for his weekend festivities."

"That doesn't leave us much time," I tell them. "Any ideas?"

A deep gurgling erupts in our collective silence. We all turn to Kibbey who is holding his stomach.

"I could eat something, too," Dylan says.

I look down at my dirt covered skin and the crude dress made of roots. "I could use a shower and real clothes."

"Your rooms are still the same," Herman tells me. "Everything is there. Go change. I can make you both something to eat."

Dylan and I stand together, not wanting to leave each other. We walk the familiar castle hall to Dylan's room so he can get a change of clothes. Then we head down the hall to my room.

"It's strange, being here," Dylan tells me, just as we reach the door to the room where Baal kept me. Pushing the door open reveals that the room remains exactly as I left it, except the window has been fixed. Dylan's eyes move to the shelf that holds Nixie's tank. It's still there, the water thick and stagnant, green with algae. "What happened to her?" he asks.

"She saved us." I tell him how Baal tried to throw her out the window, and how she puffed up, stabbing him with her poisonous spines. "It didn't faze him for long, the poison, just long enough for me to pull our strands of hair from around his neck and throw them."

"Was that when you yelled for me to run?"

"Yes."

"I remember that. Feeling the freedom."

"I was so afraid I would never see you again," I tell him.

"I would have never left you," he reaches for me, pulling me close. "I searched for so long." He pulls my hand up, placing it on his chest. I look at my fingers, noticing I'm still wearing the engagement ring Baal placed on me. I pull it off and leaving Dylan's embrace I walk to the window, placing it on the sill.

"I have to shower," I tell Dylan as I walk to the wardrobe and open the large door. All the clothes are there, the ones Baal gave me, even the ones I brought here. I pull out my old sweater and a pair of black pants. I catch Dylan locking the bolts on the door as I push the bathroom door closed.

I turn the shower as hot as I can stand. I pull at the root dress, peeling it off my body as one long whip. I leave the root on the floor and step in the shower. A year's worth of dirt and grime collect at the drain. I wash twice with the soap. I scrub under my fingernails and wash my hair three times. By the time I'm done my skin is rubbed red, my hair stripped. I dry myself off, dress myself in the clothes and brush my teeth.

I'm beginning to almost feel myself again, even though the thought of trying to defeat Baal looms over me, even though he said I wasn't human. I open the bathroom door to find Dylan sitting in the window seat. He stands as I walk towards him.

"I sat there," I tell him, pointing my finger at the window seat and watching it shake. "Every day, watching you swim away, waiting for you to come back."

"You smell much better," he tells me, changing the subject, the corner of his mouth rising in a half-smile.

I stare at him, blinking a few times as he reaches out, pushing the damp hair away from my face. "I think you broke my heart a little when you told me I was just another one of Baal's harem."

Dylan's hand stops moving. He drops his arms to his sides and stands. "I shouldn't have said that…" He gazes out the window.

"I just-" I start to say as he turns to me and interrupts.

"Do you remember Saratoga?" he asks.

"Every minute."

"I wish we could go back to that time," he tells me as he bends down, pressing his lips to mine, pulling me close to him. I close my eyes, never wanting it to end. But the moment does end, by a knock on the door. Dylan answers it as I pull my leather boots on. Kibbey stands in the hallway, tapping his foot at us. When I don't move fast enough he throws his arms up in the air and starts walking down the hall.

Dylan looks at me with questioning eyes.

"He's cranky," I tell him, standing up straight.

Dylan holds his hand out and I step forward, placing my hand in his, welcoming the warm feel of it. We walk to the small kitchen near the library to find Herman has set up a lunch of sandwiches with a tall pitcher of water. He pulls two pieces of shrimp out of the freezer and sets them on a plate for Kibbey. The Vassal stares at the shrimp, a scowl on his face-he must be wishing for more. He carries his plate towards us, sits in the seat next to me and eats both shrimp in one bite. The look on his face is dissatisfied; he leans back in the chair and closes his eyes.

We eat in silence, all of us thinking and planning.

"I think I'm going to build a forest," I tell them when we are done eating.

Dylan nods his head. "I'll bring you some seeds from the mainland. There aren't enough here."

"No," I wrap my hand around his wrist, "you can't leave me."

"I have to take Herman," he says. "He can't stay here. Something about this place has damaged his memory. And he doesn't have any powers, he can't help us, he needs to go."

Herman nods his head. "I think it is best I go. I would only be in the way."

"What about the Vassal?" I ask.

"We can try to bring them," Herman tells us. "But this is their home. It's always been their home. I get the feeling they will stay."

As we clean up, Herman leaves to collect a few things for his trip to the mainland. I walk them to the boat, Kibbey in tow with a row of the Vassal. Herman steps on the boat first.

"Come on then, Kibbey," Herman calls to the Vassal, motioning for them to get on the boat. None of them budge. Instead, they wave to Herman and march back to the castle.

"I guess they're staying," I say.

Dylan gets on the boat and starts the engine.

"Be back in a few minutes," he tells me.

I sit on the stone wall above the dock and watch Herman's face as the boat cuts through the water, the choppy waves of the seaway slapping against the its sides. The further away he gets, his expression changes, changes from a look of unknowing, to something, something else. I wish I were on that boat with him because I can see it spread across his face. He knows something, he's remembering. The spell of this island, Baal, the castle, it's losing its hold on him.

I stand, walking up the stone walkway to begin my work. I start with the trees that are already here, emptying their pine cones and seed pods onto the soil, pushing them under the ground. I grow their roots, strong and deep, and by the time I am done Dylan has returned. In his hand he holds seeds and buds from the mainland flowers, there are even a few packets of seeds.

"I grabbed what was left at the dock store," he says. "I hope this will work?"

"It's perfect," I tell him.

He pours the seeds into my cupped hands. I toss them into the air, directing them into the soil all over the island. Soon they have roots and buds, stems and leaves. I grow the trees tall, the ivy long, the flowers dense. When I am done, the only bare spots are the stone walkway and the castle.

"What are you going to do?" I ask Dylan, who has been standing by my side the entire time, watching quietly.

"I have water waiting," he tells me as he glances towards the night sky.

I follow his gaze, noticing the full moon and the way it illuminates his blue eyes. I try to hold in a yawn, feeling suddenly exhausted.

"We have tomorrow left to prepare," Dylan tells me as he takes my arm and leads me towards the castle.

"Where are the Vassal?" I ask as we walk into the front entrance.

"Look at the time." Dylan points to the clock, it's one thirty in the morning. "I bet they're hiding."

We walk up the marbled staircase and down the long hallway to my room. I bolt the door just as the hall clock strikes two.

"Should we sleep?" I ask Dylan, trying to suppress another yawn.

"We should try, at least." His eyes seem to soften as he looks at me, making my heart flutter a little faster.

I lay on the bed, fully clothed, turning to face Dylan.

"You should rest," I tell him.

Since my body has been resting in the ground for a year, I think that there will be no sleep for me. Even though I feel tired, I find it hard to close my eyes. I tell myself I can stay up and watch him while he sleeps. I can remember what it was like before Baal tore us apart and maybe those memories will give me the strength to help defeat him.

Dylan doesn't close his eyes; instead he stares into mine, his face turning soft, thoughtful. He reaches for me, pulling me closer to him.

"All these years I've spent thinking you were meant for someone else." He kisses me softly, pulling my body close to his, running his hand down my side and up my back. I wrap my arm around his strong shoulders, shoulders thick with corded muscle from years of swimming. Running my fingers up the back of his head and through his silver hair, I feel a shiver run through him.

"I missed you so much," I mumble on his lips.

"I missed you," he replies, "before you knew I even existed."

"Does that mean you knew about me?"

"I knew of you. Only that you existed, and-"

"How is it," I ask, "that you knew of me and I knew nothing of you?"

"I'm not sure." He tangles his hand in my hair. "But I won't hold it against you."

"And…"

"What?" he asks, his gaze returning to my face.

"You said *and*, but you never finished before I interrupted you."

"Oh yes." He pulls me closer to him in one smooth motion, pressing our bodies together. "And I had to see you, touch you."

His lips brush mine again, soft at first and then harder, the kiss deepening with a gentle eagerness that quickens my heart rate, making my body ache even more for him. Dylan moans softly. Our lips part in unison, his tongue claiming mine much like Baal had done, but this is so much different. Dylan isn't forceful or demanding, he progresses at the pace of a painfully slow exploration. One that I don't mind at all since he tastes so good, just as I remember, clean fresh water with a hint of spearmint.

I press myself closer, arching my back, pulling at the bottom of his shirt. He leans into me, pressing me down onto the bed, his body half covering mine. This time, the feeling of him kissing me isn't like being struck by lightning; it's something stronger, deeper, a strange feeling I can barely recognize but so strong it seems like the force of gravity which keeps the planets in sync. I need to feel him, more of him, unable to fulfill myself from the emptiness of my time in the ground alone.

He pulls his lips from mine, raking his teeth over my bottom lip as he leans away. An unexpected moan escapes my throat and I catch the hint of a smirk on his face as he moves to my jaw. His lips graze down my neck and across my collarbone.

A weakness too wonderful to explain spreads throughout my entire body. I can't wait any longer, not with what he's doing to me and the thoughts of confronting Baal tomorrow. If anything happens… I know I can't go on without him.

Dylan must've sensed this in me as his hand moves to my hip, kneading it with his fingertips. He pushes my shirt up revealing a flash of pale skin. His head dips lower. He kisses the soft skin of my stomach then my hip sending shock waves of tingling heat throughout my abdomen. I feel my breaths quicken as his hand rakes up my side, across the sensitive skin of my ribs and around my back. He pushes my shirt up further, trailing his mouth across my ribcage. I arch my back, pressing myself against him, offering more, unable to wait one more second. I reach down, pulling at his shirt, pushing my hands under the fabric and spreading my fingers across his hot skin, skin that I've always wanted to touch.

All that time, watching him strip down on the pier in front of me before a swim; now, I realize my awkward blushes and the shielding of my eyes had only revealed the truth: I have always wanted Dylan like this.

He moves his face in front of mine, pressing himself to me. I can feel the rapid beating of his heart next to mine. Desperate to feel more of him I press my lips hard onto his, let my hands run down his firm stomach and over the hollow space between his hip bones where his shorts hang, pulling him closer. He moans from deep within his chest just before pulling away.

"Now?" he asks, uncertainty in his blue eyes.

I know what he's asking: am I sure, am I sure I want to do this right now, after all we've been through and what waits for us tomorrow?

Of course I do.

"Yes," I manage to get out in a breathless whisper, knowing that if either of us don't make it tomorrow, if we fail at defeating Baal, I will never forgive myself for passing up these moments with him.

He pauses, giving me a chance to reconsider, both of our eyes heavy with desire. We've been waiting long enough for this. I wrap my leg around his back, pressing him closer to me.

"Okay," he murmurs, pressing his lips back on mine with a hurried kiss. I feel his hands run down my body, across my exposed abdomen which quivers under his hot touch. He stops at the sensitive skin just above the button of my pants. He fumbles for a moment, his breath quickening. I reach down, ready to help him, but I stop short, our eagerness interrupted by a thunderous roar echoing throughout the castle.

"The beast," we whisper to each other.

He kisses me again, ignoring the sounds of the beast, continuing with his attempt to get my pants off.

I try to ignore my thoughts of the beast. It roamed the halls before. I remember the way it breathed heavily outside my door at night. The thick locks keeping it from entering. The room vibrates. I pull away from Dylan.

"It's running," I warn him.

"How can you tell?" he asks on a hurried breath.

"That's the same noise it made when it ran at me in the library."

"You've seen it?" His fingers stop.

"Yes, Herman rescued me, it was the night you played and sang. I hid in the library." I push myself up so I'm sitting and pull my shirt down.

Dylan sits up on his knees, his face flushed from what we were about to do. "You stayed out in the castle past-"

His question is interrupted by a loud thud on the bedroom door. We both look to the locked door. We can hear it pawing and sniffing at the bottom of the door. It roars again. There is another loud thud on the door and the groan of the old wood bending in, bulging under the pressure of the beast. It must be pushing against the door. It's never done this before.

"Do you think it will get in?" I ask.

"I don't-" Dylan starts, only to be interrupted by another booming thud. A crack starts across the middle of the door. We must both see it because we scramble out of bed at the same time.

It roars and scratches at the door. Then it stops. Nothing.

"Do you think it left?" he asks.

"Maybe-" this time I am interrupted, by the thunderous sound of the beast running again. "It's coming back."

"That door's not going to hold."

"Come on." I pull on Dylan's hand, headed for the bathroom closet.

Dylan stops. "That closet won't protect us. It will break down the door in no time." He starts to pull away.

"No! There's a hidden passage behind the closet," I tell him. "Herman took me through it before."

"Really?" he questions me.

The beast hits the bedroom door, this time we can hear the sharp cracking of the centuries old wood.

I pull Dylan to the closet and we search frantically, running our hands along the lacquered wood. We push at the walls and knock in the corners. The beast hits the door again. This time, there is a sharp snap. It's broken the door. It roars, the sound echoing through the room, making our eardrums ache.

"Oh god," I whisper out in a terrified breath.

Dylan pulls the closet door behind us, enveloping us into darkness. I move along the wall, hurried, my fingers trembling. We can hear the wet breaths of the beast as it searches the room. The bed creaks, followed by crashes and loud snapping sounds coming from the bedroom. My hands tremor now and I move toward the middle of the closet.

"Have you found anything?" Dylan whispers, his voice moving closer to me.

"No."

"Keep-" I hear a loud *thump*. "Shit!" Dylan spits.

"Are you okay?" I ask in the darkness. I hear a slight squeaking noise and push my hands forward. They no longer meet on the closet wall. Instead there's open space. I walk forward, recognizing the dank smell of the hidden passage. "I've found it!" I reach behind me, grabbing for Dylan's arm, dragging him with me into the hidden passage. It's just as dark as the closet. I can't see anything and I'm not sure which direction to go. On a hunch, I turn left. We run and stumble down the enclosed hallway. The echoes of the beast demolishing the room trail behind us. When we are far enough away that I can barely hear the sounds, I slow and wrap my hand around Dylan's.

"It smells in here."

"I know," I reply.

"I can't see anything."

"Neither can I." We walk along the passage, hand in hand, both of us feeling along the rough walls. "What should we do?" I ask.

"I'm not sure. I just wish I could see something. How did Herman move in this darkness?"

"He had a light."

"Great," Dylan mutters. "Let's keep walking."

We continue with our hands on each other and the walls, afraid we might separate in the darkness.

"Herman said this castle has a way of making people lose time."

"Yes," he responds. "I've noticed this."

"Why haven't I?"

"I'm not sure."

"Baal said you keep secrets from me."

He only responds with silence.

"Dylan?"

"There are many things here that I don't understand. Baal likes it that way."

"He says he knows what we are, Dylan. He says that we could be Gods if the humans, the people, if they knew about us."

"Yes, that sounds like something he'd say."

"What do you think?"

"I'm not sure I know what to think anymore. I only know that I have you again and I don't want to lose you."

The darkness continues. A few times we pass along a section of the hidden hallway where it brightens, only enough so we can make out where the wall is and I can see the shadow of Dylan's figure next to me. It must be from a light left on in the outer rooms. It doesn't happen as often as I would like.

"I'm surprised we haven't come across any stairs, yet," Dylan says in the darkness.

Just as he finishes speaking I step forward, noticing that my foot doesn't hit the wooden floor instead it drops down lower. A small noise escapes my throat.

"I've spoken too soon," Dylan mutters before I can say anything.

I let go of him, reaching for the walls, trying to steady myself, the old wood is too worn and smooth to grasp. From the noise next to me it seems Dylan is trying the same. Neither of us is able to stop, we tumble down the dark stairs. I think I get an elbow to the face, and more than once I feel my knee hit something softer than the wood. I hope that it isn't Dylan's face.

When I finally get the sense that we aren't moving any longer I try to stretch my arms but I am only met with a sharp spasm of pain. Dylan moans next to me, one of his appendages rests heavily on my leg. I take a deep breath only to be met with another spasm of pain. My head hurts, my body aches. I feel exhausted. I close my eyes. *Just for a moment*, I tell myself.

CHAPTER TWENTY

I wake to find Kibbey kicking at my leg making some squawking noise. Whatever he's trying to tell me it must be urgent. I turn to find Dylan still unconscious, his leg across mine, and his left arm bent at an awkward angle. I shake him until he starts to move.

"Dylan," I whisper. "Get up. We have to get moving"

Looking around the dark hallway I realize that it must be daytime because I can see light streaming through a few of the boards on the wall. Dylan mumbles something unintelligible. Kibbey pulls at my arm, helping me to stand. I no longer feel the pain and aches of having fallen down the stairs. The sleep must've healed us.

I pull at Dylan's arm, helping him to stand. There is a blue streak across his forehead. It must be a deep bruise. It seems he didn't heal as fast as I did.

"Are you okay?" I ask.

"Yeah." He rubs his eyes and face. "I think so." He flinches as he touches his fingers to the mark on his forehead.

Kibbey pulls at my hand. "Come on," I reach for Dylan, dragging him along with us.

Kibbey leads us along the passage. Bright light seeps between the wall boards. He stops, pushing on the wall, mumbling something in his Vassal chatter. As I pass through the wall I recognize where he has brought us: the library. I look at the old clock on the wall.

"It's already eight at night!" I tell Dylan, noticing the sun starting to dip behind the trees outside the window.

"Baal will be here in no time." Dylan rubs his arm. "So much for planning."

Kibbey screeches at us, sounding like an injured seagull.

"What's wrong?" I ask.

He points out the window.

A deep fear shivers through me. Baal is already here and he's watching us from outside the castle. With the backdrop of the thick foliage I grew yesterday, he resembles some feral jungle creature ready for the hunt.

"Run!" Dylan pulls at my arm.

I follow him, running out of the library, headed for the stone hall.

"We have to get outside," I tell Dylan. "I can't do anything in here, there's too much stone."

We turn hard at the end of the hall, running for the front door. It's already open for us.

"This feels like a trap," I tell him, almost out of breath, my legs aching.

"No choice, we have to get outside."

We run through the door, over the stone walk, and into the thick forest that now covers Dark Island. We stop at a small clearing that's nothing more than a few of the trees spaced further apart than the rest.

"My pets!" Baal greets us, appearing in front of us without warning. "I just knew you'd be back." He leans on the amethyst-topped cane in his hands.

Dylan takes my hand, squeezing it so tight it hurts.

Baal waves a finger at us. "Uh, uh, uh," he warns. "No tricky stuff."

Taking a quick gasp in, I find that we are frozen in place. I was hoping that he wouldn't be able to do this anymore after I flung our hair out the window. But like Dylan suggested, it seems those were only a way for Baal to find us should we try and escape him.

"What do you want?" I ask Baal, trying to control the shudder in my voice. It seems I am still quite afraid of him.

"What I have always wanted, my bride." He smiles, opening his hand in front of me. The sparkling diamond engagement ring hovers before me.

"You will never have me!" I yell at him. "You are nothing but a liar. I was never meant for you-"

He draws my left hand up, spreading my fingers. The ring hovers towards my hand. I close my eyes, my mind racing, trying to figure out what to do next. And then, I feel it, just as strong as when I first moved to Saratoga: the trees beckoning me, bending, the ivy stretching. I realize that Baal may control our bodies right now, but not our powers. I whip a string of ivy from the forest, curling it around the ring and pulling it back, burying it in the ground deep within the forest.

Baal simply smiles. "I see you've learned some new tricks!"

"Thanks to you." I smile back at him, trying my hardest not to look scared to death.

The trees bow over us like a hundred monks readying themselves for prayer and I tell them what to do. Their branches whip down, smashing at Baal. He skirts from side to side, the branches barely missing him. He holds onto the staff with both hands, his knuckles gripping tight. I know he is trying his best to control us, but it seems his power is dissipating.

"Do something!" I yell to Dylan.

A wall of dense fog surrounds the island. I try to hit Baal with more branches but he seems to evade them. Clutching the staff he laughs mockingly at us. I grasp him with the strands of ivy, curling it around his arms but he rips the ivy off him in one quick motion.

It's not strong enough. I need to find something else.

"Watch out," Dylan warns me.

A great downpour erupts from the sky and a fast rushing waterfall flows onto Baal's head. The weight of the rushing water pushes him to the ground onto his knees. I wrap more ivy around the staff and rip it from his grasp. I feel his hold on us let loose completely as I pull the staff into the forest, hiding it on the other side of the island, pulling it up to the tops of the trees and wrapping it in the thick leaves.

Baal starts to raise himself up and I hear a deep gurgling laughter from within the waterfall. "Oh my, little water boy," Baal starts, his voice gurgling out of the water. "Each day your gifts tend to amaze me a little more. But really, what more could a father ask of his son."

The water stops. Dylan's face changes from one of fierce determination to that of pure shock.

"After all this time you never put the two together," Baal continues. "And here we are now. I shouldn't be surprised, though, really. Isn't this how it always ends? The son always tries to kill the father."

"You're lying!" Dylan yells at Baal. "This is just another one of your lies!"

"Don't listen to him," I tell Dylan.

"You know," a deep chuckle starts from within Baal's chest, "your mother was quite beautiful but she was never very smart, which is why she left you on that beach. What would a mortal woman do with a child like you, a child of the Lord of the Underworld? You were bred of death and evil. I'm sure you've felt it brewing inside you after all these years."

"Stop it," Dylan tells him through gritted teeth. "All you do is lie."

"Why would I lie to my son? Why would a *God* lie to his son?"

"If it's true, if you are a God, then that would make me-"

"A Demigod," Baal finishes Dylan's sentence.

"And Demi?"

They both look at me. I shrink back, trying to hide myself as the branches and vines collect around my feet.

"Ah, my son, Demi is something quite special. Something very special indeed. I will admit Olympus has had some strays over the years, but the Gods have always found these ones," Baal's finger juts towards me, "and put an end to them long before they ever stepped foot on this earth. But Demi… Demi had very smart parents, very smart indeed. Although, that is what we would expect from a Muse and a Nymph, being the sneaky creatures that they are. It seems one of their offspring slipped through, hidden amongst the population of blubbering humans. And so we have Demi, the verboten hybrid as we like to call them. Forbidden for one reason, her powers will become stronger than that of your own, *son*, she will learn to out skill you and her very existence risks the lives of all the demigods and Gods alike. And *that* is why I am taking her as my bride. I am taking her with me back to the underworld where she should have been sent in the first place, where she can't harm us."

Dylan looks to me, his features changing again. I see a flash of mistrust, of fear.

"Don't listen to him," I tell Dylan, shaking my head, barely believing what I just heard. "He lies. I told you where my parents found me-"

"Yes," Baal interrupts. "What better place for a Nymph to hide her child than in a blossoming park. And what better parents for a

Muse to choose than your very own mother. Did you ever wonder where she developed her skill for the dance? Have you even thought of your name and what it means? *Demi. Earth mother.*"

"I don't believe you!" I yell at him.

Baal smiles a deep dark smile that makes me shrink back into the trees. And with the bright glow of moonlight now above us, I can just make out Baal's retaliation: he sends a streaming length of smoke into the air, it twists and turns and snakes in the sky. Internally, somehow, I know that this is something we have to escape, this is something we can't let touch us. The black smoke from a thousand burning fires, from the fires of the Underworld I am sure, filled with the screams of the dead which will do nothing but make us weak, too weak to defeat him.

"Go!" I yell to Dylan.

He pauses for a moment, watching me, just before we run in opposite directions. Dylan throws himself into the seaway and I bury myself in the ground, wrapped in a tangle of roots.

I wait in the ground, hearing nothing but my own breaths and all of what Baal just said screaming in my mind. All those fairy tales I read, all the wondering I've done. I finally have some answers. And they weren't at all what I was expecting. Not at all. I'm not even human, not even close. And Dylan, he's some sort of a Demigod. A Demigod of the Underworld of all places. I was hoping to just defeat Baal so we could have peace again. But I could see it in Dylan's face, the understanding of what he is, and now the mistrust of what I am. It seems Baal does nothing but try to pull us apart.

As I hide in the ground things start to make sense, the references to godless humans and this strange island where time seems to stand still. I'm hoping, as I lie buried, hiding, that maybe Herman is someone great also and maybe he can help us.

I hear the echo of footsteps above me. They stop. Perhaps it's Dylan, waiting for me, maybe he's finished it already. I feel the ground around me turning soggy and sodden with water. Remembering what happened when I was stuck in the rain and fell in the lake, my breath catches in my throat. I have to get out of the ground. I can't let myself get surrounded by the water-it will only weaken me. I release myself from the roots and soil, pushing myself above ground.

Focusing my eyes in the moonlight, I instantly realize this was a bad idea. It's not Dylan standing so close to my side, it's Baal, and I've done nothing better than offer myself up to him. Before I have a chance to react he reaches out, grabbing me by the hair.

"There you are," he says to me. "Little Fiancée."

I try to pull away from him, the action ripping hair from my scalp.

"Let go of me," I scream at him.

"Not on your life," he sneers. "I see my son has left you alone. Again. I would never leave you," he promises.

"I wish you would," I tell him, searching the forest in front of me, searching for a way to get free, to escape, to get him to leave me alone. *Leave me. Leave.* I know just what to do! I pull the roots from the ground and begin to wrap myself with them in a tight cocoon, just as I was in the dungeon.

"What do you think you're doing?" Baal asks, his dark eyes flickering with excitement.

I smile at him as the roots wrap my arms, my chest, my neck. The root pushes his hand off the back of my head as it wraps me, sealing me inside. I can hear his deep voice outside the roots, circling, knocking on the fibrous material, trying to figure out his way inside. I wait until it stops, until I feel the vibration of his footsteps as he walks away.

I contemplate my next move. I know Baal will be on me as soon as I leave the root. Which leaves me only one choice, a choice that scares me to death; I have to leave my body just as I did when I went searching for Dylan.

I make the root squeeze me, its tiny fibers bore into my skin just as they did in the dungeon. I take a breath and *leave.* I travel along the root, into the tree that stands next to me and see Baal sitting a few yards away. He's watching the cocoon that protects my body, his fingers rest on his chin as he contemplates what I've done. Thankfully, it seems, he doesn't know that I've left my body behind, that right now I am nothing more than a soul travelling through the trees.

I leave Baal to stare at my roots as I travel the island, searching for Dylan. I don't see him, nor do I see a ripple in the water. I'm afraid he has left me, again. Baal has filled his mind with distrust for me and what it is I might be able to do. It's all I can think. I wait, watching the seaway.

It's not long before I hear a tearing sound, the sound of tough fibers and wood being broken apart. I rush along the roots to where I left my body, only to be met with an abrupt stop, the roots end before I can get back to my body. I panic, whatever energy my soul is right now it panics and I want to scream. I rush into a nearby tree, a small sapling, to see what has become of me.

"*Nooooo!*" I scream to myself, to whatever I am.

Baal has ripped the roots off of my body, chopped them away with an ax. I watch, powerless, as he lifts my lifeless body off the ground. I look around myself unsure of what to do. I whip vines at him. I lash branches at him. But each time he seems to sway them off. And since I am afraid of harming my soulless body, I stop.

Baal walks to the edge of the island, my body hanging over his shoulder. Wanting to follow him, I'm torn at my current situation-I have no body to contain me. Fearing for my soulless body, I lean toward Baal as he stands at the edge of the island. I stretch the sapling. I stretch its roots. I extend its tiny branches until something so strange happens. The sapling starts to move, it starts to run! I look down to see that I am truly running, the roots skirting across the ground just as an octopus scales the seafloor. My soul has a form now; it's not my body, but it will have to do for now.

I scurry after Baal, a tiny sapling roaming among the tallest trees. I should have used one of them, one of those tall strong trees instead of this.

The seaway starts to bubble. Steam rises from the edge of the island. The water turns red and turbulent in a rapid boil. I scamper faster trying to reach him, trying to reach my body which hangs over his shoulder so carelessly. But just as I reach the edge, he jumps in.

No! No, no, no, no! I stare in horror at the boiling water. Defeated, alone, my body gone.

The feeling of dread and shock running through my sapling form is interrupted by the crunching of leaves behind me and the soft thudding of feet on the ground. I turn just in time to see Dylan run out of the forest and dive into the water after Baal.

~ ~ ~

I look down my new body; the thin torso, the root feet. I hold my hands in front of me. They are branches now. Soft, brown twigs with tiny budding leaves. If I knew how to produce tears like this I think I might cry. I might scream and run in after them. But that will surely kill me, if my body isn't already dead wherever Baal took it.

I pace along the shore, feeling the soil under my roots, unsure of what to do, realizing that there is only one thing I can do. I have to trust that Dylan will find me. I wander to the front door of the castle. My roots linger over the stone walkway, bringing me to the front steps. I stand, waiting, unsure of what to do with myself now that I am nothing but a tree.

"Now, where is that?" I hear a whisper coming up the stone walkway.

I lean forward, the bark on my back creaking. I see Herman wandering towards the castle. He scratches his head and looks all about him.

"Where could it be?" he asks himself. "My caduceus, my caduceus, where did I leave you?" He steps into the forest, pushing away the branches and shrubs. "Where are you?"

I would like to ask him what a caduceus is, but I have no voice. "Where, where, where…" Herman mumbles to himself. Just as he reaches the front step, he turns back around, staring into the woods. "A staff among sticks. I will never find it here. I cannot be the messenger without my caduceus."

A staff? A staff… Baal's cane!

"This is rather unfortunate," Herman continues to himself.

I pull the cane from the treetops where I wrapped it for hiding and deliver it to Herman's side.

"Ah! There you are." He reaches for the staff. I pull it away. He reaches for it again. I pull it towards me, so he can see me. I lay it at my feet, my roots, actually. Herman bends down to pick it up. He raises his head, just a bit, and sees me, a tree, standing at the entrance to the castle.

"How strange." His eyebrows rise as he leans in, sniffing at me. "How very strange indeed." He reaches his free hand towards me, for the tiny leaves that poke from my sapling arms. I reach out with my branch arm and swat him on the hand. He recoils, holding his hand close to his chest.

"What the…"

I cross my branch arms and shake my leaves at him.

"Is that you?" he asks.

I shake my leaves again.

"Demi?" he scratches his brow and squints his eyes.

I shake my leaves, yet again.

"It seems as though you have lost your body."

Already furious with my current position I give him a very unladylike gesture with my branch arms.

His eyes widen and then he smiles. "Oh well, come, follow me."

He stands up straight, the staff in his hand, and heads for the castle doors. I follow him, my roots scuffling along the smooth stone. I hear a hiss as I enter the castle and turning, I see Kibbey in the corner baring his pointy teeth at me. I might be eye to eye with him right now, in this sapling form, that is, if I had eyes. And he could probably use me for a toothpick. At the thought of that I scurry after Herman as he opens a hallway door.

"Looking, looking, looking," he mumbles to himself. He searches the rooms, the drawers, closets, even behind the curtains. After the fourth room, he turns, noticing me again. "I'm looking for a hat, have you seen it?" he asks me.

Having no idea what he is talking about, and still being without words, I rustle my leaves at him.

He continues his search, the staff glowing in his hand. "It's a special hat, made of precious metals, smelted in the hottest of fires. Have you seen it?" he asks me again.

I try to wave myself back and forth as though I'm shaking my head no.

"Hmm," he scratches his head. "It does magical things. It hides, it hides, it hides something, somewhere, someone…" He moves onto the next room.

"Are you sure?" he looks to me again. "I can't remember…" Abruptly, he turns toward the window. "Someone is coming. You must go! I will continue my search for the hat, er… the helmet!"

I can feel it too, something disrupts the shoreline grasses. Something is returning to the island, someone is pulling themselves from the seaway! I skirt my way out of the castle, my roots moving as fast as they can. The moonlight is bright, illuminating everything as I return to the shoreline where I watched Baal and Dylan jump in the water. There seems to be nothing but a damp trail leading into the forest. I follow it, my roots sinking into the mud.

I slow as I hear a voice.

"Demi?"

I creep forward, seeing Dylan huddling over my body which lies on the ground. His skin looks to be scorched in places, there are black and red burns covering his arms and legs, soot camouflages his face.

"Demi?" he shakes the shoulders of my lifeless body.

I creep forward, trying to get closer.

"Demi, come back, come back, please!" He pulls my eyelids back with his thumbs. Whatever he sees, it can't be good. He bends over me, his body shudders. "*No*," he whispers.

I creep closer, my root-feet disturbing the soil. He whips his head up, glaring at me, ready to react, his eyes red and gleaming.

I reach out with my branches.

"Is that you?" he whispers.

Being without words, still, I rustle my leaves.

"Yes? Hurry, you need to get into your body, he's coming." Dylan leans over, looking behind me. I can hear the rapid bubbling of the seaway as it starts to boil again.

I scuttle to my body, standing next to it. It looks like a corpse; pale and lifeless. I'm not sure what to do or where to start. I touch it with my branch-arm, then with my root-foot. Nothing happens.

"Hurry!" Dylan tells me.

I stand, pressing my sapling roots back into the ground. I grow them and split them; one part grows deep in the ground, the other towards the surface. I wrap the roots around my body, tight, pressing the fibers into the skin of my pale arm.

"*Hurry!*" Dylan urges me, his voice waning.

I can see the seaway boiling behind me. I can feel its heat. All too soon Baal rises from the water. Dylan stands, he runs in front of me, placing himself between me and Baal.

"Demi, now!" Dylan shouts at me.

I press the root fibers harder, boring into the pores of my lifeless body. I travel away from the sapling, along the roots, back to my body where I belong and I slam my energy into my human form.

CHAPTER TWENTY-ONE

Dylan must be running with me in his arms. I hear the sound of his winded breaths as I come to. My eyes open, I move my arms.

He looks down at me, his eyes frantic. "Are you awake?"

"I think-"

He drops me to my feet and turns, his arm secure under my shoulders.

Now I can see why he runs, Baal is following us. But he's changed. He no longer resembles a handsome business man. Instead he's dark, scaled, his eyes have changed to a red slash of pupil, his clothes nothing more than black wisps of torn fabric.

"I know why you run, *Son,* because you liked it. Didn't you?" Baal bellows to Dylan. "While you were digging her corpse from the depths of the Underworld you felt what you were made of."

"Stop." Dylan reaches out, the sky rumbles and a waterfall pours down onto Baal. I catch the spray of it on my lips as the torrent halts Baal. It's not the fresh water that he used before, but dense, salty seawater. It seems to stop Baal from moving any further.

I pull a tree branch down, and sitting on it, I raise myself up into the heights of the tree. Dylan is now surrounded by his element as the water pools at his feet.

"You can't hide it. That feeling will continue to eat away at you until you give in." Baal laughs from inside the waterfall, gurgling on the salt water. "I am a God. I am your father. My own flesh and blood. You cannot defeat me. I will find you again!"

I look down to see Dylan's face twisted in agony. Either from Baal's words or what he's doing, I'm not sure. I just know I have to help. I have to do something. I know the ivy isn't strong enough, so I summon from the ground the only thing I know to be stronger: the trusty roots. I start at Baal's feet, wrapping, just as the root did to me in the dungeon. Wrapping, twisting, growing. I pull more roots from the ground, securing his arms, wrapping and twisting the root, growing it thick and strong. I grow it stronger than it ever was when it encapsulated me. I keep wrapping, encasing and enclosing him.

Dylan slows the waterfall and soon it is just a heavy rain, then a small trickle. Just as I reach Baal's head, wrapping the root around his face. The root bulges with the force of Baal's movements inside and his attempts to fight his way out. I squeeze him, as a snake would its prey. I wrap the root tighter and thicker.

The water stops.

The root ball shudders as I force it into the ground, securing it.

I look down at Dylan.

He smiles up at me, soot creasing his handsome face. I try to ignore the dim look in his eye, the feeling that he's fighting something dark inside himself.

"We did it!" I tell him, triumphant.

I start crawling down the tree, to the next lower branch, stopping when I hear a thunderous roar from inside the castle. I turn back to Dylan.

He looks up at me, eyes wide. "Stay where you are!" he shouts.

He turns, running for the edge of the island. I hear his footsteps followed by the heavy footsteps of the beast, running. The tree quivers and I see a flash of fur in the moonlight as it runs under the tree headed straight for Dylan.

The beast roars. The trees waiver and bend as its large body pushes up against them. My heart catches in my throat. It's going to get him! After all this time I spent finding Dylan and defeating Baal, I'm going to lose him again. I can't let the beast have him.

I can see the beast on Dylan's heels, the only thing slowing it is the trees. I try to grow a few in its path, but the beast is too fast. I work at entangling it with the ivy, but the beast is too strong, the strands breaking almost instantly. I can see the edge of the island is near and Dylan's almost there. The beast still on his heels, he jumps, realigning his body midair, diving into the seaway. The beast stops, huffing at the edge of the island. It snorts, pawing at the ground. Pacing. It waits for Dylan to return.

I let out a breath of relief and wait.

Just as I start to think he may not return, I see movement near the edge. Dylan pulls himself from the seaway, his arms full of silvery flopping fish. The beast runs at him.

"No!" I yell from my perch high in the trees.

Dylan opens his arms at the beast, flinging the fish into a pile on the ground. The beast stops, bending, shoving fish after fish into its mouth. Dylan dives back into the water and moments later he returns, his arms full of more fish. He drops them at the beast's feet. The beast continues to devour the fish, chomping as a hungry dog at its bowl.

As the beast eats its fill, something strange starts to occur. It seems the beast begins breaking apart. Large chunks of the creature fall off, resting on the ground for a moment before wiggling and shuddering.

Dylan brings back another armload of fish. The beast starts to slow, looking around as it eats. It stares at Dylan. More globs of the beast's body fall off, its form shrinking before our eyes. Dylan reaches his arm out towards the beast. It glowers at him, chomping on what looks to be a large tuna. The beast bows its head and Dylan touches it, stroking its giant head.

I start climbing down from the tree, sensing that something has changed in the beast. It no longer seems so ferocious and ready to eat us. By the time I reach the ground the beast is nothing but a dozen or so small, furred creatures. I walk to Dylan's side. He hands me a fish. I hold it out, watching as a small furred beast baby takes it from me. It looks into my eyes and I recognize these creatures.

"The Vassal!" I exclaim. They are nothing but unclothed Vassal.

"Baal should really learn to feed his pets," Dylan says, water dripping off his hair and down his face.

"How did you know?" I ask.

"Remember when I dove into the seaway each day?" he asks.

I nod my head at him, remembering all too well those long days without him.

"I was sent to fish, to get food for the Vassal."

I remember Kibbey always trying to eat Nixie, begging for her, and how he devoured the plate of shrimp every weekend while we hid from the parties. The beast was nothing but a pack of starving Vassal. Kept at bay before, when there was someone here to feed them adequately.

I turn to Dylan. He's changed again. I can easily sense it in the way he carries himself, as though there's a pile of bricks hanging off his arms. Something happened down there. Something bad.

"Dylan?" I ask.

"What?" he responds, distracted,

"Are you alright?"

He runs his hand through his hair. "I don't know. I just..."

"What?"

"Don't ever do that again." He grabs my shoulders, his fingers pressing firmly into my skin. "Don't ever leave your body like that. I can't… I can't go back there again. Ever."

"Where?"

"He took you to the Underworld. He took your lifeless body and I was so afraid that you were gone." He lets out an exasperated breath. "I didn't even think, I just ran after him."

"Thank you," I whisper to him.

"Promise me," Dylan shakes me a little. "Promise me that you will never leave your body like that again."

"Ok, ok, I won't. I just had to get away from him, and I was alone, there was no one here to help."

"I know." He lets his hands run down my arms.

I take his hand, looking at the burns spread across his arms. "Do they hurt?"

He shakes his head. "I can't feel them right now."

I control the urge to comfort him, to close my eyes and press my lips to his. Now is not the time. "Thank you," I tell him. "For saving me, again."

He looks at me, hard, and I can see the torment in his eyes from whatever he saw down there.

"Oh!" I remember, "My parents! I almost forgot about my parents." I run back towards the front doors of the castle with Dylan at my heels.

"What are you talking about?" he shouts after me.

I make my way to the library, flicking on the lights. I search the corner where the glass box once stood. It seems someone has cleaned up the smashed box, but I can still see the glint of glass shards along the wall.

"Mother?" I crouch down, peering under the shelves. "Father!"

I search for any sign of movement. Any sign that they may still be here and not relocated by whoever it was that charmed them and put them in the box. It's been a year, after all. The figures could have been picked up and relocated somewhere else. I stand, running my hands over my face, realizing that I should have searched for them first. I should have found them and hidden them so they would be safe when I came back.

"What are you doing?" Dylan asks.

"My parents, they were in this glass case, there were little carved figurines. But they weren't really figurines." I walk along the wall and crouch down again to look under another section of shelves. "They came to life, they spoke to me."

Dylan gives me that look, the one where he's thinking I'm crazy, even after all that just happened. "Are you sure?" he asks with a hint of skepticism in his voice.

"I'm as sure as I ever was, about anything."

I crawl to the couches on my hands and knees. I flip up the fabric that hides the hollow space between the floor and the couch. I call their names again, squinting in the darkness. All I see is a collection of dust bunnies which float away on my breaths. I crawl to another couch and look under it, nothing. I search under the chairs, coffee tables, carpets. Nothing. I stand up, now searching the room for Dylan.

I find him standing by the fireplace, his body tense, his eyes bloodshot. Whatever happened to him down there, whatever he experienced, it changed him. He saved me. He risked his life and it seems as though it has ruined him. I reminisce, for just a moment, about the summers we spent on the pier. Both of us happy, exploring, innocent. It seems like it was so long ago, and my heart seems to ache. Just for a little bit, it aches at the fact that we can never return to that time.

Dylan reaches out, grasping the bookshelf ladder, and begins climbing.

"They won't be up there," I yell to him. But he ignores me, and continues climbing. I watch as he reaches the top and pushes at the ceiling, retrieving the hidden book. Then he climbs down and walks to where I am standing.

"I think we should take this," he holds the old book in front of me.

"Yeah, okay." I look around the room, distracted, hoping to notice something I didn't before on the first search through the room for my parents.

"What's that?" Dylan asks, pointing to my feet.

I look down to see a tiny white sheep bow out from under the ottoman we stand near. It bays and a stream of tiny people and animals exit the space, among them, my parents. There's a mouse-like chatter as the figurines speak amongst themselves. I reach down as my tiny parents walk to me. Holding out my hand, they step up onto my palm. I straighten myself, holding them in front of my face, smiling. They smile back, waving their arms, looking at each other and saying something I cannot hear.

"See," I tell Dylan. "My parents, enchanted into tiny figurines, somehow. They weren't eaten by a bear. Baal had them the entire time. I just don't know how to turn them back."

"Who are the rest of them?" Dylan asks, motioning the cluster of tiny people on the floor.

"I'm not sure, maybe the book has something."

We sit on the couch, being careful not to step on the people and animals. I reach down with my open palm and my parents step off onto the coffee table in front of us. Then Dylan and I take turns reaching down and lifting the rest of the people and animals onto the coffee table.

"Ouch!" he complains as we lift the last group.

"What?"

"I think this horse just bit me." He uses his free hand to rush the horse and sheep off of his palm and onto the table.

"Seriously?" I chuckle at him while opening the book. "*Demigod*, we just defeated Baal and you're complaining because a tiny horse bit you."

"Yeah, yeah, yeah," he replies, inspecting his thumb.

I watch the tiny horse whinny and stomp around the table, shaking its head in the air as though it were laughing. I open the book. My parents and the other people line up across the top of the book, watching as I flip through the pages.

"I wish I could read this," I tell Dylan.

"Yeah, me too." He scoots closer to me, his shoulder pressed up against mine. For the first time I can smell him, the scorched skin, the ash. I try hard not to wrinkle my nose.

I raise my eyes to see my parents watching us. Mother tugs at Father's sleeve, nodding her head towards us. I smile at them, hoping not to get a lecture on boys if I ever get them back to normal.

I pass a few more pages filled with words I cannot read and drawings I don't understand. The little people chatter amongst themselves. One, a man in a white robe, reaches out, stopping me from turning the pages. He gestures at the page and I lean closer, trying to make out the words. Dylan does the same thing.

"This is so frustrating," I say. "I don't understand what is written here."

I hear a noise in the hall, footsteps. I place my hand on Dylan's arm, feeling the raised burns I pull back, noting that he didn't even flinch when I touched his wounds.

I sense a change in the air. "Do you feel that?" I ask.

"Yes," Dylan replies.

We both stand, waiting to see what it is.

Kibbey enters the room, now fully clothed. Herman follows closely behind him.

"I think, I think, where could it be?" Herman is pacing, just as he was before. "The hat, the hat. No, it's a helmet. A helmet you fool. Ah!" he holds his finger up. "I remember." He walks to the cupboard near the fireplace and opens it. We watch as he pulls out a black bag, which seems to be holding something heavy and round. Herman looks down at the bag and smiles. His features changed, he seems to have gained some wisdom being off the island. Or maybe it's the things he has found since he returned, the staff in his hand, and now the heavy sack.

"Do you remember something?" I ask.

"Yes. Yes. I have."

Herman walks towards me.

"You should put this on." Herman reaches into the bag and pulls out what looks to be an old helmet. The metal is aged, tarnished, with longs sides that look as though it may cover my head and my ears.

"What is that?"

"Put it on. The Gods are coming." He tells me.

"I have to hide. Baal said the Gods will kill me. That I'm not even supposed to be alive!"

"Put on the helmet," Herman urges. "It will hide you from their view."

I take the helmet from him, apprehensively.

"That will keep her safe?" Dylan asks Herman.

"Yes."

Dylan looks at me, his eyes pained. "I think I should go then."

"What?" I ask.

"I think it's for the best."

"God damn you, Dylan!"

"Gods."

"What?"

"May the Gods damn me, and they already have."

"Stop it," I tell him through gritted teeth, angered beyond belief that he could choose this moment to try and leave me again.

"Stop what?"

"Whatever it is you are thinking."

"I just need some time to sort this out."

"No! You are not going to do that to me again." I grip the heavy helmet in my hand, wanting to throw it at him.

"Why? You don't need me, Demi. Look at you, what you are, and look at me." He holds his burned arms out. "You are something so special. I saw it down there." He points to the floor. "And I… I am the Demigod of the Underworld. I felt what I was made of down there when I brought you back. And a little piece of me, a tiny piece of me, *liked it.* This has yet to work out in our favor, us being together. What makes you think now, that right now could be any different?"

Herman holds his hand up, interrupting us. He grabs Dylan by the shoulder.

"Gods have many sons and many daughters. None as special as you two." He leans towards Dylan, staring into his eyes. "Hades, Baal, Father, whatever you call him, he has provided the earth with *hundreds* of Demigods. All of them have reached differing levels of greatness and inferiority. For thousands and thousands and thousands of years, *we* have waited for *you.*"

"How can you be sure it's me?"

"You have gifts and strengths, greater than those of any human, but you are not expected to follow in the path of your father. Didn't you see the book? Do you remember? Demi needs you. And now is not the time to forget who you are. We have much to do, and if you truly want to save her, then you need to help hide her while I discuss with the Gods what awaits your fate." His grasp shakes Dylan's shoulder. "We have waited for you *both*."

Dylan blinks. "Both?"

"It was written in the book by the fates, ages ago, that there would be two, a child of the earth and a child of the Underworld."

"But Baal said I am evil. And I *felt it*, so strong down there. And she, she is meant to die." Dylan holds his arm out in the direction I am standing, the pained expression has returned to his face.

"Not all Demigods of the Underworld are meant for evil purposes."

"But I felt it when I was down there. I felt something so…" Dylan closes his eyes and curls his hands into fists.

"You felt what you were made of, not what you are destined to be. Those are two very different things."

"How do you know, how can you even know?"

"Because *I* am a God," Herman responds. "I know what is destined for you."

Dylan moves swiftly, standing in front of me, guarding me.

Herman smiles. "I am no danger to either of you. I am just a messenger. But, you need to put that on, Demi." He points to the helmet in my hand.

"Why?" I ask, "If there's no danger."

"The others, they may react differently. After all this time Hades has been hiding. He's used the caduceus and the helmet to hide for years, adding the souls to his Underworld, preying on the godless humans, the ones that have forgotten about us. It's been many years since they last worshipped someone, or anything for that matter. Either way, the Gods are not happy."

Dylan reaches for the helmet, lifting it onto my head. The metal is cold, and so heavy that I can barely turn my head.

"That's amazing," he whispers.

"What?"

"I can't see you."

"Nor can I," Herman says. "Go, hide in the forest. I will call for you after the rest have settled."

Kibbey lets out a hiss, stopping us before we leave. I had almost forgotten he was in the room.

"Wait," Herman raises his hand again. "It's too late, they're already here. Stand behind me."

We watch in awe as eleven towering figures enter the room. I can't say they're human. They are barely human-like, ducking their heads to enter the room, their height reaching far above the door frame when standing fully erect even though they still seemed slightly hunched. They have faces, in a sense, their skin almost transparent. It seems as though their heads are mostly skull and bone, with a thin skin stretched tightly over it. They wear long robes and there's barely a substance to the cloth, a dark gossamer. It seems more like they're draped in a dusky fog. Their hands are as much the same as their faces, long finger bones jutting from underneath the thin skin. They seem ominous with their stature and appearance, as I peer at them from behind Dylan's shoulder

"Brothers, Sisters, I hope your journey was well," Herman greets them.

"Hermes," one of them speaks. "We have been searching for you."

"Yes, brother, much time has passed. It seems the world is very different from the last time I saw you all."

"Hades has been working against us."

"Tell me, why have you ventured down from your mountain today? We have dealt with the likes of Hades before. He is always planning some spoof to throw us off."

"We came to meet the child."

"The son of Hades? The Demigod? You've met plenty in the past."

"We know about the boy. We've been watching him. This is different, you know, you have read the book. We want to see *her*."

I shrink back, afraid that they may be able to see me.

"Who?" Herman jests, his lip twitching at the corner.

"The child of the earth, the forbidden Nymph child, where is she?"

"Do you plan to harm her?" Herman asks, leaning on his staff.

"We only want to make sure she is of good mind, that she is ready for the task at hand."

Herman nods his head and walking a few paces away from where we stand, he continues, "She has already defeated Hades, wrapped him in a root in the ground. She's clever. But, Zeus, master of thunder, she is pure of heart, her mind weakened by lies from Hades. She needs time to heal before she fulfills her destiny."

I grip Dylan's hand tight, my heart beating fast. I notice my parents and the other figurines on the coffee table watching.

"We just want to see her," the one who Herman called Zeus responds. "Hades has already stolen one of my daughters. I dare not let him take another, especially one whose destiny is so great, even if she is not of my blood."

Herman pauses, looking to each of the tall figures. "Very well then. Demi, come out!"

Dylan turns to me as I pull the helmet off my head. The Gods seem to take a breath in and murmur amongst themselves as I appear out of thin air before them.

"Demi, I would like to introduce you to the old Stones of Olympus, the Gods," Herman tells me as he points to each figure. "We have Zeus, Hera, Poseidon, Demeter, Hestia, Apollo, Artemis, Aphrodite, Hephaestus, and yours truly. The twelve Olympians."

"Holy crap," I mumble.

CHAPTER TWENTY-TWO

"You see." Herman turns to the Gods, his aged face wrinkled in smile. "Just as you asked, she stands before you."

They stare down at me, their figures so tall in the room.

Dylan reaches his burned arm across my stomach, pressing me to his side as though he might protect me from them.

"We will not harm you," Zeus says as he steps back with the others. "We do, however, understand your confusion, your mistrust of us, and we have a tale which should clear things in your mind."

One of the Gods reaches out with his spindly finger, pointing towards the book on the coffee table in front of us. The pages flip back and forth, without actually being touched; stopping at the page with our likeness, the page that I knew said we were meant for each other.

"Hades has played these games for centuries. He desires to control this planet and its inhabitants, to quench his never ending urge to add to the souls of his Underworld. It is unfortunate that he intervened at such an early time. You were to be left to grow and learn on your own, before an intervention was made to show you your true destiny."

"What is our true destiny?" I ask, speaking for the first time to these Gods.

"There has to be a balance between good and evil. When this balance falls out, devastating events occur. You were created to prevent this from taking place again."

"This has happened before?" Dylan asks, his hand fanning across my stomach, pressing me closer to his side.

The pages of the book flip, again, this time to the front of the book, to the old etchings of the solar system. We watch as the drawings of the planets are pulled off the page and float in front of us.

"This has happened many times," they continue. "Before we learned about you, the one who would learn to control the earth, there was just the Gods of Olympus and the God of the Underworld. We fought to keep the balance. There have been plenty of other Demigods and wars. But Hades has always been tricky; he's found ways to deceive us, ways to destroy the balance. He uses the helmet to hide amongst the mortals and the caduceus of Hermes to control mortals as he pleases. Hades has one desire and that is to fill his Underworld with souls. Do you know this planet?" they ask.

I see the red planet pulsing in front of us.

"Venus," Dylan and I respond.

"Earth's sister planet. A long time ago, before we seeded the earth with life, Venus was much like this place. It wasn't always so desolate and lacking life."

We watch as the planet changes; as it turns in orbit the opaqueness, the swirling clouds, they all disappear. What replaces it all is a green planet, dotted with small blue patches. "This is the Venus before you, before the humans rose from the primordial seas of the earth. This Venus grew green, it was lush with life, plants, animals, and creatures much like the humans here. They prayed to us and in return we helped them make great advances in science and medicine. It was almost perfect, except that the life forms of Venus were so pure of heart and soul that they never questioned themselves, they never questioned each other, they never questioned the Gods. And when Hades sent his demons to plunder, the humans of Venus never thought twice to think of them as bad. But we couldn't see the demons, nor could we see Hades, they had already stolen the artifacts that gave them the ability to hide from us and control their surroundings."

The planet starts to swirl before us, changing, and in the whirl we can see the images of what happened. Images of the past. Images of families flash by us, human-like figures reading, teaching, playing. The planet swirls faster, and we see great machines roaming about, spewing black smoke. They rip up the trees and plants. Sludge pours into the water as they build towering buildings and soon the skies fill with a dense, dark smog. The human-like creatures change also, their clothing turns to armor, some turn to tattered cloth. There are scenes of war. Battles with blood soaked fields and cities. The planet continues to change as it turns. We see explosions, bombs, the green turns into shriveled brown and red sand. The water dries. Soon, there is nothing left but a desolate, milky planet, inhospitable to life.

"You see what happens when the Underworld takes over, when the planet gives up?" the Gods ask. "This is why you are here. Keepers of order, groomers of the Earth, gifted with powers of the most important essentials of this planet, the water and the plant life. And that of entertainment, to remind the humans that there is more life to enjoy, should the Lord of the Underworld tempt them again."

The planets sink back into the book and the Gods fold their hands in unison.

"When it is time, you will make a change here. Your duty is to reign over the population of earth when they start to get out of control. This is the reason for your sensitivities to their pollution. It is so you will know when it's time. Listen to the earth, she will tell you. And soon, the godless humans may worship again."

I try to wrap my head around all the information just given to us. But to tell the truth, my head is spinning and nausea has crept into my stomach. All I was hoping was that we could defeat Baal, or Hades, or whoever he is, and go on with our lives. I wasn't planning on this. I wasn't ready for this, and truthfully I don't want it.

"But Baal said I was dangerous to you and that is why he wanted me."

Their hollow eyes seem to narrow in on me. "You are dangerous to us if you don't complete this task, without the prayers of the humans we would simply disappear into nothingness. Lack of prayer makes us weak."

"But Baal-"

"Baal's compliance can be easily bought with one thing: Souls. Give him his souls and he will leave you alone."

"But I-" I start, pausing when I feel Dylan squeeze my side.

"In time, you will see what we are speaking of. It could be a hundred years, it could be a thousand, but in time, the earth will beckon you and you will answer it."

"What do you mean, *I will answer it?*"

"You control the living things of the earth, with the plants, and Dylan with the water."

I remember what Baal told me, how he wanted me to help him rule the world. "But I don't want to hurt anyone."

"You were allowed to live for this reason, for this purpose. If you refuse you may return to the Underworld where others of your kind dwell."

Dylan squeezes my hand, hard. I look to him, seeing the torture in his eyes from whatever he saw there. I do not want to go to the Underworld.

"Okay," I tell them.

"We have waited for you. Both of you. And when it is time, when the earth calls you, you need to be ready."

I lean into Dylan, suddenly weak from the information overload. I look down, noticing my parents and the other tiny people have been watching and listening the entire time.

"What about my parents?" I ask.

"They are human," Hermes responds. "They have lived a human life, as with the rest of them. Hades enchanted them for his own reasons, we may never know those. But their time is done here."

"So what will happen to them?" I ask.

"I will escort them to the Underworld when I return Hades."

I look down at them, realizing that they will truly die this time and I will have to continue on without them. I feel hot tears well up behind my eyes at the thought of their deaths.

"Can't I see them one last time?" I ask.

"Very well," the Gods reply.

One of them reaches out, pointing to my parents and the others on the coffee table. They return to their natural state, all of them, the coffee table breaking underneath the weight of ten people.

My parents rush forward and I reach for them. They squeeze me so tight I can barely breathe. "Oh, Demi," Mother whispers. "We were so scared for you." Father brushes my hair back and kisses me firmly on the cheek.

"I'm just glad to see you both," I tell them, hugging them back in a cautious happiness.

I look around the room as the people hug each other and talk loudly in their excitement of being turned back to their natural form.

Included are the sheep and horse, which bay with excitement.

"Let's move outdoors," one of the Gods suggest.

We follow them without question. They stoop down, avoiding the top of the door frame, and stay stooped in their walk through the castle. The other people follow us, as well as the sheep and horse. We follow them through the forest, to the thick root which I trapped Baal in. It is still and no longer bulging under his attempts to get out.

"You will need this." One of the Gods hands Hermes a thick golden chain. "It will help you take him back. Hephaestus forged it in his own fires."

Another of the Gods nod their head and says, "It is stronger than any mortal metal."

"You need to make sure he can't get out during the travel," Zeus tells me.

I push the root into the ground and I grow a large tree above it, but unlike the trees I've grown all over the island, this one turns a blackened brown, the leaves refusing to bud.

"From the evil within," another God suggests.

"Hermes is strong and with the help of the others he will drag Hades back to the Underworld," Zeus tells me.

"What happens if he gets out again?" I ask.

"I sense, soon, his Underworld will have a swell in souls and this will quell his thirst for some time. And without the artifacts to hide him from our sight, he should remain where he belongs." He pauses, tipping his head to the side. "I think we are done here," Zeus tells Hermes. "We will be watching over you."

"I will be in touch." Hermes waves his staff. "Now that I have this back."

The tall figures seem to step into each other and a great bright light erupts from their center as they disappear before us.

"And so I remember many things," Hermes starts, he walks around us, searching the ground.

Now the sun is starting to come up, the sky begins turning a bright pink. Hermes reaches down, picking something up from the ground and brushes it off on his shirt. "There we are," he says. I see the ring in his hand, the one Baal placed on my finger with the promise of marriage. Hermes taps it to the stone atop the staff, a spark springs from the ring.

He makes his way to Dylan, and I catch a glimpse of the ring, which is now clear and just as transparent as a normal diamond should be. "Here, my boy," Hermes closes Dylan's hand around the ring. "I sense you may need this one day."

~ ~ ~

We return to the castle, Hermes invites everyone in. "Except the beasts!" he hollers just before we pass the door. The Vassal, who had rejoined us, gives a unified groan in disappointment. "No, no, not you," Hermes replies. "The horse and sheep." He points to the horse. "I remember you, trouble maker!" The horse gives a scoffing whinny in response.

Dylan pokes my arm. "I told you he bit me," he says, flatly.

We follow Hermes to the ballroom where Baal had his parties each weekend. Hermes speaks with the other people who were transformed from the wooden figurines. Most of them seem to speak in different languages.

"What do we do now?" I ask.

"We would like to go home," Father answers, wrapping his arm around Mother's shoulders.

"It's been years," I tell them. "Since you've been gone the Sheriff thought you were eaten by a bear."

They look to each other, slightly confused. "It didn't seem as though that much time passed," Mother explains.

"They cannot return home," Hermes enters our conversation. "As with the others, they must go elsewhere."

"What will happen to them?" I ask.

"Just as the Gods said, I will guide them to the Underworld, this is my duty."

"Oh!" Mother throws her arms around me, Father follows her. I feel the sting of tears behind my eyes and Mother's body shudder.

Father lets go of me, turning to Dylan, he pats him hard on the back. "You will take care of her?" he asks Dylan, trying to hold in a sad smile.

Dylan looks at me, the darkness leaving his eyes for the first time since he brought me back. "Yes," he tells my Father. "I will take care of her, with my life."

~ ~ ~

Dylan helps Hermes wrap the golden chain given by Zeus around the blackened tree trunk, the one which holds Hades. He secures the chain to the horse, the sheep, and the others each put their hands on the chain.

I turn to my parents who stand at my side. Mother smiles a sad smile.

"We love you." She leans forward, kissing me on the cheek. "You were such a wonderful child and now we know why."

I grip my arms tightly around her neck. "I'm so sorry for all the bad things I did," I whisper to her, remembering my planned escape and moments when my powers slipped out.

"You did nothing more than be yourself, a child who didn't know what she was. I'm just sorry we didn't know more about you, and what you were meant for."

"Demi," Hermes interrupts us. "It's time."

I feel Father's hand on the back of my head as he pulls me into his chest. "I love you, Demi," he tells me.

They let go of me and turn to walk towards the chain. They place their hands on it, ready to help drag Baal back where he belongs.

Dylan returns to my side and we watch as Hermes and the others pull the chain. The tree croaks and creaks with each heave. At first the tree doesn't seem to budge. They continue, the great chain digs into the black bark, breaking a few of the branches. I reach out, willing the roots of the island to expel the blackened tree from the soil, and just as Hermes and the others give another pull, the tree slides out of the dirt, landing hard on the ground with an earth trembling thud.

We follow them as they drag the tree through the forest towards the shoreline. And as we get closer, in the early morning light, I notice a row of Vassal standing at the edge of the rocky shore, watching.

The Seaway begins to boil. The water turns red, steam rises. Hermes holds out his hand and the water seems to part, revealing a hole and a stairway. The line heaves, pulling the tree with them as they each step down into the seaway, destined for the Underworld.

I get one last glimpse of my parents, waving my hand at them, a feeble last attempt at goodbye. I catch a smile from Mother, although tears are visible running down her face. It seems as though Father cannot bear to look back. He pulls along with the others, his back to me. Dylan and I watch as they descend, the tree bouncing off each step.

Hermes returns to the top of the stairs. "Stay on the island until I return," he yells to us. "The Vassal will guard the door."

Then, they all slip away. The seaway closes. The water returns to its natural state. Feeling a sudden gush of emotion, I can no longer hold back the hot tears or the awareness of what I am and what I am meant to do. My knees begin to buckle and I fall to the ground.

CHAPTER TWENTY-THREE

Opening my eyes, I notice the softness of a mattress under me and the heat from the body next to me. I sit up, looking around the room. I am still in the castle and from the bedroom window I can see that it is night, which can only mean I slept the entire day.

The body next to me stirs.

"She wakes," I hear Dylan's voice in the darkness.

"So it seems. And I was hoping it was all just a bad dream, a really, really bad dream." I feel myself shiver in the darkness.

I feel him sit up next to me. "Even the part about me?" he asks.

I look at his form in the darkness, apprehension tearing through me as I remember him threatening to leave when the Gods were coming. When he thought he was meant for nothing but evilness.

"I'm still slightly angered with you."

"I'm sorry," his voice lowers.

"Has Hermes returned?"

"Not yet." He moves closer to me on the bed.

Feeling another shiver run through me, I rub my hands over my arms and I notice my sweater is gone. I throw the covers back and run my hands down myself, only to find that I am no longer in the clothes I wore earlier but some laced nightgown.

"Where did this come from?" I ask.

"I found it in a bag, under what was left of your bed. Remember, the beast crushed it."

"Yes, but that doesn't explain how I got into this!" My fingers grip the satin fabric.

"Well," Dylan moves closer, "you were tired, so I helped."

"Dylan!"

"What?" His tone lightens with a bit of laughter.

I swat at him.

He holds his palms up. "Just, don't hurt me, *Oh forbidden child*."

"You took my clothes off and put me in this trash?"

"I thought it looked nice." He shrugs his shoulder at me.

I pull the covers over myself, hiding the flimsy gown and my mostly naked flesh.

"*Demigods*." I shake my head. "You're so… so…"

I lean back on the pillows and cross my arms. Dylan follows, his face in front of mine, his hand pulls me towards him into a soft kiss.

"Can you ever forgive me?" he asks on my lips.

I try to think of a way, but it's hard to concentrate with the heat from his lips and his fingertips grazing down my neck.

"I will forgive you if you do one thing."

"What?"

"Sing to me."

"Now?" He pulls back.

"Yes."

"What do you want me to sing?"

"That song from the ballroom when I danced. Before we found out what we truly are."

"Hallelujah?"

"Yes, just… just don't sing it so sad. Okay?"

He sits up and crosses his legs. As the blankets fall off of him I notice he's just wearing a pair of thin sleeping shorts, his chest bare. I see the burns have healed, replaced with smooth skin covering taut muscle, just like I remember him. I train my eyes on his face, thanking the darkness so he won't see my reddened cheeks.

Dylan sings, the melody of his voice permeating my chest, straight into my heart. Just as he finishes the moonlight brightens the room and I hear the bedroom door groan as though something has leaned up against it.

"What was that?" I ask.

"The beast. It sleeps outside the door."

"Has it been fed?"

"Yes."

"Are we in danger?"

"You're safe, from the beast..." his voice trails off as he turns towards the door.

"What are you saying?"

"I said you're safe from the beast. But not from me. Not while you're wearing that."

I look down to see the sheet has fallen, revealing much more of my skin than I'd like. I reach for the sheet to cover myself but Dylan's hand grasps my wrist, stopping me.

"I chose that gown because I like it," he whispers in my ear, rekindling those feelings I had for him the last time we were lying in a bed together. "I think you should have put it on for me a long time ago."

This time no one interrupts us, not even the beast.

~ ~ ~

"Do you think we could get them back?" I ask Dylan.

"Who?"

"My parents. Do you think Baal would ever release them from the Underworld?" I ask as I lay with my head on him, feeling the muscles of his stomach contract under my head.

"I don't see how anyone could get out of there..." His voice seems to drift off.

I reach for his hand that's stroking my hair, and pull it towards my face, searching for the burns that once scorched his skin. All that remains are light pink spots. "Your burns are gone."

"Yeah." He pulls his arm away and leans down, kissing my temple. "I think we should get up."

"Okay," I agree with him. I look down at myself. "Um, did you get me any clothes while you were picking out racy nightgowns?"

"What do you think I am, an animal or something?" he grins at me. He points to a bag on the floor. "Of course I brought your clothes."

I wrap the sheet tightly around myself and crawl out of bed to retrieve the bag and pour it out. Thankfully Dylan brought some jeans and sweaters. It looks like he slipped a dress in there too. I search the pile of clothes for underwear, only to find the thin lace pieces Baal had delivered to my room.

I let out a breath of exasperation.

"What?" Dylan asks, pulling a shirt over his head.

"I wish you would have brought some *real* underwear."

"Those looked pretty real to me."

I choose an outfit, a pair of jeans and a shirt with a sweater over it. Just as I slip my boots on, I hear Dylan unlocking the door to the bedroom.

He turns to me. "Ready?"

"I think so," I tell him.

We walk in silence through the halls of the empty castle. Though neither of us discussed where we were going, we end in the library. Hermes is there, sitting in a chair, legs crossed, sipping from a mug. I notice he looks slightly younger than he did yesterday.

"Ah! You're up!" He greets us. "I trust you slept well." He winks at Dylan.

I sit on a nearby couch. "What do we do now, Hermes?" I ask.

"What do you mean?"

"I mean, now, until our destiny comes calling, what do we do?"

"Whatever you choose," he responds with a smile.

I turn to Dylan.

"Where do you want to go?" he asks me.

"I want to go back to Saratoga."

"Will you dance again?" he asks.

"I don't know. I left without telling them. I'm not sure they'll want me back. And it seems if I do go back it won't be for long. People will start asking questions about us."

"You have all of eternity to decide," Hermes tells us.

~ ~ ~

We returned to Saratoga, Zeus's warning fresh in our minds, both of us well aware that it may be only for a short time. For so long I missed the only real home I knew and what we had there. There was no other place I could think of wanting to go.

It takes me almost a week to work up the courage to visit to the dance center to ask about my job.

"I am surprised to see you here," Mr. Pavlova tells me as I walk into his office.

I open my mouth to say something to him but I can't seem to find any words. I find myself wishing I had thought of a good excuse before I came here. Something other than the excuse of being trapped in a castle by the Lord of the Underworld, because I doubt Mr. Pavlova will believe that story if I told it to him.

"You left without warning." Mr. Pavlova begins cracking his knuckles on his left hand. "You gave no notice or phone calls. Do you know how hard it is to fill your spot on such short notice?" He moves on to cracking the knuckles in his right hand. It's an intimidating gesture, makes me wish I never came here to speak to him. "I'm guessing you're here to beg for your job back?" His thin dark brow rises, waiting for me to finally speak. "Hmm." He smirks. "You're all the same, beg for a job, work your little tails off until some man comes around to take care of you, and then when it doesn't work out you come begging for your job back. I must admit, Demi, I would have expected this from one of the other girls but not you. You were… different." Mr. Pavlova stops in front of me.

Yes, I was very different and now I am even more different. I realize that coming back here and working again, it would just put mine and Dylan's safety at risk-someone could find out.

I look up at him, the tall limber man who helped me polish my dancing here, and think of what to say. "I'm sorry," I finally get the words out. "I shouldn't have come here."

I turn around and reach for the door handle, my heart sinking at the acknowledgement that I can never have my old life back, no matter how mundane it was. The Gods have already informed me of my purpose here and now thinking about it, I'm not sure how I could handle knowing that I will be responsible for harming the people closest to me.

"Demi?" Mr. Pavlova starts, but I don't wait to hear what he has to say. I run down the hallway and out of the building. When I reach the main entrance, someone is holding the door open. I don't even stop to thank them.

"Demi?" I hear a familiar voice ask.

I turn to find Swayzee standing on the sidewalk, still tall and lean, still with her long, raven-red hair, still with her wide perfect smile. She opens her arms pulling me into a tight hug. "Where have you been?" Swayzee asks, surprised to see me.

"I've been away," I respond, taking the sight of her in.

"What, did you go on one of those trips where you find yourself?"

she asks with her sarcastic tone.

I smile, looking towards Dylan's truck in the parking lot. "Something like that."

"Did you ask for your job back?"

"Yes."

"What did they say?"

"Nothing. Pavlova spent most of the time telling me how disappointed he was. And then I left. It was a mistake coming back here. I should've known better."

"I'm sorry," she tells me, adjusting the bag on her shoulder.

"Me too."

"Demi?" Swayzee asks.

"Yeah."

"Whatever happened, you...you seem… *happy*."

"Thanks," I say. But what I really wanted to tell her was to stay away from me because she is one of the Godless humans and I already know their future is limited.

"Are you going to stick around? We should get together."

"I'm not sure." I tell her, eyeing the sky as it starts to turn a dusky blue.

"Can I tell you something?" she asks, leaning towards me and smiling.

I focus on the dark hair that curls at her shoulders, remembering that there was a time when I wanted to be just like her. "Sure," I respond.

She holds her left hand up in front of my face and it takes me a moment to focus on the ring. "Jed proposed!" she tells me with a slight squeal.

"Oh my." I pull her hand with the glistening diamond ring towards me so I can inspect it. The rock is tiny, no more than a pebble when I compare it to the ring Baal put on my finger. Jesus, I want to tell her everything that happened. Instead, I settle for best wishes. "Congratulations!" I hug her, probably for just a moment too long. I know I will probably never see her again.

"It's so amazing, right?" She asks me excitedly. "Are you going to stay in town? I'd love to have you in the wedding."

"I…" I look back to Dylan again in the truck. "No, I'm sorry, Swayzee, but we aren't staying."

She pouts her lip in one of her dramatic gestures. "Looking for work elsewhere?"

"Yeah." I shrug. It's a total lie. I'll never work again.

"Well," Swayzee reaches for the door, "I have to get in there before Pavlova comes looking for me. You know how he hates it when we're late." She winks, reminding me of the time when I showed up late.

"Yeah."

She reaches out and pulls me in for a hug. "Okay, it was good to see you." She rubs her hand over my back. I savor it, knowing it will be the last time. Things can never go back to the way they were before I learned what I am.

I walk to Dylan's truck. "What do you want to do?" he asks as I get in the passenger side.

I look around the parking lot, feeling completely lost. "Let's go to the pier."

He gives me a devilish grin and his eyes sparkle with mischief as he puts the truck into gear and drives down the road.

This time I don't need to run down the dirt path that leads between the trees to the pier. I'm able to control it and keep the plants at bay. When we reach the end of the path and the pier stretches before us, I gasp in remembrance, it looks exactly the same as we left it and all the memories come flooding back.

As we walk I can sense Dylan getting antsy, the lake water calling to him. "Just go," I tell him, rolling my eyes.

"Are you sure?"

"Yes."

The weathered wood creaks under Dylan's feet as he runs, stripping off his shirt and shorts and dropping them onto the old wooden pier. He looks back at me, his lip curling in a smile just before he dives into the clear water, barely disturbing the surface.

I sit at the edge of the pier, dangling my toes in the water, waiting for Dylan to return. When he does, his head emerges by my feet.

"Want to see something?" he asks, grabbing onto my ankles.

"I'm not sure that's a good idea," I tell him hesitantly. "Last time you asked me that I had to risk my life to pull you from the lake bottom."

"Just trust me." He smiles.

"Fine."

I shriek and close my eyes as he pulls my ankles, pulling me into the water with him.

"Dylan!" I shout, "I can't swim in the water."

"Look around you, there's no water."

I open my eyes and see it's true. The water surrounds us yet it doesn't touch us. My clothes and hair remain dry, as well as Dylan's.

"See." He pumps a triumphant fist in the air. "I am the master!"

"Nice trick, water boy."

"Come on," he takes my hand, "I have something to show you."

He swims, strangely since there is no water touching us, but he swims just the same, pulling me along with him to the center of the lake and then down under the water. Fish swim by, followed by painted turtles and frogs. He dives deeper, the water becoming darker and it gets harder to see where we are going, until finally, he stops.

"Just wait a few minutes," he tells me. "Once the moon is out, you'll see."

I can feel the lake bottom under my feet and the pressure of all the water above our heads. Dylan stands in front of me dry as a bone. I can see the outline of his handsome face, his now shaggy hair covering his forehead. I reach out and brush the hair away.

"What did the dance center say?" he asks.

Pulling my hand back I remember that I never told him. "They said no."

"Are you okay with that?" he asks, taking a step towards me.

"I don't know. I thought coming back here would make it better, I thought this was the answer after all we went through..."

I feel the grip of Dylan's hands on my shoulders. "We have each other, Demi," he tells me, his voice low. "If that's not enough, I'll do anything, everything, for you to be happy-"

"No," I cut him off. "I'm fine, really." I force a smile and remember what he looked like when he dragged my body out of the seaway, the burns on his skin, the smell of smolder and brimstone all around him. "It's fine."

The water around us gets darker and darker, until I can no longer see Dylan's outline in front of me. But then, just like he said, the moon starts to shine, its pale light illuminating the bottom of the lake.

"Do you see it?" he asks.

I look around, my eyes focusing on everything around me. We float in the middle of a town. An old town with just a few buildings made out of water-aged wood, the fish swim in and out of the broken windows and I can just see the outline of a street and sidewalks, complete with benches and old trees which are now nothing but secured driftwood.

It's calm and eerie.

"What do you think?" he asks.

"This is creepy, Dylan."

I look around me and as I turn back to him a powerful shudder runs down my spine. He watches me, paling as a look of concern spreads across his face.

"Can you take me back to the top?" I ask, suddenly finding it hard to breathe.

He nods and pushing off the lake floor he launches us to the surface before I can blink and erase the image of the creepy underwater town from my memory. We continue rising, above the lake, and I watch as he turns the surface hard just like he's done before, smooth as glass, setting us down on top of it. We walk towards the pier.

"I'm sorry," Dylan starts. "I didn't think it would upset you."

"No, it's just…" I turn to him. "It just reminds me of what Zeus said we will have to do. I just don't want to hurt anyone. I can't see myself as they see me. I don't feel like some forbidden creature allowed to live for the sole purpose of controlling mankind."

"I don't think we have to worry about that anytime soon. They said it could be a hundred years or a thousand."

"I know."

"Come on, what do you want to do tonight?" He runs his hand down my arm and the gentle tingle from his fingertips pulls me from my thoughts. I try to think, remembering that most of our time was spent at the lake, because I could never control my powers. A smile starts to spread across my lips.

"What?" he asks.

"You're it," I tell him, swatting his arm before taking off and running down the pier towards the forest.

I hear a deep laugh erupt from Dylan, one that I haven't heard in so long. I smile, running faster

He must have given me a head start because I don't hear him running behind me until I reach the forest. Trees and brush sprout up behind me, erasing my path. I giggle, hearing him utter a few curse words. I keep running, across the road and into the forest on the other side. Soon I arrive at a cornfield, with neat rows of tall corn standing stiff as soldiers. I run between the stalks, letting my hands brush up against them until I'm in the middle of the field. I wait for a moment, out of breath, to hear Dylan catch up. Spotting him on the edge of the field, I wave, begging him to catch me. He starts for me and I see the moisture of the night air collect around him, dripping on the corn stalks as he passes, watering their thirsty roots. Just as he's about to reach me I pull the stalks across the rows, weaving them into a mat, trapping him.

Dylan laughs loudly and seeing him like this, after seeing him tormented by Baal for so long, it warms me deep inside.

Maybe, I think to myself, *maybe I could do this.* Forget what they want us to do and enjoy life, the life I wanted back.

CHAPTER TWENTY-FOUR

Time passed and with it grew some strange need inside of me. One that I couldn't describe or quench with my time spent with Dylan.

I left him sleeping in bed, my pillow pressed against his side where I usually sleep as I crawled out of bed and snuck out of the house.

The bad part was I planned this and remembering the guilt I felt when I snuck out of my parents house that one sunny afternoon as a child, I knew this was going to be worse. Dylan may never forgive me for what I was about to do.

I run to the edge of the forest. A place we've passed plenty of times. I knew it was the perfect spot because I could see the roots of the pine trees as they pushed above the soil. I hid under a wild blackberry bush, knowing its density and thorns would keep any animals away. Laying down, I pulled the grasses and roots over me, wrapping them just as tightly as I did on Dark Island. And then, I did the only thing Dylan asked me never to do, ever again: I left my body.

Since we have lived these past years in seclusion, avoiding questioning glances towards our inability to age, I have no knowledge of what the world has become.

We traveled sometimes, always keeping to the back roads, finding someplace warm for the first few winters, and then the cold winters ceased completely, it's actually been years since we've left this area. I had to see what the world had become, if the godless humans were really destined for such a poor future as described by the Gods.

For some reason Saratoga had hardly changed, the people were all still here, people I recognized from the store and the dance center. And when I found Swayzee, I could see that she had barely aged also.

Something is wrong here. Dissatisfied with my observations I pushed on, moving away from Saratoga and towards the cities and towns that were further away. This was when I found that things were very different. It seems Saratoga had become enchanted, much like Dark Island, and I wondered if perhaps the rest of the world remained the same, and there was no need for the destiny which loomed over us.

The cities were larger, the pollution worse, and the humans… the humans were changed and I had no words for what they had become. I just know it made me feel sick, even without my body I could feel the fear and the shock deep within my soul. The Gods were right. It was happening.

~ ~ ~

"Where were you?" Dylan asks as I open the door to the cabin.

"I just needed some air," I tell him, looking around the living room, avoiding his eyes.

"Is that how your clothes got all dirty?"

I look down at myself, noticing the few twigs hanging off my shirt and the dirt marks on the hip of my pants.

"I guess," I tell him.

"Is there something you want to tell me?" he asks, rising from his chair.

"No," I turn around, headed for the kitchen, avoiding his glaring eyes.

"Demi?" he asks, his voice strangely thick.

I give in and turn back to him. He's wearing that blue shirt I like, the one that makes his blue eyes stand out. It doesn't help what I am about to say.

"I just feel so… so trapped."

"So you did the only thing I have ever asked you not to do? I found you, or what was left of you, that thing that's left behind, your soulless remains. Do you know what it's like to come across that in the woods?" He starts walking towards me. "I asked you never to do that again. You don't understand what I went through to get you back!"

"I'm sorry. I just… I just wanted to see them again."

"Who?"

"Swayzee, the others at the dance center, and… and *people*."

"Demi, this is what we are." He holds his hand over his chest, right where his heart is. "You wanted to know for so long and now we do. What is all of this? Are you not happy with me?"

"No, it's nothing like that."

"Then what is it?"

"I just don't know." I look away from him. I can already see the pain on his face.

"We can go anywhere, we can be anyone. If you want more friends, we can go out and meet people."

"It won't be the same." I shake my head at him.

"Why?"

"Because, I know that I will be responsible for their deaths!" I shout at him. He looks at me with what can only be described as severe disapproval. "Stop."

"Stop what?"

"Looking at me like that." I take a few steps back.

"Why? It's obvious I'm not enough, that I am not good enough for you. Or else you wouldn't be out searching the town with your soul in a sapling."

"You just don't understand."

"What?" he asks sharply, taking a step towards me. "What don't I understand?"

"You don't understand what looms over my head every second of the day. What the Gods told me is my destiny."

"I don't?" He scowls. "Because it's my destiny too, or have you forgotten what they told *both* of us?"

"Just stop."

"I won't stop, Demi. You don't know what I saw down there. I keep telling you that it wasn't good. Do you want your fate to change? Do you want Zeus to come back here and deliver you to Hades, to my father, is that who you'd rather spend the rest of eternity with? Because from what you're doing, it doesn't seem like you want *me* any longer."

"That's not true." I lean towards him, fighting the urge to pull him towards me.

"It seems to be the truth to me," he responds, his voice a low growl. And with a few quick strides he is out of the room and slamming the door behind him.

I throw myself onto the plaid couch and picking up one of the throw pillows, I scream into it as loud as I can. I can't explain why I feel this way, why I've started treating Dylan so poorly. After all, he risked his life for me. And I know I love him, more than anyone, more than anything.

I stare out the window at the waterfall which seems to plummet off the porch into the lake. The day went and the night came, and all the time I sat and stared. I didn't think, because the thought of hurting Dylan had already made me numb.

Lights brush across the front of the cabin and I hear the crunch of Dylan's truck tires on the gravel driveway. I wait for him to open the door so I can stand up and apologize to him for not seeing that he shares this burden. Except… he never opens the door, not even after the headlights from his truck turn off.

I stand and walk towards the door. Turning the handle and pulling the door open, just a crack, I hear Dylan's voice and that of someone else I recognize.

"Oh no," I whisper to myself.

They must hear me because they each turn in my direction. I leave the house, walking towards Dylan. A dark fear grips me as I take in who stand in front of him.

The Gods have returned.

CHAPTER TWENTY-FIVE

"I told you that we would be watching you," Zeus tells me as I approach them.

"I know," I respond.

Dylan gives me a hesitant look. I notice Hermes is here also, changed from his normal butler attire, now wearing a loose cotton suit.

"It seems you are faint of heart." Zeus continues. "That feeling of unease, it means that the time is close."

"It just doesn't feel right," I tell him. "It doesn't feel like this is something I can do."

"You can't or you won't?" Zeus asks.

"I'm not sure." And I'm not. I know my heart feels heavy with the guilt of knowing what I have to do, it's eating me away inside.

"You are aware of the alternative," Zeus tells me. I watch the wind blow through his fog-like robes as he speaks. "Perhaps a small viewing of what Dylan went through to save you, perhaps this will help you make your decision?"

"No." Dylan shakes his head at us. "Don't do it."

Even in the moonlight I can see the redness of his eyes, the agony on his face. And I realize I've been so selfish only thinking of myself and not what he went through.

Zeus reaches his bony fingers towards my hand.

"No!" Dylan shouts, reaching for us, but Hermes holds him back and we are gone in a flash of lightning.

~ ~ ~

We stand on a rocky shoreline. A damp breeze caresses my face. Zeus grips my hand. When I look around I notice we are back on Dark Island.

"What are we doing here?" I ask.

In an instant day turns into night. I hear the clock from the castle ticking, and then the chime I recognize, as it strikes two am.

"The beast will be coming," I warn Zeus.

As soon as the words are out of my mouth, I feel its thundering footsteps shaking the ground beneath my feet. The trees waver, birds flutter from their roosts into the night sky. The panic hits me, the way I felt when it ran at me in the library. I feel myself tightening my grasp on Zeus's bony appendages, preparing myself for impact. I know it's nothing but the Vassal, but I have no fish to calm them. I only have a God at my side.

The beast clears the woods, growling and spitting and barking. It shakes its head, and just like before it seems to have three heads instead of one. Zeus holds out his free hand, the one that I'm not holding in a death grip. In his hand he holds a giant bone, dripping with flesh and blood. He waves it at the beast.

"It eats fish," I warn Zeus.

"Not if you want it to let you out. If you want the beast to let you out of the Underworld, then it eats meat."

Zeus flicks his wrist, throwing the bone and flesh to the middle of the island. The beast gives us one last horrific yap before running into the darkness to find the bloody carrion.

I hear the bubbling of water behind me and when I turn I see that the water has begun to boil and steam, turning a dark red. Zeus tugs at my hand, starting for the steps but I stop, digging my heels into the rocky island. Zeus takes another step forward and the Seaway opens up, revealing a dark stairway.

"I can't go in the water," I warn him, knowing what happens, what always happens: I get weak, too weak to do anything but sleep.

"We aren't going into the water, we are going under it."

He pulls my hand and I follow him.

The stairway seems to descend forever and while Zeus seems to float over each step, I fear that I may trip and fall into the walls which are nothing but pulsating water, threatening my existence.

The walls start to change, the water stops pulsating, the air becomes warm and thick. Soon, the walls turn into pebble gravel, then a smooth rock. Then the walls disappear altogether and we descend into a giant cavern. Except, it isn't a cavern, in a cavern I might be able to see walls, or rocky cliffs, or even stalactites. Instead, all I can feel the open space disguised by a heavy smog.

The stairs come to an end, in all their ricketyness, and Zeus leads me forward. We follow a short rocky path before stopping. Now I can hear the sound of water slapping up against something, just like when I would lie on the pier and Dylan would be swimming. Same sound, very different surroundings.

Slowly, as though it's doing its best to cut through the fog, I hear a horn, low and dense, nearing where we stand. The fog swirls as something nears us. The object creaks and groans and makes a hollow sound when it pushes against the rock we are standing on.

The fog clears and I see before us there is a wooden boat, large enough to hold hundreds of people. The fog swirls and before us appears a strange creature holding an oar. Its face is wrinkled and worn, its ears are pointed and there is a strip of dark hair down the top of its head. Its clothes are tattered and covered in black splatter marks. It holds its hand out to me, and I see the skin of its hand is very much the same as its face. A wrinkled shoe leather, with tufts of long black hair, and sharp pointed nails.

"Give him the coins," Zeus tells me.

I look up at his skeletal figure. "I don't have any coins," I tell him.

"Open your hand."

I raise my arm and I open my hand, which has been curled into a fist, there are two golden coins in my palm.

"Give them to Charon. It is our fare."

I place the golden coins in Charon's wrinkled hand. Making sure my skin doesn't touch his, afraid that it might hurt or I might catch his ugliness. Charon takes my coins and Zeus gives him nothing but a nod of his skeletal skull as we walk onto the boat.

Zeus leads me to the far edge of the boat and I feel something hollow crunching under my feet. When he stops I look down and see strips of cloth and a spattering of bones layering the floor of the boat. I hear a deep moaning sound from behind us. I turn, seeing that there is a line of people-no not people, souls-handing their coins to Charon and walking onto the boat. Some look very dead, their skin pale, their eyes sunken, their lips cracked. Others seem as though they may actually be still alive. The rest, they look horrific. Their bodies consisting of shredded flesh, blood drips down their pale bones and whatever is left of their clothing hangs in shreds over what is left of their bodies.

I back up, my back pressing up against the ghostly figure of Zeus.

"What happened to them?" I ask.

"Some were not given a coin to pass the river. This is what happens when the humans forget about the Gods. They don't prepare their loved ones for the Underworld."

"Why are they all torn apart?"

"They tried to leave, to find their fare for the ferry ride, and the beast shredded them as they tried to exit."

Somehow, they must have found a coin, because the tattered and shredded souls each press a golden coin into the hand of the farer and enter the boat. I think of my parents, whom I did not give a coin to as they left me standing on the island, as they helped Hermes drag Baal down here. Maybe the golden chain was enough for them to pass and they were not one of those souls which were shredded by the beast as they tried to escape and search for their own coins to pass on into the underworld.

When the line has ended and the boat seems half-full, Charon lumbers to the front of the boat with his oar in his hand. He dips it into the murky water, guiding the boat away from the shoreline.

I see nothing but fog, hear nothing but the waters of the river slap against the side of the boat. Turning, I find the souls staring intently at me and the figure I am standing next to.

We are out of place here.

Charon rows and it seems to take forever. My knees begin to feel weak under my body. Zeus' grip remains tight on my hand. I want to sit and rest but I'm afraid that the hungry hollow eyes which bore into my back might be waiting for a sign of weakness and devour me.

Finally the boat stops, the fog clears, and it seems we have reached land. Zeus leads me off the boat and to the side. We watch as the souls exit the boat. Some seem to float off and disappear, others form lines, each headed in a different direction.

All I can feel around me is heat. Heat and angst and there's pain in my ears as screams tear through the air. If it even can be considered air, because it's hot and heavy and when it blows across my face I feel as though it's taking layers of my pale skin with it.

I feel the heavy grip of a hand on my shoulder and when I turn I am startled to see Zeus's figure has transformed into that of a man, a tall man wearing nothing but a wisp of cloth across his groin. My eyes search his body, noting the thick layers of muscle, the fair spattering of hair on his body, and golden skin. When I reach his face I notice the thick beard and curly blonde hair. And when my eyes finally reach his golden irises, the corners of his eyes are crinkled in amusement.

"And now you see why we chose our other form to visit you." I step away in shock. "Let's go, Demi, before I succumb to my temptations and we both regret this adventure."

I feel my cheeks flush with embarrassment, and at his insinuation, because it can only mean one thing. I've seen it with Baal, these Gods take pleasure whenever they desire it, no matter whom it may harm.

"Welcome to the Underworld." Zeus stretches his arms out before us.

The heated wind blows again, bringing the stench of burning skin and bone and screams to my face and ears, only louder this time. My hands fly to my ears. I look around us seeing nothing but scorched earth, flowing rivers of flame, and a rocky mountain in front of us.

"Here." Zeus holds his hand out and I notice he has the helmet Hermes made me wear, the one that makes me invisible. "You will need this soon. Follow me."

Zeus starts walking. He follows some meandering path which seems to avoid the rivers and the fire. But I am still accosted by the horrid wind and the screams.

"Where are we?" I ask.

"The fringes." He stops, pointing to the left. "That is where the souls enter." I follow his hand to see a long stretch of flaming river. Floating in the flames is a large boat filled with what can only be more souls. The flames lap at the side of the boat, threatening to catch it on fire. It licks and laves until one flame gets high enough to wrap around a soul that's waiting on the edge, pulling it down into the flaming depths of the fire-river. I watch, horrified, as the soul burns, just as a hot ember would, before disappearing under the flames.

"And there," he points to his right. I find another river, this one seems to scream louder, and inky arms reach out of the water, grasping at the souls standing on a thin platform. The arms grab at their feet, at their arms, pulling them into the water, which can only be described as a screeching swath of flowing bodies.

"And there." He points behind us. The waters of this river make no noise at all. There are no flames or fogs, just bodies, bodies floating and awash as though they have forgotten what they are or why they are here.

"And there." He points in front of us. I find yet another river; it seems we are encircled by them. This river is just as dire as the others. The fog floats within the water, not above it, and moans and cries rise from its strange waters. There is no boat, only a platform where the souls stand, their faces twisted in pain and sorrow. Some stand still, some cry, and others scream as they drop themselves into the river.

"Come," Zeus beckons me.

I follow him, trying my best to keep up. But Zeus is so tall and my legs are so short. I have to jog a little to keep up with him, afraid of being left behind. The mountain looms before us, getting larger with each step we take. I start to sweat like I've never sweat before. Staring at the golden-skinned back of Zeus I begin to wish I had only a small piece of cloth to cover myself, that it may help me survive this unrelenting heat.

"Put the helmet on," Zeus tells me as we near the mountain.

I do as I'm told.

"Don't wander, child, for I cannot see you with that on," he warns me.

I would like to reach out and hold onto him, but there is nothing for my hands to grasp, there is only glistening skin and a tiny piece of cloth. It is the body of a God before me, one that I dare not touch, not with his comment of succumbing to temptations. The image of Dylan's pained expression is fresh in my mind, reminding me that I'd rather get lost down here than risk hurting him that way. No, I will not touch Zeus. I slow and let him get two steps ahead of me. He glances to the side, his lip curled in amusement. For a second I wonder if he can hear my thoughts? His smile widens.

Zeus brings us to a heavy metal door, secured in the side of the mountain. He pushes it open and walks inside. The cavernous hallway is dark and even hotter than the air outside. I follow Zeus until the hallway opens further at its end where there is an even larger cavern.

I wish he had warned me, as we walked into this cavern, I wish he had told me to cover my eyes or shield my view because there are horrid and ghastly things going on.

There are souls here, and they cry in agony, even louder than outside the mountain. For the first time Zeus slows, taking in the scene before us, the blood coating the floor, the torturous tools and machines, the stench of burning skin, and even more things that I can't even put into words. He meanders, I'm sure on purpose so I can get a good look of my future should I not fulfill my destiny.

When I think I can't take it any longer, we reach another metal door. He opens it and as we pass through, it seems we leave those horrible images behind, only to come upon a shocking scene.

Baal, or Hades, or whoever he is, pleasuring himself on a large bed with a group of small women. It's indecent, all the moaning and gasping.

"I see you have stolen some Nymphs!" Zeus announces to the room.

The tiny women shriek as they hurry to cover themselves with bits of cloth and rush out of the room leaving trails of soft petals falling from the flowers woven into their hair.

"What do you want, brother?" Hades asks Zeus as he sits up, obviously annoyed.

Hades stands, wrapping a sheet across his naked waist. He doesn't resemble the horrible creature I wrapped in the roots. He is no longer horned, or scaled, he has returned to the alluring man whom I almost wed in my ignorance.

"Oh, I just came to check up on you and make sure things are well here. Is the Underworld ready for an influx? Have you hired more cronies to care for all the extra souls you are about to receive?"

Hades throws his head back laughing. Then he stops abruptly and turns his head to the side. He takes a deep breath in through his nose and his dark eyes flick open, his flame irises return.

"You brought her?" He asks, his tone lightening. "Has she changed her mind?"

"She needs a little *encouragement*."

Since it's obvious they are speaking about me I lift the helmet from my head.

Zeus scowls as I appear.

"You are not looking so well." Hades laughs at me. "Are you

enjoying my son? Has he shown you what he's made of yet? Or are you still too busy fearing your destiny? It's not so easy, is it, being responsible for all those other souls, for their deaths?" Hades laughs, even harder this time. He turns back to Zeus. "Who did you leave my little water boy with? Aphrodite or Athena?" His amused eyes flick back to me for an instant. "Are they stroking his pained soul right now as he pines for his missing girlfriend? Did she see them in all their luscious beauty?" I notice Zeus's lips pressed into a thin line. "And still," Hades continues, "she ventures here without him? Does she not fear what those Gods will do to her lover, what they do to all the handsome Demigods and simple men for that matter?"

Listening to his insinuations brew a jealous rage that burns deep inside me. I want to leave. I want to be gone from this place and these Gods with their horrible games. I want to live in peace with Dylan and I hate myself for not seeing it before, for subjecting both of us to this.

"I will deliver your souls," I tell Hades, "as soon as the earth asks me to and not a moment before. And then I will be done with you, with all of you." I swipe at them both with my arm.

"You see, oh Brother Zeus." Hades points his finger at me. "I told you she was dangerous. Just think of all the damage she could do when she figures out how to truly harness her powers. I told you to give her to me. She belongs down here with the rest of her kind."

I think of the Nymph women we just witnessed him with and a shudder runs down my back thinking that I could replace one of them.

"I want nothing to do with you," I tell him. "Either of you."

Hades laughs again. "Until the next time, until the Godless humans return and we have to play this game all over again. They always do, they always turn into Godless humans again no matter how God fearing they start out. It happens every single time. Doesn't it brother?"

He turns to Zeus who simply shrugs his bare muscled shoulders.

"Can you do one last thing for me, earth child, could you dance for me just one last time?" Hades asks me in his most seductive voice.

I clench my hands into fists and narrow my eyes at him. "No!"

Hades throws his head back laughing wildly.

"Now, what is the real reason you are here?" Hades asks.

"She needs to see," Zeus tells him.

Hades seems to raise his eyebrows in humor. "See what? She needs to see what her lover went through to save her? Are his words not enough? Does she not believe him?"

"She needs to *understand* how dire their fate will become should they not fulfill their destinies," Zeus tells him.

"Very well," Hades replies.

He walks towards me, staring intently at my face. Remembering the hell he put us through on that island I try to look away from him but my eyes lower to his shirtless torso and the sheet which seems to dip lower on his hips with each step, threatening to fall off.

I step back as he nears me, turning to look at Zeus. He nods his head and I take that as a promise that Hades won't hurt me. Zeus watches as Hades takes my hand. I straighten my back and try to fake courage.

"Are you sure you don't want to reconsider my offer?" Hades asks as he raises my hand in his, smoothing his fingers over my palm. "Aren't you even the least bit tempted to become a goddess of the Underworld? We could do wonderful things, you and I."

"Stop," Zeus tells him sternly.

"Fine, just a parting kiss then."

I lean back, afraid that he may try and kiss me on the lips. But instead he raises my hand to his lips and turning it in his hand he presses his hot lips to the soft skin of my inner wrist.

∞ ∞ ∞

"Nooo!" I hear what can only be the anguished cries of Dylan.

I look around, no longer seeing the cavernous walls of the mountain of the Underworld, images flash before my eyes.

"Dylan!" I shout, looking around me.

I find only his image playing before me as though I am stuck in a movie.

He is on Dark Island, chasing after Baal who carries my soulless body over his shoulder. Now I see what I didn't see before, when I stood as a sapling waiting on the shoreline.

The seaway parts, the stairway appears, and Hades seems to float down the stairway to the Underworld just as Zeus, but Dylan jumped head first, he dove in after us, flying through the air, down into the depths of the Underworld.

When he came to the bottom he was able to right himself and land on his feet. I watch as Hades steps onto the boat of Charon. Dylan tries but having no golden coin Charon won't let him board. Dylan tries to push and shove the creature but Charon fights back. He grunts and pulling back his deeply wrinkled fist he punches Dylan hard in the middle of the chest. Dylan flies backwards, landing on the hard ground, hitting his head. I see blood seep out onto the stone under his skull.

No! I whisper to myself.

I am fully aware that he cannot see or hear me. This is just a memory, a memory of the Gods and of the Underworld. A memory to be written in the books, reminisced and discussed at dinners and parties, about how the Demigod Dylan followed Hades into the burning pits of the Underworld to retrieve the soulless body of his true love.

Dylan stirs, he wakes, sitting up just in time to see the ferry boat leave the shore in a curl of Underworld fog. He stands, running to the shore, pacing, shouting to Hades. "Bring her back! Bring her back to me!" he screams across the river.

Hades replies with nothing but a deep laughter that echoes over the water.

Dylan looks back to the stairs which rise back to the world of the living, the world of the Godless humans, then he looks back across the water. He paces to the stairs and just as I'm thinking he might give up, he turns, and sprinting, he runs at the shoreline of the river Styx, throwing his body into the strange waters, diving with a force I've never seen from him before.

Suddenly, there is a new sensation. I can feel what he feels, as he swims through the waters of death. With Hades laughing, the murky waters suck at Dylan, they stick to his skin as though he's swimming in a pit of tar. It doesn't stop him. He swims, harder, faster, on the echoes of Baal's laughter. I start to feel a familiar sense, the leeching of his energy, just as the waters of the world above do to me. Dylan starts to slow, his muscles aching, his head foggy, but he doesn't stop, he continues on until he reaches the rocky shore.

The ferry boat has already docked and unloaded Hades with his precious cargo. Charon gives a threatening hiss as Dylan drags himself out of the water, and then, getting back onto his ferry,

Charon leaves to collect more souls.

It seems if one has the courage to swim across the river Styx they do not need their golden coin for payment.

Dylan lets his body fall to the dusty rock. Rolling onto his stomach, he searches the land for Hades's figure. He finds it, floating towards the giant mountain, my pale body flopping against his back. With his last bits of energy Dylan raises his body and, running across the dusty earth, he chases after Hades. But this earth is strange to Dylan; it seems to move under his feet, the land rolls, the burning grasses entangle his legs. Dylan stumbles, he falls, and regaining his stance he continues running.

As he finally reaches Hades, he prepares to act. I can feel his muscles coiling, his body tensing as he prepares to fight for me. But Hades senses Dylan and turns before he can do anything.

"You want her back?" Hades sneers at Dylan.

"Yes, give her to me." Dylan holds his arms out.

"It's not that easy. Did you think you could just come down here, to *my* world, and I would hand her over to you? If you want her back, you take the path of the souls." He points to the rivers of death. "Choose one. Prove to me that your love for her is stronger than the anguish felt by all of those other souls. And when you've reached the depths of my mountain, if you are strong enough to reach my castle, then we will discuss your payment for her."

With the snap of his fingers Hades vanishes, taking my body with him.

Dylan looks to the surrounding rivers, the paths that the other souls take. He crouches to his heels, observing, judging, trying to choose which path to take. There's the river of woe, of lamentation, of forgetfulness, of fire, the same rivers described to me by Zeus. I can't hear his thoughts, but I can feel when he chooses. He stands, shakes his arms and starts running. And for reasons I may never know, he runs to his left, headed straight for the flaming river of fire.

No! I yell at the image in front of me, knowing that he cannot survive in the fire, even with all that he is. There is not nearly enough water down here to protect him from those flames.

He stops on the river's edge as the flames lap at him. He reaches into his pocket and pulls out a small bag. He opens it and pouring it into his hand I see it is a small amount of water. He coats his body and dives into the burning river.

His trick seems to work. Dylan swims swiftly, the flames dragging souls from the shoreline beside him. He ignores them, there is one thing on his mind and that is to save me. I can feel this in his mind just as I feel the heat as it penetrates his body, as it sucks the water off his skin. The current seems to pull him further away from the dark mountain where Hades has brought my body. Dylan swims harder, ignoring the pain in his muscles. But then, just as I had feared, the dry heat from the flaming river starts to take its toll. It starts to boil the water Dylan has coated his skin with. And I can feel it, the heat, the burning sensation. I watch as his skin turns pink, then red, then it begins to burn. Strips of his skin seem to fall off into the water. He grits his teeth and emits a deep groan of what can only be immense pain. Just before he thinks he may not make it, his hand makes contact with the hard ground.

Dylan pulls himself from the flaming river. His skin burned, his clothing shredded. And lying on the riverside panting, his insides writhing in pain, he closes his eyes. *Just for a moment*, he tells himself.

Just like Dylan, I see darkness and no longer feel the burns on his skin. Instead it's replaced by a soothing soft feeling. He opens his eyes to find he no longer lies on the shore of the flaming river, but in a luxurious bed, with satin black sheets covering his body. He lifts them, confused, to find that his clothes are gone, as well as most of the burns, although he can still see the damage to his body where the bright pink scars are. The bed gives as someone sits down next to him. He turns, facing the form.

"Demi?" he asks.

"No," replies a beautiful voice which seems to sing and echo throughout the room. It is a woman so beautiful he cannot take his eyes off her. Her eyes are green, her hair golden flax, twisted and plaited and piled onto her head in a great beautiful tangle. She reaches out, stroking his face, his chest, stretching her hand under the satin sheet.

He pulls himself away from her. "Who are you?" he asks.

"Why, I am Persephone, Goddess of the Underworld." She smiles sweetly and licking her lips she bows down and kisses him full on the mouth.

"Get off me!" He pushes at her.

Persephone leans back, staring at him, blinking. "You do not want me?" she asks, her beautiful lips turning to frown. "I should have known, especially when my own husband desires the one you love." Persephone stands and turns, the white gown she wears swirls around her. "She is quite beautiful, in a nymph sort of way. I should have known you could not be swayed. Not with what you just went through."

Dylan looks around the room, finding his tattered clothes on the floor and a door for escape. He raises himself out of the bed, dragging the silken sheet with him. He fastens it across his body trying to cover most of his naked skin, as he reaches his clothes. Dressing himself in the tattered shorts and shirt, he kicks the sheet away and steps towards the door.

"Oh, Dylan," Persephone calls to him. "If you are looking for her, make sure you take a left outside of the door and run, fast, her body cannot go on much longer without her soul intact."

Dylan runs for the door, the handle feeling hot under his palm, he pulls the door open and finds himself confronted with the same torturous images I saw when entering the mountain.

The images waft away and as though I am blind and I can no longer see what Dylan sees, I can only feel the burning pain, the holy agony from the torture they inflicted on him. I can't help but cry out, because it hurts me just as it hurt him. Suddenly, it stops, and the images return. It seems the Gods have spared me from experiencing everything Dylan did.

Now Dylan kneels on the floor, his hands tied behind his back with some heavy lead chain. Hades stands in front of him, smiling.

"I see you are strong," Hades tells him. "Or just stupid to run after this forbidden being as you have. She could end you," Hades warns.

"She won't," Dylan retorts.

"It could have been easier. I could make it so much easier for you, *son.*"

I can tell that Dylan's skin has returned to being scorched, dirty. And now his skin is glistening with sweat, a trail of dried moisture crackles the skin near his eyes. "I don't want whatever it is you're offering," Dylan tells Hades, his voice low.

"You don't?" Baal asks cheerfully. He motions to my lifeless body which lies on his bed, the same bed I saw him just a few moments ago with the Nymph women. "You don't want her shell back? You don't want to take her back up there and fulfill your destiny together?"

"I do want that," Dylan tells Baal, his voice now deep and venomous.

"Then I will trade you." Baal clasps his hands together. "I will trade you her body, for your soul."

"But you said I am immortal, we both are."

"Yes, you are immortal, until you are no longer immortal. It always tends to happen, somehow, someone finds a way to kill an immortal being, whether it's drowning them in water, or chopping off their head, or stabbing them with an iron stake. Eventually there will come a time when someone will want you dead, and you will be immortal no longer. And then, instead of your soul floating up to Olympus as payment for all that you've done, to go on forever with those other *Gods*, it will waft down here to me, and I will do with it what I please."

Dylan stares hard at Hades, contemplating the deal.

"*No*!" I shout, knowing that he can't hear me, but I still try. "*Don't do it*."

Dylan stands, and bowing to Hades he says, "Deal."

"Ah!" Hades claps his hands. "See, I knew you got your smarts from me!"

The chains are removed from Dylan's wrists. Baal holds his hand out, Dylan places his hand in his fathers, and they shake in agreement.

"I can go?" Dylan asks.

Baal flicks his wrist and lowers his eyes to glance at my form on the bed. "Yes, you may go."

Dylan walks towards my body. Picking it up, he turns searching for a way to leave the room.

Strangely, Hades looks to his wrist as though there may be a watch there.

"Oh, *son*, just a hint, you may want to run. It won't be long before her body can no longer receive her soul. I'll give you a ten minute lead."

"What?" Dylan asks.

"If I catch you, I get both of you. Now run!"

"That wasn't part of the deal."

"Gods don't make deals," Hades replies with a sharp-toothed grin.

A spattering of curse words erupt from Dylan's mouth as he grips my body tightly and runs.

∞ ∞ ∞

I look around, noticing that I am back to where I was before, with Zeus standing at my side and Hades still holding onto my hand.

I rip my hand from his grasp and hold it to my chest.

"Have you seen enough?" Zeus asks.

I think to myself, *I've seen too much.* And yet, my skin is not scorched, nor my body covered in ash. Whatever else Dylan encountered down here, Zeus has only shown me a fraction of it, but it's enough to make me regret how I've acted.

"Yes," I tell him. "I want to leave."

"Very well. Good-bye brother," Zeus flicks his wrist as he speaks, "until next time."

Zeus takes my hand and we are gone.

~ ~ ~

Zeus delivers me to the driveway and returns to his gossamer and smoke form. "We will be watching," he warns, before disappearing in a flash of light.

I stand in the driveway, staring at the cabin, waiting for the right words to come to me for when I face Dylan. I can think of none. I give up and head inside.

Dylan sits at the small kitchen table where we share our meals. He doesn't bother turning around when I open the door. Instead, he pours himself a glass from the Jack Daniels bottle that sits in the middle of the table. It's not a shot glass, or a half of a glass, it's a full drinking water glass. He takes a long swallow. He's barefoot, there's a new tear in his jeans, and the collar of his shirt is ripped.

"You're alone?" I ask.

"Of course," he answers in his smooth baritone voice that sends a tingle down my spine. "Who else would be here with me?"

I had anticipated Aphrodite or Athena might be here, stroking his tormented soul into ecstasy just as Hades had suggested. And then I remember he no longer owns his soul. He gave it up for me. I feel like a jerk.

"I'm not sure," I tell him.

"So, what did you learn about yourself while you were visiting my father? Did you change your mind?" Dylan asks. He doesn't bother turning to look at me. Instead he drains the glass and pours himself another. "Did you learn something about me, or Hades, or yourself?"

"I… I learned something about myself."

"Oh yeah," Dylan chuckles into his glass, "what was that? Did you change your mind about us? Are you ready to change *our* destiny? Are you ready to send me back to my father?"

"No," I whisper to him.

"Then what did you learn down there in the boiling pits of the Underworld? I'm sure you've seen what will happen to me. I no longer own my soul. I gave it up, for you. When our immortality is over Hades will own me."

"I know."

He frowns into his glass.

"I'm sorry. I was wrong." I take a hesitant step towards him. "I was selfish. I truly didn't understand what you did for me. And, and…" A feeling starts to well up inside of me, so strong that I can barely contain it. "I can't live without you. I'm sorry. I'm so sorry. You didn't have to do that for me."

He turns, finally, his eyes even redder than when I left with Zeus. There is a split in his lip and bruises to his face.

I gasp. "What happened to you?"

He drains his glass before standing. "It seems Hermes is stronger than I thought. Old punk. I guess the Gods will always overpower a Demigod, whether it's with wits or force."

He staggers towards me. I can smell the alcohol on his breath, feel the ache radiating off him in hot waves.

Although his features have not changed in the ten years which have passed, his face seems to be heavy with pain at this moment. And now I understand why, even if I only saw a small bit of what he went through when he retrieved my soulless body. He's afraid of losing me and returning to his father. It makes me wonder why I couldn't see it before and why I did exactly the one thing he asked me not to.

The thought of losing him, of seeing where I would go, it would drive me mad and I'm sure my reaction to losing him would be much worse than downing a bottle of Jack. The Gods might regret allowing me to live, even with what is expected of us.

Suddenly, I understand this strange feeling that's been brewing inside of me, masked by the pull of the trees and the fear of our destiny. I love him, more than anything.

"Did you hear me?" I ask him as he wanders closer to me. "I can't live without you." And I don't know why it's so hard to get the words out, but I say them, for the first time, "I love you, Dylan."

It seems with each step he becomes more sober. His eyes more clear, his anguished features lessen a little. "Finally," he says, just before he reaches for me and pulls me to him into a crushing embrace.

I press my face into his chest. The smell of burning flesh in my nose gone, replaced by his scent of sweet fresh water and mint. I feel his fingertips press into my skin as though he's trying to convince himself that I am here and real.

"I'm so sorry," I tip my face up to look at him.

He doesn't respond. He simply leans down, pressing his lips to mine with a hungry kiss, one that takes my breath away and makes the deep part of my stomach ache for him.

CHAPTER TWENTY-SIX

We both knew this time was coming. I saw it that day I left my body in the woods and I could feel it before Zeus took me to the Underworld to see Dylan's sacrifice.

Dylan sits beside me on the porch swing that overlooks the river behind his cabin. He's holding an acoustic guitar made of dark wood, plucking tenderly at the strings and singing softly, barely above a whisper but loud enough for me to ache at the remembrance of the moment I found out how skilled he is with music.

He stops playing and turns to me. "What was it like out there?"

"Bad." I look away, kicking off of the porch below my feet to make the swing move. "How did you know what I went to see?"

He shrugs, moving to lean the guitar against the porch railing. "Your body was there for a long time. I sat by that blackberry bush and watched over it. I was afraid that you'd never come back. I was there the entire day so I figured wherever you went, it wasn't just a short trip around town."

"It wasn't." I watch the waterfall near the porch ripple and crash to the rocky riverbed below. "There's something I don't understand," I tell him, remembering.

"What's that?"

"Time here has slowed. It's like they're enchanted, all of them living a slow unending life, just like… just like at the castle. Swayzee looks the same and so does everyone else in town."

Dylan looks away and over the river. "You didn't tell me."

"I didn't get a chance."

"They're keeping us happy, leaving this place the same, the way we want it. I guess we should consider it a gift from the Gods."

"I don't think I want their gifts. They always seem to come with some horrible attachment."

Dylan sighs. "Well, are the humans as godless as they described?"

"Pretty close."

"We can start now, before it gets worse. Or wait. What do you want to do?"

"Let's wait. Just a little bit longer."

Dylan stretches his arm behind my back, pulling me close to his side and rocking the porch swing.

~ ~ ~

"It's getting worse," Dylan tells me as I lie on the couch.

He reaches for me, sweeping a few strands of hair off my face, only for them to drop off onto the floor like dried hay. His eyes grow a shimmer to them, not like when we danced on the lake, or when he would chase me through the fields. It wasn't a joyful shimmer, it was one of pain, one of loss, of the fear of losing someone you love. I saw it on his face when he chased his father into the Underworld to retrieve my body.

The truth is Dylan was feeling it too. But he hid it well. He has always been stronger than me. Still, I could see the dark circles under his eyes and that he had lost weight.

Just as Zeus had warned, the earth was calling us. Our biggest fear loomed before us and I had promised that I would deliver those souls to the underworld and fulfill Hades' quota.

"I can't watch you go through this anymore," Dylan says, standing. "I'm going to get Hermes."

I lay on the couch, shivering under the heavy wool blankets and staring at the roaring fire in front of me. I hear his truck start and the sound of the tires kicking up rocks as he drives away. By nightfall Dylan returns, rushing into the house with Hermes at his heels.

"Are you okay?" Dylan asks, his eyes wide with fear as though I may have passed while he was gone.

Hermes comes to my side, crouching down so that he is face-to-face with me, inspecting me. After a moment he stands.

"It seems as though the time is here."

Dylan and I both sigh. We know what he means, the earth is calling us to rein in mankind.

Maybe it's because I didn't want to be responsible for hurting people, those poor godless people. Maybe that's the reason why I didn't hear it as clearly as I should have. But Hermes is right; we can't take this much longer, if any longer at all. We have to do something, we have to stop it, or we might actually die or worse, the Gods would send us to the Underworld just as they had promised. And the earth would perish, and the Gods would move on to another planet and start over again.

Hermes turns to Dylan. "You know what needs to be done. Go, before Zeus returns and your fate changes once again."

Dylan runs his hand through his hair, looking at his feet and then back to me. "Okay, okay."

Hermes helps us pack a few bags, supplies and changes of clothes. We look like nothing more than travelling college students. But the truth is, we are about to do something much more dire than head for some intellectual campus and spread our wings.

They load the truck as I watch from the swing on the porch.

When they are done, Dylan carries me to the passenger side, buckling me in. He stops for a moment, his face in front of mine. "It's going to be okay," he tells me, pressing his lips to mine.

We drive south; Dylan creating great downpours as we pass through the countryside. Every few moments he would pull to the side of the road, concentrating hard. I didn't ask him what havoc he was creating, but I could tell it was working, with each mile we drove I was starting to feel better. By the time we reached the state border I was able to sit up and pull the blankets off myself. I was able to feel what Dylan felt, a deep growing burn in my gut, the earth calling me to do something drastic, to save it. Just as the Gods had warned me would happen.

Finally, I used the powers I inherited, the ones the Gods allowed me to live with, with the promise of using them. I made the plants reclaim the roads, the buildings. I wilted the crops and stopped them from producing fruit. I pulled the roots from the ground and hillsides crumbled; shorelines broke away, no longer held together with the strong roots and soil.

When the truck ran out of gas we left it on the side of the road, taking just a few bags.

I remove my shoes at the roadside, tucking them into my bag. Dylan takes my hand, squeezing it hard. I nod, straighten my back. I remember what he did for me, he gave up his soul. I have to make this work. I have to deliver those souls.

"Focus," he whispers in my ear.

It was hard, very hard, because I could see what loomed before us.

We had left our enchanted town of Saratoga and now those Godless humans stood before us, a thick line of them. It seemed a hundred deep and miles long. They were all waiting, no longer resembling what we had remembered humans to be. They were worse than what happened to the humans of Venus, with their armor and tattered clothing. These humans, they were something more vicious, as though the Underworld had opened up and released all of its demons. These were not God-fearing humans, they were barely human at all. They sneered at us. They growled and bared their teeth. They yapped like vicious, rabid beasts. It was like they knew we were coming. As though someone had warned them, just as the earth had warned us.

My breath caught in my chest, frozen with fear. Oh, how I wish I had a starving horde of Vassal to help us right now.

I used the vines, the roots of the earth, grasping them around their ankles. I pulled them deep under the ground, where their souls could be closer to their final resting place, and their decomposing bodies could feed the flora.

Dylan poured the water from the oceans upon their heads; he drowned them as they stood before us. With each row that perished, another row would replace them, by the hundreds it seemed.

And then, it was like the old Stones of Olympus might have heard my prayers when the Godless humans continued to descend upon us. I felt a great thundering from behind, and when I turned I saw the three-headed beast in its full form. It ran for the horde, ripping and tearing at their flesh, stripping them down to the bone. And it was just enough help for Dylan and I to regain our strength before we had to face the next onslaught.

~ ~ ~

With the sea of the dead spread before us, we could continue our journey, reclaiming the earth. The sky began to rain giant golden raindrops. Dylan held out his hand, collecting the drops in his palm. He had no control over these; he couldn't manipulate them as he usually did the rain, because they were golden coins.

"For the ferry ride," I told Dylan, knowing that Charon would not let these souls pass into the Underworld without payment.

It seems Hades will get his souls, many of them, since the world has grown very different and darker from what I last remembered.

~ ~ ~

It seems some humans began praying again and this must have made the Gods cheerful. In return, they rewarded us and every so often we would come across a warm fire, or a basket of food, or armored clothing.

We continued on with the beast at our side. Every so often Zeus would drop coins from the sky-I noticed this after particularly deadly battles.

"This is killing me," I tell Dylan as he stands from making a small fire.

He stares at me, hands on his hips, looking every bit the warrior he had become. "We have to do this. If we don't do this, if we don't finish this, they will take you away. I'm not letting you go back to my father."

I sigh and wipe at my face. Pulling my hand back I find there is a layer of dirt, not just any dirt, this is thick, like lumpy pudding with a dark red hue.

"Oh-" I start.

"Don't," Dylan warns me. "Close your eyes."

It's all he has to say. I close my eyes so I don't have to look at it any longer. I feel him coat my face, the temperature of my skin cools as he pulls the blood soaked dirt off my face with the moisture from the air.

"It's done."

"Thank you." I force a smile at him.

The beast growls from beside the small fire, turning its head towards the woods.

"What is it?" I ask.

Before Dylan can answer the beast leaps to his feet and dashes into the dark forest. We hear the sound of running feet, growls and screams, the beast chomping something in its jaws. After a few moments the beast returns and lies by the fire once again. I watch it, noticing the fresh blood gleaming from its jowls.

I get the feeling that if the Gods don't send us away, these Godless humans will. This isn't the first time they've come for us in the night.

Turning, I look at our current camp. Each night we have to make a new one. Sometimes we find an abandoned house or an empty cavern or a spacious freeway overpass to shield us from the night and the humans who seem to be searching for us.

"What do you think happened to them?" I ask Dylan.

"I don't know. But whatever they've turned into, they know about us, they know what we've been sent to do."

There is another noise, a soft thud from behind Dylan. We turn to see a pile of cloth on the ground. A delivery. Dylan bends to open the satchel, pulling out soap, bread, blankets, and thick leathered body armor.

I watch as Dylan holds up the armor, separating it into two piles. "Those look like something from ancient Greece," I say.

He raises an eyebrow. "Maybe it is."

He separates the backplates and breastplates, the bracers and greaves, the thick soled leather boots. One small pile, one large pile.

The fear grips me. "Dear God," I blurt out.

Dylan looks up.

"It's going to get worse. Isn't it?"

He tosses a leather strap into one of the piles and stands, pushing his hair out of his face. "We're almost done." He walks towards me.

"How much?" I count the cities and towns in my head, remember the path we've taken, north, then south, around the continent, across the middle…

"There's one city left." Dylan walks closer, his arms out. "One place we have left to venture into." He stops in front of me, holding my upper arms. "New York is all that's left."

"But…" I start, remembering all the years spent there, remembering what it's made of. There was a park in the middle of the city, Central Park, I could have used that, but it's gone, They demolished that park when I was a child. "I can't go into that city, Dylan. It's all rock and steel. There's nothing green there for miles and miles. I'll be useless."

"It has to be done." He presses his lips into a thin line.

"Can't we skip that city? The Underworld has to be bursting with souls. Hades doesn't need anymore," I plead.

Dylan turns away, reaching for one of the blankets and spreading it down next to the fire. He draws me to him and down to the ground. I catch the beast rolling one of its six eyes at us.

"Don't think of the city," Dylan suggests as he brushes loose strands of hair behind my ear. He brushes his lips against mine.

The beast lets out a heavy sigh that makes the fire flicker, then rolls over, facing away from us.

I feel Dylan's lips smile on mine. "Don't think of the city," he says again. "Just think of you and me and eternity."

"It's so hard-"

He pulls back. "Hard to think of me?"

"No." I shove at him. "Hard not to think of that looming city."

"I'll help you forget it," he kisses me, hard and hungry this time. "Just this time, I'll help you forget it."

~ ~ ~

I wake to the smell of toast. Rolling over I find Dylan crouched by the fire, roasting bread on a stick. He winks as I sit up.

"Where's the beast?" I ask, looking around.

"He got a head start on the day."

Dylan stands, bringing the bread to me and I notice he is already dressed in the armor that was delivered to us last night.

"You're dressed?" I ask.

"I know you would prefer it if I walked around naked all day, Demi, but I can't. So I got dressed. It takes a while with the armor. Eat and then I'll help you."

I cross my legs and eat the roasted bread, watching Dylan as he packs up the camp and stomps out the coals from last night. When he's done he stands next to me.

"Ready?" he asks.

I raise my arms and let him pull me to my feet. "I'm not sure."

He grips my chin and pulls my face up, towards his. He doesn't have to say anything, I can see it in his eyes, the fear of spending an eternity with Hades.

I straighten my shoulders, force a smile. "I love you," I tell him, reaching up on my toes and pressing my lips to his. He releases my chin and I bend down, picking up a piece of the armor. "Now, how do I wear this?" I ask.

I try to stand still as Dylan secures the armor. My body jerks as he cinches the leather straps of the breast plate and back plate. I hold out my arms as he secures the bracers. I point my toes as he tightens the greaves around my legs and he laces of the tall boots.

"You know," I tell him. "This is how I used to put on my tights." I tap my toe on the ground.

"I know," he smiles, "I used to watch you."

"I wonder if I'll ever dance again?" I think out loud.

"You'll dance again." His hand lingers behind my knee, sending a tingle up my leg. "If not for them, you can dance for me every night when we are done with this."

We push on, heavy vegetation cropping up in our footsteps. I cover our path with vegetation, vines, tall grasses and towering trees. Dylan makes the air wet with a heavy fog. The ponds, rivers and streams all overflow, washing away everything, including mankind and their belongings, just as we had intended, just as was expected of us.

Dylan keeps his hand tight on mine, keeping the water away from me just as he did when he brought me under the lake to see that abandoned town.

"What is your weakness?" I think to ask him, feeling a little dejected that I have to count on him to protect me from the water.

"I only have one weakness," he squeezes my hand.

I have never seen him fear anything or anyone. "What's that?"

"You."

I stop in my tracks. "You're scared of me?" I ask, the taunts of Hades fresh in my mind when he told Dylan that I could ruin them all.

"No. You are my weakness. If anything happened to you…"

Feeling like an idiot I wrap my arms around him.

"Come on," he urges. "We're almost there."

We stand on the outskirts of the city. Dylan's face is set, hard and planed as he contemplates how to rid the huge city of steel and stone of its Godless residents. I do the same. Since there is no soil or plant life left in there I'm not sure what I can do.

Just then the thundering footsteps of the beast interrupt our thoughts as it runs up to us. The beast drops on the ground, panting, his face coated in fresh blood.

"What do we do?" I ask.

"We'll flush them out. It won't get them all, but it's a start."

I watch as a huge thundercloud collects above the city. Thunder cracks, lightening strikes. I watch in awe as a downpour begins.

It doesn't take long for the people to emerge. They pour from the city, their cars spewing exhaust.

"Do it!" Dylan urges. "Before they get too far."

I pull them down, cars and all. I sink them into the soil, I push them to the Underworld where Hades wants them. The beast takes off running, catching the stragglers before they can make it too far.

I watch as the city floods, the ground begins to mound, filled with bodies.

"You could wait out here," Dylan suggests. "On the outskirts. I can finish this alone."

"No." I reach for him. "Zeus and Hades said I need to do this too, we need to do it together."

I walk towards the city with Dylan with a growing sense of unease filling my chest. The floodwaters recede as we walk the streets I remember as a child. We pass stores, towering apartment buildings, the old dance center storefront where I learned to dance with Mother. We pass the plot of land where Central Park used to be, now filled with apartments and cement. We near the center of the city, looking out of place here, dressed as Roman warriors in the fashion capital of the world.

Dylan stops, reaching out to grasp my arm.

"What's wrong?" I ask.

He turns his head, just as the door of a storefront opens and out walks Hades.

"What are you doing here?" Dylan practically growls at him.

Hades grins and loosens his tie. "Just checking up on my *son*."

"Get out of here," I sneer at Hades.

"You're stealing our prayers," Hades tells me.

"What are you talking about?" Dylan asks.

"You've taken so many of them, you've killed so many of the Godless humans that some of them have started praying to someone else." His eyes narrow on me.

Dylan steps in front of me. I place my hand on his back, feeling the smooth, thick armor that covers his torso.

"You told us to do this," I tell Hades. "You told us we had to do this."

"Yes. I also warned Zeus that this would happen."

"What?" Dylan demands. I feel his muscles flex under his shirt.

"They have started praying to the earth, to their *mother earth.*" Hades' gaze falls on me again. "You feel it now?" he asks. "You're stronger. I can tell. This is how Gods attain their power, from prayers."

"What do you want us to do about that?" I ask. "We've delivered your souls, just as you've asked."

"I know," Hades smiles, his eyes gleaming flames. "And they have made me strong."

He reaches out, his arm extending further than it should, faster than it should. He grabs Dylan by his neck and pulls him to his side.

"No! Dylan!" I scream at Hades. "Give him back to me!"

Hades laughs. "I already own his soul. I'm simply collecting it a little early."

"You said not until he dies!"

"I also said Gods don't make deals."

"Let him go!"

"What will you do about it?" Hades laughs as Dylan struggles in his hand, his bright blue eyes red-rimmed and bloodshot.

"Zeus!" I scream into the sky, beckoning him to help us.

Hades laughs louder. "He won't come to help you. If there's one thing I've learned about my brother it's that he could care less about the humans when he has enough prayers. And he could care even less about those who help him acquire those prayers."

"Liar!"

"Try me."

Dylan groans as Hades tightens his grip.

I feel something deep inside me, greater than the pull of the forest and the fear of losing Dylan. I can only think it must be true, what Hades said, it must be the prayers of the surviving humans making me stronger.

I stretch my arms out, feeling the tingle in my fingertips that once kept me captive in this city, captive with the fear of what I could do.

"Release him," I say. "This is your last chance."

"Or what?" Hades chuckles.

Dylan's face pales to a whiteness I've never seen on a living creature before.

I don't give Hades a chance to stop. Instead, just as I once did to my parent's house, I reach my power to the outskirts of the city, to where there is still soil and plants. I grow them tall and long and thick, and brushing my arm I cover the city in a great wave of green.

The sky turns dark. The air stagnant. The only light comes from the light pole a few feet from us.

"You see," Hades laughs. "You're stronger!"

I don't say anything back to Hades, instead I pull the great covering of green down, crushing Hades and the rest of the city beneath it. I push hard, with all of my strength. The buildings crumble, the water of the surrounding ocean rises. I run to Dylan's collapsed body, pressing my hand to his chest, feeling for his breaths. As the water rises to the small plot of cement we stand on, I feel Dylan breathe against my hand. His eyes flutter open, landing on me before he looks around us.

"Where are we?" he asks. "There is only water. Where is the city?"

"I sunk it," I tell him. "Pressed it under the ground, under the ocean, with Hades."

"So now he has the whole city down there with him?" he asks.

"Possibly. If it didn't crumble on the way there."

"Demi?" Dylan asks, coughing. "I think…"

"What?"

I watch as a trickle of blood falls from his mouth. "I think it's too late." He coughs again.

"Dylan!" I shake his shoulders.

His hand reaches up, pressing to my cheek. "I love you," Dylan tells me and I watch as his face pales further, a blue hue appears around his eyes and mouth, and then, his body stills.

"No!" I scream at his lifeless body, feeling the sting of tears behind my eyes. I throw myself across him, feeling the block of cement sway in the water underneath us.

When the sobs recede, I raise myself, pressing my fingers to his face, his neck, his chest, searching for the tiniest sight of life. And I feel like he must have each time he found my body without a soul. The sobs turn into gasps as I try to settle myself.

A bright light appears over the water to my left. I throw myself on

Dylan, covering his body as the image of Zeus appears.

"I suppose you've come to collect something also?" I ask him.

"No," Zeus responds. I notice he is in his golden human form instead of the wispy smoke and shadows. "I've come to deliver you home."

"To Saratoga?" I ask. "It's pointless. I have no home anymore."

"Saratoga is waiting for you."

"I don't want it!" I scream at Zeus. "I did what you asked. I sent all those souls to Hades. I did everything you've asked!"

"Yes, you did. Thank you." Zeus tips his head at me. "And now your task is complete. Until the godless humans return. As Hades said, they always return."

"And if I'm not here to help you?"

"You have survived. You are immortal. You will be here for the next time."

"And Dylan," I ask, running my finger along his cold arm.

"Hades owns his soul." Zeus tips his gaze to Dylan's lifeless form. "Unless…" he begins.

"Unless what?"

"Unless someone retrieves it."

"Will you?" I ask.

Zeus frowns. "I cannot retrieve souls."

"But you brought me there before. You brought me down there to see what Dylan did to save me. Why can't you help now?"

"Dylan completed a selfless act. He went there on his own. He fought for you and made his own deals with Hades." Zeus raises his eyebrows.

I look to the surrounding water and focus on that same feeling I had earlier that I now recognize as the power of the prayers made to mother earth. I pull a vine from the mainland, growing it thick and strong. I look up at Zeus, feeling the sweat from the concentration drip down my face.

"Promise me one thing?" I ask Zeus.

"What is that?"

"Take his body to Saratoga, to our cabin."

Zeus flashes a knowing smile. "Why?"

"I have done everything you've asked. Now do this *one* thing for me. Deliver his body. Do it. Promise me."

Zeus smiles. "I promise."

I wrap the vine around my waist and dive into the water.

~ ~ ~

There were a few things I feared, one was the water, another was losing control of this power I have, and being responsible for those souls.

Now, all those fears are replaced with losing Dylan. I thought he would always be at my side to protect me from his element, the thing that he had power over. I thought he would always be there to help me gain control, now I see how wrong I was.

I grow the vine as I swim, allowing it to stretch further along with me, the deeper I swim. I follow the crumbling city as it sinks. Grabbing onto a loose piece of sinking cement, I let it drag me down. I don't focus on the leeching of my energy, as I have before when I was under water or trapped in the rain. I focus on one thing: finding Dylan's soul.

Soon the water warms, it bubbles and turns hot and just as I wonder if this was the right route to take to get to the Underworld, the sea floor seems to open, dropping the remains of the city into an open cavern. I fall through with the cement.

Letting go of my sinker, I use the vine wrapped around my waist to lessen my fall. I stand on the rubble, amazed that it all fit down here. But then, as the souls rise and form their line to cross the river, the rubble seems to dissipate and disappear as though some supernatural force is clearing it.

I tighten the vine around my waist as Charon's boat pulls away. Searching the souls on deck, I find the one I'm looking for, his blue eyes stare back at me. Remembering what Dylan did when he came after me, I don't bother waiting for the boat, I run to the river Styx and dive in. I use the vine to keep me from sinking and my arms to propel me forward. I reach the rocky shoreline, after Charon's boat has unloaded. Charon stands at the stern, gazing down at me. I stand and let the putrid water drip from me. I pull the vine tighter across my abdomen, feeling it cut into me.

The prayers must have worked, a swim like that would have knocked me out before.

I look back to Charon and find his wrinkled paw pointing. I follow its direction with my eyes and see Dylan's silver-haired soul walking towards the back door to the mountain, just as Zeus did. I run, my vine tethering me to the murky sky

Running for his soul, faster than I ever have run in my life, I reach to my side, pulling a piece of the vine away, growing it long and strong in my hand. When I get close enough, I whip it at Dylan, circling his waist, tethering him to me.

He turns, his eyes sunken and sad. "You can't bring me back," he says in a hollowed voice.

"I will and I am."

I jerk the vine, pulling him close to me. Wrapping my arm around the main vine I turn, ready to pull us away.

"Where do you think you're going?" I hear the voice of Hades.

Turning, I find him standing next to us, his hand grasping Dylan's arm.

"His soul is mine, he promised it to me."

"You don't make promises," I sneer at Hades.

Letting go of the vine I tear another piece of it and throw it at Hades. He catches it mid air, deflecting it onto the dusty ground. "Your green cannot grow here," he laughs, tugging on Dylan's arm.

"Are you sure about that?" I smirk at him.

Hades' eyes widen, he looks down and starts to move, but it's too late. I've grown the vine he tossed on the ground, wrapped it around his feet and legs and torso and arms before he can respond. I wrap it around his neck, pulling it tight until I can see his face redden.

"I don't make promises either," I tell him as I wrap his head and seal off the vine. "I've delivered your souls, but this one you can't have!"

I pull Dylan to my side and grasp the vine, pulling us up, away, and out of the depths of the Underworld.

~ ~ ~

I wasn't sure if Dylan would know what to do when I brought us to the cabin, but he dove into his lifeless form as though it was a refreshing body of water. When he gasped back to life and his eyes fluttered open I was there, hovering over him as he did to me on Dark Island when he brought me back from the Underworld.

"Hi." Dylan smiles.

"You died," I tell him, feeling the shudder of my voice.

"I know." He smiles again.

I grasp his wrists as his arms reach for me. "You shouldn't be smiling. I went to get you."

"I know," he replies, still smiling, looking every bit like that young man I met in the baseball field who gave me the confidence to make a snowstorm out of dandelion seeds.

"I'm not sure if I can do that again." I drop my arms, still weak from the energy I used to rescue him.

"I won't hold it against you," he says, pulling me closer.

"I can't live without you."

"I know this, Demi."

"Just don't ever promise your soul to anyone else, ever again."

He presses his lips to my temple. "The only one I'll ever promise my soul to again, is you."

"*Demigods*." I shake my head. "You're so… so…"

"In love with you."

Dylan lets go of my hand, and reaching into his pocket he pulls something out and holds it in front of my face. I recognize it as the diamond ring Hades once gave me. But it was a dark brown then.

"Demi?" Dylan asks. "I've been saving this for you, waiting for the perfect time and that time must have passed by hundreds of times, and then it was too late. All I could think of when my soul left was that I never asked you, I never gave this to you."

After all this time he's proposing, now. "Will it matter?" I ask, looking down as he twists the ring between his fingers. "Will marriage matter when we are the only ones left?"

"It matters to me, to us. I've waited long enough to ask you."

"You waited for me-"

"I waited for you before… before you knew I even existed."

I press my lips to his, and wrapping my arms around him I whisper, "Yes."

~ ~ ~

We were free in Saratoga. It was just us, in our enchanted town. We danced on the lake, kissed in the moonlight, and all was well when the earth went back to being green and blue and this made the earth happy.

Still, I know I should have felt something, maybe sorrow or guilt. But I didn't. They had done this, those Godless humans. They had caused the damage to the earth. They were ready to ruin this place just like the events on earth's sister planet. We had only completed the task that was destined for us. Those humans that survived, they found it in their hearts to worship the Gods again, and this made the Gods happy. But they worshiped the earth also. And this made us strong.

ABOUT THE AUTHOR

M. R. Pritchard is a lifelong inhabitant of upstate NY. When she is not writing she is a NICU Nurse, wife, mother, gardener, aquarist, book hoarder and science geek. She holds degrees in Biochemistry and Nursing. Visit her blog: secretlifeofatownie.blogspot.com, where she writes weekly posts about life, writing, and Zombies.

Meredith would love to connect with you. Like her Facebook page *facebook.com/MRPritchard*, follow her on Twitter *twitter.com/M_R_Pritchard*, or follow her on Pinterest *pinterest.com/mp30/boards/*. Visit any of these sites for information regarding previously published works and upcoming projects.

Thank you for reading SARATOGA. I hope you enjoyed it! Since there is no better way to share the love of a book than by word of mouth, please take time to leave a review or tell a friend about SARATOGA or THE PHOENIX PROJECT SERIES.

ACKNOWLEDGMENTS

Many thanks to my co-editor, my reviewer, my beta reader, my graphic designer, the one who I bounce ideas off of, who puts up with my craziness, the one who has supported me every step of the way on this crazy journey, and who sometimes cleans the snow off my car, Jorden. I love you.

There is no way I would have ever found the courage to complete this book, and continue on with more, if it weren't for my encouraging fans, friends, and family. I thank you all from the center of my heart.

Lastly, there are not enough thanks I could give to Kristy Ellsworth. Thank you so much for all of your hard work and dedication on this project and all of the rest.

WANT MORE SARATOGA?

Check out the Saratoga Pinterest Board:
http://www.pinterest.com/mp30/saratoga/

Or the Saratoga Blog Page:
http://secretlifeofatownie.blogspot.com/p/saratoga.html